These
Violent
Delights

These Violent Delights

Delights

A Novel

MICAH NEMEREVER

HARPER

An Imprint of HarperCollins*Publishers*

This novel is a work of fiction. While historical
events inspired the plot and some basic details, this work
should not be interpreted as depiction of, or commentary
on, these events. Any references to real people, events,
establishments, organizations, or locales are intended
only to give the fiction a sense of reality and authenticity,
and are used fictitiously. All other names, characters, and
places, and all dialogue and incidents portrayed in this
book are the product of the author's imagination.

THESE VIOLENT DELIGHTS. Copyright © 2020 by Micah
Nemerever. All rights reserved. Printed in the United
States of America. No part of this book may be used or
reproduced in any manner whatsoever without written
permission except in the case of brief quotations
embodied in critical articles and reviews. For
information, address HarperCollins Publishers,
195 Broadway, New York, NY 10007.

HarperCollins books may be purchased for
educational, business, or sales promotional use.
For information, please email the Special Markets
Department at SPsales@harpercollins.com.

FIRST EDITION

Library of Congress Cataloging-in-Publication Data has
been applied for.

ISBN 978-0-06-296363-5

20 21 22 23 24   LSC   10 9 8 7 6 5 4 3 2 1

To Ollie

I know my fate. One day my name will be associated with the memory of something tremendous—a crisis without equal on earth, the most profound collision of conscience, a decision that was conjured up against everything that had been believed, demanded, hallowed so far. I am no man, I am dynamite.

—FRIEDRICH NIETZSCHE

These
Violent
Delights

BY THE time Charlie punches out it's well after midnight, and everyone else has long since gone home. He switches off the lights and watches the long aisles cascade into darkness, then pulls the roll-up door shut behind him. When he steps out from under the awning the rain drapes over his umbrella like a shroud.

The air clots around his breath. At the far side of the warehouse a train wails past. Charlie thinks about knitted blankets and hot chocolate, half-forgotten childhood comforts he's a few years too old now to admit to missing. The others all have families and wives and happy plans for the holiday; Charlie just has matinee tickets and Lucy begging for scraps of his TV dinner. He's exhausted, he thinks, because it's easier to remedy than being lonely.

As he turns onto the side street he fumbles, thick-fingered, for his keys. When he opens his car door a crown of rainwater disperses from the roof and scatters. The air inside is even colder than outside—Charlie blows into his cupped hands and hopes the chill hasn't seeped between his bedsheets.

He starts the ignition. The engine screams. The rasp of tearing metal is followed by a heavy death rattle. Charlie quickly shuts off the engine and holds the wheel in white-knuckled hands. He's accustomed to dead batteries, flat tires, engines too stubborn to start in the cold, but whatever just happened was far worse.

He's drenched by the time he remembers his umbrella. He

lifts the hood with a squeal, hoping there's a miracle waiting in the unreadable mess of his engine. But Charlie has never been much of a mechanic. There's nothing in there for him to see.

He steps back and heads toward the phone booth, but stops in the middle of the street—he squints through the rain and sees the receiver swinging from its cord. For the first time Charlie lets his dismay tip upward into anger.

"Fucking—*teenagers*."

He will have to return to the telephone in the warehouse break room. He exhales hard and stalks back to the car, leaning inside to grab his umbrella. There's the germ of a headache now, just behind his eyes.

Charlie slams the door and straightens. When he looks out into the street again, he is no longer alone.

"Are you okay?"

A battered black car has appeared in the street beside him. Rain slicks down the windows and roof, but the passenger door hangs open. A boy is leaning toward him, one arm braced above the doorframe. His dark hair is artfully untrimmed, but he's dressed well. Argyle pullover, toffee-brown jodhpur boots; a suburban choirboy in halfhearted revolt.

Charlie stares at him, and he smiles.

"That looks like fun." The boy nods toward the steaming hood of Charlie's car. "Have a wrecker on the way?"

Charlie slowly shakes his head. "Phone booth's out of order."

The boy gives a sympathetic wince and turns toward the unseen driver. Then he nods and turns back to Charlie.

"We can give you a lift home if you want," he says. "Car's not going anywhere—you might as well call the tow from someplace warm."

Charlie lifts the hood again to take one last, hopeless look into his engine. He sighs and slams it shut.

"I'm in Polish Hill," he says. "Is that out of your way?"

"Not at all."

The boy slides to the middle seat, and Charlie shakes off his umbrella before he gets inside.

The driver is a kid, too, copper-haired and slim. His clothes are as well cared for as his friend's, but they're conspicuously cheaper; his plaid flannel shirt has a generic plainness to it that makes it look as if it had been sewn at home from a pattern. Behind the boy's Malcolm X glasses his dark eyes are solemn, and when he greets Charlie he does not smile.

He stares just a second longer than he should, then catches his friend's prompting glance, chews his lip, and looks away into the road.

"He's shy," says the dark-haired boy. "Don't mind him."

Charlie nods, unoffended. The boys are younger than he'd thought, maybe even still in high school. He wonders what these two were doing, driving around all by themselves. Honor-roll types, clean-cut, out for a midnight joyride. It's a poignant thought, almost charming. Charlie was a different kind of teenager—lousy grades, on the football team but never great at it, a lumbering straight man to the class clowns. But he knows what it is to wonder what everyone else is doing differently in order to be happy; he knows what it is to skirt at the outermost edges of friendship. He can still remember the companionable quiet, the fleeting warmth, of the moments teenage boys spend being lonely together.

The wipers click and the vents breathe hot. The redhead steers with his hands at ten and two on the wheel, as if he hasn't been driving for very long. The other boy reaches across Charlie's knees and takes a thermos from the glove box. The contents smell of hot broth and rosemary, something Charlie's grandmother might have made when he was sick as a child.

"Want some?" the boy asks. "It's chicken and rice."

"Nice of you," Charlie agrees.

He holds the metal thermos mug steady while the boy carefully fills it. The first mouthful burns Charlie's tongue, but it shocks the cold from his bones, and it tastes all right. At first there's the barest tang of soap, as if the mug wasn't rinsed properly, but after a moment he can't even taste it.

The dark-haired boy takes a sip from the thermos and offers it to his friend, but the driver shakes his head curtly and keeps his eyes fixed on the empty street.

It's quiet for a while. Charlie finishes his soup and rolls the mug between his hands. His scalded taste buds are starting to itch.

"What are your names?" he asks. He'll forget the answer as soon as he hears it, but he's grateful for the promise of home and the weight of hot food in his belly, and he wants to be courteous.

The boy beside him thinks before he answers, like he's deciding whether or not to tell the truth. He looks apprehensive, but doesn't appear to know it.

"I'm Julian," he answers finally. He gives his friend a pointed look. The other boy is silent for a moment, as though summoning the will to speak. His jaw is a nervous taut line. This one gets on Charlie's nerves a little, as anxious people often do. Shyness he can forgive; cringing dread is harder to stomach.

"Paul," the driver says, blank-faced, so quietly Charlie almost can't hear him.

Charlie looks between them, at how differently they are dressed and how Paul avoids meeting Julian's eyes—how little they look or behave like friends. Once again, more insistently now, he is curious what they were up to before they found him. But there's no reason for him to be uneasy. They're just kids, and he's on the verge of reaching home. Once he's there, it won't matter anymore.

His fingers are too warm around his empty cup. The heat from the vent suddenly clings like his childhood Ohio summers. He fumbles with the zipper of his parka, but his fingers are rubbery and fever-fat. The thermos cup is rocking on its side between his ankles before he even knows he's dropped it.

Julian grins suddenly and elbows his friend's arm, as if to include him in a joke.

"Where exactly are you in Polish Hill, Charlie?" The sudden clarity of Paul's voice is startling. There's an echo of Murray Avenue in his vowels, but he overenunciates as if he learned to speak by reading—in the middle of *exactly*, where Charlie has never heard it before, there's the precise, conspicuous click of the *t*.

"Uh, north of Immaculate Heart," Charlie answers, "if you turn right on—"

The numbing heat is trickling through his hands and up his arms, from his burnt tongue outward to his lips. He brings a hand to his face and smears his fingertips across the line of his mouth. He feels nothing.

The car is idling at a railway crossing, waiting out the clang of the bell. The boys watch him with unblinking eyes. Julian is still smiling; Paul looks as if he never has.

They're both wearing gloves. They've shed their coats in the stifling warmth, but they're still wearing their gloves.

"My name." His tongue is so thick he could choke. "I never told you my name."

In the moment before he manages to smother it, Julian dissolves into sharp, jittery laughter. But Paul doesn't flinch. His eyes are bright and pitiless. His every word is tight and mannered, as if he's practiced in front of the mirror.

"Do you think the neighbors will notice that you're gone, Mr. Stepanek?"

Charlie tries to will his unfeeling hands to the door latch. His arm lands hard against the door, and his body slumps uselessly in the corner of his seat.

"You don't want to do that," says Julian. It isn't a threat. He speaks as if he's trying to coax a reluctant child. "Could I see your wrists, Charlie? Behind your back, if you don't mind, it'll only take a few seconds."

He tries again to wrest his body back under control, but he lurches forward and falls against the dashboard. After that his limbs will no longer obey him. He can't even hold still.

What's going to happen to Lucy? It's his only intelligible thought.

At Julian's request, Charlie's arms move as automatically as if he still controls them. He can just barely feel the loops of rope around his wrists and the tug of a tightening knot—a nagging, distant feeling, like someone gently pulling on his clothes. The car trembles from the passing weight of the train.

"Thank you," Julian says. "See, that wasn't so bad. You *like* following orders, don't you? No matter what they tell you to do."

"We've read all about you." Paul's voice is soft. "We know exactly what you are."

But Charlie doesn't know what he is, not anymore. Maybe he never has. Fear makes you forget everything—turns you into something that only knows it can die.

He's felt it before, and seen other people feeling it. He knows what it looks like from the outside, and from the boys' faces he knows they see it too. In this cloying heat, smothering as the Vietnamese sun, he remembers the relief of deciding not to see.

When the train is gone, it leaves a ringing emptiness in its wake. Julian coaxes Charlie to sit upright and refastens his seat belt for him. Paul watches, stone-faced, then draws a deep breath and shifts the car into drive.

The numbness bleeds into Charlie's vision. He sees everything through the veil of a dream. The widening black between the streetlights; the silent strangers alongside him looking out into the dark. They're kids—just kids. He doesn't understand, and he never will.

The boys still won't meet each other's eyes. They're afraid, both of them, of what they might see.

Part I

I.

THE PILLS let his mother sleep, but they didn't help her do it well. They left her lower eyelids dark and thick, as if she hadn't slept at all. Paul could tell when she was taking them because she became sluggish instead of jittery. Most sounds still startled her, but they reached her at a delay, enough that she could brace herself first. She moved languidly, low-shouldered, as if through water.

It wasn't much of an improvement, at least not for the rest of them, but Paul wasn't the only one who had given up on that.

She was sitting by the living-room window, where she had always claimed the light was best. The winter light cast her face in the same creamy gray as her dressing gown. Paul watched her sweep her fingertips under her eyes; the shadows vanished beneath a film of concealer.

"There's nothing wrong with your present," his mother was saying. Her eyes were turned toward the compact mirror but not really watching it, as if she had surrendered her movements to muscle memory. "It's beautiful. Bubbe Sonia's always loved your artwork."

Paul was already dressed for the party, in the brown corduroy suit and knit blue tie he wore to every party. The blazer had grown too tight across his shoulders, little folds of fabric biting into the flesh whenever he lifted his arms. The sleeves were too short by an inch. Paul hated the look of his own bare wrists, with their shining blue veins and the skin stretched too thin to hold them in place. They reminded him that his body was a thing that could be taken apart.

"She won't love this," he said. "If I were her I'd hate it. It's a slap in the face."

"Who puts these awful ideas in your head?" His mother had the doleful dark gaze of a calf. When he forced himself to keep looking at her he felt a dull, insistent ache. "You're forever assuming the worst. I don't know how I feel about those books they're making you read."

"No one puts ideas in my head," said Paul. His voice was sharp, but it took a moment for her to wince. "It's an objective assessment. She'll despise it, and she'll be right to do it."

His mother slowly clicked her compact shut. She smiled at him, but with a weary finality designed to end the conversation.

It was snowing, large wet flakes that were stained gray before they even hit the ground. Outside the window, the family Buick hydroplaned in the slush before pulling to a stop. Audrey ducked out of the driver's side, shaking her long strawberry-blond hair out of her face, and sauntered up the walk with a paper bag swinging from one hand.

"Well, it's the fanciest I could find for the money," Audrey said by way of a greeting. She shook the wine bottle free of its bag and inspected it. "Whether it's fancy enough for Mount Lebanon people is a whole other matter—Ma, Jesus, are you ever planning to actually get dressed for this thing?"

It had once been the job of Paul's mother to play the sheepdog, to chase everyone into place and keep an eye on the clock. Now it had fallen to Audrey, who up till a year ago had always been the one stumbling from the basement in half-tied shoes while their mother fretted at the head of the stairs. Audrey was ready in time today, bootlaces pulled tight, but she was still so skeptical of the idea of punctuality that she struggled to convince anyone else of its necessity. By the time she'd coaxed their mother upstairs to get dressed it was clear that they were going to be late.

The three of them waited in the front hallway in their party clothes and winter coats. Paul stood very still, elbows tucked in, trying not to fidget with his cuffs. Audrey kept lifting her sleeve to look at her watch; Laurie, ignoring them both, leaned against the railing and listened to her transistor radio.

"I'm going to go see if I can give her a nudge," said Audrey after a while. "Paul, what's that face? You look like you're going to cry."

Paul glared at her back as she made her way up the stairs. Laurie took out one of her earphones and heaved a sigh. She was doll-like and scrubbed pink, wearing T-strap shoes and a flowered pinafore dress their grandmother had sewn for her. She looked much younger than her twelve years, but she had already adopted an air of adolescent lofty irritation.

They exchanged a long, wordless look. Paul summoned a wry smile; Laurie deliberately didn't return it. When a door finally swung shut above their heads, she tensed almost imperceptibly.

"God," she said. "This thing is going to be a drag and a half."

Audrey drove, a little too fast. His mother rode shotgun, gloved hands folded in her lap, watching the window. She didn't complain about Audrey's driving, or her decision to take the interstate; she didn't even mention the unseen tangle behind Audrey's right ear. Whenever the car entered an underpass, the reflection of his mother's face became visible in the shaded glass. Paul took measure of her—the blankness of her eyes and the fine lines at their corners, the way her lavender knit hat cinched into her dark auburn hair. It was easy for him to hate her; it was almost primal.

They were late enough that the rest of the fleet of cars outside their aunt Hazel's house were already dusted with snow. After Audrey parked she drew a deep breath, then turned to give Paul and Laurie a sardonic grin.

"Okay, gang," she said. "Let's go pretend to be normal."

It was just like every other family gathering—filled with well-meaning, exhausting people, eager to pull Paul's scars open and uniquely qualified to do so efficiently. Hazel's husband, Harvey, who adored Paul without reservation, had a way of behaving as if Paul's every interest and gesture was outlandishly wrong for a boy. Today he rattled Paul's shoulders and asked, as if even the premise of the question were a laugh riot, "So when's your next butterfly-hunting expedition?"

"They're all dead at the moment," Paul answered, forcing a smile, "but thanks for checking in."

The family treated all four of them with conspicuous delicacy. His mother was pillowed on all sides by his aunts' soft voices and gentle pats on the arm, so that nothing too sharp stood a chance of reaching her. When Paul and his sisters drifted too close to any group, conversations became artificially light. Younger cousins, who had clearly been instructed to be careful, fell silent altogether rather than cause offense; they exchanged panicked glances, then retreated in a flurry of whispers.

There was something different about the way the family dealt with Paul; there always had been. But now it had distilled—the fascination, the wariness, the anxious undercurrent of worry. He tried to be polite, which was the nearest he could get to making himself too small to see. He forgot conversations as soon as they ended; all he could remember was what people said as he was walking away. *Ruth says college isn't doing any better for him as far as friends go. No surprise—it's not his fault, but he's a little intense, isn't he? Oh, it must be so hard for her, he looks more like his father every day . . .*

His grandfather caught him creeping into the pantry, where he'd been hoping to gather his thoughts. He gave Paul a knowing smile, which Paul couldn't find the energy to return. Just past his grandfather's shoulder Paul could see Hazel, resplendent in her first-generation suburban finery, trying to convince Laurie to taste a spatula of frosting.

"It's a bit much, isn't it?" his grandfather said. "All this fuss."

Paul pressed his shoulders against the dry-goods shelves and shut his eyes. He didn't need to nod. He and his grandfather had repeated this exchange at every family party since he was five.

"Holding up all right? You've got no sort of poker face, Paulie."

"Everyone's treating me like a time bomb," Paul said, more frankly than he would have dared with anyone else. "So there's that."

His grandfather made an amiable, dismissive noise at the back of his throat.

"It's in your head," he said, as if this would be a great comfort. "What, you think anyone's still upset about that business with the Costello kid? Boy stuff, the whole thing. That was nothing— ancient history. Your mother might feel a little different," he added, "but she wouldn't know, would she? A boy has to defend himself."

He was deflecting and they both knew it, but Paul let him believe he hadn't noticed. After a moment his grandfather gave his arm a quick shake.

"Come on," he said, "why don't we go show Mamaleh what you've painted for her?"

He'd put it off as long as he could, but there was no avoiding it now. His great-grandmother had been placed in the den, her wheelchair folded and set aside to give her a place of honor in one of the good armchairs. She looked like a baby parrot, kindly faced and vulnerable, tiny beneath her blankets. The air around her had a sweet, powdery smell of decay.

When Paul leaned down to kiss the rice-paper skin of her forehead, she clasped a hand around his fingers. She looked toward Paul's mother and nodded, so feebly that the gesture was almost invisible.

"You and Jakob had such beautiful children, Ruthie," she said, and Paul felt a rare moment of kinship with his mother when he noticed the falter in her smile.

An awkward hush fell over the room as his great-grandmother struggled with the wrappings. When the paper fell away, the silence didn't lift.

Paul had based the painting on the sole photograph to survive his great-grandmother's adolescence in Lithuania. He had invented from it a proud, handsome girl with long black hair, and a smile—not unlike Laurie's—that had a trace of mischief in it. He had meant to make the painting happy and gentle for her, something to brighten her dimming days. He watched her adjust her thick glasses to look at it more closely, little hands shaking like thorny branches. He knew, even before she spoke, that it was the cruelest thing he could have given her.

"It is very strange," she said, accent distilled by memory. "Strange to think that I am the only person who remembers me this way." She smiled at Paul, peaceful and resigned, and Paul wished he could fade into the air. "It is always the same, you know, in my mind. No matter how old, when I look into a mirror, this face is what I expect to see."

He couldn't hide his dismay, but she was too nearsighted to see it. She reached for his hand again and squeezed it; her skin was feverishly warm.

"It is a beautiful memory," she said. "Thank you."

He retreated as soon as he could without drawing notice. He found himself in his aunt's bedroom, where the dwindling sunlight was blotted to a thin stripe by the curtains. It was cold; Hazel still wasn't middle-class enough to leave the heat running in an empty room. Paul sat in the window seat, stretching out his thin legs and trying to forget that he existed. His only companions were the shadows of family photographs and the quiet, snuffling snores of the cat at the foot of the bed.

The door slivered open, and Laurie edged inside. She put a finger to her lips, grinning, and installed herself beside him on the window seat.

"This is so fucking boring," she said, reveling in a word that hadn't yet lost its novelty. She swung her stockinged legs up to drape over his; Paul only gave her a halfhearted shove before yielding to the intrusion. "Hazel wanted me to find you and tell you there's cake in a few minutes. It's gross, though, the frosting is full of coconut."

"You're the only one who doesn't like it, weirdo," said Paul automatically, but he couldn't muster any enthusiasm to tease her.

Laurie rolled her head to one side and touched her temple to the curtains. The family always noticed Paul's likeness to his father, but no one remarked on how much stronger a resemblance there was in Laurie. Alone among the Fleischer children, she had missed out on their grandfather's red hair. Her face was fuller than Paul's and far more kind. But the others didn't expect her to take after their father—it was something only Paul noticed, something that now and then could strike him breath-less with grief.

"Are you okay?" Her eyes met his, and she made a quick, matter-of-fact assessment, nothing like the rest of the family's self-interested concern. "You look really sad."

Paul was tired of being asked, but he was also tired of pre-tending the answer was what everyone wanted it to be.

"Aren't you sad, too?"

Laurie made a noise that was a shade too angry to be a laugh.

"I miss Dad," she said. "He messed everything up."

"Well." Paul tucked his glasses into his breast pocket and shut his eyes. "You're not wrong."

2.

HE REMEMBERED the boy from freshman orientation—months ago now, but the memory still lingered. Paul had only seen him from a distance, then; he was a laughing dark-haired blur with a straight spine, perpetually surrounded by people as if he took for granted that he ought to be. He'd reminded Paul of the golden boys he knew in high school, the state-champion track teammates and stars of school plays. Paul remembered writing an elaborate life story for the boy in his head while he picked at the label on his soda bottle and spoke to no one. He couldn't remember any details of the story now, but he hadn't chosen them to be memorable. Paul assumed such people had the luxury of leading uneventful lives.

The boy had come to class alone, which looked unnatural on him. He sat a row back from Paul, carefully draping his satchel and wool winter coat over the back of his seat. He wore his sleeves folded back from his forearms, which he leaned on as he listened, attentive to the point of impatience. His hands were very like Paul's, long-fingered and lean, blue delicate shadows of vein just visible. There was a winter-faded smear of freckles beneath his skin, and his watch (burgundy leather) was a shade too large for his wrist.

The professor was making a list, ETHICAL ISSUES IN THE SCIENCES. Paul turned forward again at the squeal of the chalk. He thought he felt the other boy glance toward him, as if he'd finally noticed that he was being watched, but Paul didn't dare look back.

"So many eager volunteers," said Professor Strauss. He picked up the class roster again, holding the chalk between his fingers. He wore a film of eraser dust on his hand like a white laboratory glove. "Let's see, how about—Paul Fleischer, Biology. Perhaps you can think of a pertinent problem in experimental ethics?"

His classmates were looking at him, not staring, but in that moment the distinction felt very fine.

"Well," he said, "there's the fact that doctors keep medically torturing people in the name of science whenever they feel like they can get away with it."

All the air left the room. Strauss took a moment to shake himself.

"Human subject experimentation," Strauss said to the class, "is an excellent example of what we'll be talking about in this class. The places where the demands of scientific inquiry come up against the boundaries of human need—"

"Pardon me for interrupting," said the boy behind him suddenly, "but I don't think that's what he was saying."

Paul turned, slowly, to look at him. The boy sat at attention, turning his pen between his fingers. When the other students' eyes landed on him, he hardly seemed to notice.

"Of course it's an example," the boy said, "but it's not *his* example. I think what Fleischer is actually getting at is a widespread failure of the scientific conscience to consider the humanity of its subjects at all."

"Yes," said Paul, "yes, that's it exactly," but he was speaking so quietly and the words felt so thick that he didn't think anyone heard him.

"I think that's sort of a melodramatic way of putting it," said a voice from the front. Paul knew the speaker slightly—Brady, an upperclassman in Chemistry who had been the student assistant in Paul's laboratory section the semester before. There couldn't have been more than five years between them, but he was decisively a man rather than a boy; his hands were broad and thick-fingered, nails wider than they were long. "This isn't the Third Reich," Brady said. "Scientists here operate under ethical standards."

"Yes, and those standards work so well," said Paul acidly. "That's how we get, what, only a few *decades* of letting innocent people die of syphilis in Tuskegee before anybody thinks to complain—"

"Sure, there are problematic studies, conducted by a few bad apples who manage to avoid notice, but we're *doing* something about it. With institutional review boards and the like, we're imposing—"

"But you can't impose morality from the outside." Paul knew anger had seeped into his voice, but he didn't care. "The whole idea of an *infrastructure* of ethical oversight is a symptom of the—the 'failure of the scientific conscience.' I'm saying there's something about the way we conduct scientific inquiry that's actually appealing to people who want to slice people up just to see what happens. Because they sure seem to do it the second they think the infrastructure won't notice."

"A review board is just a hedge on liability," said the boy behind him. "We can't and shouldn't pretend it functions as a conscience. Let's not delude ourselves that we can send Mengele on his way with a stack of consent forms and pretend that solves the problem."

"Spirited debate!" said Strauss with a clap of his chalk-streaked hands. "Highly preferable to dull-eyed terror. Hold that thought, gentlemen, because the readings for week seven in particular will prove pertinent . . ."

Paul sank back into his chair and exhaled slowly. As the conversation shifted, he felt a stir of movement at his side. The dark-haired boy had gathered his belongings and settled at the desk beside him. Paul watched him, but the boy's eyes were trained on the professor. They were the same shade of green as sea glass—a soft and striking color but very cold, an eerie contrast with the dark of his lashes.

Strauss had moved on to a girl from the Physics department, who suggested nuclear weapons research. Paul only half listened to the discussion as he sketched a skeleton with Brady's barrel chest and wide jaw. He blackened the bones and haloed them from behind with the shadow of a mushroom cloud. *Further achievements in American ethics*, he wrote underneath. *A superior system.*

Something tapped at his ankle—the toe of a jodhpur boot, stained with a faint crust of sidewalk salt. The dark-haired boy was looking over at his notebook, leaning forward so he could see past Paul's arm.

Paul felt his face flush. At first he considered turning the page, or tucking his arms around the notebook to conceal it as he'd done countless times, protecting his sketchbooks from the singsong girls who liked to pester him in the cafeteria.

Instead, scarcely recognizing himself, he pulled the page free and placed it in the boy's hand.

"We haven't had an example from you, yet."

Paul jumped, but Strauss was talking to the boy beside him, with a teacher's well-worn glee at catching a student unawares. The boy hid the drawing under his desk and smiled, unabashed.

"Just two names to go, and I have to doubt you're Ramona," said Strauss serenely. "So you must be—"

"Julian," answered the boy. "Julian Fromme."

"I see." Strauss glanced down at his roster again. "And I see I have you down as 'undeclared'—surely the lives of the indecisive are beset with ethical quandary."

A polite titter made its way around the room. In his place Paul would have wanted to melt into the floor, but Julian Fromme endured it without a trace of distress.

"It's Psychology, actually, as of yesterday," Julian said. "And I'm interested in social psychology in particular, which is inherently problematic. Every method of social research does some kind of harm. If you observe social phenomena from a distance, you often only see evidence that conforms to your hypothesis—'objectivity' is a lie scientists tell themselves, even in the hard sciences, and with qualitative research, forget it. But if you observe from up close, then your presence alters the nature of the data. And social experiments in controlled environments have certainly been *conducted*, but they all require some degree of deception to get untainted results—which may or may not cross ethical lines," he added with a glance at Brady, "depending on the particular conscience your IRB has imposed on you."

"Am I to understand, Mr. Fromme," said Strauss, "that you want 'social psychology in general' listed as an ethical debate in the sciences?"

"Just put me down for 'confirmation bias,' 'observer's paradox,' and 'informed consent,' please," said Julian briskly. "I believe that's the order I cited them in."

Strauss raised his eyebrows and smiled. "Very well, Mr. Fromme," he said. "I suppose we won't throw you to the wolves just yet."

Strauss turned toward the blackboard again, and Paul watched with alarm as Julian casually set the drawing on his own desk. He looked down at it for a moment, stone-faced and calm. Then he wrote something in the margins with a lazy flourish.

By the time the drawing arrived back in Paul's hands, Julian's scarlet ink had bled straight through the cheap paper.

Crime rate reduced to 0%, Red Menace permanently defeated—an apocalypse for the greater good.

(Sign this. I want to keep it.)

IT DIDN'T occur to Paul to wait. At the end of class he pushed his books into his knapsack and zipped his army parka up to the throat. Beyond the second-story windows a soft snow was falling. With the stain of soot blurred by distance, flakes paler than the dark sky, it almost looked white.

He lingered at the top of the stairs to uncurl the ball of his knit wool gloves. Brady pushed past him. When Paul heard someone call out behind him—"Hey, wait a second"—he thought at first that Brady was the one being pursued. It took the sound of his own last name for him to turn and look back.

Julian Fromme smiled when he caught Paul's eye. His gait was brisk but unhurried; he slung his scarf around his neck as he approached, a single languid movement that betrayed an unthinking sureness in his body.

"In a hurry?"

"Not really."

"Could've fooled me."

Julian joined him at the head of the staircase, fastening the last button on his double-breasted coat. He looked meticulously cared for, like a rare plant in a conservatory; Paul felt abruptly shabby beside him in his anorak and snow boots, too careworn and practical to be worthy of attention.

"You look familiar," Julian said. "Did we see each other at orientation?"

Paul had forced himself to forget, the memory too humiliating to dwell on. They were supposed to remain strangers—the other boy had been meant to forget him, because Paul couldn't be the first or last person he'd ever caught watching him. He remembered Julian's faint smile, the slight rise of his left eyebrow. That eyebrow was sliced through by a thin scar near its outer edge, an incongruous imperfection Paul had noticed with sudden ardor and then stowed away.

He'd spent the rest of the mixer on a bench outside, waiting out the ninety minutes he had promised his mother. He remembered wanting the strange boy to follow him, but of course he hadn't. They never did. That was how it was always supposed to end.

"I don't really remember," he replied, and reflected in Julian's face he immediately saw the weakness of the lie. "I didn't stay very long, those things give me a headache."

Julian smiled, but he didn't answer. He started down the steps, watching Paul impassively over his shoulder. He didn't use the railing; Paul tried to ignore it himself, letting his fingertips skate along the edge on the way down as if he paid it no mind, but he'd been nervous about heights all his life and couldn't quite force his hand to fall.

Once he was certain Paul was following, Julian smiled again and looked ahead. "You're one of those people who worry all the time, aren't you?" he said, and it was as much an accusation as a joke. "You've got that look."

Paul hurried to catch up. He turned up his hood as they emerged into the snow, but Julian's head was bare, so he quickly lowered it again. "I don't worry," he protested, and when Julian looked skeptical, he dug in his heels rather than let himself be mocked. "I *ruminate*. They're distinct actions."

"Are they?" said Julian. "From this angle . . ."

"Worrying," said Paul, "means you're afraid it's going to happen. Ruminating is when you *know* it will, if it hasn't happened already. One is neurotic, the other is fatalistic, and fatalism is supported by evidence. It isn't the same."

Paul didn't notice his own tension until it receded when Julian laughed.

"That's the most goddamn German thing I've ever heard," he said.

Paul retrieved his bicycle from its berth outside and walked it alongside them, the fresh snow squeaking beneath its wheels.

"Speaking of German." There was a note of keen interest in Julian's voice, muted but unmistakable, and Paul's chest tightened like a coil. "That thing you were saying, about the infrastructure of ethical oversight. Where did you get it?"

Paul's excitement faded. "I don't have to *get it* somewhere," he said defensively. "I can think for myself."

"Of course you can. Don't be so eager to get your feelings hurt, it's boring and beneath you."

Something in the spiteful impatience of the remark put Paul at ease, far more than a more earnest reassurance would have. Julian coughed on a mouthful of cold air and pulled his scarlet scarf a little tighter. Against the dull gray of winter he was the only bright thing.

"Did you really just make that up?" said Julian after a pause. He didn't sound disbelieving, though the fascination in his eyes was still remote and clinical in a way Paul didn't entirely appreciate. "Didn't they give you any of the world-weary Continentals in Phil 101?"

"Um—we did the *Symposium*," Paul offered in dismay. "And some Descartes, a little bit of Kant."

"That's not philosophy, that's paleontology." Julian spoke with a sardonic grandness that couldn't quite conceal his enthusiasm. "You're better than that, you need a philosophy that's equipped to grapple with the moral reckonings of the twentieth century—you're already most of the way there, you obviously ruminate better than most. Is that your last class of the day?"

Paul was so dizzy on the compliment that it took him a moment to parse the question that followed. He noticed odd notes of likeness between them—the shape of their hands, their heights within an inch. It made him feel better about how dissimilar they were otherwise, as if he might really be worthy of notice.

He nodded, belatedly, and Julian grinned.

"Good," he said. "Come on. I need to lend you some books."

On campus tours, the college always showed off its handful of spotless, intensely modern dormitories with poured-concrete walls and façades pitted with plate-glass windows. The building where Julian Fromme lived was not one of these—it was ancient and drafty, built in the same cheap brick as an elderly elementary school.

The kitchen was a dank subterranean room with grills on its squat windows. The dim light was a mercy, since it spared Paul from seeing too clearly how filthy every surface was.

"I'm not seeing any ginger ale," said Julian, peering into the fridge. "Barbarians. Is Coke okay?"

"Sure." Paul glanced over his shoulder toward the group of boys sitting at the kitchen table, who were eating beans on toast in their boxer shorts and sweatshirts. Julian had serenely ignored them, breezing past them as if they were furniture. Paul wasn't convinced they were returning the favor.

"Don't mind them," Julian said quietly. He handed Paul his soda and glanced dismissively at the strangers. "They don't deserve your attention."

Julian didn't belong in this place. He was like a dart of clean bright light, alien and vibrant.

He led Paul back into the hallway and up a staircase through the atrium. Someone had misplaced a volume of Hegel on the landing; Julian paused over it with feline disinterest, then deliberately kicked it the rest of the way down the stairs.

"You don't live on campus, do you?" he said as he searched for his keys.

"I live with my mother." Paul realized the moment he spoke that he couldn't have phrased it any more like a Hitchcock shut-in. He quickly tried to paper over it. "—and my sisters. I wanted to be in the dorms, but my scholarship doesn't cover housing, and we only live a couple miles away."

"Well, as you can see, you get a lot for your money." Julian gave his door a shove to free it from the damp-swollen frame. "Come in, make yourself at home."

Paul did his best to pretend he did this sort of thing all the time. He tried not to linger too long over the details, lest it become obvious that he was trying to commit them to memory. There were no family photographs—just a picture of Julian himself, several years younger, arms flung around the neck of a large brown dog. There was a small stereo by the window, but no television. Instead the little room was dense with books, which spilled over from the shelves and sat in crooked stacks on the dresser and floor. Many of the spines were titled in French, and a few, with their spiky half-familiar alphabet, looked like they had to be in Russian.

A portable chessboard lay open on the desk, pieces scattered in full combat. Paul stared at it to see if he could make sense of it, but when Julian looked at him, he turned away and seated himself tentatively in the desk chair.

"Arendt is mandatory," said Julian. He tossed his coat over the end of the bed and began gathering books from the case. "She's brilliant, I Greyhounded up to New York last semester for a talk she gave at the New School. She gets at *why* behavioral norms can't function as a conscience—the purpose of social norms is to *norm*, not to attain moral perfection—oh, let's get some of old Fritz in here too, why not, the Teutonic bombast will stick to your ribs. Your other friends don't give you homework, do they, Fleischer?"

"I wish," Paul said faintly. It startled him, perhaps more than it should have, for Julian to use the word *friend*.

"You'll regret saying that by the time I'm through with you." Julian had dropped the books at Paul's elbow and was rifling through his milk crate full of records. "I was led to believe," he said, "that college was a haven for the intellectually curious. Turns out that it's really just about acculturating you to academia—which is *fascinating*, petri dish of maladaptive behavior that it is, but still."

"Is that even true? I thought it was about drugging yourself into a stupor."

"I think they prefer to pronounce it 'seeking enlightenment by way of the chemical expansion of the mind.' How else are they going to feel self-righteous about it?"

Julian flung himself onto his bed. Paul felt an odd thrill, not unlike relief, when he saw that Julian was grinning. He was

terrified Julian would notice that he spoke too haltingly around
the remnants of his childhood stutter—that his thoughts were
ugly and incomplete and insufficiently well-read.

"How old are you, anyway?"

"Uh—I'll be seventeen in March."

"Ha! I knew it." Julian retrieved his soda from the windowsill and settled back on his elbows. "I can always spot a fellow
runt. I skipped third and seventh—ruined my chances of ever
playing varsity sports. My father was furious."

He could have resisted the impulse to be honest, but he chose
to yield. The surrender made his body feel light and cool.

"I just had to graduate early, because otherwise they wanted
to expel me."

"Get out," said Julian. "What did you do?"

He had never said it out loud before. It occurred to him, as he
was speaking, that it ought to feel stranger than it did.

"I hit a guy in the face with my locker door."

"The hell you did!"

"He needed about fifteen stitches." Paul couldn't decide if
Julian looked enthralled or horrified. "He had it coming," he
added, but Julian waved him off.

"I can imagine. God, If I'd known *that* was all it took to get
out of high school, I'd've done it myself. Did your parents hit the
roof?"

Paul scrambled for an excuse to avoid Julian's eyes. He busied
himself making room in his knapsack for Julian's books; the di-
version felt transparent, but he couldn't think of anything more
sophisticated.

"My mother doesn't really . . . she just gets *sad*," he said. The
truthfulness was beginning to burn like an overextended limb.
"That's all she does anymore, she worries at you and asks 'Why

are you doing this?' and sits around feeling sorry for herself where she knows you can see her, so you feel like you have to do something about it—which is what she does anyway, she's a house-widow, all she's good for is cashing the pension checks and making people feel bad for her. So it was just—more of that. And I guess I got grounded, but I don't go out much anyway, so I didn't really notice."

In the brief silence that followed, Paul still couldn't bring himself to meet Julian's eyes.

"Sorry," he mumbled. "I didn't mean to just . . ."

"It's a raw nerve," said Julian evenly. "You're allowed them. For what it's worth, there's a reason I decided to go to college in a town where my parents don't know anybody."

Paul noticed distantly that he didn't much care for the record Julian was playing. It was a girl singing in French, nothing he could object to in substance, but the cadence was poppy and simple in a way that he felt Julian oughtn't to care for. The dislike elated him—it gave him something, however trivial, that he could politely overlook for Julian's sake.

"Where are they?" he asked.

"DC." Julian paused, then corrected himself. "*Near* DC. My father works at the State Department, but they live in a little village on the bay that 'keeps the riff-raff out,' as he says. Of course, according to the town charter, *he's* riff-raff, but we're pretending to be Episcopalian so that we'll be allowed into the country club."

Paul tried to conceal his fascination. "That's," he said carefully, "I mean, it's very—"

"Don't be diplomatic about it, it's disgusting—I think he only married my mother because he was hoping the kids would turn out blond," said Julian. "Not that she's any better than he is, or she'd be chum in the water. She's from France. Her father owns a bunch of department stores there—money's so new you can still smell the ink, but they're swimming in it. She's on the board at MoMA and owns a gallery in New York, because I guess she needed a hobby."

A few details in the room that had struck Paul as strange at first sight now began to make sense. The string of maritime signal flags pinned to the wall above the bed, clashing brightly with the room's general asceticism; the crisp new wool of Julian's winter coat and the conservative, prep-school shape of his clothes. These details rang false because they had been chosen by someone else, someone who lacked Julian's wit and energy and his ability to ignore everything beneath his notice.

"It's not tragic, or anything," Julian was saying. "Don't get me wrong. It's just *tedious*. I hope you won't hold it against me— being, you know, a half-shiksa trust fund baby who's never had to work for anything. I usually lie about it."

Julian's vulnerability was more calculated than it pretended to be, but Paul decided not to fight it.

"I'd never hold it against you," Paul said. "I've actually been thinking this whole time how I can't really make sense of you. You're nothing like anyone else, and now I know it's not because of where you come from. Nothing made you. You just are."

He didn't know before speaking how nakedly earnest the words would sound, but he only regretted it for a moment. One corner of Julian's mouth went a little higher than the other when he smiled; Paul remembered something he'd read in his art history class last semester, about how the Japanese believed there was something poignant and endearing about asymmetry.

"Damn you, Fleischer," said Julian. "Now I'm going to have to try and live up to that."

3.

PAUL COULD only forgive himself for keeping a journal if he told himself he was documenting history. He wrote it for an audience, one who would only read it after the end of a life he'd made significant. He imagined a future biographer poring through his juvenilia for the signs of future greatness, and how that person would perceive the moments of weakness and self-indulgence in between. In hindsight his frustrations and fears would be taken as evidence that he was still human—but in the present, before he'd made anything of himself, they meant he was *only* human.

A few weeks after his father's death, Paul had launched and begun to document a variety of self-improvement projects designed to increase his mental and physical vigor—running times when the weather allowed, swimming times when it didn't, synopses and excerpts from the enriching books and essays he read between the horror and science fiction he secretly preferred. Every few weeks he took himself up the Mount Washington funicular, resuming alone a ritual his father had led when Paul was little in an attempt to cure him of his fear of heights. When he reached the top, Paul had to stand on the observation deck, close enough to the railing to touch it with his elbows, until he was so shaky and light-headed that he had to retreat. His father had always rewarded this so-called bravery with an ice cream or a packet of baseball cards, no matter how much of a fool Paul had made of himself by running away or crying. Nowadays Paul brought his stopwatch with him, and he recorded the minutes and seconds he lasted before his crashing heartbeat pulled him back from the edge.

On bad days, there were no improvements to write down. On worse days he couldn't even try to make himself better. But he wrote every day, even when all he could do was pick fights with a dead man. He resurrected long-ago arguments about his schoolwork or spats with classmates, things his father would never have remembered. He searched his memory for lies his father had told him, the gentle coddling lies parents always told their children, and none was so small that he couldn't dissect it down to threads. When the fury burned so bright that he couldn't bear to look, Paul curled over his desk with his head bowed close to the page, watching the pen move from the corner of his eye. He wrote long, ruthless lists. Reasons to stay alive, however little joy it brought. The same words appeared every time, *duty* and *defiance* and *refusing to submit to weakness*. Paul never let himself consider who he was trying to convince.

He tried to believe there was no shame in what he wrote, those days when he was too lead-limbed and numb to try to make himself stronger. Paul could be forgiven his unhappiness, even his fear, so long as one day he proved strong enough to overcome it. There was no surpassing himself unless he knew which parts of him deserved to be left behind. Paul imagined the summarizing sentences in his biography—how they would mark his sharpest turns of phrase, and marvel, in retrospect, at the resilience he'd showed.

The day after he first spoke to Julian Fromme, he took his journal out of the locked paint box he kept under his bed and opened it to a fresh white page. *January 17, 1973*, he wrote, more neatly than usual because he pictured the biographer making a note of it. *Yesterday I met someone I believe will prove very important.*

Paul didn't know what Julian was destined for, but the

promise of greatness marked every part of him. Even Julian didn't seem to know—throughout the first few weeks Paul watched him breeze between interests and ambitions, and he became an expert on each one so quickly that it was as if he were born knowing everything. But he wasn't aimless. His curiosity was ravenous, blazing in all directions like the sun. He wanted to write scathing treatises on human nature, empirical data on obedience and self-delusion, nocking neatly into Arendt's bleak promises. He wanted to hone his Russian to a fine enough point to read Nabokov's early works in the original, or else to become a spy. He had ideas for satirical novels about what he called the *haute-bourgeoisie,* because god knew his hometown had given him enough material. When he reviewed movies for the college newspaper, he was razor-precise, calling out long takes he liked and choppy editing that he didn't—after all, if he ever became a film director, he had to know how to do it right.

He took Paul to strange art galleries in the Strip District, where there were wild nonsensical interpretive dances or fleshy sculptures whose formless sensuality made Paul squirm and look away. Whenever Paul and Julian stood together in front of an artwork—a canvas blank but for a single fleck of blue, a collage of magazine models with their eyes blacked out—Julian would take rapid measure of it and then elbow Paul's arm. "What do you think?" he would ask, with no hint of what he wanted to hear, and Paul could never think fast enough to say anything at all.

It was impossible to keep up with him. Paul's tongue was too clumsy for wit. His thoughts were meticulous and slow, and he could never find words for them until he had milled an idea down to the grist.

There was something mesmerizing about the way Julian

moved—carelessly graceful, as if he weren't excruciatingly conscious of every atom he displaced. Paul had tried all his life to erase the anxious delicacy in his own gestures, especially the hesitant motions of his hands. For a while he thought he could teach his body to follow Julian's somehow, if only he practiced long enough. He spent hours in front of his bedroom mirror, trying to relax into that loose-limbed elegance. But Paul was fettered and careful, and even his weak imitation of Julian's posture looked wrong.

When they walked together across campus, Paul could all but see the two of them from the outside—a dark-haired Apollo painted in flowing Botticelli lines, and the ungainly stork of a boy beside him, trying to keep in step. He could tell other people were thinking it too, especially the friends of Julian's who thought themselves more deserving of Paul's place. They never hid the disbelief in their smiles as they glanced between the two of them, clearly wondering why.

Because Julian did have other friends, though Paul rarely saw them. Julian had thought of studying drama in his first semester, and occasionally the two of them were accosted on the snowy path by one of Julian's buoyant, overwrought theater friends. Other times, the interlopers were colleagues from the arts pages of the student paper—these friends spoke in an identical arrogant drawl and made insipid comments about Max Stirner, and they never seemed to realize that Julian's replies were making fun of them. After the initial introductions Paul always hung back at Julian's side with his arms folded, staring at his shoes. If the friends acknowledged him at all, it was in the third person—*your friend here*, never his name.

But no matter how mediocre or shallow the other friends were, even they could tell Julian was destined for something.

They might not understand it, but they knew. When Julian addressed them, Paul watched the way their faces opened. They smiled as if they were already thinking of what they would say years later. That they knew him when he wasn't anyone yet; that they were there before it all began.

There was no avoiding them if they approached first, but whenever Julian caught sight of his friends at a distance he would take Paul's arm and steer them out of sight. "I attract pretentious people," he explained, and there was nothing in his voice that betrayed any fondness for them. "I think that's why I like you so much, Pablo. You're so goddamn sincere."

Paul never asked where the nickname came from, because it didn't matter—what mattered was that Julian had given it to him unbidden. His real name was common, ordinary, something Julian might say and then forget saying. But *Pablo* rang like a harp string. Julian said it warmly, but it was an imperious kind of affection. It was as if this were the name he'd given a favorite belonging.

Julian moved through every part of Paul's life the same way—not entitled, nothing so crass and insecure, but taking for granted that Paul would allow him anywhere. His was an arrogant intimacy, the kind that followed Paul home without asking and spent the afternoon examining the bookcases and pantry shelves.

Neither Paul's mother nor his sisters were home that first day—he had the house to himself on Friday afternoons, or else he might have refused to let Julian inside. The fact that Paul allowed him into the house at all wasn't the acquiescence Julian probably thought it was. He'd done it for the same reason that he embraced Julian's nickname for him—the same reason he didn't flinch away from the occasional brush of Julian's hand on his shoulder. Paul was taking something for his own, and he wasn't sure it was something Julian even knew he was giving.

"So which door is yours?" Julian asked, one foot already on the bottom stair. It didn't seem to have occurred to Julian that Paul might refuse him. Even Paul didn't know why he did. But it pleased him to hold something back, if only for now. He liked the look that came over Julian's face, the bewilderment that someone might tell him no and mean it.

"My mother's going to be home soon," Paul said, and he caught himself smiling in the brief, exhilarating moment that Julian's face faltered.

That denial only lasted another week.

He let Julian be the one to open his bedroom door, and from the foot of the bed Paul watched him help himself to the details. Julian carefully opened Paul's drawers of butterfly and moth specimens, then paused at the desk to examine a watercolor—a rib cage emptied of heart and lungs, a trio of bright tropical songbirds trapped inside. There was a copy of *The Man in the High Castle* on the dresser next to Paul's bed, and for a moment he panicked at having forgotten to hide it in favor of something more rarefied. But Julian picked it up and paged through it without apparent judgment.

"God, and I've got you reading even more things about Nazis," he said, and Paul only realized belatedly that he was supposed to laugh.

Julian hopped onto Paul's mattress and lay back against the pillows, legs outstretched, his head resting on the Leonard Baskin reproduction on the wall behind him. The sudden nearness of him was a shock—the warmth of his ankle gnawed alongside Paul's hip, so close that Paul could have closed the distance between them and made it seem accidental. He watched how easily Julian settled into the same place Paul's own body lay when he slept. Paul imagined the traces of him that would remain—a stray dark hair, fine scarlet fibers from his merino pullover.

"It's so funny the way you paint," said Julian idly. "It's like you checked out of the twentieth century sometime around Frida Kahlo, you still paint *pictures* of things . . . It's all very Paul Fleischer, isn't it? You don't care what other people think you should be doing. It's so blood-and-guts moral, so rigid. It's exactly like you."

Paul was sure Julian wasn't making fun of him—he knew by now exactly what that looked like, because he'd memorized the movement of Julian's eyebrow and the dismissive angle of his mouth. He knew that Julian took him seriously, even when Paul himself felt foolish and overreaching. But that didn't mean he could tell whether the remark was a compliment or a criticism.

"That's the way a person should be." Paul's certainty didn't waver, but the longer he spoke, the more his confidence did. "Nothing imposed from the outside. You figure out on your own what's good and what isn't, and maybe that idea ends up being rigid, but that's better than not having anything at all. I don't care if anyone doesn't like it, even if it's you."

If Julian had asked where this thought came from, Paul would have had to lie a little to claim it for his own. It was similar to something his father had told him when he was young—that there was a difference between the law and what was just, and that being a good man meant building a framework for deciding which was which. For Paul justice could encompass infinite space, far past questions of crime and punishment. But Paul wondered in his cruelest moments if the idea had extended any further than the inside of his father's own head.

"You're a Kantian to the core." Julian laced his fingers and stretched his limbs like a cat; for the barest moment Paul could feel the light pressure of Julian's leg brushing his. "I do like your paintings, by the way," he added carelessly. "I don't understand why you don't just major in art, you're good at it."

The compliment burned in his face, then at the outer edges of his ears. He didn't dare acknowledge it.

"It's like you said," he answered after a moment. "I don't want other people telling me what to do."

Julian liked that, enough that he let Paul see that he did.

"So what are you telling *yourself* to do?" asked Julian.

That was something else Paul had been holding back, at once less personal and far more intimate than the mere physical spaces of his life. He had no name yet for what he was trying to become, nothing he wanted to be able to call himself—no "renowned conservationist," no "famous painter." The early sprouts of his ambition were still so deep under the earth that he couldn't say for sure what it was.

"Whatever I do has to mean something." He hugged his knees and stared at them; it took all his nerve to raise his voice above a mumble. "I need to make something beautiful, something that *lasts*. I don't know what, but I have to, if I want my life to matter at all."

When he finally made himself meet Julian's eyes, he couldn't find any doubt or ridicule in his face. Julian believed him, and his respect was so consequential that it felt like Paul's first step toward mattering. Paul wasn't sure he would ever grow used to it—this precipitous thrill of being seen and known and understood.

"Surely it can matter even if it doesn't last," said Julian—not disagreeing, just prompting, the way he did with all their other thought experiments. "If you painted a masterpiece and then set it on fire, it still would have mattered. If you know you've made something beautiful, who cares how long it lasts? *Après toi, le déluge.*"

"I like it better the other way," said Paul. "Where it means you're leaving the flood in your wake."

Julian smiled; it was a private, elusive smile, almost as if he thought this were funny.

"You would, wouldn't you?" was all he said.

They left soon after, at Paul's insistence. It was getting dangerously close to the time his mother tended to drift back from her weekly appointment with Dr. Greenbaum. She was what he wanted to hold back the most, for as long as he could get away with.

"They can't possibly be *that* embarrassing," Julian said as Paul hurried them to the far end of the block. "And even if they were, I'd never hold it against you."

"It's not that," said Paul. He couldn't think of a way to articulate the real reason, which felt far more complex. He liked how clean the boundary was between what his family knew about him and what belonged to him alone. He had spent his entire life in a house whose doors had keyholes but no keys. It was a new sensation for him to have a secret, and he wasn't ready to relinquish it.

They made their way to the nearest deli. Paul was worried about the venue at first—it had been his grandparents' lunch spot for decades—but it was off-hours and mostly empty, and Paul didn't particularly recognize anyone, aside from the bored-looking girl behind the counter with whom he'd taken a civics class.

Paul took a while to decide on what he wanted, while Julian

quickly loaded his tray with soup and cookies and cake slices and went to claim them a table. By the time Paul had selected his meal (turkey sandwich, French fries, ginger ale, a single deviled egg), Julian had nearly finished his first cup of coffee.

He had also retrieved one of the plastic mat chessboards from their shelf over by the napkins, and was arranging the pieces—not into their starting configuration, but an elegant midgame chaos. The positions looked familiar. Paul had seen something like them on the portable chess set in Julian's room.

"Pop quiz," said Julian as Paul arrived. "Say you're playing black. What's your next move?"

It took Paul longer to contemplate this than he would have preferred; he was distracted by the belated realization that there wasn't any dignified way to eat his egg. But Julian appeared content to let the silence linger. He poured Paul a cup of coffee and placidly dropped his crackers into his soup one by one.

Finally, Paul moved one of his knights to threaten the white bishop. When Julian didn't visibly react, he began to doubt his instincts. "Is that right?" he asked too quickly. "I'm not going to pretend I'm, you know, *great* at it—"

"It's a solid move. Maybe a little conservative, but it's solid." Julian reached to return the knight to its previous place. "But watch this."

He picked up the black queen and pulled her across the board to check the king. It was an option Paul had immediately written off as suicidal, positioning the queen such that white had no choice but to capture her. Only after he saw the aftermath did he understand the beauty of it—the way the sacrifice burned the path clear, so that no matter how white chose to reply, he would find himself in checkmate two turns later.

Julian was watching him, grinning. Paul looked between him and the board in disbelief.

"Did you . . . ?"

Julian gave a sudden, dismissive laugh.

"*God*, no," he said, so ruefully that he sounded almost defensive. "I had nothing to do with this, trust me."

Julian rifled through his satchel and produced a cheap paperback, battered and dog-eared and creased sharply along the spine. He opened to a page in the middle and handed it over. *U.S. Open 1970—Kazlauskas v. Kaplan—Championship Final.* Paul's knowledge of chess notation had atrophied since junior-high chess club, but the queen sacrifice was easy enough to find because white had immediately resigned. The transcriptionist gave the move a double exclamation mark.

"The whole game was like that," said Julian. "I was there. I'll never forget that moment—the way the whole room drew a deep breath at the same time as they realized."

"What were you doing at the U.S. Open?"

Paul had never seen Julian look embarrassed before.

"Ugh—I had no business being there. I was *barely* in the Juniors section, I was cannon fodder for the cannon fodder. All I really got for my trouble was a few days away from boarding school."

He picked up the black queen and left the piece lying on its side next to the salt shaker. Paul waited for him to speak again; it felt wiser and more honest than offering an uninformed reassurance.

"It was a beautiful game. Even between grandmasters, that's not a given, there's plenty of ugly chess even at the highest levels. But *this* game, this goddamn game—the whole time you could see the players trying to take each other apart and push each other as far as they could go. And it's *gorgeous*—when chess is played at its best, by two genuinely great players, it's a work of art made from pure reason. It was . . . Watching them build that game together—and after I'd spent the whole tournament proving my own absolute mediocrity—but anyway, how beautiful it was, and how far it was from anything I'd ever be able to do, it broke my heart a little, is all." He pulled a face. "God, sorry about that, that sounds so mawkish."

"No, it doesn't." The protest sounded more emphatic than he'd planned. "Beautiful things are supposed to hurt. It's what I was saying earlier—even if you don't know *how* you're going to create something that matters, you can still want to do it so badly you can barely think about anything else—"

Paul thought, for a moment, that Julian was reaching across the table to take his hand. Then Julian retrieved the black queen, and Paul understood in a rush how foolish he was being, how little sense the gesture would have made. They weren't children. Perhaps that would have to be another self-improvement project for the journal—observing how grown men spoke and behaved around each other so that he could mimic it more effectively.

"People tell you you're 'shy' all the time, don't they?" said Julian. He watched Paul's face with a slight frown, as if he were listening to a familiar tune in an unusual key. "And then they act like you're crazy when you do speak up, just to drive the point home that being shy is safer?"

Paul didn't reply, at least not aloud, but Julian knew the answer already. He swept the board clear and smiled.

"Don't listen to them. The rest of the world might not be ready for you, but I don't know how I ever got on without you.

You play white," he added. "I want to see how you think when you have to move first."

Paul could tell he was blushing, and Julian made it known, wordlessly, that he had noticed and would take it for what it was. This often happened between them now, the silent transmission of recognition and acceptance. Paul thought that Julian must see some immense potential in him, an early glimmer of all he hoped to become. It was the only way he could make sense of Julian's willingness to forgive him.

4.

"SO HONEY, when do we get to meet your new friend?"

Paul instantly wished he hadn't dawdled so long at the breakfast table. He could tell from Audrey's reaction that this wasn't the first she'd heard of the subject. She sighed as if trying to hide her annoyance and took a purposeful swig from her orange juice.

"Which friend?" he said.

It wasn't convincing, and neither his mother nor his sisters did him the courtesy of pretending it was. His mother smiled at him obligingly and ignored the question altogether.

"Mrs. Koenig," she said, "mentioned you have a friend who comes by sometimes. She says she doesn't think he's from the neighborhood."

"*Mrs. Koenig* is hoping he's a drug dealer," Audrey muttered into her glass. "Smug buttinsky."

"She said he looked perfectly nice, very clean-cut." His mother fired Audrey a quick warning glance. "Weren't you ever going to say something? Why would you keep that a secret?"

He should have seen this coming—he'd known the boundary would have to be breached eventually, because they always were. But anger still plumed through him, and his chest felt so tight that for a moment he couldn't speak.

"It isn't a secret." He squared his shoulders and glared down at the lukewarm, rubbery scrambled eggs he'd spent the last half hour cutting into pebbles. "It's—there's nothing *untoward* about wanting to conduct my own social life without keeping you apprised of every detail."

"That's college for 'mind your business,' Ma," said Audrey.

"But it's not a detail," his mother protested, "it's an entire *person*. I just don't know why I haven't even heard you mention a name."

"You don't keep an inventory of all Audrey or Laurie's friends, so I don't see why—"

His mother wrung her hands and gave him another smile, this one much more strained.

"All I'm saying is that it's a big change for you. I'd have thought you'd say *something*. I hope," she added, as if it were an afterthought instead of the main thrust behind the line of questioning, "that it's not because you're ashamed to introduce us to your college friends."

Of course this left Paul little choice but to surrender. He harbored a vain hope that Julian would reject the invitation, and it felt like a deliberate jab in the ribs when he didn't. That weekend, inevitably, Julian arrived at the house for lunch with a box of pistachio candies and a bundle of hothouse sunflowers. He was late—fashionably, he would have claimed—and slightly overdressed in the now-familiar way that made him seem like a character in an English novel. When he took off his overcoat, Paul caught the scarlet flash of a carnation pinned to his lapel.

Paul was only ashamed because his mother had suggested he might be. The house felt smaller and dirtier now—sun-faded curtains, cheap detergent smells, a year's patina of soot and grease on the outside of the windows. As if through a stranger's ears he heard the small blemishes in his mother's grammar, and the way her working-class accent, much thicker than his own, made every vowel as blunt and flat as a woodchip.

As they were all sitting in the living room, drinking Folgers out of the good peach-blossom cups, Paul had trouble ignoring the photograph of his father on the mantelpiece. Jake Fleischer had never learned to smile like an American—there was too much tooth to it, or else they were the wrong sort of teeth, functional rather than ornamental. The picture had been taken at his father's twenty-year anniversary at the department. He was wearing his dress blues, and he held his checker-banded cap in one gloved hand as if he were gesturing with it. The pictures had come back from the printer three months later, when the remnants of the family were still surviving on sympathy casseroles and Chinese takeout.

In an empty house, when he and Julian were caught up in conversation about immense abstract ideas, it had been possible to ignore the void left in his father's wake. Surrounded by the rest of his family, though, Paul could no longer pretend the elision was an accident. Since his death his father's absence had spilled far past the carefully drawn outlines his father had occupied when he was alive. It had flowed into every available space and settled there, and there was no chance Julian hadn't noticed it. Paul had no idea, watching him, how he was managing to think about anything else.

"No, it's all lovely, Mrs. Fleischer," Julian was saying. He had been similarly effusive about the beet soup and white-bread sandwiches his mother cobbled together for lunch. Paul knew Julian was just trying to get her to stop making a spectacle of her self-disgust, but something about the politeness irritated him. Julian's kindness toward his mother felt so deservedly patronizing that Paul was embarrassed for her—and even for Julian, a little, for deigning to give her what she clearly yearned for.

"Paul's father always took care of most of the cooking," his mother said, still apologetic and anxious. She nudged the cookie tin across the coffee table as she spoke. "He came from a restaurant family, he had a real gift for it."

That was one of his parents' old lies. It was strange that she would resurrect it now, for the sake of this stranger who could never guess what it was supposed to hide. It had been a nice story until Paul thought to do the math. He'd known for years now that the war began when his father was still young, and the bohemian café in Berlin was lost long before his father was tall enough to reach the counter. In his father's stories the family restaurant stood on its own power, moving like clockwork, unaided by human hands. There were only the patrons, with their raucous conversations and pipe-smoke smells. There was winter-squash stew bubbling on the stove, its steam glazing the kitchen windows. There was bitter, soft rye bread and the sweet aroma of cinnamon coffee cakes. The woman who lifted them from the oven was such a deliberate afterthought that Paul never learned her name.

Perhaps Paul's mother thought she could keep his father alive by telling his favorite lies for him. Paul knew better, but the story wasn't for him anymore.

"Well, I would never have known," said Julian. Paul saw something perilous behind his schoolboy manners—an interest, genuine and eager, in the details of Paul's life that he was still holding back.

"It's just hard." Paul's mother, as always, was unwilling to stop talking about his father once she'd started. She sat with her elbows on her knees, cradling her empty cup like a fallen bird. "You get used to things being a certain way, and then when they aren't—"

"Ma," Paul cut in, "it's fine."

She looked as if he had struck her. The silence that fell was ugly.

Julian's hand grazed Paul's shoulder; the touch didn't last

long enough for Paul to decide if it was meant to be reassuring. At his other side, Laurie was taut as a slingshot. She was playing joylessly with the cat, teasing it with an ostrich feather that had come free from the duster.

"I really ought to get better at cooking," Julian said, brisk and bright, as if he weren't taking control of the conversation. "Dining halls foment learned helplessness, I can barely boil an egg . . ."

The air no longer felt so thick. Laurie eventually let the cat run off with the feather and settled back into her seat, less irritable now than merely bored.

Paul's mother didn't seem to notice any false notes in Julian's earnestness. Julian soon had her promising to teach him the basics of cooking, and assuring him that he was welcome to drop by whenever he wanted a hot meal. Julian handled her magnificently—flattering her without appearing to do it deliberately, steering her gently toward safer topics when she drifted too close again to the subject of Paul's father. Paul watched the process with distant fascination, not unlike what he had felt during his fetal pig dissection in high school. *This is being nice,* he thought. *This is what she wishes you were like.*

Watching Julian's performance, Paul realized he had been wrong all along to imagine his family wanted him to metamorphose into something softer and kinder and more docile. It was much simpler than that. All they actually wanted him to do was lie.

Audrey was home, but she was in and out of the living room, and showed few signs of interest even when she was present. At their mother's behest, she was washing a load of towels; once that task was complete, she had to get herself properly counterculture-looking before her shift at the record store. She only settled down toward the end of the visit, sitting in the chair by the window in her overcoat and boots. Paul thought he could feel her listening, and could even imagine the face she was wearing, but whenever he looked at her she appeared absorbed in her magazine.

"I hope you know I meant it, about being welcome at dinner," his mother said to Julian as he and Paul gathered their coats. "What are you boys going to be up to tonight?"

Julian answered before Paul could speak. "I don't know—get a soda, probably, maybe go bowling. Or see if anyone's still playing *The Godfather*, it's a crime Paul hasn't seen it yet."

He said it so casually that at first Paul doubted his own memory. Somehow it was easier to believe he'd forgotten an entire conversation than to accept that none of it was true. He couldn't fathom why Julian would have lied, but the sheer pointlessness of it convinced him all the more that it had been deliberate.

As they were leaving, Paul heard his mother and Audrey in the front hallway, speaking as if they didn't think he would overhear.

"He seems like a sweet boy."

"Yeah," said Audrey. There was a smile in her voice, but an arch one. "'Seems.' That kid's trouble."

He didn't linger. He followed Julian into the snowy streets, sprinting to catch up. Julian didn't stop walking as he lit himself a cigarette. For a moment he left the match lit, and he brushed his fingertips over the flame, one after the other, just quickly enough not to burn. Then he shook the match cold and flicked it into the gutter.

Julian's hands were bare despite the chill, but he was wearing a new scarf, courtesy of a care package from his mother—

camel-colored, some kind of exotic wool, softer than anything Paul had ever touched.

"I like them just fine," he said, looking sideways at Paul with one of his sly, tilted smiles. "I don't know what you were so worried about."

Julian smoked in shallow inhales, holding the smoke in his mouth rather than drawing it into his lungs. Paul suspected it was a relatively new affectation for him, one he hadn't yet learned to enjoy—but he'd already mastered the aesthetics of it, holding the cigarette between his fingers with the practiced, languorous grace of a film star.

"Listen—why did you lie?"

Julian raised his eyebrows in mild surprise. "When?"

"When you said we were going *bowling* or something instead of to the museum."

"Oh." Julian was unabashed. He shrugged and drew another mouthful from the cigarette. "I thought that sounded more *likely*, I suppose—more what she'd expect to hear. Going to the art museum sounds like a cover story, or else it just sounds queer. I thought you would prefer for me to lie."

For a long while Paul couldn't speak. Julian finished his cigarette at the bus stop, leaning against the signpost in the dimming gray-blue light.

"So are you going to sulk all afternoon?" he asked suddenly as their bus drew near. "It's so goddamn *boring* when you wallow in self-pity."

The snap of cruelty didn't surprise him. He'd been expecting it all along. Everything about Julian was shaded with the threat of it—even his affection felt dangerous, as if it might curdle at any moment into derision.

"I'm not here for your entertainment."

When Julian grinned, Paul felt as if he'd passed a test he didn't know he was taking.

"So I gathered." Although he was smiling, there was an edge to his voice. "Still—try and make an effort. We'll both be happier if I can find you as fascinating as you ought to be."

Paul was almost relieved to feel the sting. It meant Julian saw every weakness in him and still thought he was worth the effort of hurting.

5.

MOST NIGHTS the fifth chair in the dining room still sat empty. But even in its emptiness there was an absence occupying it that *belonged* there. Paul wished it would speak, in that soft-hard High German lilt that sounded almost nothing like his great-grandmother's Yiddish accent. Paul still wanted to tuck in his right elbow to make way for a sweeping gesture that would never come, to grimace at a pun, roll his eyes at a prolonged explanation of a request to which he'd already assented. He wanted the silence to press hard enough that Audrey would remember how to argue with it, to throw down her fork and scream "You're impossible" while their mother—always the more decisive disciplinarian—pointed sharply at the basement door. Paul wanted to feel the quiet at his side, to wait, keep waiting. He wanted to hate it for giving him nothing.

But two nights a week now the absence receded, replaced by an eager and chatty version of Julian, whose features were the only recognizable thing about him. Paul's family hurried to make a place for him, the way people always did. His family had so many spaces to fill—some they'd spent the last year trying to ignore, others that had been there so long no one but Paul seemed to see them at all. Julian found each one in turn, and Paul's family gave him little chance to hold anything back.

Julian's presence chased away the grim hush that hung over the dinner table. Only Paul felt any discomfort now. Even Audrey—who didn't think much of Julian—occasionally smirked into the back of her hand at one of his jokes. And he had won Laurie and his mother over so completely that it was hard for Paul to remember how guarded they usually were around outsiders. Julian wasn't a worried aunt or a prying, tutting neighbor; he was a blank slate, easy to talk to, endlessly interested in what they had to say but never too curious. He patiently absorbed Laurie's questions about France and her fondly cynical gossip about her friends. One day he surprised her with a few of his Dalida and Françoise Hardy LPs, and Paul knew right away he would conveniently forget to ask her to return them. At first Paul's mother was nearly as quiet as when the family sat alone, but she observed Julian attentively, and occasionally even smiled. When he asked a few questions about the Bobby Kennedy biography she was reading, she picked it up the next day for the first time in months, as if she wanted to have more to tell him next time she saw him.

To Paul's mother, Julian must seem less a human being than a miraculous apparition. Here at long last was a friend for her only son, one who could match all Paul's intelligence but who showed none of the awkwardness or fragility that accompanied it in Paul. He was respectful and charming, sophisticated but deliberately uncondescending; when a siren screamed past the nearest intersection, he didn't cringe and cover his ears like a child. She welcomed Julian with a shy, decisive warmth that made Paul feel almost as though something was being stolen from him.

Even before his father's death, Paul would have been embarrassed for Julian to know her—her wringing anxious hands, her flowery homemade blouses, the way she sometimes talked with a mouthful of peanut-butter-and-sweet-pickle sandwich tucked into her cheek. But now she was just a sorry blot of gray, so far from Julian's own energy and searing color that it was hard to believe he could even pity her. Whenever Julian spoke to her,

Paul felt such a sick wave of humiliation that he could barely stand to look at either of them. And yet Julian seemed to seek her out, engaging her even when there was no need for him to acknowledge her at all. When Paul tried to slip straight out after greeting him at the door, Julian always leaned around his shoulder and called "Hi, Mrs. Fleischer!" into the entryway. More often than not that reeled her in, and the two of them would cycle through ten minutes of the same small talk they had the last time. Paul could do nothing but silently wait them out, one hand on the doorknob, army jacket zipped to the chin.

"I'm sorry she was still in her nightgown," he told Julian once, when they finally managed to depart for their weekly visit to the art-house theater. "She's so lazy sometimes, I hate it, I wish she'd—"

"She's sweet to me, Pablo," said Julian flatly. The defensive edge to his voice somehow made Paul remember that Julian wasn't actually any older than he was.

Paul tried to grow accustomed to the visits. He tried to enjoy this other version of Julian, if only for the flashes of humor and wry grace that managed to break through the false earnestness. He tried to think of the dinner-table chatter as a reprieve from his father's absence instead of an affront to it. Still he caught himself resenting this half-familiar boy at his side, making his little sister laugh and his mother smile, talking through the silence as if he didn't know or care that it was there at all. Paul knew he was unsuited to this place he'd claimed, no matter how easily he made himself fit.

PAUL'S GRANDPARENTS made a point of whisking him and his sisters out of the house on Sundays. The custom had begun not long after the shiva, back when it was ostensibly intended to allow Paul's mother a few quiet hours to give widowhood her undivided attention. Nowadays, as their daughter made it clear nothing else would ever hold her attention again, his grandparents seemed to make the overture more toward the Fleischer children themselves—a chance, however brief, to pretend nothing had changed at all.

It was such a beloved reprieve for them that even Audrey still participated. At their grandparents' house, all the unnatural seriousness would leave her. Paul liked Audrey better there, where she laughed as loudly as she wanted and told outrageous stories about her musician friends. She wasn't back to normal— none of them were—but it was enough of an improvement that they always dreaded having to go home again.

Sunday's entertainments were never elaborate. Lunch was usually Shabbat leftovers and oddments from the freezer; as far as Paul could tell, his grandparents' music collection was comprised of the same thirty jazz standards, recorded in slightly different orders and styles. But the very monotony was soothing in a way that few things in his world managed to be.

Nothing ever changed at his grandparents' house. The two of them scarcely even seemed to age, and had remained robust well into their sixties. His grandmother was a restless hummingbird of a woman, shorter even than his mother, with a cloud of steel-gray hair and a rapid Brooklyn patois. His grandfather was her opposite, tall and somber-faced; he carried himself with the lumbering deliberation of a draft horse. They liked to tell the story of their first meeting in the back of a police van in the twenties—a pair of restless idealists pouring their lives into labor activism. But in their old age they shared an idyllic stasis. They filled in each other's gaps so thoroughly that it felt inconceivable that they could exist separately; at lunch they always sat elbow-to-elbow, speaking in overlap and borrowing freely from each other's plates. Paul believed in his own death far more conclusively than he believed in theirs. He knew it must have occurred to them that one day the stasis would have to end— that one would have to go before the other, that the wallpaper would be torn down and the house sold, Ella Fitzgerald and Benny Goodman divided between their daughters' basements. But they gave no indication that they believed in endings at all, for themselves or for anything outside of them, and that was nearly enough to forget he believed, either. He remembered his parents bringing them here during the Cuban Missile Crisis. The house had had the same effect then—it could dull a cataclysm into background noise.

". . . not as if I didn't think he had it coming." Paul was only half listening to Audrey's story. "But all I'm saying, you can't kick a chair out from under some drunk yutz and claim that's a 'revolutionary action against the bourgeoisie.'"

"Never heard that one before," said Paul's grandmother as she brought her teacup to her lips. She exchanged a wry look with his grandfather, who raised his eyebrows and said nothing. "I thought your generation wanted to liberate the proletariat through peace and love?"

"No one I'd hang out with," said Audrey airily. "I have no patience for that self-righteous do-nothing flower power bullshit— sorry, Bubbe."

"Such language, Audrey," said his grandmother, unfazed. "You'll burn your Zayde's ears."

Paul let his attention fade again. His family allowed him to be quiet, which was a rare mercy, especially now. While the others picked at the crumbs of their meal, Paul worked aimlessly in his sketchbook. He was trying to plot out a painting—he had the image in his head of a human figure overtaken by flora, the torso erupting with ferns and wildflowers. But whenever he started in on the details, he decided he didn't like the composition. He sketched and erased until the paper was ragged, but he couldn't seem to force himself to give up and turn the page.

Eventually his grandmother recruited Laurie and Audrey to help her put the kitchen in order. "Let's not get underfoot," his grandfather said to him; he spoke so casually that Paul didn't detect any cause for concern until it was too late.

He gathered up his belongings and followed his grandfather into the living room, eyeing the chessboard by the fireplace. He thought about rearranging the pieces, but couldn't quite remember the configuration of Kazlauskas v. Kaplan. Even if he could have, though, the queen sacrifice felt oddly personal—as if its beauty should belong to him and Julian alone.

His grandfather switched on the television at a low volume, turning the channel dial until it landed on a static-frayed hockey game. "Your mother tells me she hardly sees you anymore," he said. He settled heavily onto the couch and motioned for Paul to do the same. "Says you're always out with friends."

"She's exaggerating." Paul sat on the edge of the cushion and tried to become raptly interested in his sketchbook. "Friend, in the singular."

"Give it time, they tend to multiply." His grandfather had an odd air of self-satisfaction, as if he'd thought of a joke he wasn't in the mood to share. "What's he like, this Julian?"

"Um—I don't know. He's cool."

"What do the kids say nowadays—he's *groovy*?"

"*Ugh*, Zayde, don't do that." Paul pulled a face rather than smile. "Not groovy, just cool."

"You two get into any trouble?"

"Of course not," Paul answered quickly, but he knew as soon as he spoke that it wasn't the right answer. "I mean, not really."

"A little trouble is a good thing for a young person," his grandfather said. "All the old stick-in-the-muds are afraid of the young people making trouble and shaking things up. Might as well give them something to fuss about."

He thought that might be the end of it. The quiet was broken only by the low hum of commentary from the television and the occasional flurry of conversation in the kitchen. When his grandfather spoke again, he still gave the impression of telling himself a private joke.

"Mind you," he said, "you do want to be careful about *girl* trouble."

"There's no girl." Paul knew that this was another wrong answer, but he was too desperate to shut down the conversation to care.

"There's always a girl," said his grandfather. "Especially once you get a couple of teenage boys together, and they have an audience they need to impress. I wasn't born yesterday, Paulie, I know what boys get up to."

His grandfather appeared to read his revulsion as mere embarrassment. Paul stared at the television and curled inward like a dying spider.

"A *bit* of girl trouble is normal. Like I said—everything in moderation. And it's good for you especially, because it'll teach you not to be shy when it comes time to find the kind of girl you want to marry. Just don't let yourself get talked into any girl trouble you'll end up regretting. Do you understand what I'm saying, here?"

The distant strains of jazz from the kitchen radio had taken on a cloying sweetness. Paul abruptly wanted to escape the safe,

62   MICAH NEMEREVER

soft confines of this house, to let himself feel everything its walls kept at bay.

"It's good, though," said his grandfather. "We're all glad you're starting to make friends, Paul. Didn't I always say it would get easier once you were out of high school? And it'll only get better from here on out—when you're a doctor and you're married to a nice girl, you'll look back on the hardest years and you'll think, 'I can't believe how easily it all came together once it really counted.' I believe that. I hope you can, too."

Paul's family had been telling him this for years. It was the only story they knew, and they told it relentlessly because they thought they were doing him a kindness. All he could do was force a smile and hope that they would all be gone before he had a chance to disappoint them.

"IT'S FINE if you don't like it. Just give it a chance."

There was a check from his parents burning a hole in Julian's pocket—for expenses, allegedly, on top of what they spent on his room and board. There was always plenty left over after the few expenses he did have, and it didn't seem to occur to Julian to save it. Instead it went toward small relentless gifts, and the movies and meals he insisted on paying for. Today he seemed to be spending the bulk of the money on records. Paul counted seven so far, and not one that he would have picked out himself. Julian was most enthusiastic about the one he'd selected now. It was a replacement, Julian claimed, for one his father had taken away and burned. The anecdote was so outlandishly cruel that Paul wasn't sure he believed it. He would have called it a lie outright if not for the matter-of-fact way Julian told him, as if he didn't consider it remarkable at all.

Awful as the story was, though, Paul nearly understood why

it had happened. The singer's photograph made him look very much like a woman, rawboned and imperious. Paul couldn't look directly at the record sleeve without feeling a flood of embarrassment, so he avoided seeing it, as if he were shying away from eye contact with an acquaintance he didn't want to acknowledge.

The listening booths were tucked away behind the jazz section, far from the front counter where Audrey and her friend were pretending to be busy. The booth was so narrow that there were only inches between him and Julian, no matter how small Paul tried to make himself. Julian, however, didn't appear to mind. He let Paul hold the stack of records while he squirmed free of his peacoat; Paul tried not to notice the way the striped fabric of his T-shirt pulled and slid over his torso as he moved.

"Ninety seconds. Not even the whole song." Julian closed the distance between them to hand him the headphones. "Either you'll be in love by the end of the first chorus or you'll never get it."

The booth walls blocked the sounds of the store, but the headphones muffled even the hush; all Paul could hear was his own heartbeat and a soft hiss of static. The closeness of their bodies was overwhelming—the shadows at the hollow of Julian's throat, the clean wintry smell of his skin. When he sidled past to put on the record, his hand brushed Paul's chest. It was an accident of proximity, but it still sent a jolt through him. He pulled off the headphones and started to recoil, but Julian stopped him with a glance.

He almost expected Julian to hit him. Instead he lifted the headphones again and placed them firmly over Paul's ears.

"Listen."

Julian watched his face, patient and prompting, as if he still cared about Paul's verdict on a song he could barely be bothered to hear. Julian's smile was impassive and absolutely opaque.

Paul had heard parts of the song before, drifting up from Audrey's basement bedroom or in snatches from the car radio. He'd thought it pleasant enough, if a little frivolous, but now he felt too sick from shame to keep listening.

"Didn't like it?"

"I'm weird about music," said Paul to his shoes. "Sorry. It doesn't mean I don't think it's any *good*, I just . . ."

Julian stopped the record and returned it carefully to its sleeve. "It's all right. We don't have to be twins." He said it carelessly, but that only worsened the sting.

They emerged into the low thrum of *The Dark Side of the Moon* playing on the PA system. Audrey and her friend Joanne looked up as they approached, but Joanne quickly decided they weren't her problem and went back to sorting the singles rack. She was tall and glamorous, with a tasseled macramé vest and an immaculate Afro. Like most of Audrey's friends, Paul could tell she'd been a kind of cool in high school that he was constitutionally unable to comprehend, much less emulate.

"Sure you don't want to take home the whole shelf?" said Audrey. It was a sharper remark than she pretended, but Julian feigned cheerful oblivion.

"I want to get his, too." Julian caught Paul's elbow when he tried to retreat. "Don't be dumb, it's your birthday next month anyway. This one still hasn't forgiven Dylan for going electric, has he, Audrey?"

"He likes what he likes," said Audrey coolly, though she'd been teasing Paul about his music tastes for the better part of a decade. "It's good that he's got guns to stick to, instead of turning his record collection into a performance of the kind of person he wants to be."

"Well, I find it very charming," said Julian, scrupulously amiable but brooking no argument. "I hope that was clear."

Paul reluctantly allowed Julian to pull his lone record out of his hands. He could feel his sister watching him, but he refused to meet her eyes.

"Do you have any idea what Ma's doing for dinner?" Audrey asked him over Julian's shoulder.

"She isn't." Not wanting to look at either of them, Paul stared at the bracelets on Audrey's wrist. "It's fine, there are TV dinners."

"Ugh, hell with that, I'll make us some spaghetti or something." She exaggerated her annoyance to conceal her worry. "Want we should do the candles this week, at least? I'll be in a little late, but no one wants to eat when the sun goes down at fucking two in the afternoon anyway."

"We're not going to be home, I don't think." It was only after speaking that Paul noticed the jarring, conspicuous *we*; Audrey's lips twitched when he said it, as if she were fighting the urge to echo it in disbelief. "Sorry—next week, for sure. I'll help cook and everything."

"Don't worry about it." Audrey slid Julian's change across the counter, but Paul could tell she was still watching him. "All right, enjoy, stay warm out there . . . See you at home, *Pablo.*"

It would have been better to pretend the jibe barely registered. Instead he froze and pressed his elbows into his sides to keep from covering his face. Audrey could only have heard the nickname by listening in on a private conversation, and her scrutiny felt all the more invasive because she treated it like a joke.

Julian paused, forearm propped on the exit door. He glanced back at Paul, eyebrows raised as if in polite impatience.

"Don't," Paul said quietly.

"What, isn't that your name now?" said Audrey with skeptical amusement, but her smile faded when he didn't laugh.

"Not to you, it isn't," he said, and he hurried to join Julian at the door before she could protest.

As they made their way along the icy sidewalk, Julian pushed down the back of Paul's scarf and rested one gloved hand on the nape of his neck. The touch moved hot through Paul's body, but Julian's eyes were serene, even cold. Julian held Paul's gaze for a long moment. Then he smiled, straightened his spine, and pushed Paul to keep walking.

"They're nice people," Julian said carelessly, and it took Paul a moment to parse that he was changing the subject. "Your family, I mean—they like you. But they don't understand you, do they?"

It was the first time he'd ever known Julian to miscalculate. It was a strange mistake for him, trying to chip away at something that wasn't there. It was ugly enough to know that Audrey thought he needed protecting; no matter how many vulnerabilities Paul had let Julian collect, he couldn't let them lead Julian to believe the same thing.

"I don't know if I want them to understand me," Paul answered, and he felt a little less powerless when he saw the falter in Julian's smile.

6.

JULIAN COULD never sit still while he was talking to his parents. He drummed his fingertips on the wall of the pay phone kiosk, biting the inside of his cheek as he listened. Paul leaned against the wall opposite him, watching the small, tense movements of the muscles in Julian's jaw and neck.

"Yeah, they're not very good." Julian spoke to his father in a flat, clipped tone. "I don't know why you're torturing yourself getting invested."

Mr. Fromme was following the college's mediocre lacrosse team in what struck Paul as a poignantly pathetic attempt to cultivate a common interest with his son. Julian had even less interest in this subject than his father did, but without it they would have had hardly anything to discuss at all.

"Did he really?" Julian looked toward Paul, rolled his eyes, and pulled his necktie sideways in a pantomime of a noose. "Well, how *nice* for him—so how does that one rate next to, I don't know, the one at Harvard? . . . I'm not, Dad, I'm very happy for him, I know both of you have worked hard for this . . ."

Julian always wanted Paul nearby for his weekly call home. At first Paul hadn't understood why. Julian never mentioned Paul to his parents, even though he offered regular updates on the childhood friends whose letters arrived postmarked from New England college towns and tony boarding schools. He would sometimes go the entire call without meeting Paul's eyes once; when he spoke to his mother he usually did so in French, which Paul knew was partly intended to prevent him from listening in.

But there was inevitably a moment that Julian would re-treat to monosyllables and long silences, and the lie of his self-assurance would collapse around him. Paul knew he was being trusted with something no one else would ever see. That Julian never discussed it afterward was immaterial. The mere existence of Julian's vulnerability was an immense and terrible secret, and keeping it was as much a burden as a privilege. It sent a long ugly fracture through everything Paul knew about him, and he struggled sometimes to remember that Julian had enough resolve to hold himself together in spite of it.

Something his father said made Julian's face fall. He shut his eyes and drew a deep, slow breath. It frightened Paul how read-ily he yielded to the pain, almost as if he were so used to it that it bored him. By the time he exhaled, the grief had disappeared again; Paul couldn't tell if it had passed through him or if he'd just absorbed it so completely that Paul couldn't see it anymore.

Julian didn't meet Paul's eyes, but he closed the distance be-tween them and rested their foreheads together.

"Ha ha. I suppose so." His skin was warm, but the overhead lights cast long shadows under his eyelashes that made him look sickly and cold. "I'll try. Thanks, Dad."

Calling home always put Julian in a volatile mood. After he hung up, he broke away from Paul unceremoniously and sidled out of the booth, rolling his shoulders as if he were shrugging off a too-tight jacket.

He lit a cigarette as he climbed the stairs to his dorm room, not looking back to see if Paul would follow him. Paul thought about leaving until Julian's ill temper had ebbed; he decided, as always, that there was more honor and loyalty in enduring it.

Julian didn't slam the door behind him, which was the only evidence of an invitation. Paul lingered in the doorway while

Julian picked up an ashtray and threw himself onto the bed. He crossed his booted ankles on the quilt and blew a mouthful of smoke at the ceiling.

"If I have to deal with one more person today, I'll fucking kill myself."

Paul almost snapped at him, but he didn't want to explain why the threat made him feel sick. Instead he said, very quietly, "I can leave."

"Don't be dumb," said Julian, "*you* don't count."

That stirred something inside him, something ill-defined but instantly calming.

Paul sidled inside and shut the door. Julian watched impassively before rolling to one side to ash his cigarette. Paul pocketed his glasses and sat on the bed, still a little wary, but Julian pulled him down by the back of his shirt.

"I don't feel like getting lunch after all," Julian said. If he was sorry, he didn't sound it. He wrapped one arm around Paul's neck and held him in place.

"It's fine," said Paul. "I'm not that hungry."

They lay like that for a long while, Julian watching the ceiling, Paul watching him. He tried to pour his consciousness only into the parts of his body that Julian touched. He wanted to forget everything but the way Julian's blood ran a little hotter than his own, how the warmth of him pooled just below his rib cage and at the hollow of his throat.

"I don't understand why you haven't tried it yet," Julian said carelessly. He glanced at Paul's mouth, so fleetingly that he might have imagined it. "I wouldn't stop you, if that's what you're worried about. You could do anything to me and I'd let you."

It didn't surprise him that Julian had asked, but he still felt a shock of shame—not at the desire itself, but at the fact that

Julian could see him. He wasn't ready to be seen, not yet. He hadn't done anything to earn it.

"It just—" He started from the beginning, trying to steady his stammer. "It feels like it would be disrespectful."

"I don't need you to treat me respectfully. I'm not made of glass."

When Paul still didn't move, Julian sighed and turned his gaze back toward the ceiling.

"Tell me you love me, at least," he said quietly. "Please. I need to know *somebody* does."

When Paul shut his eyes, he could pretend someone else was speaking. Someone he hadn't become yet; someone who deserved to speak.

"I love you," he said, and once he'd spoken, the words took hold of his tongue like a prayer. Julian pulled him nearer, but he didn't dare open his eyes. *I love you. I love you. I love you.*

7.

THEIR CLASSMATES never seemed to find the film clips troubling. Distasteful, perhaps, in the same way as a flayed specimen or a foul chemical smell. When Paul couldn't stand to look, he watched the others instead, their faces lit moon-white by the screen. He'd kept an eye on the girl from Physics a few weeks ago, while the class watched Japanese children wither slowly from cancer in unforgiving black and white. Here was her discipline's crowning achievement, mirrored in the lenses of her glasses so he couldn't quite see her eyes. He should have seen shame in her face, but it wasn't there. All he saw was distant revulsion.

His classmates' faces were the same today—politely repelled, with no evidence of anything so unscientific as an emotion. Today's clip wasn't as showy as some of the others had been. There was no gore, no disfiguration, no animal vivisection in service of some "higher purpose." But when Paul watched it too closely, he could hardly stand to keep his eyes open.

The experiment was notorious; Paul hadn't heard of it, but Julian had. It was a dire practical joke, played decades ago on unsuspecting Yale boys who still wore suits to class. *They* weren't the subjects, the researchers claimed—they were just helping, seeing if they could help a fake subject at the other end of an intercom pass a quiz by punishing him whenever he got an answer wrong. A little zap of electricity, barely painful, until they were told to turn up the voltage notch by notch and the victim begged them to stop.

The victim's pain wasn't real, of course, but the subjects thought it was. The subjects squirmed, giggled with alarm, occasionally even asked the researchers whether this was really all right. But they didn't stop. Even when the dial said the voltage had edged from painful into dangerous; even when the unseen victim's pleas faded away, and he stopped responding at all. They didn't question it, because the researchers wore white coats and spoke with authority, and that meant they must know what they were doing.

The subjects weren't cruel people, the narration claimed. They just didn't think.

Before the film played, Julian had told Strauss it was the reason he'd chosen to study social psychology. Paul felt an unwanted surge of fury toward him now for having the capacity to be fascinated—for the way Julian could look at the truth, even feel it, without it overwhelming him.

The light afterward was a shock. Strauss lifted the projection screen with a clatter; behind it on the blackboard, THE MILGRAM EXPERIMENT had been scrawled large.

Strauss rested his hands on his hips before speaking. The chalk left silver shadows on his clothes.

"Mr. Fromme," he said, "perhaps you can get us started. What was so controversial about this experiment?"

Paul didn't even parse the question at first, because it was inconceivable that Strauss wanted them to argue about the mechanics of the experiment itself. It missed the point so decisively that it felt deliberate.

"What was *controversial* about it? Honestly, the fact that nobody liked the results," Julian said. "I mean, they dress it up in a lot of hand-wringing about informed consent and whether the subjects experienced undue distress and all that. But I think if the findings had made us feel good about ourselves, nobody would care one way or the other about the methodology."

"Oh, come on, we spend half this class talking about how science has a responsibility to treat 'the human variable' with kid gloves," said the girl from Physics. "But when it's *your* discipline, suddenly it's *hand-wringing.*"

"The difference is, the human variable chose its own outcome this time. The experiment was *about* the decisions the subjects would make—they made them under false pretenses, sure, but they made them of their own free will. If they got their feelings hurt because they learned they were Eichmanns waiting for a Hitler, that's on them."

"In other words, it's all right to mess with their heads because they had it coming," Brady interjected. "It's a nasty trap to spring, and I don't even think you can make broad inferences from it—it's such an artificial scenario, so to extrapolate from it into real-life applications . . ."

"And if there's really no way to gather that data without inflicting that kind of distress on the subjects, even if the data *were* informative," the girl went on, "I don't see how it's even worth it to try."

Strauss was busy making notes on the chalkboard. The room had turned decisively against Julian. Several students were nodding along; others still wore their looks of mild disgust, as if the experiment was just another film-strip horror that had failed to touch them.

Under the accumulated weight of their indifference, something inside him collapsed.

"It is worth it."

Paul's voice trembled, but it still left silence in its wake.

"You don't get to complain about a test being a 'trap' when it's your own decisions that cause you to fail it." His stammer was rising to the surface, but he didn't care. "It's—the experiment proves that people only respond to the authority, they have no sense of morality themselves—we need to know that, *science* needs to know that. I don't care how upset they got about learning what they were."

"Mr. Fleischer certainly isn't alone," said Strauss quickly, as if to smooth things over before they got out of hand, "in finding the ethical implications of the results themselves disturbing—"

"Hold on now," Brady said, affronted but calm, holding up his hands as if in self-defense. "At the end of the day, these are ordinary people. It's natural to trust authority, so of course most people do. This experiment was predicated on abusing that trust. Drawing the worst imaginable conclusions about the subjects, based solely on an extreme and contrived situation that put them under immense stress—"

"Crying crocodile tears afterwards about the atrocities you commit isn't morally exculpatory." Red flooded the edges of Paul's vision. He could feel his pulse in his teeth. "Tell me what makes them different from every Nazi who 'just followed orders' and only felt bad about it after the fact. Don't you dare ask me to fucking pity them."

The high wave of adrenaline swelled through him and then receded into the shallows.

In the ringing quiet, the others all stared. Some were irritated, others on the verge of nervous laughter, but none showed any sign of comprehension. All they could see was the rule he had broken, one of the innumerable unwritten boundaries of politeness designed to protect them.

Only Strauss was grim with compassion, as if he understood too well for his own comfort. His hands reminded Paul sharply of his father's—fine dark hairs, knuckles thickened by early-stage arthritis. It was Strauss, in the end, whose presence Paul couldn't bear any longer.

He didn't speak; he wasn't sure he could. He retreated up the lecture hall steps as quickly as he could without running. He realized too late that he'd left his belongings at his desk, but he refused to turn back. The hallway was deserted. Paul ducked into the bathroom—empty, cold, lit by fluorescence so that every detail screamed. He filled his hands with frigid water and cradled his face and throat, then lifted his glasses to splash another handful over his eyes.

Slowly, Paul turned off the faucet. There was a strange sound in the room, rapid and rhythmic, that Paul thought at first must be coming from a faulty pipe. It took him a long time to recognize it as his own breathing. His reflection looked inhuman and barely familiar.

He didn't see Julian follow him into the washroom; he just wicked into being like a ghost. He leaned against the counter, already dressed to leave, Paul's knapsack and coat draped over one arm. The harsh light clarified the filaments of artery in the whites of Julian's eyes.

"I've had all the bourgeois apologetics I can stomach for one day, I think," said Julian. "We can go once you're ready."

"Where are we going?" Paul asked, but Julian only shrugged. Paul tried to scrutinize his reflection, but he could hardly stand to meet his own eyes. "Do I look normal? I can't tell if I look normal."

"You never do," said Julian dismissively. "Thank god for it."

"You know what I mean, though, do I look—you know—"

Julian handed him his coat, gentle and impatient in equal measure.

"You're fine. Not that you need to care. Think for a second about what 'normal' means."

THEY WERE headed to the river; that was all either of them bothered to know. Paul waited in the snow while Julian conned a liquor store clerk out of a bottle of bourbon. It shouldn't have worked, but even from the other side of the plate glass it was a convincing pantomime—Julian searching his wallet for a non-existent driver's license, all apologies and sheepish smiles, until it yielded an *Okay, just this once.* "You can get away with any-thing," Julian had told him beforehand, "as long as you act like an authority on the truth." It sickened Paul a little to watch Ju-lian prove this right.

"So what happened after I left?"

They were passing the bottle between them as they walked, as if there were no chance anyone might notice them, as if they were the authority on whether or not they were visible. There was a hum of unease in Paul's body, but he didn't think it was from the drink. He couldn't remember his heartbeat slowing since they left.

"Don't pay attention to them," said Julian bitterly. "I mean it. You use other people's useless fucking opinions as an excuse to hate yourself—"

"I don't care what they think. I just need to know whether I have to drop the class."

Julian considered this around a mouthful of alcohol. Then he swallowed hard and shrugged. It was a superficially careless gesture, but Paul recognized it as the first gust at the head of a hurricane—Julian's face was the mask of vibrant serenity that always marked his cruelest whims.

"It's a very complex case," he said, but it was no longer *him* speaking. His body language was changing; his gestures became less expansive, emphatic but constrained, hands held awkwardly, as if he had been an ungainly child long ago and had never quite forgotten it. "There is, as you can imagine, a fair bit of historical resonance, some still very recent—"

"Stop that."

"—was intended, certainly, to provoke a discussion, and it's natural for emotions to run high." Julian brought his free hand to his face, as if to push a pair of wire-framed glasses up the bridge of his nose. There was no trace of him left; he'd even borrowed Strauss's voice, dropping from tenor to baritone as if the shape of his throat had changed. "We cannot fault *any* of our colleagues for responding to the real-world implications—"

"Stop it," Paul pleaded. "I mean it. It's horrible—"

"If you can't be objective, the least you can do is recognize your own bias." Julian had shifted to Brady's self-satisfaction and blunt gestures as easily as donning a coat. "Put in the effort to gain some distance, or recuse yourself before you hurt your argument by—"

"I'll knock your teeth in if you don't stop." Paul didn't know whether he was talking to Julian or to the simulacrum of Brady, and he didn't care. "I mean it, I swear to god—"

It was over as suddenly as it had begun. Julian relaxed back into his own body and flashed Paul a wide showman's grin.

"Not bad, right? That's my party trick—five minutes of observation, and I can do anyone. I do a great one of my dad. His underlings all love it, and he can't *stand* it."

Paul took the bottle and drank; it seemed the only thing to do before making what he already knew would be a mistake. The alcohol scorched the inside of his throat.

"So you'd be able to do me," he said. "Wouldn't you?"

A pause.

"I could, I suppose," said Julian. "But you wouldn't want me to."

"Don't tell me what I want."

Julian stopped walking. He looked very young in that moment, wind-bitten and flush with drink, and Paul could see the effort it took for him to keep his gaze steady. His smile had become opaque and careful.

"Go on." Paul stood in front of him, watching, not sure what he expected or wanted to expect. At his side he held the bottle by the neck; its brown wrapper was freckled with melted snow. "I want you to. I won't be angry."

He could see Julian's disbelief, then the impulsive resolve as he decided to make the mistake along with him. Without asking if he could, Julian reached forward and pulled Paul's glasses from his face.

"If you insist," he said. When he put on the glasses, he disappeared behind them.

There was nothing cruel about it, except for its accuracy. Paul hadn't already noticed all the details Julian observed in him, but he still knew instinctively that they were true, the same way he would have known his own face even after years without a mirror. He watched Julian's shoulders sag as he curled in on himself like a too-tall weed growing in the shade. He recognized the solemn bow of his head and the anxious sharp line of his jaw, and the truth in the way his hands moved, their halting delicate gestures like fine-petaled flowers bowing in a breeze.

Paul could have accepted it if not for the frailty there, the uncertainty and the overwhelming fear. He couldn't see anything about himself that was immune to yielding to the right lie—to biting his tongue and saying "Yes, okay, just this once." The transformation was perverse and unforgivable. It was evolution in reverse.

Julian only maintained the illusion for a few seconds. He exhaled hard when he let it fall.

"How do you stay sane, Pablo?" The sincerity in Julian's voice took both of them by surprise. "It's *exhausting*. Everything's so bright and sharp, it's like there's nothing protecting you—"

Paul didn't notice that Julian was reaching toward him until he'd already snatched his glasses back and turned away. He walked quickly, barely noticing the cold.

It took Julian some effort to catch up. There was a hazy echo in his breathing, like music from a dusty speaker.

"You said you wouldn't be angry," he said. He took firm hold of Paul's arm, as if to hinder his pace, but when Paul slowed down, he didn't let go.

"I'm not. Not at you."

"Don't even try," said Julian almost gently. "You know you're just about the worst liar I've ever met."

DOWN TOWARD the river. The bottle was drunk down enough by now that it sloshed like a full stomach. They crossed over the railyard on a pedestrian bridge caked in graffiti; as they made their way along the waterfront, the sidewalk gradually crumbled from the outside in, until the asphalt finally gave way to tar-blackened gravel and long gray grass.

They came upon an abandoned building. It had been a slaughterhouse once, according to the fading letters whitewashed onto the brick. Moss streaked the windows and climbed the walls; the corrugated metal doors were creased with rust. The only sign of life was a mushroom cloud spray-painted onto one of the doors, captioned, in jaunty block letters, WALK IT OFF SUNSHINE.

Julian climbed over the chain-link fence, holding his cigarette between his teeth. Paul passed the bottle to Julian and dropped his knapsack onto the gravel, then cautiously followed after him. The rusting wires shivered and squealed under Paul's weight, and it took him a moment to convince himself to climb the rest of the way.

"How long has it just been sitting here, do you know?"

Paul shook his head. Julian finished his cigarette and ashed it on the heel of his boot. With his coat collar turned up, leaning carelessly against the fence, he looked like a film still of James Dean. Paul could never decide if Julian was borrowing mannerisms from the movies or if it was the other way around—that the movies were trying to synthesize an image that came to Julian naturally.

Paul turned away and tucked his glasses into his breast pocket. Then he scooped up a rock, tossed it from his right hand to his left, and pitched it straight through a windowpane.

He thought he heard Julian speak, but a wool-thick quiet had settled over him, and no sound could penetrate. He worked his way along the bank of windows, smashing them column by column, each filthy mirror to the sky collapsing backward into black. Empty panes gaped, ringed with fragments of glass like broken teeth. He could imagine nothing beyond this moment; there was no reason, no goal. He had been here all his life.

Then the final pane fell away and he had a body again—sore muscles and roaring blood and fierce mortal heart, skin taut against the chill and damp snow. The air splintered in his chest, and what was left of his father lay in a box in the frozen earth with a tunnel through his skull, and for all that he raged against it, nothing had changed.

Paul sank down to the tangled grass and brushed the dirt from his hands. He was too exhausted to cry, or to hate himself for wanting to. He wasn't certain, once he sat down, that he would be able to stand again.

Julian stood in front of him, carrying the bottle by its throat. His lips were chapped, his nose and fingertips pink from the cold. For the first time since Paul had known him, he looked uncertain. He offered the bottle, but Paul shook his head. He couldn't put a name to what he felt, but he knew it would be dishonest not to feel it. He fought against what the alcohol was already doing; he wanted the world to stay clear and sharp and unbearable.

Julian emptied the bottle into the snow. He knelt beside Paul cautiously, as if he were approaching a wounded dog. When he touched Paul's face, the gesture seemed at least as experimental as it was affectionate.

"I don't want to talk about it."

"You don't have to." Julian brushed Paul's hair back from his face and darted forward to press a kiss to his forehead. The gesture seemed to startle him far more than it did Paul. "But there has to be something I can do. I can't stand it. What am I supposed to do?"

He didn't remember how to speak. He couldn't have given the answer even if he'd had one.

8.

HE WOULD never get used to the scar. It looked like a dead tree, milk-white, bare branches grasping. The whole right side of Julian's torso was given over to it. He claimed it didn't hurt anymore, though he'd had it for so long that Paul wasn't sure how Julian could know what his body had felt like before. The lung inside was so heavy with dead tissue that it didn't remember how to be a lung anymore. When Paul put his ear to Julian's back, he could hear the asymmetry, the way the left lung had to drink in almost more than it could hold in order to keep its twin from drowning.

He had pictured Julian's body wrought from marble, flawless and intangible even under his undeserving touch. "You said you wouldn't stop me," Paul would say, and Julian would let him take what he wanted, because he'd promised he would. But even in his most shameful fantasies, that was all Paul let himself expect. He never allowed himself to imagine Julian wanting him. In Paul's mind Julian only ever made himself an object. He was pliant and receptive; he would surrender to him as smooth unbroken skin, as hips and collarbones and acquiescent mouth. But if the imaginary Julian ever deigned to kiss him back, it was only to draw forth another unanswered *I love you*. Paul could never reach past Julian's surface, no matter what he did to him.

When he arrived uninvited at Julian's door the next day, it wasn't the unblemished immortal idol that had brought him there. Instead he came for the boy who had tried in vain to comfort him, whose kiss at his forehead had felt like an uncertain imitation of something he'd only ever seen in the movies. He came because that kiss was as vulnerable in its way as Paul's own unhappiness. Paul wouldn't even see the scar until after. It was enough just to perceive the ones that Julian carried inside him, even if they were too elusive for Paul to name.

Julian wasn't expecting him. He was dressed for warmth, wool socks and haphazard layers, more careless and aesthetically indifferent than he usually let Paul see him. He answered the door with a book at his hip, marking the page with his first two fingers.

He started to ask, then stopped.

There was a long silent moment of understanding each other—of panic crashing through, so forcefully that it might have swept everything else away with it. Then Julian took him by the arm and quickly pulled him inside.

After long desperate weeks of imagining him this way, it was frightening how tangible he was now. There was nothing divine about him. When Paul pushed him back against the door, part of him still expected Julian to withdraw into himself, yielding and passive as a doll. But through their clothes Paul could feel the spring-tight apprehension in Julian's body. Paul only hesitated for a moment. They were breathless, eyelash-close. The snow-dimmed light deepened the color of Julian's eyes like the sea under rain.

"Go ahead," said Julian, almost too quietly to hear, and when Paul kissed him it was as inevitable and instinctive as breathing.

They didn't properly undress; it was rushed and clumsy. Paul kept losing track of his own body, and when he found himself again, there was too much of him—clothes clinging to his skin, the weight of his knee making the mattress sigh. All that anchored him was the eager unhesitant way Julian touched him, the unexpectedly gentle reassurances he murmured against his mouth. When Paul couldn't bear to meet his eyes any longer, he pressed his face to the shoulder of Julian's sweater and shut his eyes tight; Julian wrapped one hand around the nape of his neck, soft and firm.

They lay together for a long time after, not speaking, the closed circuit still echoing between them. Julian lifted Paul's chin and studied his face, and Paul could tell it was a deliberate mercy that he didn't ask if he was all right.

Eventually Julian sidled out from under him. He rifled through his wardrobe, then his drawer, gathering a clean shirt and sweater that were more carefully matched than the ones they were replacing. He tugged off every layer at once, under-shirt and all. It felt nonsensically intrusive to watch him, and Paul almost looked away, but when he caught his first glimpse of the scar he froze.

When Julian looked toward him again, Paul couldn't turn away fast enough to hide his face. Whatever Julian saw there, it didn't appear to make him self-conscious, much less hurt him.

It seemed impossible that Julian was still alive. The scar all but sliced him in half, sternum to hip and midway up his back. It rendered the truth of Julian's body with startling brutality.

"Car accident, obviously. When I was ten. The most American way to die, and I nearly managed it. The door peeled back like a sardine can, a big shard of it went straight through me." Julian spoke calmly, dreamily, as if he couldn't remember the pain—or as if he could remember, but chose not to struggle against it because he knew it was part of him.

He folded the clothes over one arm and sat on the bed, and for a long moment he watched Paul's face. He was impassive, or almost; Paul could sense there was some feeling that Julian wouldn't let him see, even now.

"You can touch it if you want," said Julian. It was as if he'd put his hand to Paul's chest and felt the shape of the impulse inside. "I thought you might like it."

It should have felt strange to touch him, but it didn't, any more than touching his own body. When he'd kissed Julian for the first time, all Paul could think was *Of course,* and he would never forget the shiver that passed through Julian's chest as he gave himself over to it too. *Of course.* The feeling would have been peaceful if not for the insidious way it made its way inside of him and took root.

There was a perverse beauty to the scar, holding Julian's body together in defiance of every force that had tried to pull it apart. Whenever Paul caught sight of it, he would feel an echo of its texture in his hands, smooth and dense and just slightly cooler than the surrounding skin.

THE LOW winter sky grew heavier the longer the city bore its weight, and no amount of rain or snow could rinse the filth from the air. Paul moved through his days like a ghost, retreating to the farthest laboratory benches and the shadows under burned-out lights at the back of lecture halls. Whenever he returned from a run, there would be an invisible film of pollution on his skin, and no matter how hard he scrubbed or how hot he ran the shower, the greasy feeling never quite lifted away.

The synagogue sent them a postcard to remind them, as if they needed it. There was a handwritten postscript from the rabbi, imploring them to "please reach out without hesitation if there's anything at all that you need"; Paul's mother hung the card on the refrigerator and covered the note with a magnet.

Dread seeped through the cracks in the house. His mother

descended into a quiet, frantic misery, so that he longed for the kind of unhappy she'd been just a few weeks before. His sisters fled from the house as much as he did, seizing every excuse they could to escape.

He compounded his grief relentlessly, like pushing at a sore tooth with his tongue. He reread *Silent Spring*, then forced himself to press through *Hiroshima* and *Eichmann in Jerusalem*. During classes he would sit very still and shatter himself over and over, by flames and toxins and blunt force, until he was so numb that it almost felt like indifference. When he imagined the moment of death, he never let himself flinch. He had to look straight into the emptiness until it felt real. That was the only way he could be certain he didn't want it.

Paul could hardly stand to be apart from Julian anymore. There was little reason for them to be separated for more than a few hours, and so they rarely were—Paul only returned to his house to sleep, or for the few family dinners he couldn't avoid. When Julian was in class, Paul let himself into his dorm room and waited until he got back. If Paul wasn't in the mood to brave the public, Julian would bring their meals up from the dining hall on clam-shelled paper plates. On the days he was too miserable to eat or speak or even to sit upright, Julian curled up next to him and let him rest his head on his hip while he read aloud from a book of O'Hara or Mayakovsky. But even Julian couldn't make the dread ebb completely. It wouldn't; not on its own. Something would have to break. Last year it had been Danny Costello's face.

The yahrzeit, when it came, was bitter and bleak, the sky so dark with the threat of snow that the sun never seemed to rise. None of them had discussed what to do about it, because that would have required acknowledging it in advance. The debate over breakfast nearly turned ugly when Audrey, uneasily irreverent, suggested that they go to the movie theater.

"We could pick at the movie on the way home," she said, gesturing with her coffee cup as she spoke. "Point out all the plot holes and correct every little detail it got wrong. I think that would honor a part of Dad's legacy that he was pretty proud of."

Paul nearly laughed, and Laurie started to smile, but their mother looked so wounded and furious that they both looked away and sank into their seats.

"It was endearing," Audrey protested. "It was just such a *Dad* thing. I thought it would be nice to remember something funny and annoying that we loved about him, instead of just the parts that are—"

"Your father deserves respect." His mother's voice was clipped and airless. "He always did, Audrey. The least you could do is start showing it to him now."

Paul could see the effort it took for Audrey to bite her tongue. He wished she wouldn't, and that the argument could devolve into the fight it wanted to be. Instead it festered all morning without anyone daring to mention it.

After breakfast they took the candle to the cemetery in its little brass box. It fell to Audrey to place it at the base of the headstone because she was the only one who could stomach it. They waited in silence under the cobweb of black branches, watching the candle flame gutter in the cold.

"Shouldn't we say something?" said Laurie.

"Why?" Paul countered. "Who do we think is listening?"

But his mother was already drawing a deep inhale so that she could get through the kaddish without collapsing. He joined her along with the rest of them, because somehow there was still some comfort in following the pattern. There was no argument over who they were to each other or what the absence meant. Paul couldn't forget the size of the void on the far side of the clouds, or his sense that any being that could encompass it would be too terrible and unfathomable to notice them at all. The only thing to pray to was the agreement between the four of them, and between them and the centuries of blood and bones that came before.

And then when they left, they were sick of each other again. They had to withdraw; they had to pull themselves forward into another year of pretending to forget.

"I want to go to services tonight, I think," Laurie said tentatively in the car. "Anyone want to go too?"

Audrey said nothing, wringing her hands in front of the heating vent as the Buick sat idling. In the passenger seat Paul's mother sat very still, and he could tell she was imagining the same thing he was—the neighbors' faces turning toward them when the rabbi read his father's name. Nearly all the neighbors had been compassionate, which really meant deigning to pity. After it happened, the wives had brought trays of food, while their husbands offered to make repairs around the house and clean the gutters in the fall. But compassion didn't mean their faces wouldn't register the gravity of his father's final sin— their surprise at having to hear his father's name spoken aloud, among their own deserving loved ones, as if he had any right to be mourned the same way.

"I'm sure your grandparents will go with you," his mother said after a long pause. "I'm sorry, honey. I'm just too tired today."

Once they reached home, they scattered. Laurie escaped to their grandparents' house, Audrey to cover a friend's shift at the record store. As Paul was leaving, he saw the light flick on above the stairwell. He pictured his mother leaning over the bathroom sink, tying her hair back into its plait with a Seconal waiting on her tongue. Whenever he got home, whether in one hour or eight, he knew she would be asleep.

When he boarded the bus to campus, he was barely conscious of where he was going—he was preoccupied by fantasies of crashing, every anonymous body around him torn and battered. At first he imagined dying alongside the rest of them, agony splintering through him, perfect understanding and then perfect oblivion. He asked himself if this was what he wanted, and he kept asking until he could believe his own answer. Paul was still braver than his father. He would try to survive like Julian, defiant, holding his body together through sheer will to live.

Paul was in his winter clothes, hat pulled low over his red hair and one of Julian's old scarves covering his face, but the other boys in the dormitory still recognized him. They never got used to Paul's comings and goings. Often they muttered to one another as he passed; occasionally he heard a ring of jeering laughter.

He couldn't relax until he'd put Julian's door between him and the world outside. It wasn't that he was afraid of the others, exactly. But he remembered Danny Costello crumpled on the linoleum, blood-slick hands covering his head. He remembered how suddenly the dread had receded, how every other sensation was buried beneath the thrill of relief. Paul didn't trust himself to listen too closely to what the boys said outside the door. If he heard the wrong thing, he knew his self-control would snap.

Julian was out, but he'd left his day planner open on his desk (*group proj. mtg., 12–2ish—bring Goffman—do not concuss K. with it*). Paul shed his shoes, hat, and coat, but he kept the scarf close. It smelled like menthol drops and orange peel and a dusty trace of smoke, deeply familiar and nothing like home.

He set aside his glasses and lay on the unmade bed in his cemetery clothes, watching the signal flags catch on the eddies of heat from the radiator. Outside the window, at the outer edge of his vision, snow was finally falling.

When Julian returned, Paul drifted out of his uneasy sleep, consciousness fanning outward petal by petal with the sound of Julian's voice. There was a fresh cool weight over his body—the blanket, he realized after a few seconds, pulled up to cover him.

"I'm not sure if it's the cold or the smog or both." Julian was chatting idly as he put away his belongings. Paul watched him from the corner of his eye as he stepped out of his shoes. "But I've been a wheezy mess all week, it's mortifying. Listen, I sound like an accordion . . ."

He shut his eyes again until Julian had slid under the covers beside him. They settled against each other a little gracelessly, more intent on closeness than comfort. Paul pressed his mouth to Julian's temples and wrists and the side of his throat so that he could feel his pulse against his teeth. There were still a few half-melted fragments of snow clinging to Julian's hair, but they dissolved between Paul's fingers as soon as he touched them.

"Listen," Julian said again, and drew a deliberate inhale. There was a ringing haze in his breathing, air struggling to find a path around scar tissue. Paul feared suddenly that a fissure would appear inside the broken lung. He pictured blood bubbling up and spilling from Julian's nose and mouth.

He looked away quickly, but Julian still saw some ugly truth in his face. Paul felt Julian's fingertips press into the side of his chest, as if he were measuring the gaps between his ribs.

"Oh," Julian said. "That was today, wasn't it?"

Paul thought at first that the question perturbed him because he had told Julian and then forgotten about it. Then he remembered that he hadn't—wouldn't have, ever, even if he'd resolved to forget afterward. "I don't . . . ," he started to say.

"That was creepy of me." Julian didn't sound sorry. "I saw the postcard on your mom's fridge. I had to look up what it meant." He added, "That's one of those things my family doesn't do."

There was a jarring gentleness in Julian's voice, uncharacteristically wary, but it didn't entirely eclipse the cool verve of curiosity. Paul avoided Julian's eyes until he was certain he wouldn't press for details. He knew, or thought he knew, that Julian cared whether or not he was in pain—but there was also a part of Julian that was fascinated by how the pain worked, just as he was fascinated when Paul revealed a weakness or idiosyncrasy during a chess game. Perhaps he scrutinized it in case he needed to use it someday. The alternative was that it was curiosity for curiosity's sake, which was almost more dangerous.

"There's this idea in psychoanalysis that I've always liked." Julian pulled himself closer and rested his head in the crook of Paul's arm. "It's that what we call 'love' is actually letting your identity fill in around the shape of the other person—you love someone by defining yourself against them. It says loss hurts because there's nothing holding that part of you in place anymore. But your outline still holds, and it keeps holding. The thing you shaped yourself into by loving them, you never stop *being* that. The marks are permanent, so the idea of the person you loved is permanent, too."

Only as permanent as I am, Paul wanted to say, but being cynical in response to Julian's kindness would have been cheap.

"But I've always been shaped around you." Paul had given up

on trying not to stammer through his sincerity; whenever he became embarrassed Julian would kiss his forehead and promise to be charmed by it. "It's different, you're different, it's—I always think of a passage from the *Symposium*, this allegory about people who started off as two halves of a whole, but then something cut them apart, and they spend their whole lives looking for their other half so they can fit themselves back together. And that's how it feels, it *hurts*, it's like I lost you before I was born."

"I don't think you've ever felt anything that didn't hurt you," Julian said. "We've found each other, out of everyone else in the world. Does that hurt, too?"

Paul abruptly let go of Julian's hair and slid his hand under the layers of sweater and shirt. He felt the embossed ragged line of the scar and imagined how deeply it threaded between muscle and interstice. Julian yielded as if Paul were following his command.

"What happens if I lose you again?" Paul didn't mean to ask it aloud, but he couldn't stop himself.

"You don't."

"How do I know that?"

A sharp, inscrutable smile. "You don't."

Paul could never forget, not quite, that the closeness between them was an illusion. He had no scar to mirror Julian's, because the wound that had cut them into separate bodies was much older and deeper, invisible. When he kissed Julian, there was always a moment when he believed they could heal the division. But it didn't matter how urgently or reverently they touched each other, how inseparable they pretended to be. He couldn't trust that they wouldn't be parted again, not so long as the separation still existed.

9.

WEEKS AGO, he'd tried to tell his family that he didn't want them to do anything for his birthday. They hadn't listened last year, when the day came so soon after the funeral that it still startled him to see his reflection in an uncovered mirror. He had all but pleaded then, but they insisted. The cousins brought gifts wrapped in bright crêpe, and his grandmother baked a cake he could barely taste, and they all pretended vehemently that he still had a childhood left to indulge. If they'd been willing to make him endure that charade for the sake of their sense of normalcy, then Paul knew that this year's battle was already lost. When the day arrived, there was nothing he could do but set his shoulders, resolve to endure it, and try to convince his face to smile.

He had to get through the first half of the party without Julian. One of Julian's brothers was in town for the morning, and he insisted on being entertained. ("A long layover on his way down from Dartmouth for a crew meet," Julian had explained, "which is a *mortifying* sentence, and I could kill Henry for forcing me to utter it.") So Paul spent the hours before Julian's arrival trying to fade into the wallpaper and avoid notice, which was difficult when the festivities were ostensibly in his honor.

He could tell some of the family thought he was being churlish, no matter how much he widened his eyes or how amiable a shape he tried to make with his mouth. He did his best to absorb the small talk and best wishes, but he still caught sight of Hazel and her daughter, Debbie, exchanging a look of exasperation. *He could hardly wait to get rid of us,* one was thinking; *It was inevitable that at least* one *of those kids was going to turn out funny,* answered the other. They shared a discreet laugh, and Paul crushed his elbows against his sides until the fury faded.

Julian was late; this wasn't unusual for him, but it still stung. They started lunch without him, twenty minutes after he was supposed to arrive. Finally there was a tentative knock at his grandparents' door, then a more decisive ring as Julian figured out how to work the old-fashioned twist doorbell. He was waiting on the porch with a hinged wooden box under one arm.

"I hope I didn't miss lunch, it smells great," said Julian with breathless earnestness as he stepped into the foyer. Paul's grandparents were waiting behind him, and Paul could tell Julian was engineering a very specific first impression. "I'm so sorry, my cabbie *vastly* overstated how well he knew the neighborhood."

"It's fine," Paul said, though he was quietly trying to discern whether the excuse was actually true or just a plausible thing for Julian's persona to say.

Paul's grandparents had crept up beside him. His grandmother gave his shoulder a quick, prompting tap, and Paul scrambled for the script he was supposed to follow. "Um, right, so this is—I would like to introduce—Julian Fromme, he's my friend from school, Julian I would like to introduce my grandparents Maurice and Flora Krakovsky—"

"A solid effort," said Paul's grandmother fondly, "although for future reference, it may help to *breathe*. How are you, Julian? Let me take your coat, we've got your plate in a warm oven . . ."

When his grandparents had drifted back out of earshot, Julian caught Paul's eye and smiled—his real smile, sly and electric.

"'I would like to introduce,'" said Julian. "Poor Pablo. You're so square, you're a cube."

"Remind me, how much money did your parents spend on those nice straight teeth?" Paul countered, and the smile became a grin.

"My brother says happy birthday, by the way," Julian added. "Nice of him, I suppose. When he's President, you'll be able to tell all your friends."

"God, is *that* what he wants to be? Is he out of his mind?"

"Oh, our Henry wants whatever Father tells him he wants. There's not a single thought in his head that wasn't bought and paid for by someone else, so it's really the perfect job for him."

Paul soon forgot he'd ever been annoyed at Julian for being late. He even forgot how anxious his family had made him all morning. If they paid him any attention now, he no longer noticed; he imagined that in Julian's presence they had gone sunblind, and that they would only perceive Paul himself as a faint blur at the periphery. It freed him to speak, because anything he said would be forgotten as soon as he'd spoken. Whenever Julian answered a question, Paul caught himself joining in, trying to focus Julian's brilliance to a fine, searing beam. He tried to coax Julian into venturing past the bland, polite persona designed to placate Paul's mother. He prompted Julian to tell his most eloquent stories, to talk about topics Paul knew he was so passionate about that he wouldn't be able to contain his enthusiasm. When Julian failed to divulge an interesting detail, Paul did it for him, eagerly, as if the life he described were his own.

After the meal, the party began to dissipate. Charlie Parker faded out to soft static, and neither grandparent hurried to replace him. A young cousin had a temper tantrum, and his parents whisked him and his siblings home for their nap. The Mount Lebanon cousins made their goodbyes next, pleading traffic, and drove away into the torrent of late-winter rain. The rest of the group drifted into the living room, where there was a fresh Duke Ellington record and more coffee. Paul's grandfather made a great show of cagily adding a splash of whiskey to each mug (Laurie received no more than a teaspoon).

Julian had fallen quiet. He gave the impression of being serenely unguarded. Paul lingered in the doorway to observe him, trying to decide whether he was looking at the machinery or at the ghost that turned its gears.

He watched Julian reach toward the sugar bowl, the movements of his hands and the way his shirt shifted over his shoulders. As he was collecting a third sugar cube, he looked up and met Paul's eyes with a ready smile. There was no evidence of a shift, but Paul also knew better than to think he would be able to detect it.

He returned the smile, wary and sincere, and sat alongside Julian in the armchair.

"Anyone mind if I smoke?" Julian asked the room. He settled back as he spoke, draping one arm carelessly around Paul's neck. When no one objected, Julian held a cigarette between his teeth and lit it one-handed. Paul tried to imagine his own body moving with the same fluid grace.

"You never opened the one Julian brought," Laurie pointed out after a while. Sure enough, the box sat undisturbed in the front hallway. Paul had set it there with the opened gifts, the inevitable hiking socks and hand-knit sweaters and books that were almost, but not quite, the kind he actually liked.

"I figured, you know—later," Paul said to his shoes, but she was already rising to retrieve it. "I don't like turning it into a performance."

"It is later," said Audrey. "All the cousins are gone, there's nobody here but us chickens."

Paul hesitated before opening the box, wishing the others would take pity on him and look away. He lifted the lid just far enough to parse the contents—then shut it again and quickly fastened the latch.

"Are they the wrong kind?" Julian asked, with a guilelessness that might even have convinced Paul if he hadn't known better. "I can take them back and get different ones, I just got the brand my mother said was good."

"You know *perfectly well*," said Paul quietly, but his stammer overtook him and he couldn't summon any words beyond that.

There was no preventing it. The box was pulled from his hands, its contents inspected; there were appreciative murmurs and shared looks of tight-lipped alarm.

Paul had hoped they wouldn't know enough to understand, but they had the same memories he did. A few summers ago he'd saved up for weeks, pulling weeds and washing windows up and down the street, so that he could go to the art supply shop near Carnegie-Mellon and buy a single tube of real carmine red. He'd used every scrap of it, flattening the tube down to a sliver and then slicing it open to scrape out the remnants. It hadn't even been quite top-of-the-line, not like these; the mere presence of the word *artist* instead of *student* on the label had been so daunting that he was afraid to open it once he had it.

"Don't you dare fret about 'wasting' them," said Julian. "I like your weird paintings, I want there to be more of them."

If Julian had detected Paul's embarrassment at all, he was atypically oblivious about where it might have come from—misattributing it, apparently, to mere modesty. There was nothing to do but forgive him, but it didn't happen without effort. It came slowly, breath by breath, before Paul could finally manage a smile.

Paul's grandfather was sitting in the other armchair, watching the two of them. He held the box open in his large hands while Paul's grandmother perched on the arm, reading glasses held aloft as she looked inside. Their faces were shrewdly calm, as if they were waiting for the right moment to share a piece of bad news.

"You have a very generous friend, Paulie," said his grandfather gravely.

They took advantage of the chaos as the party was finally ending. While the others gathered their coats, Paul's grandparents ushered his mother into the dining room, then shut themselves away behind the louvered French doors. Paul only listened in for a moment; it was all that he could stand.

"It's just that he's so lonely. He pretends he isn't, but he wouldn't *try* so hard if he weren't. It's hard on him the same way it is on Paul, they're both so smart, and I think that's why he—"

"Ruth—oh, Ruth, honey, it wouldn't be so bad if it were just him. Paul could take care of himself, provided he wanted to, but—wasn't there some *concern*, before?"

He could hear the panic in how briskly his mother ignored the question.

"You don't understand how good this has been for him," she said. "He's never had someone his age he could talk to before—I'm not sure either of them have. Of course they don't know how they're supposed to behave around each other, they haven't learned yet, and they're still so young—"

"He's seventeen." (His grandfather knew, of course, what teenage boys got up to.) "Two years younger than you were when Audrey was born. He isn't that young. He knows."

"It isn't healthy to let him carry on like this. You need to do something, or this is going to get out of hand."

"Jake said he would grow out of it." His mother held his father's name in her mouth as if the shape of it could cut her tongue.

"For god's sake, Ruthie," said his grandfather. "Look at the way he *looks* at that boy. This isn't going to go away by itself."

Paul tightened the belt of his raincoat as if to cinch his fluttering insides into place. He turned away and stalked out; his sisters were both still waiting in the front hallway, but they recoiled quickly and didn't try to stop him.

Julian waited in the back seat of the Buick, door hanging open, droplets dusting the inside of the glass. Paul threw himself inside and slammed the door. He could feel Julian watching him, but refused to look his way.

"Are you—?" Julian started to ask, but Paul's last nerve finally snapped. He wasn't even aware of hitting the back of the passenger seat until the shock was reverberating between his elbow and his fist. He hadn't broken anything, he knew that right away, but there was a ringing jagged pain in the bones of his hand that told him it had been a close thing.

"Okay," said Julian coolly. "Thank you for your clarity."

Paul stretched his hand to let sensation flow back into his fingers. His knuckles ached with the slow promise of a bruise. "Shut up. It isn't about *you*."

He expected Julian to snap at him, but he didn't. He just set his jaw and shut his eyes, the way he did when he had decided to absorb an insult from his father rather than pick a fight. It was unfair of him to be hurt, unfair of him to put himself deliberately in the way of Paul's anger. Paul looked away quickly and stared at his knees, wringing his injured hand to worsen the pain.

"I don't want to take it back." Julian looked at his hands as he spoke, so carelessly that Paul couldn't tell whether he was avoiding his eyes. "It's supposed to be a vote of confidence. You're always saying you want to create something that matters—I wanted to show you that I know you can. I just want you to believe me when I tell you you're *worth* something."

"I don't *want* you to tell me that. I'll believe it when it's true. And in the meantime this sort of thing is just—just so conspicuously unearned, it's so obvious that I haven't done anything to deserve it that I—"

"Spare me, Pablo," said Julian acidly. "This isn't a transaction."

He had never wanted reassurance. When Julian finally lashed out at him, it was a relief.

10.

HE EXPECTED a confrontation at home, but it didn't happen immediately. His family handled him with kid gloves, the way they always had. "They're nice people," Julian had said, as if it were an amusing peculiarity rather than evidence of cowardice. His grandparents still had him over for lunch on Sundays, and even if the questions about girls had grown more frequent, they asked them so carelessly that Paul couldn't tell. Julian was still welcome at his mother's kitchen table. He still watched with performative raptness as she demonstrated how to fry mushrooms or sew on a button; Paul's mother still laughed, quietly but sincerely, at the stories of prep-school whimsy that were too sunny to be the whole truth. When she walked past Julian, she would often squeeze his arm gently, as if he were one of her own children.

The strangeness of it sometimes took Paul aback. What existed between them shouldn't share a reality with the world outside; it should be its own truth, self-contained and defined on its own terms, the same way that a dream was true. But at odd moments the two realities converged as he watched Julian's body move through the world and remembered how recently and how intimately they had touched. He would notice the angle of Julian's wrist as he turned a doorknob and remember twisting that wrist behind his back—letting his teeth cut a slim black bruise into the flesh of Julian's shoulder, only hours before, a wound so fresh that Julian must still feel it sting. Now and then there was a stray note in Julian's laugh that rhymed with the way the right touch could make his voice break. The familiarity drew an uncanny bright line between two moments that should never have been able to reach each other. Look at you, Paul would think, in a voice he despised because it imposed itself from the outside. Look what you're doing. What's wrong with you?

But when they were alone, he could promise himself that he and Julian were each other's birthright, and that the only unnatural thing was the fact that their blood was divided between two bodies. He could believe that even calling it "sex" was incorrect, because it wasn't about anything so shallow as physical desire. They wanted each other in the way of flesh wanting to knit itself together over a wound.

AS WINTER faded into a dreary spring, Julian grew more tense with every passing day. Tentative summer plans to watch a professor's house had fallen through—his parents were demanding that he accompany them to visit his grandfather in France at the very least, and the professor decided that his orchids required a house sitter who could provide continuous care. As the end of the school year grew nearer, there were no other opportunities. Julian pretended to find the topic merely irritating, but his dread was clear from the sheer number of times he mentioned it.

Eventually Julian couldn't talk around it any longer. He'd been in a volatile mood all day, snappish and brittle and not making any effort to hide it. They had the house to themselves, but as usual they had barricaded themselves in Paul's room. Warm, dirty rain glazed the window; Julian was sitting up beside him, watching it fall.

"This summer is going to kill me."

Paul felt a twist of annoyance at him for speaking. He wanted to keep pretending that the full extent of space and time only reached as far as the walls of his room. When Paul pulled the blanket over his head, he could pretend in the dull light that their skin was the same color, no freckles or veins or scars to break the illusion. He could convince himself not to know that his own limbs belonged to him and Julian's didn't. Both their hands were the same lean shape, indistinguishable in the dark.

"I hate being there," said Julian. Paul listened to his voice moving through his chest, the eerie way it rang hollow on one side but not the other. "I hate their creepy Stepford town. I hate the dinner parties they throw for their war-profiteer friends. I hate how when we go to the country club, my dad always wears the same *fucking* sunglasses that he thinks distract people from the bridge of his nose. Three months of them, without a real human being for miles around—if I don't take a hammer to every last one of them, it'll be a miracle."

Paul noticed with a sudden, sickly chill that Julian had said nothing about missing him.

"You could come stay with me if you get too tired of them," he said, trying to convince himself as much as Julian. "Or I could even come visit for a few days, just, if you wanted backup—"

Julian laughed so dismissively that Paul didn't dare keep talking.

"What you *can* do is write to me," Julian said. It didn't sound like anything he actually needed so much as an acquiescence to Paul's childishness. "And keep an eye out for anything— anything at all—that might get me back up here before August. The rest is *my* problem, not yours."

Carefully, half certain that it was a mistake, Paul pulled the blanket down and propped himself up on his arm to meet Julian's eyes.

"Listen," he said. "What do they do to you?"

Julian looked as if he'd never heard such a pathetic question.

"What do they *do* to me?" he echoed, singsong and impatient. There was something a little flat about his vowels, and with a twist of self-disgust Paul recognized it as an imitation of his accent. "God, Pablo. It's not fucking *Peyton Place*, they don't have to 'do' anything."

"So why do you feel so sorry for yourself?" It sounded much nastier out loud than it had in his head, but he pressed on, desperately, as if that might achieve anything besides making it worse. "Either you're lying to me, and they're worse than you say, or what you're going home to isn't much worse than what I'm going to be stuck here with all summer, so I don't—"

Julian's gaze was ice-cold.

"You don't have the first idea what you're talking about," he said. "Shut up before you make a fool of yourself."

Paul let the ugly silence settle over them. He disentangled his legs from Julian's and put some space between them, lying on the edge of the twin mattress with his arms folded tight. Julian shrugged back into his unbuttoned shirt and sat hugging his knees. His fingertips brushed his lips now and then, restlessly, as if his hands were itching for a cigarette.

"I just thought—I don't know—that if I were around to look after you, it wouldn't be so bad."

Paul imagined Julian imitating him again and didn't dare let on that he meant every word. Even at a murmur, he sounded so ridiculous that he couldn't have blamed Julian for making fun of him. But he didn't; his mercy was just as capricious as his cruelty.

"I'm going to miss you, too, you know," said Julian—resigned, or else indifferent, and Paul didn't dare try to decide which. "But the sooner we stop fighting it, the better chance we have of getting through it in one piece. It is what it is."

Paul knew this was the closest he was going to get to an apology.

OVER THE course of finals week, Julian's room wrung itself empty. The signal flags ended up in the same trash bag as a year's worth of worksheets and discarded calendar pages. The bookshelf was disassembled and taken, along with its boxed contents, to a storage unit in the Strip District. When Paul arrived the morning of their last exam, the wardrobe was hanging open, and when they spoke their voices rang from the high white walls. Stripped of everything that had given it the illusion of permanence, the room filled Paul with the muffled, eerie sadness that he associated with Cape May motel rooms and his great-grandmother's suburban rest home. It was designed to be forgotten and to forget.

He would be staying with Paul for the next two nights, which Paul's family had allowed without protest. Sunday morning, very early, his grandfather would drive Julian to the airport—had volunteered to do so, with a prompt benevolence that looked a bit too much like eagerness. Paul could tell his family had pinned their hopes on the separation. They intended to keep him occupied with his annual volunteer position at the butterfly garden and a job at his grandfather's repair garage. The plan, he knew, was that he and Julian would slowly lose interest in each other.

Julian had consoled him in fits and starts, far too wrapped up in his own dread to expend much effort. He gave Paul a book of airmail stamps and the address to his grandfather's summerhouse in the South of France, but he refused to share his parents' telephone number; he frequently extracted promises from Paul to write twice a week, but only rarely did he make the same promise in return. The last day of finals, Paul knew better than to expect any reassurance. Julian was full of nervous energy, his voice bright with false cheer. As they sat at either end of his bare mattress, he gestured expansively and talked without pause.

"I haven't given up on coming back early." Julian lit a new cigarette with the stub of the last, leaning over the empty waste-basket to catch the ashes. "Once we're back from France, I'll be able to commit to house-sitting engagements—that *can't* have been the only one in the entire city."

Paul had never met anyone who employed a house sitter in his life, but he didn't dare say so. Julian's overnight bag sat at the outer periphery of his vision; its presence nagged at him even when he looked away.

Their last final was with Strauss. Julian finished early, as always, while Paul's handwriting compressed and his thoughts ballooned past the boundaries of the mimeographed page. He saw Julian lingering at the desk, chatting quietly with Strauss; both laughed at something Julian had said, but when Julian turned away, he caught Paul's gaze and rolled his eyes.

Paul was nearly the last to finish; when he brought his exam and term paper to the front, there was nothing to distract Strauss from his approach, and Paul knew he wasn't going to get away as easily as Julian had. He tried to summon something banal and trivial to say, something that demanded a response he'd be able to roll his eyes at as well. But he couldn't think of anything, and Strauss wouldn't have let him get away with it anyway. All he could do was watch silently, shouldering his knapsack and chewing the inside of his cheek, while Strauss lifted the essay's cover sheet with the end of his pen.

"'Morality as Social Control and the Ethics of Obedience'— straight out of the gate, we know this is a Paul Fleischer creation." He said it amiably, even with affection, but Paul blushed and furiously avoided his eyes. "I do look forward to straining my eyes at those great, galloping Germanic sentences of yours—with you it's never a boring read . . . You've taken the Milgram example rather to heart, haven't you?"

Paul picked at a loose thread on his knapsack strap and stared at the corner of the desk. "It didn't say anything I didn't already know," he said in a flat monotone. "Other people might understand too, if they weren't so—so lazy and atavistic they don't bother thinking for themselves, if they were smart enough to pay *attention*. But then of course the results would be different—"

Strauss lowered the cover sheet again. His smile was solemn and infuriatingly patient, as if he were trying to talk down a fretful child.

"I understand," he said, "that yours is a meticulously researched pessimism. Justified, even, to a certain extent. The trouble lies in the same thing that makes it seductive, especially at your age—a certain heady isolation in believing that you, and you alone, are burdened by the truth. That's what concerns me about your approach, Mr. Fleischer. It tips into nihilism if one isn't careful."

The door behind him pulled like gravity. When he glanced over his shoulder, he expected to find Julian waiting, but he'd already gone.

Strauss was watching him expectantly. Paul tried, very weakly, to smile, but he took a step backward even before he spoke.

"Have a good summer, Professor," he said.

Sunlight sliced through the hallway. Julian was leaning next to the window by the stairwell, cigarette in hand. When he caught sight of Paul, he seemed unsure what he ought to do with his face; after a moment he settled on a smile, but it was too nervy and joyless to be convincing.

"Ma's making you that thing with the mushrooms for dinner."
Paul watched Julian closely as they descended the stairs. Usually
when they walked together, they fell effortlessly into step, but today Julian was moving just a shade too quickly. "She insisted," he
said, "so I hope you weren't lying when you told her you liked it."

He had intended the remark to be a benign distraction, but
Julian stared at him as though the news had struck him silent.
"Why would she do that?" he said. He had an odd, fierce look,
as if he were trying to hide his alarm.

Paul couldn't make sense of it, so he shrugged and tried to
pretend he hadn't noticed. "She was just trying to do something
nice for you, I guess."

Julian's mood abruptly changed after that, though Paul didn't
dare ask why. He became very quiet and still, speaking to Paul's
family only when prompted. The nervous energy didn't leave,
but he kept it under tight control. He was polite but far less effusive about the meal than Paul's mother had likely planned. After
dinner he helped Laurie with her French homework in the living
room, but he didn't tease her as usual or theatrically read the text-
book passages aloud—he didn't show the slightest enthusiasm for
the task at all. Laurie seemed to decide this was a personal insult. When they'd finished, she mumbled her thanks, then picked
up the cat from Julian's lap and carried it upstairs to her room.

"Well, *I* thought dinner was lovely," Paul heard Audrey tell
his mother. They were in the kitchen, tidying up before their
detective show. "Teenage boys, for god's sake, nothing ruder on
this earth. I'm sorry, Ma."

Even from the hallway, he could hear the weight of his
mother's pause.

"He was just sad, honey," she said, as grimly as if she were taking this into evidence.

II.

FOR THEIR last day together, Julian had unexpectedly asked to accompany Paul on a hike. Barely believing his luck, Paul had offered more palatable alternatives in case it was a bluff, but Julian insisted. "I want to see what you like so much about it," he'd said, just skeptically enough that Paul was able to believe him. Now that their few dwindling hours together had actually arrived, Paul suspected that what Julian was really after was novelty. It was something Julian's own family had never done, so drastically unfamiliar that it might distract him from his flight in the morning. Julian's mood was so tense and unpredictable that the slightest friction could make him snap, and Paul could hardly sleep the night before because he couldn't stop imagining the mistakes he might make to set off Julian's temper. If they parted on bad terms, he knew that would be the end of it. His family would get their wish.

Julian slept far more soundly, so much so that Paul suspected he'd stolen one of his mother's sedatives. When the clock radio went off at half past four, Julian barely stirred; Paul kissed the nape of his neck, but he didn't seem to feel it.

They had slept in a tangle, sheets kicked to the foot of the bed, the sleeping bag pristine on the floor. When Paul got up to shut the window, he noticed his door was slightly ajar, as if it hadn't latched properly; the cat, predictably, had taken the opportunity to install itself under his bed.

He showered and dressed as quietly as he could, but when he reached the kitchen he found his mother awake. She sat alone at the table, soft hands wrapped around a tea mug. The only light

came from the dying bulb above the stove, painting the edges
of her face in yellow. Paul noticed for the first time that they had
the same full upper lip, the same kittenish upturn at the outer
corners of their eyes. For an instant, before she moved, his face
wasn't entirely his father's; then she turned to look at him and
the resemblance disappeared, as if it had never been there at all.

"You're up early."

"I'm looking for specimens today," he reminded her. He suspected she would forget again as soon as he stopped speaking.
"I'm taking one of Zayde's loaner cars."

She smiled at him wanly, tucking a stray lock back into her
braid. No pill last night; he could tell from the uncanny outline
of her hands, as if they were trembling just a shade too subtly
for the movement to be perceptible to the naked eye.

She started to get up, but Paul quickly waved her back to her
seat. She was wearing an old lavender cardigan over her nightgown, and the flat mother-of-pearl buttons clicked against the
kitchen table as she sat back down. At first she pretended to ignore him while he prepared a thermos of Campbell's soup and
a stack of sandwiches, but now and then he could feel her eyes
on his back.

After a while she pushed herself to her feet and arranged two
slices of white bread in the toaster. For a long while she leaned
against the counter, sipping from her second cup of tea. Her
silence had become apprehensive.

"Your friend is going with you, isn't he?"

Paul knew instantly that this was going to be a fight—his
mother's usual kind, wrapped in so many layers of earnest concern that she could pretend it wasn't a fight at all.

"Maybe, if I can actually get him out of bed this early." He stared at his hands and pretended to be raptly focused on the task of wrapping the sandwiches in wax paper.

Another long silence. Paul stacked the sandwiches in a bag; his blush receded slowly until it lingered only at the edges of his ears. His mother stood with her back to the counter, taking tiny bites from her toast. She hadn't put anything on it, not even butter; Paul wondered if she was sick to her stomach.

"Paul," she said, and her careful tone made his own stomach drop. "You know I'll always love you. We all will."

He had to stand very still. All his energy went toward reassuring himself that the ground hadn't really pitched beneath his feet.

"It's just that it's hard to explain to the neighbors why you and Julian spend so much time together," she said, setting aside her dish. "Because it's—well, it's *strange*, Paulie. If it were a group of boys, it'd be one thing, but just the two of you . . . And we're all a little worried about you, because you really only have the one friend—and I'm proud of you for starting to make friends, I really am, but—"

"But what? Spit it out, Ma, what are you actually asking?"

At first she made a vague gesture and looked away, but he could see her fighting against her own cowardice. She drew her spine a little straighter and met his eyes.

"When you two go out," she said, voice shaking, "are you trying to meet girls? Or is it just the two of you, off in your own little world?"

"I don't think that's any of your business." His tongue tripped on the *b*, one of his childhood enemies. He knew better than to hope she wouldn't notice.

"Just tell me." She was on the verge of tears, which he felt was monstrously unfair. "Just tell me there's a girl—I won't get angry, if you two are out there chasing shiksas, you wouldn't be the first, just *tell* me so I'll know at least you're a normal boy—"

"I'm done talking about this," he said, or meant to say, but he couldn't hear his own voice and wasn't sure the words made it out intact.

"Just tell me I'll be able to look the neighbors in the eye without being *ashamed*. Please, Paul. It's been hard enough for us this last year, I'm begging you, don't make it worse."

From a great distance, Paul heard a loud *bang*, as if a car had backfired two streets away. Only belatedly did he realize he had slammed a cupboard, hard enough to scar the doorframe.

"So you're *ashamed* because of Dad?" He was so furious that he didn't even stammer. "All this time I thought you just missed him, but no, I was giving you too much credit, the whole show you're putting on is so the neighbors will know how goddamn embarrassed you are."

His mother's mouth fell open in shock. When she didn't answer, he pressed on ruthlessly rather than let it go.

"The only person who should feel any shame did a pretty good job of ensuring he never had to answer for anything again. So what, we have to fucking apologize to the neighbors because he's not here to do it for himself? Or are we 'ashamed' because we're supposed to have driven him to it?"

"No." It was less a word than a pained exhale, as if he had struck her in the gut. "No, honey, that's never—it isn't your fault, no one thinks it's your fault, no one would *ever*—"

"Maybe *they* drove him to it." Paul heard a laugh, but it couldn't have come from him; it was too sharp to have left his lungs without slicing them apart from the inside. "Ever think of that? All most people care about is pretending everyone is exactly the same as they are, and he *wasn't*, he couldn't be, he knew too much about what the world really is. Those people don't care about anything except reinforcing their own *fucking* normalcy by making you reflect it back at them—"

His mother exhaled hard.

"*Paul.*" She didn't quite snap at him, but he could see the effort it took not to. "Honey, there were a lot of things going on with your father, and I don't . . . You might not believe me, but I get angry, I do, I get terribly angry that people can't understand. But there are limits," she said desperately, "to what you can expect people to understand without living it, and that's not something they're *doing* to you. You can't fight everybody all the time, you still have to live with them—"

"Hell if I do." His voice nearly broke, but he didn't dare let himself fall silent lest the weakness reach his face. "I'm done trying. Dad tried, he spent his whole life trying, and I *refuse* to end up the way he did."

At first he felt a miserable thrill of adrenaline. He hadn't let her turn her suffering into a problem for him to solve. Perhaps he had finally proven to her that he wasn't the malleable, fearful child she assumed he was. But then the fury cleared, and he saw that she wasn't actually the relentless crush of need he always felt from her; she was just a woman, sad-eyed and small in her faded cardigan. As if for the first time, he realized that she wasn't only his mother, but a widow. That once she'd been only a couple years older than Paul was now and had fallen in love with a boy, never knowing that the boy would wait alongside her for twenty years before taking his service pistol into the garden shed.

There had been a note pinned to the shed door; Paul knew because he'd heard his grandparents talking about it when they thought he couldn't hear. It was nothing elaborate, just a plea to call the police rather than look inside. He'd thought at the time that it was foolish and pathetic of her to disobey, as if she had merely disbelieved the warning. Only now did he understand that she hadn't failed to comprehend the horror. She had faced it knowingly, without question, because even the slimmest hope outweighed the lifetime of nightmares. It was such a profound act of love that it agonized him even to imagine it.

"I'm sorry," he said, and the apology was as inadequate as the belated, horrifying empathy that accompanied it. "Ma, I'm sorry."

He could see the effort as she pulled herself back inside her outlines, swallowing the pain to fester inside her. Had she learned that trick from his father, or had they taught it to each other?

"I hurt you," she said. *I hurt you as much as you hurt me*, was what it really meant. "Forget I said anything, sweetheart. Please. It was never supposed to hurt you."

He didn't answer, or even look at her. When he gathered his belongings and hurried up the stairs, she made no attempt to stop him.

12.

"I'VE ALWAYS thought this might be where he first saw an opening," said Julian.

Paul glanced over to the passenger seat. Julian looked sickly in the dull morning light, shadows deepening the crescents under his eyes until they echoed the hollows of bone underneath. He'd brought the chess book with him, and Paul knew even without looking that he had returned to Kazlauskas v. Kaplan. Other games caught his interest now and then, but only that one held it.

"You can't tell from the notation," Julian went on, "but Kaplan took the longest time to answer this move from the white bishop. It was a great move, but not so aggressive that he'd think he was in really serious trouble. I've always wondered why he took so long, and then to decide on such a standard reply—but god, how can this be it? It's a strong move, black spends the next few turns trying to dig out from under it, it's not as if Kazlauskas made a mistake."

Paul didn't really follow, but he knew he wasn't meant to, particularly; Julian talked himself through this game whenever he wanted a distraction, and Paul could hardly begrudge him for needing one now. He let Julian's voice wash through him, pleasant and familiar even in the absence of comprehension, just as it was when he spoke French.

"Kazlauskas does everything right. *Everything*, I can't find a single flaw. Playing black against him should be like trying to climb a sheer cliff. So why is he doomed? Where does he go wrong?"

As Paul steered the borrowed car around a curve in the road, the rust-streaked mass of a steelworks emerged from behind the hills. He noticed with a jolt that he had been given far more power than he wanted, and for a moment he wasn't certain he could stop himself from using it. He could slam the accelerator and swing the car off the road into the ravine alongside the steelworks—smash it into a tree and kill them both. There was nothing Julian could do to stop him.

"Maybe he doesn't do anything wrong," Paul said, tightening his hands around the wheel. "Maybe Kaplan's just so good that white is doomed no matter how perfectly Kazlauskas plays."

"That isn't how it works." Julian held the book between his knees as he peeled the wax paper back from a tomato sandwich. "No. Jury's still out on whether he wins or draws—it's a big debate in chess theory—but in perfect play, white doesn't lose. That means somewhere in there, no matter how good each move looks, Kazlauskas made a mistake. *Something* is imperfect, and I want to know what it is."

"Or it's just less perfect than black's game, rather than being imperfect."

"There are degrees of perfection," said Julian airily, "the same way there are degrees of being dead."

They fell into an amiable silence. Julian finished his sandwich and rested his head on the window, watching drowsily as the landscape grew wilder. The steelworks faded into the distance, and with it the remnants of the industrial smog. Paul sometimes forgot how blue the sky could be outside the city, especially in the moments before sunrise, when it was just barely too translucent to blot out the stars.

Just over the state line they passed a roadside stall where a few sleepy hippies were peddling anemic apricots and bunches of crumpled arugula. By then Julian was asleep, arms folded loosely around his waist. Stillness and vulnerability were so foreign to Julian's body that sleep looked unnatural on him. Awake, he was all edges, from the aristocratic line of his nose to the stark, eerie contrast between black eyelashes and light green iris. It was only when he was sleeping that Paul could tell how much of the sharpness was a performance.

When they paused at a railway crossing and the roar of a coal train failed to rouse him, Paul finally yielded to the impulse to wake him. He brushed Julian's hair back from his face; Julian's eyes opened just slightly, but the alertness didn't return.

"We're almost there," Paul said, but Julian's eyes had closed again.

He saw the sun crest the horizon just briefly, searing and merciless, before the car slipped into the park and the light was swallowed by trees. He was fully and fiercely awake by now. He rolled down the window as he drove and breathed in the damp clean smell of dewy earth and new leaves. For a moment after he parked he sat still and alert. Then he shouldered his bag and stepped out onto the gravel.

Julian was slow to stir, so Paul leaned back into the car and punched his arm before grabbing his net and thermos from the back seat. "You coming or not?"

"I'm going to push you off a cliff, you fucking Boy Scout."

"Well, hop to it, then."

Anticipation was almost indistinguishable from panic. The speed of his pulse, the tightness in his tendons—the anatomy of it, by any objective measure, was the same as the anatomy of fear. The difference lay in the sense of purpose, which reshaped the nervous tension into something electric. This was how he

imagined Julian feeling all the time, free from fear, able to regard the world with a predator's detached fascination.

The parking lot was empty except for the loaner car and a
solitary Park Service pickup truck. Julian finally joined him at
the trailhead, moving a little stiffly. He threw a glance back at
the car before turning to face the woods.

As they descended the path, the forest tightened around
them, the heavy organic quiet broken only by the occasional
far-off trill of a bird. Julian had dressed slightly wrong—canvas
tennis shoes, a shawl-collared pullover with a tiny anchor embroidered at the breast, the sort of clothing Paul imagined you
were supposed to wear on a sailboat. He slipped once or twice
on the carpet of rotting leaves, so when they reached a fork in
the trail, Paul chose the easier path for Julian's sake. The park
punished him for it. All they saw before noon were a few flick-
ers of false hope, whites and buckeyes and plain little sulphurs,
never worth the effort of pursuing. Midway through the morning Julian pointed out a potential target, and he was so pleased
with himself that Paul didn't tell him spicebush swallowtails
were so common he'd often practiced on them in the backyard as a child. But even this was a disappointment; the butterfly
seemed to sense danger before he had even lifted its net, and it
flew up out of reach.

They followed the path to a creek bed at the bottom of a shallow ravine. Julian crept along the water line, his tennis shoes
blackening around the edges. Paul watched him pause to gaze
down at a clutch of tadpoles, delicately fascinated, as if he hadn't
actually seen them before outside of a cartoon. Jagged walls of
bare limestone and shale followed the creek's path back through
the forest. The sun was higher now, its light filtering down from
the canopy in mottled green.

"They can always tell when I'm trying to impress someone." Paul leaned against the ravine wall and rifled through his knapsack for a sandwich. "All the interesting ones hide, so I look like I'm out of my mind for enjoying this. We're taking a break, by the way, so smoke 'em if you've got 'em."

"Nah, not out here." Julian picked his way along the creek bed, grinning, and plucked the second half of the sandwich from Paul's hand. "You *are* out of your mind, in a charming, Caspar David Friedrich sort of way. But I can't tell which butterflies are interesting in the first place, so I'm enjoying myself just fine."

Julian's lungs were still buzzing faintly from the hike, so they made no immediate move to return to the trail after finishing the sandwiches. They sat together at the base of the low cliff, watching the skittering paths of birds overhead.

In lieu of smoking, Julian took up the restless, Sisyphean task of trying to unmoor a rock that was embedded in the earth. Like many of his movements, it looked so careless and kittenishly destructive that it took Paul a while to recognize it as nervous at all. It unnerved Paul to see him appear out of his element, fidgety and short of breath in his ill-chosen shoes. He was about to ask if Julian was sure he wasn't miserable—if he wouldn't like to go back to the city and do something else with their last few hours, even if they just lay on the grass at Schenley Park and did nothing at all.

But at the edge of his vision, tiny and nearly imperceptible, he saw a flutter of movement. It was small, about the size of a half-dollar coin; he should never have been able to see it. But against the murk of the creek bed, the butterfly's underwings were bright as a misplaced brushstroke. Sea-glass green, soft and cool.

It fluttered from rock to rock, low over the shallow water.

It picked its way toward a lonely shaft of sunlight; when it settled there, it basked, opening and closing its small wings as if to drink in the warmth.

Paul picked up the net and got to his feet slowly, casually careful. Julian kept very still, watching; he didn't try to follow.

Most insects didn't have more than a rudimentary ability to feel—his father had asked, once, and Paul looked it up to assure him that they didn't. Fear was too complex an emotion to attribute to them, so it stood to reason that pleasure was the same, too sophisticated for a neural structure so simple it could scarcely be called a brain. But as Paul watched the butterfly linger in its patch of sun, pulling the light into its tiny cold body, it was impossible not to feel an echo of sunlight in his own skin, and to imagine, against all he'd been taught, that it enjoyed the sensation as he would. Human consciousness was more animal than its arrogance liked to pretend; perhaps the opposite was true. Perhaps somewhere in the microscopic folds of its ganglia, the creature felt something akin to joy.

He was ready when it vibrated its wings and rose to fly away. It was dull brown on its upper side, the same muddy color as the creek, and for a split second he nearly lost sight of it—but his movements were so fluid and practiced as to be all but instinct, and he never truly feared that it would escape.

He had to work quickly after he trapped it, before it could destroy its wings in the net. With his thumb and forefinger he took hold of its bristly body through the fabric and squeezed it, just tightly enough to push the air from its thorax. When it stopped moving, he looked more closely, examining its underwings through the mesh. It was a gem of a specimen, nearly every scale pristine; the shimmering light green was scalloped with hazel that glinted gold when the sun touched it.

Julian finally approached, a little hesitantly, Paul's knapsack slung over one shoulder. "Is there a jar?" he asked, eyes flitting from Paul's hands to his face. "Should I—"

"I don't use jars for this. It's already dead."

Julian's eyes returned to Paul's hand, to the tiny corpse in its mesh shroud. There was a peculiar look in his eyes, too elusive for Paul to name.

"Can you open up the zipper pocket?" Paul said. He retrieved a triangle of folded glassine from the pocket and sat on his heels. "Thanks—anyway, jars work great for beetles, but the specimens go ballistic inside the jar before the poison kicks in. Beetles are pretty durable, but leps are delicate, they ruin their wings trying to escape. Better to make it quick, so they don't have time to panic. A little squeeze to the thorax kills them instantly."

Julian watched as Paul transferred the butterfly to its paper wrapping, then rested it in the box of cotton gauze and camphor that would keep it safe until he could relax it. He shut the lid, but Julian lifted it again to look inside.

"What was he? Or was it a 'she'?"

"Juniper hairstreak. Male." Naming it was what made it feel as if it belonged to him; it had a place waiting among the other Theclinae in his third-highest specimen drawer, and an acid-free blank label waiting to be inscribed in Latin. "They're not that uncommon, but they can be a little tricky to catch. I've been missing a male for ages."

Julian lowered the lid, with a sharp exhale that turned into something like a laugh. Paul carefully returned the box to his knapsack. "Unlucky bastard," said Julian. "A noble sacrifice for science—or *was* it for science? Is there even a scientific end to justify the means?"

"Science just helps me do it." Paul steeled himself before admitting what he had never said aloud before. "I kill them because they're beautiful, and it's the only way I can keep them."

Julian didn't laugh. Paul belatedly understood the odd look he'd given him earlier. Apprehension was so foreign to him that Paul barely recognized it.

"I don't know how I can be the first person to notice how twisted you are." Julian smiled coolly as he spoke.

"You're the only one who's never wanted me not to be."

They returned to the path, back the way they came, and the ravine sank away behind them. Julian walked ahead, nearly silent. It might have passed for pensiveness, if not for the way his every movement carried a charge.

When they reached the fork in the trail, Julian didn't continue toward the car. He turned to follow the steep second path, then stepped away from it after a few yards and disappeared behind an ancient oak tree. Paul hesitated before following him. He set his knapsack down beside the trail sign, moving slowly so as not to jar a scale loose from the specimen's wings. His pulse was violent and quick—now it felt much closer to fear.

Julian was standing with his back to the tree trunk. His eyes were unreadable and cold; not for the first time, Paul wished intensely that he could touch them.

"Take off your glasses," said Julian quietly. When Paul had complied, he spoke again, fiercely serene, every human part of him out of reach. "Make me beg you to stop."

A current of compulsion moved through Paul's hands. He let them fall and hang at his sides—not because he was uncertain, but because it frightened him that he wasn't.

"I don't . . ."

Julian looked at him down the fine planes of his cheekbones, the cool arrogant look that Paul was usually spared. "Yes, you do." He didn't smile. "You've wanted to all along."

He wanted to believe Julian didn't know what he was really asking. He wanted to believe that some part of him was still impossible for Julian to see. Because it wasn't as if they'd never hurt each other before—between them it was a kind of tenderness, writing themselves onto each other's bodies with every mark they left. It was a promise; *I'm here, I've always been here.* Pain was a necessary consequence, but that was all it was.

Paul knew all the vulnerable places on Julian's body, and when he'd touched them before, it was with a gentleness born of fear. He could decide to be gentle now. He could bare Julian's throat and kiss the thin skin between his collarbones; he could follow the ragged scar tissue with his lips and pretend as he always did that he felt no desire in his teeth.

Only fear had ever held him back. He wanted to tear through Julian's skin and map the shapes of liver and lungs, to memorize the path of every artery with his fingertips. He wanted to break Julian's body open and move inside it alongside him, rib cages interlaced around a single heart. There was an emptiness inside Paul that would take and never stop taking. He should never have believed that Julian couldn't tell it was there.

Paul told his body to move. He took a cautious step closer and lifted Julian's chin as if to kiss him, watching the green glaze of canopy light slide over his face. Paul wanted him to waver, but he didn't—there was no trace of doubt in his eyes.

"I'm sorry," said Paul quietly, and he hit him as hard as he could.

It was sickening, watching Julian instantly regret it. Paul had forgotten the way the shock of a blow rang through the entire body—that sudden unnatural snap of movement, fear fanning outward like a wave of radiation.

Julian was slow to turn back toward him. After a long moment he wiped his mouth with the side of his thumb; the blood came away in a sweet, bright line. All Paul could think of was pinning Julian to the tree by his throat and biting his lip until his blood was all either of them could taste.

When Julian met his eyes again, he smiled, as if in defiance, but all his arrogance had left him.

"Keep going," said Julian. Paul couldn't move. He felt a spasm inside his chest, almost like wanting to cry, and he hated Julian for making him feel it. He hated himself even more for not wanting it to end. "What are you waiting for? Do it."

"I can't." Even before he said it, he knew it was a lie.

"I'm not asking." Julian didn't seem to realize his voice was shaking. "Do it, fucking *do it*, don't be such a girl—"

The world went blazing white. Paul was barely aware of hitting him again until he realized he wasn't stopping.

Julian couldn't pretend it was a game any longer. It didn't matter anymore whether he still wanted it, or if he ever had. Paul didn't let himself listen too closely to Julian's voice—the way he strained for an authority that wasn't convincing, then slid into an insistent "Paul, I mean it, *stop*" whose panic he could tell was real by how fiercely Julian tried to hide it.

There was nothing left of Julian now but the parts of him Paul couldn't take apart—he was sharp hipbones, white strings of nerve, muscle and soft tissue. Paul couldn't tear him to pieces with his bare hands; he wasn't strong enough. He couldn't pull Julian's scar open and peel the skin back with his fingertips. He couldn't bite hard enough to reach past flesh to bone. He still tried.

Julian's protests faded away. He stopped attempting to squirm free. When Paul pinned him down, he fell back, still as a corpse against the base of the tree trunk, blank-faced, arms limp. Here at last was the passive acquiescence that for so long had been all Paul had allowed himself to want. For all his pathetic ill-formed ambitions, for all his eager desperation to be better, this was still all he deserved.

Paul couldn't feel his hands. All he could feel was the slim fragile line along the edge of Julian's rib cage, the promise that if he pressed hard enough the bones would snap. Desire moved through his body like a shudder. He could barely breathe for it. He'd never been more repulsive.

When Julian met his eyes, he was glazed and unfocused. He brushed his hand experimentally along the inside of Paul's thigh, up between his legs. It was only at his touch that Paul finally let go.

"Don't," Paul said. He pleaded with himself to recoil, but the need was too savage to overcome. "Don't, please, I'm sorry—"

Julian looked up at him as if all he could feel any longer was distant curiosity. He held Paul's waist and gently coaxed him to stand. As he sat up straight and unfastened Paul's belt, he never looked away from his eyes.

"This is how you want me." Julian's voice was toneless and quiet. "Just take what you want."

He tipped Julian's head back by his hair and pushed hard into his mouth. He shut his eyes tight, but he could still feel the artery-warm film of blood on Julian's lip.

It was as if he'd stepped out of himself and settled three inches to the right, just barely enough to remember he was still there at all. His body's every response was purely mechanical; any pleasure he took from it was remote, barely worth feeling, like the unconscious relief of breathing. *I won't stop you, anything you want and I'll let you*—Paul hadn't seen it for the threat it was.

It was over quickly. He was only able to open his eyes when he turned his face up toward the canopy. New leaves whispering; the sky a patchwork of cloudless, searing blue. He could feel tears on his face. Somehow his fear and shame and remorse were more humiliating than every other nightmarish part of him that lay bare.

He pulled back and sat next to Julian among the dead leaves. Julian didn't look at him right away. He usually hurried to console Paul if he wept, no matter how trivial or foolish the injury. It was only now that he withheld the comfort that Paul understood the full power Julian held over him.

He couldn't bear to look at Julian, so he looked. The only other mark Paul had left on his face was the early shine of a bruise at his temple. But from his collarbones down, dark blood flooded beneath his skin. Paul could have pressed his hands to the marks and found their exact shapes outlined underneath.

The scar looked different now. It would never again mean what Paul wanted it to mean. It was no longer the unbreakable seam that held Julian's body together. Now it looked like a fault line, as if the slightest pressure could shatter him.

For a long while Julian didn't meet his eyes at all. He absorbed the torrent of pleas and apologies as if he barely heard them. With imperious calm, he buttoned his shirt over the contusions and the lacerations from Paul's teeth and fingernails; he gazed impassively at his bruised wrists as he refastened his shirt cuffs, then shook the leaves from his sweater before tugging it back over his head.

"Please." He begged himself to shut up, but he couldn't. "I'm sorry, I'm so sorry, I was just doing what you wanted."

From the shallow movements of Julian's chest Paul could all but feel how much every inhale must ache. "What I told you to do." Julian plucked his collar straight, still gazing ahead into the trees as if he didn't particularly care that Paul was there. "Not what I wanted."

Paul could barely draw breath without sobbing. His throat burned with bile, but he couldn't make himself throw up, even when he pressed his forearms hard against his stomach. He was fragile, weak, pathetic, every hideous thing he had labored so relentlessly to keep Julian from seeing.

When Julian finally looked at him, there was no malice or resentment in his eyes; nor was there pity. Slowly, gingerly, he put his arm around Paul's shoulders and pulled him close. Paul only understood how much of the calm was a performance when he felt how violently Julian's heart was still racing.

"I didn't want to like it," Paul said miserably. He felt a flare of hatred toward Julian for kissing his forehead then, as if he were still a human being. "I love you, oh god please promise you'll forgive me, I'm terrified you're never going to."

For a moment Julian seemed to consider giving him that unequivocal forgiveness. Instead he smiled, solemn and unreadable, and told Paul the truth.

"Of course I will, Pablo."

WHEN THEY returned to the car, they sat for a while with the radio on, not speaking. Paul stared at his face in the rearview mirror, scrubbing his skin meticulously with his cuff until all the dirt was gone. Julian smoked one-handed, his other hand pressed firmly to the nape of Paul's neck. His lower lip hadn't quite stopped bleeding. It left a rust-red impression at the end of his cigarette.

"Thank you for trusting me with this," said Julian quietly.

All along it had been Paul who was meant to plead for mercy. The real violence was in how gentle Julian was—how near his reassurances came to absolution while stopping just short of granting it.

Part II

I.

PAUL'S FAMILY was deeply patriotic, in the same way that his father had been a loving parent: their warmth and pride was accompanied by high expectations, and they made it known when their standards weren't met. As Americans they were disgusted by Watergate—the queasy spectacle of the President and his administration being investigated by the Senate on national television. But as left-wing trade unionists who had loathed Richard Nixon for two decades, they were also enjoying themselves far more than they pretended.

They followed the hearings with enraptured revulsion. Paul's grandfather listened on the radio at work and hurried home at lunch to watch them on television. The whole extended family took to watching Dick Cavett's evening discussion panels and then telephoning one another in the morning to debrief. Watergate overtook the weather and the Pirates' playoff chances as their favorite topic of conversation. For years the news had been a nightmare of assassinations and massacres and Technicolor war crimes—at long last, America had given them a bloodless scandal, and they were so relieved that they turned it into entertainment.

Paul spent most of his working hours alone in the repair garage business office, the scandal reduced to a chitter from his grandfather's radio outside. Politics couldn't hold his attention, but few things could nowadays. The work itself certainly didn't. The previous manager had left behind a snarl of ledgers and faded vendor receipts on carbon paper, and in five years of running the business himself, Paul's grandfather had never had the time to untangle them. It was a task Paul quickly learned required repetitive precision but almost no brainpower. By lunchtime the nagging crackle of frustration would grow into a directionless, burning anger. Now and then, he would reach down into the file drawer and slam it on his arm until the pain made him see stars.

On their way to his grandparents' house for lunch, Paul's grandfather usually stopped at the newsstand to pick up the latest edition of the *Washington Post*. It was one of the few by-products of their obsession that didn't irritate Paul, though he didn't dare let on why. He let them believe that his interest in the paper was the same as theirs. They only had eyes for the news itself, and after he left, they never noticed that the paper's back pages were missing.

"Was he sweating as badly as it sounded?" his grandfather asked by way of a greeting as he and Paul sidled through the back door into the kitchen.

"You know, he *was*, the poor dear," his grandmother answered from the living room, gleefully and without pity.

Against their every stated principle, his grandparents had lately taken to eating lunch in front of their television. His grandmother was already done eating, but she'd left two lunches in the refrigerator for them—bottles of ginger ale, twin hard-boiled eggs and liverwurst sandwiches under pink plastic wrap. Paul's grandfather took his plate into the living room to join her, leaving the *Post* on the kitchen table. Paul took a cursory glance at the headlines, just in case his grandparents quizzed him later. Then, once he was sure they were both settled, he opened the paper to the classifieds.

He hadn't answered Julian's latest letter. The Frommes had returned to Maryland from France, which should have meant Julian's letters would grow more frequent, but they hadn't. Paul was lucky to receive one letter for each of his two—and they were far shorter than Paul's, written in an odd breezy tone that he couldn't square with the dread Julian had shown before he left. This latest letter mentioned his father, but only in the context of Julian's take on Watergate (*Daddy's still waiting by the phone for a subpoena like a virgin on prom night—I think it's hurt his feelings terribly that nobody invited him to the conspiracy*). Even this small acknowledgment of one of his parents was a departure for Julian, who generally only mentioned them in passing. His specific grievances with his family were mostly directed at his brothers, and even those were only included for humor. His parents flitted in the background like moths too quick and erratic to identify, and the elision was so consistent that it made Paul nervous.

Much of the letter, just like its predecessors, had the impersonal dashed-off quality of a postcard. Paul could imagine Julian copying entire paragraphs verbatim and sending them to all his rich childhood friends, the Greenwoods and Desjardins and Lockhart-Schmidts whose offerings had filled his dormitory mailbox. The indications that the letter was meant for Paul in particular were small enough that anyone else might have missed them. There was a chess notation in a postscript, Julian's next move for their correspondence game; the salutation was addressed to "Pablo," and the closing claimed to miss him terribly.

And beside the final paragraph—the only one that replied to Paul's letter directly—Julian had drawn a little caricature of him. *Compulsive working-class hero that you are, it shouldn't surprise me that you're keeping busy.* The drawing wasn't half bad, and if it had portrayed anyone else, Paul would have thought it a charming likeness. The figure was curly-haired and round-shouldered, gangly as a heron, laboriously dragging a cartoonish five-hundred-pound anvil. *I hope you'll relax at some point, if only as a personal favor.*

Paul was indeed keeping busy—forcing himself to do so, for fear that he would seize up like a torn muscle if he held still. He ran every morning, swam at the community center every night, ruthlessly filled his time with work and volunteering and constructive reading projects. For the first few weeks of summer Paul had written extensively to Julian about what he was doing and what he hoped to achieve by doing it, as evidence of his commitment to reshaping himself into something worthy. Sometimes he transcribed entire pages from the beginning, trying to make his handwriting look more ambitious and self-assured. But when Julian noticed his efforts at all he treated them as a novelty, or worse, a joke. In retrospect, Paul saw that these were actually an unwitting confession to the crime of mediocrity—a plea, pathetic and damning, for an approval he didn't deserve.

Concierge, nights. Paul didn't dare circle any of the listings until he was alone in his room, so he memorized where they were on the page so he could return to them later. *File clerk. Dishwasher, room to advance.*

"Do you have anything fun planned for this afternoon, Paulie?"

Paul quickly flipped back to the news pages, but his grandfather wasn't looking at him—he reached into the fridge for the pickle jar, big hands creased black with stubborn remnants of motor oil.

"I don't know," Paul said, gazing unseeingly at the paper to avoid eye contact. "I have got some books I should finish before they come due."

"Uh-huh." At the periphery of his vision, his grandfather shut the refrigerator; Paul could tell he was being watched, but pretended not to feel it. "Not going to the woods much this summer, are you?"

Paul was silent for a moment. For weeks now he'd been afraid to do anything he loved; he avoided hiking, just as he avoided painting, because he was terrified to discover he could no longer enjoy it. He had tried just once—the same loaner car, the same West Virginia forest preserve. The woods were lush with summer, silvery dime-sized azures darting through the grass along the roadside. Paul had sat for a while in the gravel lot, waiting for himself to get up and walk the path, before he finally gave up and left. His hands never left the steering wheel.

"There's not a ton of local species left on my checklist," he said with a shrug. "I'm at the point where I have to start traveling if I want anything new."

"You're getting withdrawn again." When his grandfather's hand settled on his shoulder, Paul had to steel himself to avoid shrugging it off. "It's good to have a work ethic, and you've been such a help getting the garage under control—but you need to do things for *fun* sometimes, too."

Paul summoned all his energy to look up at his grandfather and smile. It wasn't safe to let his unhappiness become so conspicuous; if his family could see it, they could source it too.

"Stuck in school mode, I guess." He tried to sound cheerful, but to his ear his voice was childishly cloying.

"Well, knock it off." His grandfather gave his shoulder a shake before letting go. "Go to the movies, chat up a few girls, maybe paint some rude words on the side of a train. Be a kid while you still can."

Over the last few weeks, Paul's appetite had ebbed away to nearly nothing. As his grandfather retreated, Paul pushed away his plate and returned to the classifieds. There were neighborhoods where minimum wage was enough for a living, if he didn't care about adding to his savings. And he would be far from his family and from the soot-stained city, far enough that the curvature of the earth would blot out the shadow his father's absence had left behind.

When Paul included Julian in these fantasies, he did so hesitantly and shamefaced, as if Julian were only an afterthought and not the nucleus around which the entire impulse had formed. He knew very little about DC; beyond its landmarks, he could only imagine it as a blur, in whose hazy streets Julian stood alone as the only solid and tangible thing.

Paul took the classified pages home with him, tucked into the cover of one of the Western-canon landmarks he was forcing himself to read. He was building a stack of classifieds under his bed, a collection of futures circled in red. A payroll assistant at the Museum of Natural History, going home to a furnished efficiency in the attic of a town house; a night clerk at the Georgetown law library, with blackout curtains in his studio apartment so that he could sleep during the day. Unglamorous work in illustrious places—and Julian, always Julian, the promise of him so bright that Paul didn't dare look directly.

He didn't give himself a chance to think better of it. He unspooled his reasoning thoroughly but haphazardly, as if he were answering an essay question with one eye on the clock. He needed to try living somewhere besides fucking *Pittsburgh*; Washington was the capital of the free world, rich with culture, and history was writing itself there before their eyes. And any-way, maybe Julian would enjoy having a friend so close, a safe haven and a sympathetic ear when his family became (Paul chose these words carefully) too *tediously bourgeois* to bear. He knew Julian hadn't liked his previous proposals for seeing each other before the end of summer, but this one was better, eas-ier to conceal from Julian's parents. It was just an idea, and he might be missing some key detail—but that was why he was writing to his cleverest and most knowledgeable friend, who could turn Paul's half-formed impulse into a plan.

It was stamped and in the mail before panic caught up with him, but he was excited enough that he managed to swallow the fear. Julian was taking several days to reply to his letters; Paul forbade himself from compulsively checking the mailbox, telling himself that the reply would be worth the wait. In the meantime he thought of the plan whenever he was obliged to summon a smile, or when he needed a reason not to succumb to frustration at work. The dream was painful, but he preferred it to everything else that pained him. If nothing else, it gave the bruises on his forearm a chance to fade.

Julian's reply caught him off guard. It arrived very quickly, as if he'd composed his answer to the letter the day he received it. Paul came home from a volunteer shift at the botanical gardens and found the envelope waiting on his bed. It was the same sta-tionery Julian had apologized for in his first letter—a gift from his mother, dove-gray, each page decorated along one edge with a motif of nautilus shells.

His hands shook so hard that he almost couldn't open enve-lope. The letter itself was brief; he propped it up on his pillow and tucked his arms tightly around his body as he leaned down to read it.

Pablo—

If Washington were your introduction to the world outside of Pittsburgh, I fear you might never be persuaded to move anywhere else. Please be advised that the damn thing is built on a swamp ("air you can wear," as my preternaturally witty eldest sibling likes to say). Not a good swamp, I hasten to add, because I know you have an unfathomable fondness for the muddy and mosquito-plagued. The odious creatures known as civil servants which shamble through its streets would not be at all out of place in such an environment. It's abysmal, and if I allowed you to inflict it on yourself I could scarcely call myself your friend. Sorry—I know this isn't what you wanted to hear. But you can't have failed to catch on that it's my dearest ambition in life to leave.

As I write this I am kicked back in an Adirondack deck chair, wearing my fucking tennis whites and drinking a Horse's Neck, which I'm afraid means I might have finally left the pupa and become a real WASP. They're having a crab boil, "just a little get-together for a few close friends," which means a lot of radiantly white and very distinguished legs are currently being exposed to the air for the first time since August. The weather is absolutely foul, the dragonflies aren't pulling their weight as regards the mosquito population, and I would love nothing more than (and am thus not allowed) to hide away inside with the fans until the nightmare is over. One of the guests brought a dog, at least. She's a nice dog, a little black spaniel; pity the owner is a cryptofascist. (You'd recognize his name, though sadly not from any impending indictments.)

This is about all I can get away with writing when I'm supposed to be advancing the charm offensive, so I'll sign off for now. Best to everyone, and chin up—now you're free to daydream about running away to a real city, instead of the worst goddamn company town on earth.

Thank you for writing to me so diligently. I do mean that.

As always, your faithful servant—

—J.

The fantasy lingered a second longer than it should have, before curdling his yearning into self-disgust.

He couldn't bring himself to destroy the letter, as much as he wanted to. Instead he crumpled it into a ball and shoved it to the back of a dresser drawer. But when he went out for his swim that night he took his collection of classifieds with him, and burned them, page by page, on a footbridge over the creek in Schenley Park. He wanted to forget he'd ever yielded to the weakness of wanting anything. He wanted to scrub away any evidence that he existed outside his own head at all—that he was a visible object that anyone else could see and mock and judge.

He tried to tell himself that Julian would laugh it off and forget about it, and that the out-of-character promptness of his reply was a sign of boredom instead of alarm. But he couldn't relax knowing Julian still had his letter and could refer back to it whenever he wanted to remind himself why Paul wasn't worth his time. If they ever saw each other again, he resolved to steal that letter and burn it, too. The weight of the *if* was almost more than he could bear.

JUNE 2, 1973

Hello, stranger.

Even from 200 miles away I can hear you sulking. I never said, nor intended to imply, that you ought to stop writing, so either you're up there wallowing in self-loathing or you're giving me the silent treatment on purpose, as punishment for having the gall to say "no" to you. Both have the effect of turning your crisis of self-worth into a problem I am supposed to solve for you, and I don't think I've made any secret of finding that fucking tedious.

Or perhaps you've been too busy to write, in which case I'm being unfair. Still, I hope this will serve as your impetus to make the time if you don't already have it. Or (ahem) to emerge from your sulk a better man. I will not actually be able to tell the difference, and if you reply in due haste I'm happy to give you the benefit of the doubt.

Things are bad here, so I won't write about it. It isn't anything specific, nothing I'd know how to explain to you in a way you'd understand. And even if I could, I wouldn't want to, because it isn't your problem and it's not for you to take on. I can't put it any more plainly than that, so if you're holding your breath for an apology, read this again. Believe in the things I try to tell you instead of the things you think you deserve to be told.

Keep writing. It doesn't matter what about. Please keep writing.

—J.

2.

HE DID as he was told. It was all he could do. Even though Julian's letters still arrived just once a week—usually on Tuesdays, as if he'd set them as a weekend chore. Even though Julian concealed every fragment of his own life, piece by piece, until Paul might as well have been writing to a constellation of opinions and ideas rather than a human being. The anecdotes about Julian's brothers shrank away to nothing; the already rare mentions of his parents disappeared altogether. Paul only found out after the fact that Julian had had a birthday in mid-June ("Don't feel bad, I didn't tell you")—and there was no mention of what he'd done to mark the occasion, if anything. Vague as the letter was, it stated plainly that Paul shouldn't send a present. If he insisted, Julian wrote, he should wait till August and give it in person.

At the beginning of the summer, Paul had at least been able to situate Julian in some kind of context. There were details he could extrapolate from, even if they were sparse. The lavender-sweet French country air at his grandfather's summer house, a relief after months of Pittsburgh pollution; in Maryland his family had a garden, humid and immaculate (Julian had seen an orange butterfly he hoped Paul would be able to identify from a hazy description). Until now Julian's relatives had been as indistinguishable and carefully posed as mannequins, but at least Paul had known they existed. Now, for all Paul could tell, the Frommes' family home was completely empty. The house itself might not even exist at all, not since Julian had stopped acknowledging the deck chairs or the wallpaper or the shutters battened against a gale.

Worst of all, there was no indication of what was going on inside Julian's head. The only emotion he would ever name, or even allude to, was boredom. Paul knew by now that Julian used this word to describe any form of discontent, however acute or persistent it might be. It could indicate genuine boredom or something far more malignant.

As Julian's family receded from view, they became all the more monstrous. Paul could no longer believe, if he ever had at all, that they were merely shallow and cold in a way that exasperated Julian but didn't hurt him. They couldn't keep Julian from him like this unless there was something more to them, something worse. When Paul summoned an image of them now, they were no longer mannequins in fine white tennis clothes. They melted—plastic buckling, distorted and inhuman—into hateful misshapen faces and greedy, clutching hands. Paul remembered Danny Costello's father sitting in the hall outside the principal's office, his hard gin-blossom face, his bloodshot eyes unfocused and glaring—the flare of compassion for the other boy that Paul had felt, then decided not to feel. He felt it for Julian now, as he built a new picture of Julian's father as a man capable of keeping such a tight grasp. His ugliness might be dressed in a suit and tie in the name of patrician civility, but his eyes were just as cruel. Paul's father had talked about men like this, whose hands were steady even when they were drunk and who knew how to hit their wives and children without leaving a mark. The law couldn't do much with them; Paul's father dealt with them by returning after his shift and bruising his knuckles on their jaws.

With Julian's every letter Paul drummed himself into a rage against his imagined version of Julian's father. He pictured smashing in that vaguely defined face, sometimes with his baseball bat, sometimes with his hands. He would arrive on Julian's doorstep, knowing he was needed, knowing he was wanted there. One by one he would break the grasp of every hand that tried to hold Julian in place. He hated them, and his hatred would make him brave.

But despite his fantasies, Paul knew too little, and Julian gave him nothing. Julian tried to conceal the distance between them by pretending he hadn't noticed it at all, much less engineered it. As he withdrew, his letters became warmer, filled with doodles and inside jokes and effusive thanks for whatever Paul had sent him most recently. He answered every question Paul asked him except the important ones, and Paul eventually gave up on asking if he was all right. "I'm worried about you," he allowed himself now and again, but Julian didn't acknowledge these asides, either.

Writing turned into a compulsion. Two letters a week became three, sometimes four. When Paul didn't have much to write about, he filled his envelopes with small watercolor sketches and magazine clippings. Julian always responded to these offerings with such a complete performance of delight that Paul had trouble believing he really meant it. One week Paul sent him a copy of the Conservatory's brochure for the summer butterfly garden; Paul himself was featured on the front flap, showing an Atlas moth to a cluster of gleefully horrified children. Julian replied with a now-predictable outpouring of teasing and whimsical caricatures. As always, Paul wanted to be charmed—but it was a kind of affection Julian had never shown when they were face-to-face, and it kept Paul writhing at the end of the hook so helplessly that he could never quite believe it wasn't by design.

The next time he felt the urge to ask whether Julian was all right, he decided it was better to be angry than afraid. *Sometimes*, he wrote, *I feel like what you're really hiding is that you're sick of me.*

Julian's reply, uncharacteristically direct: *If I were sick of you, believe me, you'd know.*

Paul had to resign himself to the fear, to the helpless fury he could never find a reason for. The dread settled into place just below his stomach. At night he tried to focus his attention on the space that curled up against him in the dark, to imagine merely missing Julian rather than fearing what his distance might signify. He tried to remember how it had felt to believe that he and Julian knew each other more profoundly than either of them knew themselves. But if that were true, he knew now, he wouldn't have to guess what Julian was keeping from him. There was nothing mutual about their understanding and never had been; he'd only been convinced otherwise by how perfectly Julian understood him.

It wasn't until Audrey confronted him that he realized how visible his suffering was from the outside. For all the pains Paul was taking to hold his unhappiness below the surface, some part of him was grateful to be seen. For Audrey to notice meant that he was still tethered to reality, if only by a thread.

She sprang the conversation on him while they were in the car, an old trick of their father's when he wanted to trap them in a lecture. Audrey had finally saved up enough for a car of her own, a little green Volkswagen whose interior smelled persistently and inexplicably of fennel. She was proud as a peacock of her new acquisition, and took every possible excuse to jingle her new keys and take the car for a spin, so he didn't think anything of it when she offered to pick him up from his volunteer shift at the Conservatory. Still, when the bait-and-switch came, it didn't entirely surprise him.

They crammed his bicycle awkwardly into the back seat and rode in silence. Audrey kept lollipops in her glove box, and was worrying at one of them as she drove. Paul couldn't quite ignore the noise the hard candy made whenever it clicked against her teeth.

"So," she said as the car emerged from the park onto Forbes Avenue. "You know I try to pretty much stay out of your business, right?"

"So you tell me whenever you're about to pry into it."

"When I have to, sure," she said, unabashed. "Like when I see you tying yourself into knots over someone who can't be bothered to give you *half* as much attention as you give him. I wouldn't say anything if it weren't obviously upsetting you, but . . ."

He had tried, clumsily, to conceal the imbalance in how often he and Julian wrote to each other. He hid his own letters between outgoing bills, or else covertly walked them downhill to the nearest street-corner mailbox. But Audrey—protective, impatient Audrey—had of course noticed it anyway.

Audrey let the silence fester. When they had to stop for a red light, she reached forward and hesitantly squeezed his forearm. She was trying to look gentle and maternal, traits that were utterly foreign to her.

"Poor little bug," she said with awkward tenderness. "Listen, I've been there, it's a fucking drag."

He couldn't think of a way to defend himself without confiding in her, and this infuriated him.

"You don't know what you're talking about," was all he could say.

Audrey sighed and let go of his arm.

"Believe it or not, I kind of do," she said carefully. "I know sometimes you can be really invested, and the other person is just sort of . . . trying on a new idea of themselves, and you end up as collateral damage once they get sick of playing dress-up as someone more interesting than they actually are. Don't ask me how I know, but—"

"There's something going on with his family." He felt as if he'd broken a confidence. "I don't know what it is, but I can *tell*, he isn't being—it's not like you were saying, it's not that he doesn't want to, it's more like he *can't*."

But the longer he spoke, the less certain he was that it was true. Perhaps Julian wasn't hiding anything at all, and was pushing Paul away not out of necessity but because he was nearing the end of his patience. Perhaps the airy house by the sea still stood, and perhaps its residents' worst sin against Julian was to annoy him. The possibility cast a bitter pall even over Julian's demand that he keep writing. He might have devoured Paul's need for him with such unfettered hunger that he had made himself sick on it. Everything else eventually bored him. There was no reason for Paul to think he was any different.

Audrey must have seen the doubt in his face, but she was either too kind or too cowardly to acknowledge it.

"If you're right," she said, "I wish he'd at least tell you what's going on so you can stop running yourself ragged."

He didn't dare tell her that he wished for the same thing, but not because he craved relief. It was because he was certain he could only feel whole again if Julian gave him a reason to show up on his doorstep and slit his parents' throats.

JULY 6, 1973

Paul—

I just can't imagine you on a beach. I picture you lurking under the boardwalk like a barnacle, wearing long slacks and your army coat and one of those countless black turtlenecks. Just a pair of dark eyes peering out from the shadows, perhaps with a sketchbook open on your knees, casting judgment on the heliolatry of the philistines beyond. The sunburn you mentioned is no obstacle to this image, because if the sun touched you even for a moment you'd go up in flames like a vampire. (I grew a plant in the dark once for a science project, and it came up so skinny and pale. When I put it in the sun it died.)

I wish I'd known you were in Cape May before you were nearly gone. We were at the same latitude down to the minute, did you know that? When I got your postcard I went down to the dock for a while and looked due east, straight at you, wondering if you would turn around and look back.

For reasons I won't detail, I've been thinking a lot lately about our old pal Milgram. There's a variable he didn't account for, and it's that he was at fucking Yale. All those nice Mayflower Society boys, who went to prep schools just like mine and who were Ivy League–bound before they could walk. And here is what I learned about these boys: the haute bourgeoisie is a perpetual motion engine of in-group compliance, and all who fail to conform to the masculine norm in particular are to be met not only with disdain but with violence.

It isn't just that the young man of means is conditioned to obey (though he certainly is—Daddy always knows best, and the nice fellow in the white coat probably does, too). It's that he is also conditioned not to particularly care about the collateral damage of his obedience. Of course most Yale boys would turn up the watts—what do they care about the poor bastard on the other side? Their fathers make their fortunes pouring poison into the sky. What's a little one-on-one torture when you know the world is yours to ruin?

(There was only one of Milgram's participants who immediately clocked what the experiment really was. Funnily enough, he was Jewish—one of the few who managed to squeak past the quota.

Amazing what a difference it makes when you know how easily it could be you at the business end of the buzzer.)

I'm trying to remember now what it's like when we speak in person. Your voice changes when you're angry—something in the sharpness of the consonants. But your handwriting doesn't change at all, and it makes you seem more dispassionate than you're capable of being. But I know I can always count on you to maintain your revolutionary fervor. It's the two of us, contra mundum, looking down into the machinery. All I've ever learned to do is survive it, and that just barely. I've always admired your ardor in wanting to smash the gears.

What a lonely, dreary thing it is to know the truth. What a relief it is that now neither of us has to be alone in knowing.

I hope you looked west while I was looking east, and that for a moment you met my eyes without knowing it. I know you never look away, even when your eyes are closed, but I'm never certain you can see what's really there.

I miss you to pieces.

Yours always
—J.

3.

HE WOULD swear in retrospect that there was a shift in the air, that day in mid-July that the rupture came. He could never explain what about it was different. It was much like the ugly summer days that had come before it, smog-dreary and maddeningly still, heat trapped under the dome of the low beige-blue sky. Paul had retreated to the swimming pool the last several mornings, ever since an abortive run left his chest aching. The only thing that should have distinguished that day was its agonizing monotony, the boredom and stir-craziness of a filthy city in high summer. But part of him knew, or would remember knowing. It was a feeling in the same fold of soft tissue in his chest that experienced a sense of foreboding the day his father killed himself—the place inside him that had once, and sometimes still, believed in God.

He worked an uneventful morning shift at the butterfly garden. The latest Atlas moth was dying, but that was no surprise; they were larger than the other saturniids and lost strength more quickly, no matter how relentlessly they had eaten when they still had mouths. This one was six days old now, sluggish and docile in the way of a starving creature that didn't expect to eat. Paul could see the early signs in how it moved its wings, as if they hung from a rusted hinge. At the end of his last demonstration, he released his grip on the moth's abdomen, but it didn't retreat to its usual perch beside the skylight. It rested in his hand for a long while, very still, its soft strange weight balanced on his palm. He pitied it in a way that he never felt for the ones he killed.

Outside the gardens, the world was quiet, all its sounds muffled. The streets were unusually empty as he bicycled home. He was insensitive at last to the anxious misery that had thrummed through him for weeks. What had replaced it was a profound and unmistakable sadness. His nerves were cool, the world's edges sanded smooth.

When he arrived, he found the house in chaos. His mother's car was gone, and Audrey's sat by the curb with both its doors hanging open. Laurie was sitting on the stairs inside, hugging her knapsack, while Audrey careened from room to room like a disoriented fly.

"God, where've you been?" Audrey remembered the answer to her question before she had finished asking it. "You need to pack an overnight bag. We're going to Hazel's, Bubbe Sonia had a stroke."

"Is—?" he started to ask, but she had already darted back downstairs. He turned to Laurie, who looked at him blankly before she parsed the question he didn't want to ask.

"Not yet," said Laurie flatly. "But she's ninety-two, so . . . yeah. Not yet."

He remembered how small and sad his great-grandmother had looked at the end of his last visit to her rest home—sitting alone in her little white room, watching with solemn rheumy eyes as they left her behind. His body suddenly felt ungainly and out of place, an awkward distraction from the gravity of the news. But the fog of anticipatory quiet hadn't lifted, even in the turmoil. Without it he imagined he might grieve, or at least feel pity. Instead the only feeling he could identify was the claustrophobic dread of being trapped in the middle as his family circled the wagons.

Paul hadn't quite finished packing when the phone rang,

and he tried to ignore it until he remembered that they were expecting news. His sisters were waiting in the car, so he ran downstairs to pick up, his half-zipped knapsack and a black collar shirt bundled in one arm.

"Hello?" He was ready to hear any voice but the one that answered.

"Hey, Pablo."

Paul was so overwhelmed by elation and impatience and sheer, savage relief that he thought he might collapse. Then he realized there was something wrong with Julian's voice. He was affecting a carelessly cheerful tone, but it sounded tinny and flat even through the echo of the line.

"What happened?" Paul asked quickly. "What's wrong?"

A brief, crackling silence.

"Oh, it isn't that something's *happened*, really," Julian said, every word more airless and atonal than the last. "I just thought you might like to come stay for a few days."

The reversal was so abrupt, and Julian's urgency so badly concealed, that Paul felt a flare of suspicion. But he played along, reflexively, because he couldn't imagine any catch that wouldn't be worth it. "When?" he asked. "It's just that I—"

"Soon—tomorrow, ideally." Julian gave a sudden, sharp laugh. "I actually already called the airport, they have a flight a little before noon. Once I'm certain you're coming, I'll call them back to buy your ticket—"

"Tomorrow?" Paul heard Audrey tap impatiently on her car horn, so he hurriedly stuffed the shirt into his knapsack. "I don't know if I *can* that soon, we're having sort of a family emergency—can I call you back later?"

"Oh—no, naturally, of course you can." There was something like sympathy in Julian's voice, but it wasn't quite convincing, as if he were taking measure of his position and trying to hide it. "But you'll need to call tonight at ten o'clock sharp, it's the only time I'll be able to . . . What's going on, anyway? Anyone I know?"

Paul scrambled for a pen; Audrey tapped the horn again, more insistently. "No," he said. "No one you know."

They were on the interstate ten minutes later. In the urgency of the moment, Paul had written the number on a napkin; its folded mass was thick and awkward in his breast pocket, impossible to ignore no matter how many distractions his family offered him. Laurie slumped wordlessly beside him in the cramped back seat, but the shock had put Audrey in a relentlessly chatty mood. She narrated the familiar drive to Mount Lebanon as if she were afraid to stop talking. "'Waiting at Hazel's,' isn't that so messed up?" she said more than once, as if the callousness of it had surprised her anew. "*Waiting.* It feels so sick to sit around waiting for someone to die." When Audrey was distracted by a left turn, Paul turned toward Laurie and mimed throttling their sister to shut her up. This teased a weak smile to Laurie's face, but it didn't linger, and after a moment she looked away again.

What followed, in the suburban quiet of Hazel's house, felt like an uneasy marriage between sitting shiva and a children's slumber party. Hazel's daughter, Debbie, went out for a case of beer and some cheap Chinese food, and the cans and cartons slowly migrated from the kitchen to the far corners of the house. The young children were in the den, watching *The Sound of Music* on the color television. The older cousins chatted around the tension and drank more than any of them usually liked to do.

Every now and then Hazel's telephone would ring, and a bleak, nebulous update would make the rounds. Paul deliberately forgot the details as soon as he heard them. He wanted to remember his great-grandmother as something other than a withered fragile creature in a hostile world, but she had been right—only her own memory knew her as anything else.

When they couldn't bear it any longer, Paul and Laurie retreated upstairs to look at the progress of the bathroom Hazel and Harvey were renovating. Paul made fun of the new orange-and-gold floral wall tiles, which coaxed another small smile from Laurie. They sat cross-legged at either end of the plaster-dusted bathtub, eating from a carton of tepid sweet-and-sour chicken. The television downstairs was muffled but still audible; every silence between them was accompanied by tinny, distant singing.

"Can I have some of that?"

Laurie wasn't quite smiling as she gestured toward Paul's nearly full can, but there was a trace of her usual mischief in her face.

"I'd be a really bad influence if I said yes," Paul said, leaning forward to hand it to her. "It's vile, though, fair warning."

Laurie held the can delicately and took an experimental swig. "Totally vile," she agreed, but gamely sipped again anyway. "I've got to get one of those, um—the little bottles they put in gerbil cages or whatever, but human sized and full of beer. Because," she said with sudden vehemence, "if I have to go to another *fucking* funeral and not be blotto, I'm going to throw up."

Paul thought about telling her that this one would be different. He could have said that some tragedies were socially acceptable, and when the neighbors offered condolences for a natural death in old age, they weren't secretly asking *Yes but why? What did you do to make this happen?* But he couldn't articulate it without revealing too much of his own anger, so it wouldn't have been much of a reassurance.

For a long while they didn't talk. Paul picked through the carton with his chopsticks but couldn't force himself to eat anything; Laurie smoothed her skirt against her knees and drank skeptically but steadily from the beer can.

"What time is it?" she asked.

Paul lifted his cuff and checked his watch. It was already a quarter to ten. He hadn't forgotten his promise to Julian, but he remembered in the way he might remember a waking thought in the middle of a dream. The hour might have passed entirely before he noticed.

"Almost ten." He handed Laurie the carton of chicken as he stood. "I need some fresh air—if anyone asks for me, tell them I'll be back soon."

"Well, if anyone asks for *me*," said Laurie with theatrical pathos, "I'll just be sitting here alone, drinking beer and eating cold Chinese food in an empty bathtub."

"Well played." Without really knowing why, Paul leaned down and gave her shoulder a shake. "Do me a favor and don't tell anyone I let you have that, all right?"

The air was clearer in the suburbs, but muggy and clinging. Paul followed the sloping sidewalks to the neighborhood baseball diamond, where there was a bank of pay phones parallel to the right-field line. He'd played a few away games here with his Little League team; he remembered one of the telephones ringing once when there was a development in one of his father's cases that couldn't wait until the start of his next shift.

The operator had barely put Paul on hold before Julian answered. His voice was hoarse and soft, as if he were trying not to be overheard. "Pablo?"

There was a faint clattering sound in the background, muffled voices heard from a few rooms away. It was more context than Paul had received in weeks; he imagined Julian excusing himself from dinner, shutting himself into a back room, and waiting to pick up the phone before it had a chance to ring.

"I don't think I can do it tomorrow." He fidgeted with the metal-wrapped coil of the phone cord and watched a moth circling the streetlight—small, brown, too indistinct at a distance to identify. "She—my great-grandmother—the funeral will probably be the day after tomorrow. I could come after that."

Julian was silent for a long time. Paul could hear his fury even before he spoke.

"I'm so sorry to hear that." He spoke with such stringent courtesy that Paul could see the way his hands were shaking. "Of course I was hoping to see you sooner, but . . . Are you close to her?"

He didn't quite ask, but Paul could hear him not-asking. He only acknowledged the tacit question; the one Julian had asked aloud, so much more benign, was also far too complicated to answer.

"Everything used to revolve around her," he said coldly. "She's my grandfather's mother, he's crazy about her, so is my mother. It would upset a lot of people if I tried to get out of it, if that's what you're asking."

"It *isn't*," said Julian, too defensively for Paul to believe him. "I was only asking if you were all right—"

"It's fine, Julian, I'm not mad." Paul laughed as if to prove that he meant it, but it came out as more of a nervous exhale, and suddenly the words wouldn't stop coming. "God, don't you think I *want* to get out of it? I'd rather have a root canal, the last funeral I went to was—but they'd never let me live it down, ever, no matter what I tried to tell them. They already think I'm a freak, all I ever hear from behind my back is how I'm too quiet and give people the creeps and don't know how normal people are supposed to act, and oh, he's *always* been like that, and remember how he wouldn't even go to poor Bubbe Sonia's funeral—"

"So stay," Julian interjected. "Stay as long as you need to, I'll be fine without you until then."

"Of course you will. You're always fine without me. You've made that very clear. Obviously this time wouldn't be any different—as usual you were probably just hoping I would drop everything in order to come *amuse* you, because you're always so fucking bored and obviously that's all I'm good for."

"You're being ridiculous." All the annoyance had left Julian's voice, replaced by something that almost sounded like panic. "Why did you think I told you to keep writing? You can't know how lonely it is here, you've been helping me stay *sane*—"

"I hate it when you lie to me."

The silence swelled through the static. Julian was the first to break it; he spoke so quietly that it took Paul a moment to parse the words.

"Please tell me what you want."

For weeks now he had felt unnecessary, useless, pouring his devotion into a void. At last he had a chance to demand better, and he seized it.

"Say you need me to come."

"I thought that was obvious," said Julian acidly, but Paul stopped him before he could say more.

"No. It's not a yes-or-no question." His own voice was so cool and imperious that he barely recognized it. "Tell me you need me. In those words. I won't come unless you say it."

Julian took a long time to answer. Paul wasn't sure at first that his pride would allow him to speak at all.

"I do need you. I *need* you. All right?" Paul would have doubted his sincerity if he hadn't sounded so disgusted with himself for yielding. "As soon as you can possibly get here. I can muddle through for another day or two if I have to, but I need to know when to expect you. *When*, not if, or I'll never forgive you."

Part of Paul would have been disappointed, even a little repelled, if Julian ever said outright that he loved him. It was more natural for Julian to be loved than to love. If Julian were to love him, it would feel like something he deigned to do. It meant more to be needed. That, far more than love, gave him enough power not to be completely at Julian's mercy. He hated for Julian to be in enough distress to need his help—of course he did. But the exhilaration of Julian admitting it was so intense that Paul could ignore the worry for now.

"No, it's all right, tomorrow is all right, I'll think of an excuse." He'd forgotten ever being angry. He felt gentle and endlessly patient; if Julian had asked, he would have happily cut his chest open and handed over his heart, his lungs, every part of himself piece by piece. "I'll be there as soon as I can—I'll pay you back for the ticket."

"Don't worry about the money, it's nothing." Julian didn't thank him, but that was no surprise. He had already given more than Paul had dared expect.

"Can I tell you something," said Julian after a pause, "that I'm all but certain you won't believe?"

"Try me." It was a peace offering, tentatively teasing.

The barest pause. "I never lie to you, but sometimes I wish I could." He sounded surprised, even frightened. "You never let me pretend the truth is all right when it isn't."

"You're right, I don't believe you."

He was trying to joke, but Julian didn't laugh.

"I know," he said. "You never do."

WHEN PAUL returned to his aunt's house, he found the conversation replaced by a tense, artificial hush. He knew what it meant, even before he heard Debbie on the phone in her father's study. Audrey had finally lost her voice; she sat at the kitchen table with the older cousins, fidgeting with her bracelets, an empty can folded in front of her. The television in the den had gone dark.

"Was that it?" his cousin Myron asked Debbie when she emerged. It was the sort of callous thing Paul would never get away with saying, but because Myron wasn't thought of as cruel or cold or strange, nobody would say anything about it.

Debbie was already carrying herself with the grim dignity that would complement her funeral dress. "She passed away peacefully about half an hour ago. Uncle Frank is swinging by to pick up his and Susie's kids, but I think our moms will all be at the hospital for a while longer."

Audrey wordlessly followed Paul up to the second floor to retrieve Laurie. The three of them sat for a long while in the car, waiting for the vents to cool the fennel-smelling air. None of them spoke, though Laurie opened her mouth once as if she thought she might.

Paul just thought about the girl from the photograph, whom he'd tried to paint as a living person even though her likeness looked like an artifact under glass. Two years after she traveled to the portrait studio in Vilnius, both her parents were dead. He imagined her packing her entire life into a garment bag, preparing to cross the ocean and marry a man she barely remembered, with the soil from her parents' graves still damp on the heels of her shoes. Leaving so soon after their deaths was a cold decision, no less so for its necessity. Age had sanded away every visible trace of that hardness, but Paul imagined it had still been inside her somewhere; she would never have survived so long without it.

When his mother returned in the morning, Paul was already showered and dressed and waiting for her in the kitchen. He pleaded his case as she prepared her breakfast (cold cereal dressed with a fistful of frozen blueberries). He lied that the invitation from Julian had come before the news about Bubbe Sonia, and that the plan had already existed, the ticket already been bought, and he had just put off telling her about it. Then he explained, patiently, that he couldn't bear to go to a funeral. "Not yet," he said, "not so soon." He didn't specify after what; it wasn't necessary, and he didn't want to make her cry. But he would stay in town if the family needed him—of course he would—and he made sure to use the phrase "putting his plans on hold," because he knew that was the phrase she would use if she wanted to insist that there was no need.

He need not have expended the effort; his mother was tired and in no mood to fight back. He didn't even get to the end of his script before she waved him off.

"You're going camping for a couple days," she said flatly, "so you can clear your head. Anything else would break your Zayde's heart."

Her acquiescence briefly struck him silent.

"But I'm going? You aren't saying no?"

She chased a blueberry through the milk and sighed.

"You'll still be back before the end of the shiva," she said wearily. "Do what you want."

It was well after he'd boarded his bus that he understood that

"Do what you want" wasn't the same as "Yes." There would be consequences. She'd all but promised it.

And it would be worse than merely offending the whispering aunts and uncles or making the neighbors gossip. He remembered all the times he'd confided in his grandfather, how often both of his grandparents had shut the others down about Paul when their worry over him tipped into needling. Setting the cousins to chattering was one thing, but abandoning his grandfather was a genuine betrayal.

Paul slid down in his seat and reminded himself, ruthlessly, that his grandfather had betrayed him first. *This isn't going to go away by itself.* He forced himself to remember the aversion in his grandfather's voice, repeating it in his head until it distilled into hatred. He was no different than the rest of them.

4.

WHAT HE hadn't dared admit, lest Julian think less of him, was that he'd never been on an airplane before. The flight was little more than an hour, and Paul spent nearly every minute of it with his eyes shut tight against the impossible distance of the earth below, certain every patch of turbulence would send the plane into a spiral. He still wasn't sure he would ever remember how to use his legs again, and the drive to Julian's house wasn't doing him any favors.

The girl who had met him at the airport was named Joy Greenwood, a rail-thin doe of a girl who drove as if she'd learned by watching *The French Connection*. He knew a little about her, because Julian had mentioned her once or twice; now and again she had sent packages to Julian's dorm, filled with candied ginger and Dutch chocolate. She had picked Paul out of the crowd by comparing his face to the picture on the butterfly garden brochure, and announced within moments of meeting him that she was nursing a hangover. When they reached her convertible, they were greeted shrilly by her dog, a grotesquely tiny auburn puff that was canine in name only. Paul couldn't tell if its name was really Sweetpea or if that was just a nickname, but it inexplicably decided to sit on his lap as they drove.

"Julian's told me so much about you."

The countryside spilled past them in a blur. Joy steered one-handed as she lit a cigarette—a peculiar one, long and skinny, with a striking resemblance to a lollipop stick. Paul stared at her, trying to decide what she might mean by "so much."

Joy looked at him sideways and seemed, quite suddenly, to take pity on him.

"He says you're absolutely brilliant," she went on. "And that you do wonderful creepy paintings of moths and dead things, and that he wishes you'd major in art instead of—oh, I forget, it was something dreadful—"

"It's ecology," he said a little defensively. "It's not dreadful."

"Oh! Thank goodness, I thought it was *economics*. That's what Daddy does, something at the Treasury, and he despises it."

Joy was his age or even younger, but her clothes, like Julian's, were refined and overly grown-up. She had a cashmere sweater tied around her shoulders and a red silk scarf folded over her dark hair. She would have given the impression of being older than her age if she hadn't been a little frayed at the edges. The beds around her painted blue fingernails were chewed raw, and she had deep circles under her eyes that the layers of shadow and mascara didn't quite conceal. She had a profound, elusive sadness about her, for all that she chatted and smoked and fawned on the dog in his lap. Paul caught himself failing to dislike her, somehow, even when she darted into the next lane without signaling.

"I'm Jewish too," she said, speeding past the car she'd been tailgating for half a mile. "Well, sort of—only a quarter, but it used to be 'Grunwald,' and around here that's more than enough. It's *so* much better in New York—I can only stomach coming here once or twice a year. I'd love to see Daddy more, but it's about all I can take. The fewer people you talk to while you're here, the happier you'll be."

"I probably won't talk to a lot of people outside Julian's family," said Paul, trying to conceal his dread. "So it should be fine."

Joy was visibly horrorstruck. She took a long drag from her cigarette to cover her silence.

"He's—*warned* you about them, hasn't he?" she said carefully.

Paul avoided her eyes. Instead he looked at the dog, which grinned up at him as its paws pressed into his thigh. He wasn't sure if there was a correct way to pet dogs the same way there was with cats, so he patted its forehead gingerly with the tips of his fingers.

"Of course," he said. It was true in that he could read between the lines of what little detail Julian had ever given him, but he knew that this wasn't what Joy meant.

If Paul had expected anything at all of Julian's hometown, it was that it would be something like Mount Lebanon—tonier and tidewater-flat, but built to welcome school buses and children's bicycles. But those suburbs had fallen away behind them ages ago, treetops shining in the sun alongside the highway. For a long while afterward it was all farmland—lush orchards ringed by split-rail fences, verdant fields of what Joy identified as tobacco.

Joy wasn't forcing Paul to hold up his end of a conversation, which he slowly recognized as a deliberate kindness. She talked in fits and starts, amiable monologues about her parents or her boarding school that allowed replies but didn't demand them. Her silences didn't ask anything of him, which was hardly ever the case, even with people who knew him well.

When they pulled off the highway, the country road followed the contour of the coast. The bay glinted in and out of view between houses that were now a little closer together, but Paul kept waiting in vain to encounter anything that resembled a town. There were no schools or baseball diamonds or even shopping plazas. There were only the driveways fanning out from the road, and at their ends the houses, bigger and more grandiose with every mile. The houses perched on their empty lawns like headstones, or else were cloaked in gardens so opulent and elaborate that they had to require an entire team of gardeners to maintain.

"They're not . . ." He grasped for a way to phrase the question that wouldn't inadvertently insult her, then decided he was too desperate to care. "God, they're not *that* kind of rich, are they?"

Joy plainly had no idea what he was talking about, but that didn't stop her from making a sympathetic face and guessing, far wide of the mark, at what might soothe him.

"It's climber central back there, that's why it's so gaudy and gross," she said kindly. "But *they've* got a lot of real aristo neighbors to impress, so their house is nicer—you know, less tacky. The harpy queen has good taste, at least. Ugh, his dad would be hopeless without her, there'd be Corinthian columns on the *gazebo* . . ."

The dog had been dozing, but it woke up with a reproachful yap when Paul miserably slid down in his seat.

The car stopped at a driveway flanked by brick columns. If Paul's hand hadn't remembered the shape of Julian's address so well, he would have been certain they were in the wrong place. The house wasn't even visible from the road; the driveway plunged into a thick stand of pines, toward the water and out of sight. The iron gates sat open as if they were merely too polite to be closed. Joy turned up the drive without hesitation.

The house was a regal colonial, red brick crisscrossed with ivy, with the expanse of Chesapeake Bay glimmering at its back. The front garden was bright with emerald grass and pearl-white starbursts of magnolias; beyond the house, the lot sloped down toward the water, where he could just make out the sun-painted mast of a sailboat.

Paul would have been far happier if they had stopped at one of the garish houses farther up the road. However loathsome, those belonged to a kind of exuberance in plenty that he could nearly understand. The very tastefulness of this place made it far more offensive than if the Frommes had succumbed to new-money excess. It gave the impression that they breathed their wealth as carelessly as air.

Joy's car barely had a chance to idle before the front door flew open. Joy pushed her sunglasses up and waved, beaming; if she hadn't, Paul might have mistaken Julian for one of his brothers. His hair was cut short and combed back from his face, ruining the fashionable length that had been nurtured by months of careful neglect. He was wearing crisp, summery, Kennedyish clothes Paul had never seen him in before, and with the alien mass of the house behind him, he looked for a moment like a stranger. Then he bounded down the steps like an eager kitten and the illusion shattered.

Paul got out of the car quickly. Julian stopped short of embracing him; instead he pressed one hand between Paul's shoulder blades, insistently, as if to hurry him along.

"You're just in time," he said, so vehemently cheerful that Paul's stomach dropped. "I've got everything ready—is that your only bag? Good—thank you for rescuing him, Joy, you're an angel, come on inside and I'll make you a drink—"

Joy was in no particular rush, which clearly made Julian impatient. She struggled to hold the dog; it huffed and strained with wild eyes as if to break free and leap at Julian's throat. "We can't stay *too* terribly long," she said. "I wish we could, but Daddy wanted to—"

"Of course! Just one drink, as a thank-you present. I insist."
Julian smiled brilliantly and gave Paul an ungentle push in the
direction of the door. "Oh, poor Sweetpea, I *know*, I'm being so
mean ignoring you—I think we still have some of Tib's old bis-
cuits in the pantry . . ."

The world had whirled into such frenetic activity that Paul
had trouble taking it all in. He had the impression of a genteel
front hallway—walls done up in white and robin's-egg blue,
hardwood floors finished with a dark soft patina as if they'd
seen centuries of the same family's footsteps. When Joy set the
dog down, it danced around Julian's ankles until he scooped it
up and bounced it like an infant. Paul clung to his suitcase and
looked from doorway to glass-transomed doorway, then up to
the wrought-iron chandelier.

A slim, middle-aged black woman was hurrying toward
them, smoothing her gray dress as she walked. Her face was a
mask of courteous alarm.

"You were expecting visitors too," she said to Julian, in a tone
that suggested that the absence of a question mark was squarely
his fault. "I apologize, I didn't see it on the calendar—"

"It must have slipped my mother's mind," said Julian brightly.
"Joy's only here for a little bit, just long enough for a drink, we
shouldn't get in the way."

"Of course—Miss Greenwood, always a pleasure." The woman's smile was fixed and despondent. "And this is . . . ?"

Paul quickly let go of the suitcase handle and reached forward to shake her hand. She gave him a bewildered, pitying
look before taking it.

"Paul Fleischer," he said, wondering hopelessly what he'd
done wrong.

"Cecilia Stanton." She grasped his hand weakly and immediately let go; her eyes never left Julian's face. "Julian," she said delicately, "are you certain you remembered to let your mother know?"

"I didn't forget." Julian handed the dog back to Joy, who had gone very pale. "Don't worry about it, Ceci," he added fondly. "We were just going to put him in the spare bed in my room, you don't need to do a thing—I thought we'd just look in on Mother quickly, and then we'll get out of your way . . ."

Julian steered Paul up the hallway toward a set of French doors. Joy brushed apologetically past Cecilia and scrambled after them.

"Julian." She caught his arm and addressed him in an urgent whisper. "Julian, you *didn't*, please tell me you didn't—"

Whatever was transpiring, Paul had little time and barely enough context to even follow along on the surface. But Joy understood it perfectly, and what he could see of her understanding filled him with dread.

Julian looked at her impassively, then gave Paul a bracing smile.

"I can't tell you how happy I am to see you," he said, and for a moment Paul couldn't imagine, much less remember, that anything in the world existed outside the two of them.

Then Julian rapped on the French doors and pushed them open before anyone could answer.

Beyond the doors was a formal living room, simply furnished but so pristine that Paul could tell no child had ever set foot in it. Three people turned toward the disturbance in surprise, highball glasses clicking with ice. Two of them were women, both with doll-perfect sundresses and sculpted blond hair, but Paul knew Julian's mother right away. There was an ineffable likeness, something in the proportions of her face, even though the

individual features were dissimilar. Julian's freckles came from
her; she'd hidden hers under foundation, but they were still visible on her bare forearms. After a split second of incomprehen-
sion, she smiled, and the resemblance became unmistakable. It
was the exact smile Julian wore when he was beside himself
with fury.

"Hey! Sorry to interrupt." Julian slid his hand around Paul's
forearm and held tight. "Paul's here. I thought we should say
hello before I go get him settled in."

"*Julian,*" said Joy miserably, but she spoke so quietly that Julian could pretend not to hear her.

The guests graced the intruders with tolerant smiles. Julian's
eyes left his mother just long enough to grin back, a boyish and
blunt smile that didn't suit him. He was telling them without
words that nothing was out of the ordinary—that Paul was a
duly invited guest rather than a grenade he'd thrown in am-
bush. The couple, of course, were integral to the plan. There had
to be witnesses, or there would be no pressure on Mrs. Fromme
to acquiesce.

Mrs. Fromme's blue eyes flitted toward Paul. One eyebrow
lifted; she looked him up and down, the way she might look at
the corpse of a deer that had thrown itself in front of her car.

"My goodness." She set her glass aside and swept to her feet.
Her bared teeth glinted white. "You must forgive me. I had
thought that was next week."

Paul had forgotten she would speak with an accent. Not unlike his father, she used overly precise facsimiles of acquired
English consonants, the barely perceptible slowness belying
decades of familiarity. The echo made her seem more human,
but no less dangerous. He hadn't given her much thought before, preoccupied with such garish imaginings of Julian's father

that she had seemed beside the point. For the first time he fully understood how little he really knew.

"We decided he didn't need his own guest room, remember? He's a string bean," he added to his mother's guests, giving Paul's arm a shake. "All you really need for this one is an umbrella stand."

"One of your prep-school friends, Julian?" the husband asked. He was younger than Mrs. Fromme, fresh-faced and doughy and faintly familiar, as if Paul had seen him on television without committing him to memory.

"College, I think," Mrs. Fromme corrected. She sidled gracefully past the coffee table to approach him. He kept hoping she would look away from him, or at least blink, but she was waiting for him to flinch first. "How nice to put a face to the name at last, after all your letters."

The latent threat was so subtle and elegant that Paul had to admire it. *I know what you are. I've seen you all along.* She clasped both hands around his, her skin cool and smooth as alabaster. It took all his willpower not to shy away.

"I—thanks, I've—heard a lot about you, too."

Out of sight of her guests, her smile had faded. He tried to withdraw his hand, but she didn't let go.

"*Ça va, Maman?*" said Julian quietly, and she looked at him with such cold anger that it was a wonder he didn't recoil.

"I apologize for the confusion. I assure you it is not typical." Her eyes snapped back to Paul; her voice was a perfect imitation of warmth, but there was no trace of the sentiment in her face. "Make yourself at home," she said.

Julian didn't let go of him. When they were out of sight of the French doors, he slid his fingertips down Paul's arm and laced their hands together.

"Sorry about that." For the first time since Paul had known him, he sounded as if he meant it. "They've been suspicious of you for weeks. They'd never have agreed to let you come if I'd asked them."

Joy had been walking ahead of them in a daze, but she stopped in her tracks and looked at Julian in horror.

"*He* didn't even know? Julian, for god's sake, what's the *matter* with you?"

Her vehemence took Julian by surprise, but mildly. "I think he did," he said, glancing at Paul as if to confirm. "Didn't you? You knew this was enemy territory, you can't have expected a fatted calf."

"You and your"—Joy let the dog squirm out of her arms and threw her entire weight into punching Julian's shoulder—"your awful little games, you decide you're going to show off and you do absolutely vile things to get the pieces into place—"

"It was an emergency." Paul said it less to calm her down than to remind himself that it was true. Julian needed him, had said so outright; anything else paled in comparison. "I'm fine, I'm not—"

"Don't *coddle* him," said Joy, "or he'll never remember he's supposed to do better."

"Why would I bother to grow my own conscience when I've always got you around to pester me?" Julian gave Paul a wry sidelong look—*girls, right?*—and leaned down to gather up the dog.

"Poor Sweetpea is starving," he added. "I promised him a biscuit and everything. Let's get you that drink, Joy, I think all of us could use one."

In his usual fashion, Julian had regained control of the situation without the slightest sign that he was doing it. He ushered Joy into the sun-bright kitchen, where she sat wearily on one of the ebony barstools. While Julian searched the pantry for a dog treat, Paul stole a glance into the back garden. Two boys careened around the sloping lawn and tossed a football, one about Laurie's age, the other a few years younger. Both were blond and nondescript, dressed in khaki shorts and polo shirts. Beyond them there was indeed a gazebo—no Corinthian columns. The air was thick with honeysuckle and saltwater.

This place was so far from his neighborhood's careworn row houses and wood-paneled basements that it barely looked real. The adults in the living room, the younger brothers outside, even Julian and Joy, all looked less like people than like the sunny illustrations on his grandmother's sewing-pattern envelopes. He was too overwhelmed by the perverse details to take them all in, so he fixed his attention, desperately and nonsensically, on a rack of fine-necked crystal wineglasses hanging above the kitchen island. Nobody should own that, he thought, with a fury so brutal and inexplicable that it made his head swim.

Joy and Julian were bickering again, while she drank as if she'd been at the verge of dying of thirst. "When your father gets home, he's going to crucify you," she said. "Right there on the mast of the sailboat."

"Not in front of the Congressman, he won't. Pablo, I don't know what you drink."

His panic must have been visible, because both their faces fell when they turned toward him. Joy gave him a look of abject pity; Julian adopted such a perfect performance of compassion that Paul knew he was trying to hide his impatience.

"My room's up the stairs," said Julian, far too kindly for Paul to trust it. "Turn left, then it's the last door on the right. I'll be up soon."

Paul suspected he was supposed to apologize, which just made him angrier.

"It was nice to meet you, Joy," he said, and darted back into the hall before Julian could change his mind.

He'd left his suitcase at the base of the stairs, but it was gone when he returned. He found it in Julian's room, emptied into the dresser and tucked neatly under the guest bed. He was mortified to think Cecilia had done this for him, though the thought that it could have been Julian's mother was far worse. In their drawer his clothes looked shabby, folded so carefully by the unseen hands that the neatness felt almost mocking.

He lay on his bed; with the curtains drawn, the room was dim and cool. There was little sign that it belonged to anyone, much less Julian. It was of a piece with the rest of the house, tidy as a guest room, with twin nautical-striped bedspreads and blue wallpaper etched with lighthouses and gulls. The only trace of personality was the chair by the window, a folding director's chair where Mrs. Fromme would doubtless would have preferred an armchair. Paul could imagine Julian, a few years younger, making a frame with his fingers as he looked out over the bay.

It wasn't long before Julian sidled inside and shut the door with his shoulder. He'd brought two glasses, glittering with condensation, which he set on Paul's dresser with a chatter.

"I think we're even, now." Julian brushed Paul's hair back from his face and leaned down to kiss him, hard enough to hurt; his mouth was sweet and warm with bourbon.

"Don't ever make me beg you for anything again," he said quietly. "Understood?"

Not for the first time, Paul wondered if he might hate Julian a little. He wanted Julian to kiss him again; it wasn't at all dissimilar from wanting to bite his mouth until he drew blood.

"Why am I here, Julian?"

At first he thought Julian was ignoring the question. He pushed Paul onto his back and let his fingertips graze the hollow of his throat. Paul hated himself for falling for it, for surrendering control instantly and without question.

"I've missed you," said Julian, as if it were an afterthought. "And you're going to help me escape."

5.

"I CAN'T believe you never had to learn an instrument. What kind of a nice Jewish boy are you?"

"Not a particularly nice one, for a start," Paul answered, and Julian pretended not to smile. "So I never had the patience."

"I don't either," said Julian. "That's why I'm not any good."

There was an upright Steinway in the living room, varnish clouded with age. Julian was a splinter of nervous energy. He cycled through the first few bars of a Rachmaninoff concerto, pretending to ignore the party. But every few moments he looked through the glass doors that opened onto the deck, trying—thus far in vain—to catch sight of his parents alone.

They were busy with their guests, the "few close friends" carefully selected so that the Frommes could take credit for introducing important people to one another. Julian had told Paul that his mother didn't drink, but that she led all her guests to believe she did. She swanned through the crowd with her club soda and lime, laughing as if her lungs were loosened by alcohol. She kissed the wives on each cheek to win them over with her Continental charm, and whenever a guest's glass looked too empty she beckoned an attendant to come by with a drink tray. The guests hardly needed encouragement, but they accepted it with relish; these people drank so relentlessly that Paul couldn't fathom how none of them were sick.

"You sound fine to me," Paul said, though he could see what Julian meant. For all its precision, there was something too-smooth and bloodless in Julian's playing that belied the sweeping bombast of the notes.

"That's all I ever am is 'fine,'" said Julian, pretending that this didn't disappoint him. "It's how I am with any art, and *especially* how I was with chess. I excel at theory and memorizing techniques, but in the execution there's always something lacking—"

"I wish you'd listen to me for a minute," Julian's older brother cut in. He glanced toward Paul, impatient and almost pleading. "Are you sure you're not drinking, Julian? Maybe your friend wouldn't mind getting you something—"

"He's not the *help*, Henry," said Julian acidly, and began the concerto again from the top.

Henry had arrived with a few friends of his own, but after a conference with his mother he quickly abandoned them. He was angling to get Julian on his own, and seemed to have decided that the way to do this was to annoy him into submission. He followed Julian and Paul from room to room, cutting into their conversations no matter how vehemently they ignored him.

He leaned now with his arm draped over the top of the piano, holding a half-finished Southside with his fingertips. He'd been nursing it for so long that all the ice had dissolved. Henry didn't look much like Julian at all—he was tall and athletically lean, with an angular look that was at once more classically handsome and far less interesting. But their voices were eerily similar in timbre and cadence, enough that if Paul wasn't looking, he almost couldn't tell which one was speaking.

"Julian." The cascade of crashing chords had summoned Julian's mother. She stood in the doorway with one hand on the hip of her pleated skirt. Her false laugh rang like a bell. "Darling, surely you can play something less Slavonic and grim!"

She lingered, watching them. Paul saw himself through her

eyes, glaringly out of place in the new corduroy suit his grandmother had sewn for him. Under her gaze Paul became acutely aware of how little space there was between him and Julian as they sat elbow-to-elbow on the piano bench. Their bodies were supposed to abhor each other; they were supposed to be like Henry's friends, who only touched when they punched each other's shoulders.

When their mother left, Henry fixed Julian with a pointed, sanctimonious look. "Well, she's right," he said when Julian glared at him. "It's hardly appropriate."

"If you're so sure what's appropriate, would you like to take over?" said Julian with a vicious smile. "Or would you rather attend to your own guests?"

Henry grimaced around a mouthful of his tepid drink.

"I'd like to *talk* to you, quite frankly, and I think you know damn well—listen, Paul," he added suddenly. Paul thought he could see a trace of sympathy in his eyes, which made him feel a little sick. "It is Paul, isn't it?—I hate to be inhospitable, I really do, and it's nothing personal against you, but the circumstances are so irregular that—"

Paul tried to believe he was taking pity on Henry. It was less odious than admitting to himself that he would writhe out of his skin if his hip touched Julian's for another moment. The heat was suddenly stifling, the coffered ceilings dizzyingly high. It seemed impossible that such a tastefully empty place could be so suffocating, far more than his own cluttered little home had ever been—this house was a shadowbox, blank-walled and airtight, never meant for living things.

"It's all right," Paul said over Julian's protest. He buttoned his blazer as he stood, trying to conceal his body a little more. "He won't ever let you alone otherwise."

Julian threw a bitter look toward the crowd milling on the deck, but his mother was engaged again with her guests; his father, whom Paul had only seen from a distance, was completely out of sight.

"We've got to talk to my parents," said Julian. "As soon as we get a chance to corner them."

Paul could never replace an expression, only flatten it to blankness. It would be clear to both of them how much dread he was trying to hide.

"Talking to them" was as far as the plan went, and Paul hadn't dared tell Julian that it didn't sound like much. He decided he just didn't understand it, for the same reason he didn't immediately understand Julian's chess strategies until they were already in motion. Paul didn't know Julian's parents, after all. Julian was going to ask for an early return to Pittsburgh, so he could shop for a few items for his new dormitory and check out some presemester reading at the library—an excuse they could give their friends, if they liked, because that was a favorable alternative to trying to say no and having him pick a fight in public. Paul was supposedly there as reinforcement, a latent threat of resistance in case they tried to physically prevent Julian from leaving.

"This place is a prison," Julian had said. It was the only explanation he would give, no matter how urgently Paul pressed him. "I can't stand another minute here. It doesn't matter why."

Paul left Julian and Henry behind, to whisper in their identical voices about details Paul wasn't allowed to know. He couldn't breathe with their secrets pressing at his back. He retreated into the garden, toward an imaginary solitude on the far side of the crowd—a secluded corner where he could quietly watch for moths. The party spilled down from the deck and out over the lawn, beneath white string lights that crisscrossed between the trellises like a ceiling of stars. Paul had planned for the other guests to ignore him—he survived parties full of strangers by being invisible, and he excelled at it. But these strangers were unaccustomed to letting anything go unseen. The whole point was to be visible to each other, to be recognized and to recognize. When he tried to sidle past them, they paused midsentence and turned to watch him. He couldn't have been more conspicuous, and they wanted him to know it.

No one *approached* him, of course; Paul had the sense that even if Julian had been there to introduce him, they would still have been reluctant to address him directly. He passed a cluster of Henry's Dartmouth friends, vile smirking specimens of Anglo-Saxon boyhood who glanced between Paul's glasses and thin wrists as if they were only a few years too old to try and snap them. The adults were no better—behind the glaze of polite smiles, the sentiment was the same.

The hors d'oeuvres table was set up in the gazebo—lit gold by the white lights that snaked up the support posts, and overflowing with inscrutable things that Paul couldn't eat. Everything seemed to be wrapped in prosciutto or needlessly entangled with a shrimp; even the salmon-and-cucumber bites, which Julian claimed would be safe, had been topped at the last minute with a spiteful chip of bacon.

Paul could feel the other guests watching him from the corners of their eyes, as if they thought he might be contagious. It was all he could do not to put his hands on everything—to contaminate the hateful food so thoroughly that the other guests would be repulsed. Instead he just picked up a plain roll, careful not to touch the others, and pulled it in half to see if there was anything offensive inside.

"That can't be all you're having."

Paul started as if something had stung him, and he hated himself for it. It took him a moment to recognize the man as Julian's father. Paul only knew him by his beige summer blazer, which Julian had pointed out to him at the far end of the crowd. He was deep into his fifties, at least a decade older than his wife, clean-cut and nondescript. His dark hair was silver at the temples and stranded throughout with gray; his eyes were sea-green like Julian's, such an undeserved beauty that Paul wanted to cut them out of his face.

"I'm not that hungry," said Paul, but Mr. Fromme pretended not to hear. His hand landed on Paul's shoulder, and he leaned down, not letting go, to pick up a toothpicked morsel of steak.

"One of my wife's specialties." He affected the tone that intolerable men used when they spoke about their wives, that condescending cocktail of fondness and bemusement. "You've got to love the French—butter and garlic on everything, a little bit of red wine. It melts in your mouth."

"I—no, thank you. I'm all right."

He wanted to squirm away, but Mr. Fromme's hand was firm on his shoulder. When Paul refused the offering, Mr. Fromme's smile became abruptly less convincing. "I insist," he said coolly. "My wife would never forgive me for letting one of our guests go hungry."

"I'm *fine*. Thank you."

It wasn't even that Paul's upbringing had been all that strict, but there was a difference between the occasional dubiously kosher egg roll and being bullied into an unambiguous transgression. That Julian's father would even attempt it struck him as rather pathetic, but Mr. Fromme looked pleased, as if he'd caught Paul in a lie. Paul had imagined such unbreakable authority into this man, such bitter and confident volatility. But he was clear-eyed and sober—there was a palpable insecurity about him, straining for dominance without quite reaching it. He was more hateful than anything Paul's fear had conjured for him.

"Let me tell you a story."

Mr. Fromme didn't let go of his shoulder; he walked Paul back down the steps and along the garden path. Paul watched his face and gestures with clinical fascination. He'd never before met a Jew who tried to pass, and had expected to find some affectation that made the effort visible. But Mr. Fromme probably skated through less by being particularly gentile-looking than by sheer blandness. He had the steam-pressed, Brylcreemed appearance of a witness at the Watergate hearings. In order to wonder if he was Jewish, his country-club acquaintances would first have to differentiate him from every career bureaucrat who looked exactly like him.

"In my Foreign Service days," Mr. Fromme was saying, "we lived for a few years in Iran."

"When Julian was little. He told me."

"Julian and Henry," Mr. Fromme assented; it was clear which name he favored. "In any case—on one occasion I was required, along with a number of my colleagues, to attend a state dinner at one of the palaces of the Shah. Now, by and large I've always found Persian cuisine agreeable, at least the savory dishes. But I also have a particular dislike for rosewater, and I was rather dreading this dinner—because, as you may or may not know, most of the desserts in that country carry at least the threat of it . . ."

Paul noticed with alarm that Mr. Fromme had led him out of earshot of the rest of the party, toward the stuttering reflections of the dock lights on the water.

"Sure enough, come dessert, we were served something they call faloodeh—a sort of noodle ice cream, absolutely *swimming* in rosewater. I would have liked nothing more than to turn my nose up at it. And to do that, to follow that impulse, would have been a grievous offense, not to mention a liability to my employers. So do you know what I did?"

He paused, as if he expected Paul to ask for the answer.

"I ate every bite," he said. "Because that's what you *do*, young man, when you have a vested interest in maintaining a diplomatic relationship with your hosts."

Paul finally shrugged off Mr. Fromme's hand and stepped back to put some distance between them.

"I'm only here for Julian, sir. I'm not trying to have a relationship with you at all."

For a long, ugly moment, Paul almost expected Mr. Fromme to take a swing at him. For the first time, he looked capable of it. But he didn't move. He watched Paul with an incredulous fury, and then he smiled.

"No," he said. "I don't suppose you are."

Mr. Fromme pulled a checkbook from his breast pocket and flicked it open, then returned to the pocket for a pen. It seemed a nonsensical gesture until its meaning landed hard below Paul's ribs.

"What does your father do?"

"He's dead."

Mr. Fromme didn't blink; he didn't even look up from his checkbook.

"My condolences," he said blandly, writing as he spoke. "That must be difficult for your mother. Maybe you'd like to make it a little easier—or keep the money for your own purposes, that's your prerogative. And of course we'll pay for the flight back to wherever you came from, first class . . . Spell your name for me, if you would?"

Paul held his hands steady against the urge, just shy of irresistible, to knock him down onto the pebbled shore and hold his face underwater.

"Go to hell."

"I'll let you write it in yourself." Mr. Fromme signed the check with a flourish and freed it delicately from its perforated edge. "Just as well. I'd forgotten your name already; I don't particularly care to remember it."

"I don't want your money." He was too repelled even to stammer. "You're not going to *buy me off,* I'm not—"

"Of course I am. Don't be ridiculous." Mr. Fromme smiled and held out the check between his first two fingers. "Everyone has a price. I think you'll find this is well north of yours."

The curiosity was too powerful, even through the mortification. He looked down; he immediately wished he hadn't.

"You're abhorrent." He hated how his voice sounded, exactly as uncertain and malleable as Julian's father thought he was. Nothing in him wanted to accept the money, but it was humiliating to be so shaken that he needed to tell himself that at all.

"I grew up the same way you did, you know." That Mr. Fromme would admit this was a sign of how insignificant Paul was to him. "I know what this would mean for you. You wouldn't get anything better from Julian, even before this mess. And if he comes away from this with anything at all, which is severely in doubt," he added with grim satisfaction, "do you really believe that four years from now he'll even remember your name?"

The final sentence eclipsed everything that came before.

"Four years," he said before he could stop himself. "What happens in four years?"

He shouldn't have spoken. Mr. Fromme's insincere smile had given way to unconcealed triumph. He gave a low, faint chuckle; it took all Paul's resolve not to recoil.

"He didn't tell you." His eyes flitted past Paul's shoulder, and the smile became a grin. "What a *singular* oversight. Julian—perhaps you had better set the record straight."

Julian couldn't have been there long. He was a little out of breath, as if he'd rushed through the crowd, but he'd stopped short a few feet uphill. His back was straight, face blank and white as paper. His mother sauntered after him, serenely un-hurried, her high heels dangling from one hand.

"Go ahead," said Julian's father. "Bring him up to speed."

"Julian," said Paul in an urgent undertone, but Julian only glancingly met his eyes. As he approached, he took hold of Paul's forearm; Paul couldn't decide which of them the gesture was meant to steady.

"It isn't going to happen," Julian said. "There's nothing to tell."

"How do you figure?" His father didn't give him a chance to answer; he turned again to Paul. "It's a great opportunity, really. Julian's grandfather has offered to host him for a year at the Sorbonne. Under close supervision, of course, to prevent any further foolishness. And after that, well—"

"He's always had such a difficult time being away from home." As she drew near, Mrs. Fromme touched her son's face with mocking affection, and Julian tensed as if he were trying not to recoil. "He is *emotional*, our Julian. He will be happier if he can live here with us his last three years of college, until he's ready for law school . . . Georgetown, I think, we decided was a better fit?"

"Better school, too. Much more in line with your qualifications, which matters in the real world, believe it or not."

Julian swung forward to catch his gaze, but Paul could hardly see him. The world shimmered at its edges.

"Don't listen to them," said Julian. "It isn't going to happen— Paul, that's why you're *here*, that's what we're telling them, remember?"

His voice had no right to waver. He'd known all along and said nothing, had knowingly put Paul in a position to be blindsided. It was monstrous for him to be afraid when Paul desperately needed him to be brave.

"You still think you can salvage this." Mr. Fromme's attention had refocused, raptly, on his son. Julian did something Paul had never seen him do before—he broke eye contact, as if he couldn't endure it any longer, and fixed his gaze unseeingly on the water.

"I'm going back to Pittsburgh." He retreated to their script as if its flimsy words still had any power. "It's my life, I can decide where I want to go to school and who my friends are. You've no right to stop me, and you aren't going to try. I know you don't want me to embarrass you in front of your guests—"

"Let me tell you how that plays out for you, Julian," his father interrupted, "because I think you're under the misapprehension that we would continue to be as *patient* as we've been up till now." That struck Julian silent. If he felt anything at all, all evidence of it had emptied from his face. "Has it not occurred to you how much more difficult we can make this for you?" said his father. "Ungrateful, as always, for every unpleasantness we've worked so hard to spare you."

"Poor Julian. You've always been so emotional." The word was no less jarring the second time Mrs. Fromme said it. Paul might have used it to describe himself, in a moment of self-loathing, but never Julian. "The way you reacted to that little incident at boarding school, you were nearly hysterical—all our friends were concerned, and it was terribly difficult to explain. So if there were to be a public outburst, well . . . it would be uncomfortable for us, of course, but everyone knows how you are."

"You were always too spiteful to even pretend to be normal," his father cut in. "Naturally you'll never appreciate how much effort it's taken to try to mitigate the damage."

"He's delicate. Since the accident, I think—he's never been the same." Mrs. Fromme wasn't quite correcting him. "No one," she told Julian kindly, "would ever fault us for sending you somewhere quiet to recuperate."

"You're damned lucky we didn't do it years ago."

Mrs. Fromme flashed her husband a warning smile and reached, once more, for Julian's face.

"It is what any loving parent would do."

There was supposed to be another layer to the plan. It should be like one of Julian's favorite games between grandmasters, every apparent flaw a strategic feint. But Julian said nothing. Paul might have been able to hold himself steady if Julian had looked at him, given him even an empty reassurance that he knew what he was doing. But he appeared to have forgotten that Paul was there. He looked so blank and faraway that it might have passed for calm. There was no backup plan. Paul had been right—there had barely been a plan at all.

Mr. Fromme checked his watch. He smiled at them and offered his wife his arm.

"I think you know what your options are, Julian. I trust you'll choose sensibly. As for you—" Here he paused, as if to remind Paul that he hadn't bothered to commit his name to memory. "—I'll hold on to the check till morning, I think," he said with a thin smile. "After that the offer will be less generous."

"Be a good host, Julian," said his mother. "Your friend looks a little pale. Perhaps you should fetch him a drink."

They ascended the hill arm in arm, not a hair out of place between them. Paul watched Julian's mother pause to pull her shoes back on by their ankle straps, while his father waited at her side and chivalrously held her hand. Paul could pick up a stone while their backs were turned and throw it before anyone could stop him. But he didn't know which skull he would rather crack, and before he could decide, they had disappeared into the party again. There was nowhere for the impulse to go.

"Tell me what the plan is. Tell me what we do next."

But Julian still wouldn't look at him. He sank down to sit in the tall grass by the edge of the strand, bracing his forearms on his knees. He didn't seem to register that Paul had spoken. He held a cigarette between his lips and tried fruitlessly to light the match.

Paul stood in front of him, bay water bleeding into the heels of his shoes. When Julian didn't look up, Paul pulled the cigarette out of his hand and snapped it in two.

He didn't know, once he had Julian's attention, why he had wanted it in the first place. He could see his every flaw reflected in Julian's face, every insecurity and weakness and insatiable need.

"There's more to the plan." His stammer grew more severe with every word until he could barely understand himself. "Tell me there's more to the plan, because otherwise this *was* the plan, to bring me all this way to prove to me that it wasn't your idea and you didn't have a *choice*—of course it's not that you're sick of me, you *have* to leave me, it's not your fault this way, how fucking convenient for you."

Something elusive and terrifying moved through Julian's face, and he raised one hand as if to conceal it. Paul caught his wrist and wrenched it away and didn't let go. He wanted to watch Julian hate him.

"I'll die without you," Paul said. Even he didn't know if it was a plea or a threat. "You *know* that, that's what's always been in this for you. I never understood it till now, but it's the only thing that makes sense. You don't need me, you never did, you just get off on knowing you could kill me and I'd thank you for it, it's a story you can tell yourself whenever you want to feel special—"

"Paul, that *hurts*."

Regret flooded through him even before he realized how hard he was twisting Julian's arm—the unnatural angle at his wrist and elbow, as if Paul were just at the verge of breaking them.

He let go. He wanted to cut his own throat and spare them both the disgust of enduring him any longer. Julian covered his face again; it was frightening and repellent to think that he might cry.

"I'm sorry." Paul dropped to his knees and reached forward, but Julian batted his hand away. "I'm sorry, I'm so sorry—"

A sharp, bitter laugh. "I know you are."

"I didn't mean any of it, I was just—"

"Yes, you did. You know damn well."

Julian let his hand fall and lifted his eyes. Even in the dim light, Paul could tell they were dry.

"I always worry you're going to kill yourself," he said. "You're just the type, I've always known. Sometimes I wish you'd get it over with."

He had all but pleaded for it, the precision and scalpel-sharp intimacy of Julian's cruelty. He had needed to remember that they were monstrous together, merciless, twins conjoined at the teeth.

"I want to go inside." He traced the line of Julian's jaw with his fingertips and took hold of his neck. "Please, I need to kiss you."

Julian was breathless with fury. He lifted his face as if to bare his throat for a sacrifice.

"I couldn't care less what you need," he said, and he yielded to the kiss just long enough that it stung all the more when he shoved Paul away.

6.

THE PARTY dragged late. Julian shut his window, but they could still hear voices, muffled by humidity and glass. Well after the clock struck one, the imperfect hush was punctured now and then by a woman's high liquory laugh.

Neither of them wanted to open the window until the voices were gone, though the room was stifling. In the moments before Julian pushed him over the dresser, Paul caught sight in the mirror of their fever-shining faces—how the heat chafed their skin, blood swelling just beneath the surface like ink blotting through thin paper. He looked away before he could find any differences between them; he wanted only to remember how heat and despair and delirium made them look, just for a moment, as if they shared the same face.

There was no forgiving one another after, but there never was. The anger didn't ebb, or even turn away from each other completely, but it held them together against the siege. Julian became tender and soft-spoken; Paul allowed him to kiss his forehead and murmur patient reassurances, as if either of them could believe they were true. But Paul also listened for the sharp scar-burned notes in Julian's breathing—the effort it took to hold the fury tight inside him.

They'd migrated to the floor, half dressed and restless. Their only light was a lamp on the desk, and the bulb burned unbearably hot. The small fan angled uselessly toward them on the floor.

Paul lay with his head on Julian's lap, trying to map constellations into the sun-darkened freckles on his knees, while Julian combed his fingertips gently through Paul's hair. Two stories below, the voices were finally ebbing. Before Paul could stop himself from recognizing it, he identified one voice as Julian's mother—too indistinct at a distance to parse the words, but adopting the unmistakable cadence of a goodbye.

"They aren't going to come up here, are they?"

The question made the movement of Julian's hands stumble, just barely, out of rhythm. Henry had done so, hours earlier, before he and his friends headed out to a second party they'd been priming for with the first. He left soon when Julian didn't answer the knock, but the intrusion had reminded Paul how visible they were to people who didn't deserve to see them. He doubted either of Julian's parents would ever show them the same mercy Henry had.

"No," said Julian after a pause. "Mother likes people to stew for a while."

"And then what?"

"We make our goodbyes, preferably acrimonious," said Julian. "And in the morning you're supposed to go see Father in his study and accept the—how much did he offer you, anyway?"

Paul didn't want to answer the question, so he decided to be irritated that Julian hadn't answered his.

"I mean in reality. You haven't told me what's going to happen, because you never do. You told me I was coming here to help you, but you haven't told me anything I need to know in order to do it. You just keep pushing me into the deep end and then acting like I'm drowning to spite you."

"You *didn't* need to know," said Julian, as if the argument already bored him. "I'm leaving; you're helping me. Nothing's changed. All I need to do is work up my nerve."

A mosquito had bitten Paul behind his ear, unnoticed until

the itch became too shrill to ignore. Both Julian's shins were flecked pink with remnants of the same stings.

"You still haven't said what we're going to do," Paul said, but Julian just gave a low, brittle laugh and didn't reply.

Paul couldn't be still any longer. The last few voices had moved inside, perilously close; he felt like an animal shivering off a tranquilizer and finding itself in a cage. He stalked into the adjoining bathroom and drenched two washcloths in cold water, but by the time he emerged, they were already beginning getting tepid. He opened the window in time to see the Frommes coming inside, the string lights clicking dark above their heads; neither looked up. When they were finally gone, a breeze came in off the bay, but it was humid and warm and brought no relief.

Julian had settled in the director's chair, holding the cloth against his neck. Paul leaned against the foot of one of the beds and watched him, measuring Julian's latent energy and imagining how it would snap. *Working up his nerve.* But Julian's bravery was absolute; nothing lay beyond its reach.

"Tell me more about them," said Paul, and Julian winced before looking up to meet his eyes. "I want to hate them as much as you do."

"You already do, probably." Expressionless, Julian turned his gaze toward the night sky. "It'd be easier for you—they aren't yours."

Paul was sick of his evasions. He was sick of doubting that their hold on each other was unbreakable.

"They don't know how much you matter," said Paul. "They don't see it, you're the most brilliant person I've ever met and they don't even *notice*, they should be . . ." His own stammering sincerity frightened him, but he forced himself to keep speaking. He had to give Julian something of himself that wasn't needy and grasping, something that burned itself alive to exalt him.

". . . They should be in *awe* of what they've been given in you," he said desperately, "but they aren't, they want you to be just as petty and small as they are and they can't even conceive of how much you matter already."

Paul didn't recognize the guardedness in Julian's face until after it had fallen away. It was the first time Paul had ever seen such a stark echo of his own need in him. Julian devoured the adoration as if it might be the last he ever received—as if he didn't trust it not to disappear.

Julian took a moment to summon his voice. He drew a deep breath, released it in a trembling exhale.

"You're sweet when you want to be," he said quietly. Then, with a frayed smile, "It's all right, Pablo. You don't have to convince me of what they are."

But Paul was convincing himself—working up his own nerve. When he spoke again, even he wasn't sure whether he dared take himself seriously.

"Do you want me to kill them?"

Julian froze. He watched Paul's face with wide eyes. Then he burst into wild laughter.

"I mean it." Paul laughed too, anxious and grave. "They deserve it. Then you'd have your freedom back, and they couldn't hurt you for it. Isn't that why I'm here, to help you get out of this place in one piece?"

"Good god, Pablo." There was still a trace of a laugh in Julian's voice, but he spoke with a horror that was very close to eagerness. "You'd really do it, wouldn't you?"

When Paul couldn't answer, Julian turned in his chair to face him head-on, pulling one knee to his chest. His smile wavered, but it didn't fade.

"How do you want to do it?" he said. "I want to line them up all in a row and clock them between the eyes with a cattle gun—or how about a Helter Skelter kind of thing, wouldn't that be fun? We could paint gibberish in blood on the walls."

After the unbreaking fever of the last two days, Paul was ready for them to find solace in one of their thought experiments, to strike and parry until their thoughts spiraled into revelation. Offer an idea, find its flaws, build it into something better.

His solemn consideration, his very earnestness, was part of the joke. Julian had always been fascinated by his sincerity, after all, and the object of the game—the object of all their games—was to find each other fascinating.

"They'll suspect us right away," Paul said, "especially if neither of us is hurt. We'd have to slice each other up a bit, too."

"You could do it without blinking," said Julian with affection. "Just try to miss all the important arteries—I've nearly bled out once before, it's a drag."

"It still wouldn't be a sure thing, though, even if it looked like the hippies roughed us up . . . Oh, hell, and I forgot about the kids. Did you want to do them in, too?"

"Probably not Oliver," Julian conceded. "He's not too bad, and he's only ten—it might do him good to be an orphan."

"But the older one?"

"Edmund I'd be happy to kill myself." His grin was merciless. "He fits right in at my old school."

Paul remembered being the same age. He didn't need Julian to elaborate.

"Okay," he said, "that's three we have to get through—"

"Four," Julian corrected shortly, "if Henry comes home and tries to stop us."

"Four. If necessary. So we'll put the kid in the basement—"

"Wine cellar, actually, I wish I was kidding—"

"Oh god, of course it's a *wine cellar*. How do you put up with these people?"

"Not well," said Julian pleasantly, "hence the stabbing."

Paul dissolved into hysterics, and Julian clambered over the foot of the bed and pinned him facedown in the blankets. "You'll give us away," he said, covering Paul's mouth with both hands, "you're going to spoil it, all our careful planning—"

He let go when Paul elbowed him hard. They lay side by side, hands clasped tight, shaking with silent laughter. Nothing could dampen their euphoria, not even the soft indistinct threat of the things outside their walls.

Eventually Julian's lungs betrayed him in a spasm of coughing, and once it had ended they finally lay still. Somewhere in the floor beneath them, a pipe sighed with water; in spite of the late hour, someone slammed a door.

"It still doesn't work," Paul said. He didn't want the moment to end—he wanted to pitch it higher, drive them both mad with it. But the flaws were too glaring. "It's just—implausible, there's no way to avoid suspicion. You never want them to bleed if you're doing it properly, blood gets everywhere and blood is evidence. There's no way we don't get caught."

In the dim light, Julian smiled, an indulgent and affectionate smile that Paul had always hated.

"I don't know what I'd do without you, Pablo. You're just so sincerely creepy."

In the long, aching months of being able to agonize over

every word at leisure, Paul had forgotten how this felt—the humiliating realization that he couldn't keep pace. He was too meticulous, too literal-minded and laboriously slow, two steps behind every joke except the ones he then ruined by explaining them. There was no reason for Julian to take him seriously, because Paul took himself so seriously that no one else possibly could. He was an ungainly, inherently ridiculous thing, and he shouldn't expect to be seen as anything better. He was lucky to be allowed near Julian at all. Paul's body, briefly forgotten, had become more expansive than should have been allowed. He folded himself back into his usual small shape, shoulders curled in, arms wrapped around himself.

Julian watched him with impassive eyes, then sighed and turned away. He dug through the drawer of the nightstand and found a cigarette, nestled amid childhood yo-yos and packs of ossified gum. Paul's idea only took shape when he saw Julian strike the match.

He forgot his doubts as suddenly as he'd been crushed by them. Understanding moved over him like frost over glass.

"There could be a house fire," he said. "It happens all the time."

Julian didn't laugh this time. His spine straightened. He shook the match dead and set his cigarette aside.

"You'd even look like a hero," said Paul, so calmly he might have been dreaming. "Saving your little brother like that. It's a pity there was nothing you could do to help the rest of them."

He would have done anything, anything at all, if it meant Julian would look at him this way a moment longer. The green of his eyes, like white winter light vectored through the crest of a wave; the ravenous grasping for evidence that Paul loved him, and the relief and terror at finding it. Anything, so long as Julian yearned for something Paul could give him. He would never hesitate.

"Aren't you clever," said Julian. He wasn't smiling. "Talk me through it. I can't wait to hear."

7.

IT WAS as real as a dream. They tended to it with careful hands, letting every detail blossom in place and take root as if it had been there all along. With every question they answered, it grew more alive. *How easily could it be an accident?* A low flame, easily forgotten, the corner of an open cookbook just barely touching it. Careless, giddy on cocktails, anyone might make the same mistake. *How to trap them in their rooms?* A thick wedge of folded paper behind the hinges, another at the foot of the door—the sort of evidence that burned away, if the flames raged too long. *How long?* Hours. The nearest neighbors separated by sprawling lawns, jewelry-box houses guarded by high fences. They couldn't knock on doors and plead to use the phone, not here; wealthy people paid handsomely for the privilege of ignoring cries for help. *And what about Henry?* Indeed, what about him? It was up to him and his own drunken luck whether he would live or die. He knew enough that he might suspect them. It suited them just fine if they had to kill him too.

Saving the youngest boy was an attractive flourish. Paul hadn't caught a clear glimpse of his face, so he imagined trailing behind the two brothers as they hurried to the water's edge, the child visible only as golden hair and nightclothes. Julian would be in his element, the perfect embodiment of fear and frantic concern. One arm around his brother's shoulders; a quick backward glance, a silent gesture for Paul to hurry up.

I'm sorry, Oliver, he said. I'm so sorry, but we can't go back for them.

They retreated to the sailboat for safety, pushed out into the bay and stayed there, watching as the house burned. *But why didn't we sail to the neighbors' docks and try to find help?* One disoriented child; two slight teenagers, one with weak lungs and another who didn't know how to sail. No one could expect much of them, except perhaps to try (in vain, always in vain) to draw the attention of a bystander on the shore.

Perhaps Henry stayed the night at a friend's house, and returned in the morning to find police tape stretched between the gate pillars. Or perhaps he came home, drove back and forth in search of help until someone finally gave it. They had no way of knowing either way; it was impossible to see his car through the trees. *Who else might raise the alarm?* Perhaps the smell of smoke disturbed the neighbors.

And the police? Julian handled them as beautifully as he handled everyone—brave for the sake of the others, face ashstreaked and solemn, while Paul was so shaken that he and his too-honest tongue could scarcely speak.

They were above suspicion. They were above everything. Julian was free of the walls his family had built around him; Paul, courageous at last, was free of the ones he'd built around himself. It was a masterpiece they would carry forever between them, an undying flame.

What next?

Paul wanted to live somewhere wild, somewhere the air was clean. Julian needed people—an audience, a hum of activity to keep him from getting bored. But that was all right. *We'll be able to compromise.* They went north, found a college town where one or both of them could teach. They gave away most of the inheritance once Julian no longer needed to cover his expenses with it, because the money wasn't the point. They had each other now, and the clouded windows of old thread mills, and a house with a long white wall where Paul's butterfly collection could shine in the sunlight. Of course Julian wanted that future for them too. *You believe me, don't you, Pablo?*—and of course he did. Look what they'd made together. Look what they'd done to break free.

The temperature dropped. The fan still whispered, facing the floor where they had been. It was real. They kissed each other breathless between each promise. All around them the flames peeled the wallpaper back from blackened beams.

8.

THERE WAS cool soft rain and the crush of the tide. There was the shadow of Julian's shoulder blades beneath his shirt as he shut the window, and then there was quiet. The director's chair was folded to a fasces and propped against the bookcase. It was half past eight; only the way Paul's memory had folded forward four hours told him he'd slept at all.

"We're still here." It was the blue wallpaper that made him realize it, with its etched ship's wheels and twists of sailing rope. Of course it hadn't been real. It couldn't be. With their fever broken, all that was left was this grand cruel house, and everything inside it that Julian needed and didn't want to need.

Julian was already dressed, in a polo shirt and pressed plaid trousers that made him look painfully like his parents' son. His calm would have looked like indifference if not for how ashen he was.

"Not for much longer," he said. "I've got us packed already. I want to get this over with."

Paul sat up too fast, though his head was swimming even before he did.

"Wait," he said. "We haven't figured out a plan, we need more time, you don't have anywhere to *go*—"

"I've got a couch I can crash on for a few days." Julian's face was blank as a mask. "The orchid guy's house. I know the girl who got the job, I called her yesterday, she's expecting me."

Paul sat very straight, trying to stave off the panic. Beside his own suitcase on the other bed, Julian's satchel sat open; it was so thick with books that its seams buckled, but Julian grabbed another few paperbacks from the shelf and bent them smaller to fit them into the gaps.

"Just like that?" Paul couldn't admit outright that it was a bad idea, so he left it unsaid for Julian to discover on his own.

"Just like." Julian didn't look at him. With great effort he forced the satchel shut, then stalked across the room to wrench his dresser open.

"What are you going to do about the—I mean, the money thing, how—"

"I'll get by," said Julian acidly, "like everybody else does."

Paul wanted to let the silence lie, but he couldn't stop himself.

"There's got to be a better way to do it. You deserve better, you deserve a *chance.*"

Julian looked at him at last, holding a neat stack of clothes to his chest. From the edge in his voice Paul had expected him to be angry, but he only looked exhausted.

"It's decided," he said. "Stop complaining. You know damn well this is what you want."

It was the truth, but Paul didn't like to be confronted with the selfishness of it. They didn't speak again. Julian arranged his belongings carefully in his suitcase, precision and efficiency honed by a lifetime of boarding schools and family vacations. By the time Paul returned from his shower, Julian had left; their bags sat by the door beneath the shroud of his navy-blue raincoat.

Paul sat on Julian's bed and tried to ignore the voices, which shivered through the floor under the soles of his shoes until he crossed his legs to escape them. The summer rain had thickened to a gray mist.

There was a sharp knock, and the door swung open before Paul could speak. Henry's lips pursed when he saw him. He was dressed impeccably, black hair towel-dried and combed straight, but he looked as if he'd been sick all night.

"Do you know what you've done?" said Henry.

"I haven't done anything," Paul replied, and told Henry silently that he was luckier for it.

Henry made an impatient, miserable sound and dragged one hand irritably through his hair. The gesture was another uncanny likeness to Julian, and Paul quickly focused his gaze on Henry's wrist to avoid dwelling on it. He'd never known before that it was all right, in some circles, for a man to wear any kind of bracelet; it was reasonably masculine, a loop of plaited leather fastened with a brass anchor, but it was still strange enough that it helped Paul forget all the ways Henry was familiar.

"He has a *future*." The words were his father's, not his own, and the uncertainty in how Henry mimicked them made him seem very young. "Surely you understand that—surely you know what you're doing by standing in the way. He could achieve great things, if only he weren't too stubborn to accept the guidance."

"Julian doesn't need 'guidance.'" Paul smiled; he couldn't help but pity Henry, all the more because Henry would never understand why. "He'll be great no matter what, because he'll do it for his own sake. The best *they* can offer him is the opportunity to engrave a few letters of your father's name. He can do better than that."

Henry looked at him with blank horror.

"Christ," he said. "I can't tell whether he's done a number on you or if it's the other way around."

The voices downstairs were no louder, but the tone of the conversation abruptly shifted. Henry appeared to forget Paul was there. He went alert as a deer; when he hurried into the hallway, he moved like one, with the same sudden and sharp-angled urgency.

Paul tried to follow, but by the time he reached the foyer, Henry was out of sight. He could no longer hear the voices. They'd been coming from below the bedroom, but when he tried to find a path toward the back left corner of the house he kept running into dead ends. It was a maze of a house, too-large and inscrutable, like the elderly buildings on campus that hid his classrooms where he could never naturally find them.

One door opened onto a library with tall mahogany shelves, stark and neat and cold. When Paul moved on to the next door, a lacrosse stick clattered to the floor; beyond it he saw the empty bedroom of one of the younger boys, one wall adorned with a familiar string of signal flags. Eventually he gave up and doubled back. He remembered, or imagined in desperation, that there may have been a doorway in the living room—it might have a hallway beyond it, toward an out-of-the-way corner where an irritable man could retreat to his office and avoid his children. Paul didn't know what he would do when he found it, but it was just as well. He might need to tell a good story afterward, even if only to himself. It was better not to premeditate.

His memory hadn't failed him. There was a doorway just where he'd thought there was, half hidden by a thick tress of ivy from a hanging iron planter. And there was Mrs. Fromme, leaning against the frame of the open French doors, lit from behind by the gray light and the rain.

She wasn't surprised to see him. She was in weekend clothes, no makeup but a sheen of powder-pink lipstick, though she'd still dressed with care. White slacks, navy cardigan, pinstriped blue blouse. She held her cigarette the way Julian did—the same careless, graceful angle at the wrist.

When he met her eyes, she smiled, and it wasn't even an unkind smile. No warmth, but no malice. It was worse than if she had brought a knife to his throat.

"You poor boy," she said. "You really believe this will help you keep him."

The weight of his stammer was so heavy on his tongue that he couldn't speak. He drew a breath of the cool humid air and forced himself not to avoid her eyes. She didn't seem to expect an answer. She gave him a long, dispassionate look and flicked her cigarette to let the ash fall.

"You know, Adam can't make sense of you," she said indifferently. "He is too venal a man to understand anything but venality. But I've seen your letters—I know what has been done to you. You aren't the problem. You are only the weapon of choice."

Her candor was a lie, sold beautifully; so was her tone of weary resignation. But Paul couldn't stop himself from listening—even if he knew she was a liar, even if he refused to speak. It was like watching Julian put on one of his masks. The lie was fascinating for how near it was to the truth.

When he tried to brush past her, she caught him by the shoulder. She turned his face toward hers, lifted his chin so he would have to meet her eyes. Without makeup her lashes were straw-blond, cheekbones dappled amber with freckles.

"You are just as I always knew you would be," she said. "Curly hair, sad eyes. Quite striking, in your way. His sweethearts always are."

She didn't belabor it. She waited until it reached his face, then smiled as if with great pity and turned her gaze toward the rain.

"You are how he spites us, because he thinks that makes him free." Mrs. Fromme took a leisurely pull from her cigarette and exhaled a stream of smoke into the mist. "Your mistake is in believing he has any further use for you. You have fallen for the same lie he always uses—that you're the only thing in the world he will still love once its novelty has worn off."

He couldn't pretend there was no part of him that believed it, because he'd believed it since the beginning. All she had really done was bring the belief forward from its clumsy hiding place and show it to him. She took it from the hysterical reality inside his own head and placed it in the one outside. It was a familiar trick—Julian could only have learned it at her knee.

Mrs. Fromme looked out over the garden, silent and calm. She didn't watch for Paul's reaction. She knew that giving him a single questioning glance would betray all the uncertainty Paul needed from her.

A door burst open at the end of the corridor. Julian swept out, electric with fury; Henry followed close after and reached for his shoulder, but Julian shrugged off the touch without looking back. When he saw Paul, he tried to look certain and unafraid, but he couldn't settle on a persona that would make it true. He threw his mother a look of wary disgust and hurried to take hold of Paul's arm.

What did she do? his lips asked silently, but Paul swallowed his nausea and shook his head.

"We'll bring our things down," said Julian, "then we'll go. All right?"

"Julian."

At the end of the hall his father was a shadow in shirtsleeves and squared shoulders. His face, just visible in the dim light, wore a thin jeering smile that made Paul's hands itch to break his teeth.

"When you come back—and you will—you'll have to beg us to let you in the door." His voice strained for cold authority, but it achieved only spite. "Whatever pride you think you have, enjoy it. You won't keep it for long."

Julian's face was blank; he didn't look at his father so much as look through him. After a moment he closed his eyes, then held Paul's arm tighter and turned away.

"I'll drive them," Paul heard Henry say while they were leaving. "I'll try to get rid of the friend, I can still talk some sense into him . . ."

"You want to say goodbye," answered Mrs. Fromme, as if she were merely correcting him rather than accusing him of a lie.

They were bringing only a few things with them, just their suitcases and the director's chair and Julian's school satchel full of books. Henry's dark blue Chrysler waited in the drive with its doors open. One of the younger children watched from the window above the front door, small face and blond hair blurred by glass.

Henry made no move to help them pack up the car. He waited in the driver's seat, gripping the wheel with both hands. Paul thought he heard the clack of a deadbolt at the front door, but when he turned to look, there was no movement behind the glass.

The child's face had vanished from the window, and all the lights were dark. At either side of the walkway, the white magnolias shivered in the rain.

Julian joined Paul in the back seat and slammed the door. Henry's blue eyes watched them in the rearview mirror. "They only want what's best for us," he said, though he'd clearly given up hope. "You'll see that someday."

Julian drew his first shaking pull from a cigarette and brushed his thumb along his lower lip.

"Just drive, Henry."

No one spoke. The parvenu mansions beyond the woods quickly segued back into farmland, and the countryside bled across the windows like splashes of verdant watercolor. Julian finished his cigarette and slid to a slouch, bracing one boot against the back of the passenger seat. He didn't look at either of them; it was only by the insistent pressure of his shoulder against Paul's side that he knew Julian noticed him at all.

The car turned off the highway, onto a slim stretch of road with no lane markings. It didn't look familiar, but Paul didn't expect familiarity; he didn't think anything of it until Julian sat up, suddenly alert.

"Why are we going this way?"

"Just making a pit stop. Won't take long."

Julian made a peevish face. "You *should've* gone before we *left*, Henry." It was the same singsong tone Laurie used when Paul was annoying her.

"This day is already a nightmare," said Henry wearily. "You don't have to be childish on top of it."

Past the haze of loblolly pines, a driveway branched off toward what purported to be a riding school. The paddocks were sodden and empty, horses apparently confined to the barn. The white clapboard office looked filthy, though it would have been handsome in better light; the carport alongside it was almost vacant, home only to a pickup truck and a red two-door Chevrolet. Paul could picture the brothers coming here as children, their mother watching with her arms folded over the fence as they rode in cautious circles. Henry's detour might be an act of nostalgia, part of a final burst of affection in the wake of loss.

The love had been what shattered Paul after his father died—betrayal came later, willed into being to save him from the agony of loving something he couldn't reach. He remembered the way love had burned through him like a flame under glass, grasping outward, devouring what air it had left before it choked. How he hated it; how desperately he had tried to keep it burning. He didn't have to like Henry, or even understand him, to know he was capable of that same grief. He felt sick for not noticing it before.

Julian had gone very still. He was staring at the Chevrolet under the carport, red paint and windshield glazed with dust. Henry pulled up beside it, parking with scrupulous precision between the white chalk lines.

"I thought you sold it."

Henry sighed and zipped his Dartmouth crew jacket up to the chin.

"I wanted it to be a surprise," he said. "For your birthday. But by then things were already so . . . Well, anyway. I was proud of you for finally getting your license. And it'll be a saleable asset—which you're going to need, if you insist on behaving this way."

Hectoring and unsentimental as the act was in its particulars, the love behind it was starkly clear, but Julian couldn't seem to make sense of it. He didn't move until Henry, barely hiding his impatience, reached into the back seat to hand him the keys.

The luggage that had fit easily into Henry's trunk became an awkward jumble in the back seat of the coupe. The vents yielded a musty bovine smell from weeks of disuse. Paul didn't want to be privy to their goodbyes, so he waited in the passenger seat and folded himself narrow. His purpose now was to be small, even if it meant driving himself from his own body. Whatever Julian needed from him now, it wasn't strength or courage or even anger; he'd rejected that in favor of something any other devotee could have given him. Paul felt his own presence as if from a distance. He was beside the point, easily taken apart and even more easily replaced, whether or not Julian actually wanted to do it.

Neither Julian nor Henry had much to say. They mumbled between long silences, arms folded, pointedly not touching. Eventually they each nodded curtly, and Henry retreated to his car. He didn't wait around to watch them leave.

By the time Julian settled into the driver's seat, his brother's taillights were already waiting at the mouth of the drive. A brief pause to watch for traffic, then he was gone. Julian had fixed his attention on adjusting the mirrors; Paul was the only one who saw him go.

Carefully, as if he didn't trust the car not to spin out of control, Julian shifted gears. He had to pause to remember how to turn on the windshield wipers; in the moment before they clicked to life Paul thought he saw the crescent of a bruise on Julian's cheek, but it was only the shadow of a raindrop's impact on the glass.

"What did my mother say to you?"

It was the first time Julian had addressed him directly since they left. He still didn't meet Paul's eyes; he spoke very quietly.

"Nothing." He knew Julian could tell he was lying, but he couldn't tell the truth without having to feel it. "Nothing important."

Julian set his jaw and straightened his back. He'd wanted an excuse to be wounded and defensive, and had fully expected that Paul would give him one. At first Paul thought he was infuriated at being denied; he could see the imperfections in the studied blankness of Julian's face, and he braced to find anger underneath. When he felt himself being watched, Julian finally met his eyes, and there was such vicious bitterness in his face that Paul nearly recoiled. But it was only an imitation of anger, desperate and grasping, nothing like the real thing.

When Paul tried to touch him, Julian shoved him away. He seemed to regret it instantly—brusquely, without apology, he put his arm around Paul's neck and looked away from the road just long enough to kiss his forehead. Paul rested his head on Julian's shoulder and listened to the movement of the air through his chest. Ragged but steady, still in control. It had been disrespectful of Paul to doubt that he would be, and worse that he still wished Julian would fall apart for him.

"I can't remember," said Julian. "The town where we're going to live, is it in Vermont or Maine?"

He'd nearly forgotten about their northern college town, the factory windows and autumn sunlight that was to be their reward at the end of their game. Julian shouldn't have reminded him. Paul wanted to forget that he'd ever thought it possible to suture the cut that separated them, to tether themselves together and then hold still.

"One of those," he said, and he tried to close himself off to the yearning. But it was already inside him, deep in his marrow, and he couldn't pretend not to feel it.

The car emerged onto the highway, alone between the sprawling tidal flats and the low gray sky. Paul listed all the ways death could find them in that moment, while they were still young and bright and certain of each other. It found them in the wreckage of an accident, the pain shattering and quick. It found them in a smear of atomic light in the sky over Washington, and the world preparing to die with them as they sat on the hood of the car, hand in hand, waiting. It found them together in the inlet waters beneath a bridge, their bodies tied to each other at the wrist.

But they would keep driving, and Julian would switch on the radio, and Paul would page through the road atlas in search of a route home that accommodated Julian's skittish dislike of the interstate. There would be no stillness, no permanence. There couldn't be. Paul wasn't strong enough to hold Julian in place. All there was to him was that desperate, wretched need; the weakness was unforgivable. The fantasy of the house fire had brought them to an impossible truth. They could only stitch themselves back together if they did something irreversible.

Part III

I.

IN MID-AUGUST, the night the meteor shower reached its peak, they took the rural route into the foothills. Julian parked in the tall dry grass at the side of the road. He leaned on the driver's-side door and watched, heckling, while Paul spent twenty minutes adjusting the feet of the telescope stand. As the last sunlight faded they sat side by side on the bumper, working through their respective six-packs of ginger ale and Dr Pepper, until they could only see each other by moonlight. They were alone in the country darkness. Hours went by without a single passing car. The nearest farmhouse was a mile across the valley, a lone chip of light against the black.

It was the first real time they'd spent together since the start of summer. For weeks Paul had seen very little of him, because Julian refused to let him close enough that the effort might show. "Getting by" had to look like a series of easy victories, and only now had there been enough of them that Julian could devote his attention to anything else. The work-study job at the campus library, the cheap one-room walk-up in lieu of a dorm room—he'd assembled a tidy new life for himself, and once he had it, he pulled Paul abruptly back in from arm's length, as carelessly as if the distance had never been there.

Paul wasn't relieved and he couldn't quite force himself to pretend he was, but at least now the two of them could fall back into each other's orbit. Paul could lie on the hood of the car with Julian's arm around his shoulders, under a breathtaking sky that could still never blaze as bright as Julian did. He could watch the moon-painted curls of smoke leaving Julian's lips—one of those new, cheaper cigarettes he'd switched to without comment, hoping perhaps that Paul wouldn't notice the slight change in the taste of his mouth. They could talk to each other without grazing any open wounds, and somehow Julian could act as if there was nothing there to avoid at all. In that moment they were so close to the way they'd been before that Paul could almost believe it was the same.

They drove back to the city in the small hours of the morning, thick warm air sliding through the open windows. The heat shone through Julian's skin, down the length of his arms and the elegant angle where his wrists met his hands. It can always be like this, Paul tried to promise himself. But he'd never believed it, even before Mrs. Fromme told him he shouldn't.

They were deep past the city limits when Julian finally broke the silence. "I've got a good one," he said.

"Oh yeah?"

Julian looked sideways just long enough to smile. The late hour and the long drive had made him languid and calm. "So you talk yourself into the subject's bedroom—"

"I do?"

"General 'you,' you square." Julian rubbed one eye with the back of his wrist. "You tie him to the bedpost, then you empty his wallet and knock a candle onto the bed on your way out. Looks like he just got screwed over by a one-night stand."

"Your ideas are always too showy," Paul said, though he also found them so endearingly vindictive that he couldn't mind. "What if someone saw you together? What if he doesn't behave *exactly* the way you need him to? It has too many variables."

"You're such a drag, Pablo."

They never mentioned their first idea. In the light of day it had flaws enough, but Paul didn't want to dissect what was already dead. It was better to leave it in the summer, along with the unburnt house and the letters too painful to reread and every other thing they had consigned to silence. With the Frommes out of reach, their target was constantly shifting. It was always "the subject," a hateful ever-changing *him*— someone who by callousness or malice had earned the privilege of being killed, though he had never touched the nerves they both wanted to forget ever feeling.

They could never approach the perfection of the house fire, even if their newer techniques were objectively more sound. It had become an idle game, a chance to enjoy each other's cleverness. But it reminded Paul what they were capable of, even as everything else between them was riddled with the unspoken.

"Needle's getting close to empty." Paul folded his arms and watched the amber gleam of passing streetlights glide over Julian's face and hands. "Tonight was my idea, you should let me pay to fill up."

"Nice try," said Julian, drowsy and unconcerned. "It's nothing, I liked having a chance to get out of the city—"

The interior of the car was suddenly alight with red and blue. Swinging out of a cross street not far behind them, a police siren gave a single, yowling cry.

Julian sat up straight and turned in his seat. "Fuck. *Fuck*, I'm not even speeding!"

"It's fine, just pull over. He might only want you to get out of his way."

But when Julian brought the car to a nervous halt, the police car pulled over behind them. It occurred to Paul abruptly that they might actually look suspicious in the dark. Bundled in the back seat, the telescope resembled a sniper's rifle, as if they were a pair of contract killers fleeing the scene of an assassination.

"Christ." Julian had gone very tense. "Do I get my license out yet?"

"No, wait, put your hands on the steering wheel and don't do anything unless he tells you."

The officer left his roof lights on as he picked along the crumbling shoulder. He was middle-aged, about as old as Paul's father would have been. He had tired eyes and a thick mustache. The name NOWAK was embroidered at his breast. Even if Paul had met him before, he was too much like every other beat cop in the city to summon any specific memory.

Julian took a moment to find the officer's eyes in the dark past the glare of the flashlight. "Is my taillight out?" he asked. He offered a conciliatory, apologetic smile, and Paul realized with a lurch of panic that Julian was planning to treat the officer like any other adult in a position of authority—he was going to be earnest and cheerful and self-deprecating, every unthreatening quality that Paul's mother was charmed by and that a police officer would regard with instant suspicion.

Nowak didn't answer the question. The faint shape of his face grew grim in a way that made Julian shrink back in his seat.

"You boys know what time it is?" He asked it flatly, as if he didn't expect an answer so much as an excuse.

"We're just heading home." Julian still hadn't abandoned the persona, though it was unraveling at the edges. He glanced reflexively at his watch and smiled again. "There was a meteor shower we wanted to watch, we had to head out past the smog to be able to see it."

"A *meteor* shower."

"The Perseids." Paul couldn't tell if Julian thought the name would jog the officer's memory, or if he just thought it was a disarmingly eggheaded thing to say. When neither proved true, he spoke again, voice audibly pitching with nerves. "They happen every year. It's—"

"You were just . . . out looking at the stars. *That's* your story."

Paul had awful visions of a night spent in lockup with the local hustlers and drunkards—of the telescope, which had cost his grandfather a small fortune, wasting away in an evidence locker until it made its way to a police auction. He had to say something before Julian could make the situation worse.

"Don't mind my friend, he's never talked to a cop before."

Paul's voice was so firm and self-assured that Julian turned to stare at him. The beam of the flashlight moved from Julian's face to Paul's, and he was all but blinded by it. "Listen," he said. "Do you know Frank Malone?"

A long silence. The flashlight wavered just barely.

"You could've made that up," the officer said finally. "Enough cops on the force named Malone. What's he supposed to be, your dad? That red hair don't make you look Irish."

"Ha, ha. He was my dad's captain." It didn't occur to him to be surprised at his own easy candor until he saw that Julian's mouth had fallen open slightly in shock. "*His* name was Jakob Fleischer, badge number five-one-eight-four. I don't know Malone's off the top of my head, but I think he's still at the—"

"Jake Fleischer?" The officer lowered his flashlight and dipped toward the window to get a better look at him. "Your dad is Jake Fleischer?"

"Was," Paul corrected, but Nowak ignored him and gave a sudden bark of a laugh.

"Jesus," he said, "I remember you. I bet you really *were* fucking stargazing, straight-A student and everything."

Paul felt his mouth pull into a grin. "Yes," he said, "we really were fucking stargazing." He wished suddenly that he wasn't telling the truth—that he was helping them get away with some beautiful crime.

Between them, Julian held very still. But Nowak was no longer paying Julian any attention. He straightened again, bracing his forearm on the roof of the car.

"Listen, you kids better head straight home." Nowak was as gruff and dispassionate as he'd been at first, but all the suspicion was gone. "Couple teenagers out late in a flashy red car—looks like trouble, and not everyone's going to remember your dad."

"We will," Paul promised. Nowak sent them on their way with a wave, and an admonishment to Paul to look after his Ma.

They were across the river before either of them spoke. Julian's hands shivered as he lit a cigarette.

"I've never seen you like that before," said Julian. "Not once."

Giving Julian a moment of novelty meant there were still parts of Paul he hadn't seen. As long as these moments still happened, Paul could almost trust Julian not to tire of him.

"It seems like a waste, though, doesn't it?" he said. "Getting out of trouble when we weren't really getting into trouble at all."

"The night is young." Julian's mouth tilted into a grin. "There's still time."

2.

IT WAS only when classes began at the end of August that it became clear how much time together they were losing. They adapted. Or rather, Paul adapted, while Julian took for granted that he would be the one to do it. Julian's new commitments were immutable—so Paul rearranged his schedule at the garage and quit volunteering at the gardens several weeks early, because that would buy them a few extra hours together. Paul could study anywhere, so he might as well bicycle to the library in the dwindling light, lugging his homework between study carrels to stay within earshot while Julian shelved books. "You should see me trying to do this when you're not around," Julian told him once—his tone was blithe and bored, in a way that intensified the manor-born refinement of his accent. "It's so goddamn dull, I'm at death's door by the end of it. Sometimes I think about running someone down with the cart just to liven things up."

Glad I'm here to entertain you, Paul didn't say, because he wouldn't see Julian again until their statistics class tomorrow afternoon and there was no time to pick fights.

"How many times would you have to do it to actually kill him?" he asked instead, because it was the only safe way to needle him.

Julian wheeled his cart back out from behind the stacks.

"Twice," he said cheerfully. "One to knock him over, and then you just"—here he gave the cart a gleeful shove forward— "aim for the head."

Their shared statistics class was the kind of math Paul had moved past in high school, but Julian needed it for his major, so that was what they took. Whenever Paul dropped by the shabby apartment, he usually spent much of the visit watching Julian wearily rush through his homework. He would have liked to keep up with the books Julian chose for them, but Julian himself hardly had time for them. They could only inch through a book a chapter or two at a time, curled up together in Paul's bed and reading from the same copy. They had to give up on *Pale Fire* after an intractable quarrel about the order in which they ought to read it.

For his part Julian paid him such relentless attention that Paul had to reassure himself sometimes that it wasn't a cruel joke. It reminded Paul of his letters from the summer, affection overflowing, enveloping them both so completely that he could barely see Julian at all. Julian ended up with solid Cs on their weekly stats quizzes, which would have thrown Paul himself into a panic had he done the same, but the lecture seemed little more than an excuse for Julian to leave jokes and doodles in the margins of Paul's notebook. (*Strychnine!!* he wrote, accompanied by an X-eyed stick figure whose limbs twisted like corkscrews. When Paul captioned it with an unceremonious *no*, Julian kicked him.) He'd always touched Paul casually in public, letting his hand rest on his arm or his back just long enough to send a shiver through his body, but there was something different about it now, less careless, lingering a moment longer than he would have before. Now and then Julian would catch his eye and offer him a small private smile, neither aloof nor teasing, asking nothing. It looked so strange on him that Paul knew it must be an invention—not insincere, just designed, as if Julian were indulging him with a gift he didn't really deserve.

Paul tried to adapt, the way he had to everything else. He took in the affection without flinching, no matter how pathetic it made him feel. There was no time to doubt Julian, so he tried not to. All he could do was try to become the version of himself he could imagine Julian really loving this way—fierce and brilliant enough to match him, as fascinating as Julian thought he ought to be.

He decided to learn to be impulsive, which meant planning the impulse so exhaustively that he could almost ignore his misgivings. But it convinced Julian, as if he were so eager for Paul to impress him that he didn't think to question it. There was finally a day when Paul worked up the nerve to pull him into an empty classroom and barricade them inside, and the only thing that kept his resolve from wavering was the startled noise Julian made into his mouth. When he pinned Julian to the desk, Paul could feel an anxious laugh waiting inside Julian's chest, and afterward he collapsed into such wild hysterics that Paul had to cover his mouth until he stopped.

"What's gotten *into* you?" Julian asked once he'd caught his breath, but Paul couldn't trust himself to summon an answer that didn't sound like a lie.

The novelty never seemed to wear off. Julian would always grin when Paul kissed him in public and shudder now and then with suppressed laughter, and Paul was so terrified of being caught that he could barely speak for fear of being overheard. But they took every chance they could find, whenever they found a dark music room or a little-traveled stairwell. Midway through Julian's late-evening shifts, Paul would seize his arm and lead him to a secluded spot behind the bound astrophysics journals. That always felt the most perilous, somehow, not because of any greater risk of being found but because they had to return to normal so quickly. Julian would go back to his cart, flushed and jittery, compulsively smoothing his hair long after he'd put it to rights. Paul would in his nearby carrel with his pile of books, barely moving, feeling so different from the person he really was that he wasn't certain he still had the same name.

For Paul it was never just a matter of making up for the time alone that they'd lost. What was important was that for all his newfound gentleness, Julian could still look at Paul as if there were something elusive inside him—something he wanted but couldn't quite reach.

IN THE cataclysm of summer Paul had dreamed of things getting back to normal. He'd imagined that after they finished grieving, his family would fall into its usual patterns, and that, reunited, he and Julian would eventually remember their own, despite everything. In several months there would be a second candle for the father who had abandoned him, and Paul would retreat into Julian's promises not to do the same. Grief was normal enough that it felt almost safe, and Paul could imagine enduring it forever. He might be able to suspend the two of them together in amber, so long as his unhappiness remained the same.

But there was no stasis, even in the places he had always imagined it. At the end of his great-grandmother's shiva his grandfather flew into a frenzy, and every Sunday his grandparents' house became a little less familiar. A fresh coat of paint on the front door, the squeaky third stair finally repaired, a new kitchen rug woven with the image of a hen and her eggs. His grandfather had never acknowledged Paul's alleged camping trip, which was nearly the same as forgiving it, but when he mentioned "your Bubbe Sonia" there was a hint of accusation in his voice.

There was a cascade of changes in his daily life as well, no

less disorienting for being small enough he might once have
ignored them. The price of their usual brand of toothpaste went
up, and the new one had a slightly different false-mint scent.
One weekend Laurie acquired a pageboy haircut, modeled after that of the straight-haired blond daughter on some television comedy. Laurie's curls contracted the layers into a cloud
of frizz, but she claimed to love it, despite her obvious regret.
Audrey's Volkswagen had new seat covers made from wooden
beads, and no matter how deeply he searched his memory,
Paul couldn't remember noticing when she'd installed them.

But it was his mother who jarred him the most. He realized
one day that he couldn't remember the last time she'd spent a
whole day in her nightgown. Now every morning she would
unfurl her hair from its plait and comb it, and even on the days
that she didn't leave the house she took to wearing lipstick
again, tentative shades of coral pink, as if she were working her
way back up to red. The shift felt so abrupt that Paul searched
the medicine cabinet to see if she was taking a new pill, but he
found only the usual canister of Seconal between the toothpaste
and the aspirin. He decided she must have hidden whatever it
was—if she had simply chosen to feel better without showing
him how to do the same, he would never forgive her.

A particularly unwelcome change was that, after a year and
a half of gentle nagging from her parents and their rabbi, his
mother went back to attending regular Shabbat services. She
treated this as a whim of her own, which shouldn't affect her
children's observance in the least. "You can tag along if you
want," she'd say, already dressed and using her talking-to-the-
neighbors voice. But she had decided that the neighbors would
never again remark on the family's reticence and drawn curtains. There was no real choice in whether or not to indulge

her—even Audrey complied, yawning and reluctant and heavy-limbed from her Friday-night indulgences. They were all afraid one wrong move would push her back into isolation.

Bitter and irrational as he knew it was, Paul couldn't shake the feeling that his mother had made this change in part to ensure that he would spend a few more hours each week being watched. Milling around the parking lot in the same good clothes as last week, the neighbors would chat with his mother, *So glad to see you around more often* and *It does you good to get out of the house, Ruthie, it really does.* But now and then Paul could tell they were more interested in him than in her.

He would have preferred the sympathy and vicarious shame that had followed him since his father's death, or even the wary suspicion after word of the Danny Costello incident began to spread. Now the neighbors looked at Paul with carnival-sideshow curiosity. He wondered whether his mother could hear the accusation in their voices when they mentioned his name to her. Perhaps she had simply decided to pretend it didn't exist, like every other ugliness she chose to ignore.

One Saturday in August the Koenigs convinced his mother and grandparents to come to their house for Shabbat lunch. They lived across the street from Paul's family, a little farther uphill, in a row house built in a mirror of the same plan. Being in their house always filled Paul with a peculiar anxiety, as if he might walk into a room and find his double waiting inside. The Koenigs' dining room, with its robin's-egg walls and gauzy curtains and gleaming cutlery, was patterned on the same lifestyle magazines as the Frommes' house. The echo only made Paul more uneasy. The house's every detail felt precision-engineered to set him on edge.

The Koenig parents were stringently courteous, which was

part of the reason Paul had never much liked them. They complimented Laurie's new hair and Audrey's homemade paisley tunic dress, and pretended the color in Paul's face was a handsome tan rather than a sunburn. Mr. Koenig joked clumsily about Nixon because he knew Paul's grandparents would laugh on principle, and Mrs. Koenig made vague platitudes about his mother's strength and sweetness while reaching across the table to squeeze her hand.

But when Paul's family wasn't looking, the Koenigs watched him from the corners of their eyes, and their fascination and alarm were unconcealed. He remembered a distant Friday afternoon when Mrs. Koenig was watering her plants on the porch, how she'd lifted one gloved hand to wave while Paul and Julian were making their goodbyes. The Koenigs, he could tell, were doing the same thing Paul had been trained to do in his biology seminars: bringing the specimen in for examination, searching in vain for disconfirming evidence.

After lunch the party drifted into the living room with coffee and cake, and the Koenigs' teenage son asked to show Paul his baseball card collection. "I'm not going to *trade*," he assured his parents, "I just want to show him. This cheapskate won't trade for anything. He's got a mint Clemente rookie card and I've never even *seen* it, he'll tell you."

Mrs. Koenig smiled so brightly that no one seemed to notice she had gone a little pale.

"Leave the door open," she said automatically, then added quickly, for the sake of Paul's mother, "I don't want to hear one peep of haggling today."

Eddie Koenig believed he and Paul were great friends, mostly because he believed himself to be great friends with everybody. He was a year and a half younger than Paul and had played shortstop on the same Little League team, where he'd achieved widespread admiration from the other boys for eating a June beetle on a dare. He had skinny legs and rosacea, and his voice, though loud, had not yet finished breaking. His bedroom was right at the top of the stairs, where Laurie's was in the house's mirror image.

Paul reluctantly allowed himself to be installed at the foot of the twin bed, where he paged through Eddie's binder of baseball cards while his companion amiably rattled off batting averages. After a while the texture of the conversation downstairs grew smoother, as if Mrs. Koenig no longer had one ear turned toward the stairwell.

"So listen," said Eddie suddenly. He was speaking more quietly than usual, though his voice still rang. "What exactly do you guys do over there?"

Paul lingered unseeingly over a grainy color image of Dock Ellis, grasping a ball behind his glove.

"Same thing you do over here," he said, a little too sharply to sell the lie. "What kind of a stupid question is that?"

"You know what I mean." Eddie glanced over his shoulder at the open door and leaned across the bedspread to whisper. "When that weird friend of yours goes over when you're alone. Is it grass? Where does he get it?"

"He doesn't." He probably ought to have lied, but he was too irritated to care. "It's nothing like that. How about you mind your own business?"

Eddie leaned back against his headboard again, as calmly as if Paul hadn't snapped at him. Eddie's even temper had always infuriated him—there was an unblemished, unquestionable maleness to Eddie, as if he'd never felt any emotion strongly enough to let it shake him. Downstairs, Paul's grandfather told the punch line to a joke with a familiar rhythm, and the living room erupted with laughter.

"I'm just saying," said Eddie, cheerfully needling as always. "My folks think you guys are homos. Maybe buying pot isn't so bad."

Eddie had clearly expected him to react with revulsion—to counter the accusation with a protest, or to turn it into a joke by returning it in kind. What Eddie clearly didn't expect was for Paul to freeze in horror, wide-eyed and silent, heart beating so hard that he couldn't speak.

Eddie's grin faltered. He took the binder back and held it gingerly, as if he feared Paul's touch had contaminated it.

It would have been easy in that moment to pretend the conversation had never happened. They could have both retreated into the fiction that Paul was invisible, Paul flattening himself into nothingness while Eddie laughed him off and forgot everything. The sheer unfairness of it sent a shiver through Paul's chest.

"So how much do you want me to tell you?"

Eddie tossed the binder onto his dresser and looked at him in confusion. "What?"

Paul didn't allow himself to waver. "You asked 'what exactly we do.'" Paul held his body taut to keep from shaking. "Are the generalities sufficient," he said, "or do you want to know specifically who does what?"

He took a vicious satisfaction in the silence that followed. Eddie stared at him, saucer-eyed; by the time he remembered how to shut his mouth, he'd given up on mustering a protest.

"I'm for a soda," Eddie said. He was deliberately slow as he got to his feet, as if he were fighting the urge to recoil. "You coming?"

Eddie clearly didn't want to leave him unsupervised in his bedroom, but Paul couldn't face the others. While Eddie took the stairs down two at a time, Paul shut himself into the bathroom across the hall. The tile in the Koenigs' bathroom was green instead of yellow; they still bought the Fleischers' old brand of toothpaste. Mrs. Koenig had left a tube of lipstick on the bathroom counter, the same vermilion that marked the rim of her drinking glass. Paul pressed his shoulders against the half-familiar wall and watched his reflection in the mirror over the sink. He practiced neutral expressions, trying to ignore the patter of conversation downstairs, until he finally found a version of his own face that he thought he might be able to keep steady.

3.

WHEN SHE felt Julian had missed too many family dinners, Paul's mother sent him across town with a casserole dish full of cold lamb chops. Paul hadn't told her anything was wrong—when Julian explained his new arrangements to her, he'd been indefatigably cheerful, and he made the shift sound like an idle experiment in self-sufficiency that he could abandon the moment it began to bore him. ("My dad's always on me about 'what it's like in the real world,'" he'd said, the mention of his family so casual that it made Paul jump. "I figured I should get an idea of how things actually work so I can get on his nerves by correcting him.") But even Julian couldn't convincingly lie about how well he was eating when he was out of her reach. While she was filling the casserole dish, Paul's mother quietly scolded Julian in absentia, a muttered monologue about vitamins and protein that she normally directed at Paul himself. "Does he like tzimmes?" she asked Paul a little accusingly, and when he shrugged she made a small disapproving noise and scraped the leftover vegetables into the dish anyway.

Paul expected it to be a rushed, tense visit—Julian hurrying to get ready for an evening shift, and Paul left as usual to sit at the Formica table with his chin in his hands, waiting to absorb any stray flares from Julian's temper. From the moment Julian opened the door, it was clear that he was as brittle and irritable as Paul had expected—after their eyes met, there was a long, exhausting moment in which Julian tried to force calm into his body, as if he were doing Paul a grudging favor that he might withdraw on a whim. He looked at the dish in Paul's hands with his head tilted slightly, as if in kittenish curiosity, but the rest of him was so tense with impatience that Paul wished he hadn't come.

"Ma misses you." Paul gestured sheepishly with the dish—it was olive green and baby blue, emblazoned with cartoon daisies, and if Julian had been in a better mood Paul might have been embarrassed to be seen with it. "She's still reading that *Burr* book," he added when Julian failed to react. "You shouldn't have asked her about it, she has opinions for you now."

"That's kind of sweet," Julian said, but he didn't even try to smile. He lifted the lid off the casserole dish and peered in skeptically. "Ugh, those fucking carrots . . ."

Julian didn't invite him inside. While he was arranging the dish in his empty refrigerator, Paul sidled unbidden through the tiny front hallway. The entire apartment was little bigger than Paul's bedroom. Bookshelves overflowed, and every cooking pan sat out on the stove because there was nowhere else to put them. There was no room for a couch, so two papasan chairs sat jaw to jaw. The only decoration was a cluster of potted plants on the windowsill—cloth and plastic, every one, because Julian couldn't keep real ones alive.

The dining table had to double as a desk. When Paul sat down, he was careful not to bump the teetering textbook-stack centerpiece, but he did pick up the smear of papers and tap it straight. He half listened to Julian telling him he'd called in sick—"You'd better stick around awhile," he said offhandedly, as if he didn't actually care one way or the other, and for a moment Paul hated him for making him dread staying.

When Paul set the papers back down, he realized one of them didn't belong. Among the notebook pages and mimeographed journal articles, there was a single sheet of stationery. It wasn't quite the same as Julian's nautilus-shell paper—blue instead of gray, with a motif up the side of soaring terns. Henry's handwriting was tidy and boyish, very little like his brother's, but midway through the first sentence Paul started hearing the letter in the voice they shared.

I must insist that you put this directly into savings. I will send more as my own expenses allow. If I find the checks have not been cashed, I will be forced to make a personal visit and escort you to the bank myself. As I'm sure you're aware, this would put me in a potentially uncomfortable position, and I trust that if only for my sake you will have the

Julian snatched the letter out of Paul's hand so sharply that its edge sliced a stinging line up his palm.

"Ouch—I'm sorry, but it was *there*, you left it out, I didn't mean to look—"

"Sure you didn't."

Even after the weeks of his relentless affection, Paul could have painted the real Julian from memory. He could use those expensive oil paints to remember the arching scar-darted line of Julian's eyebrow, the way his mouth and the planes of his face rendered the subtle shift from expressionlessness to disdain. Paul never stopped expecting that look, no matter how long Julian withheld it. In painting him, his hands would always know that sudden coldness in Julian's eyes—how his irises could chill even the warmest light the moment it touched them. What Paul had lost was his tolerance for the way it felt. He'd forgotten that whenever Julian looked at him this way, it left a fresh cut. It reminded him he was something Julian wanted but rarely needed.

Julian only let contempt overtake him for an instant, but it was enough. The anger faded quickly, but the frustration didn't. He watched Paul's face a moment longer, then carefully crushed the letter in one hand.

"He's an idiot," he said with curt resignation. "But if this is how he wants to spend their money, I'm not going to try to stop him. At least it's good for a laugh."

Paul hid his hands under the table and clasped them together. He lay his thumb along the cut on his palm and pressed hard, but it refused to sting as much as he wished it would.

"Are you—is the money thing a problem?"

The only reason he'd hesitated was that it sickened him how desperate he was for the question to hurt. If Julian willingly allowed him a glimpse of pain, Paul might feel for a moment that he really mattered—that he could help or offer comfort, find a need in Julian that he could reshape himself to fill.

But Julian's face didn't falter. He leaned against the chair and brushed Paul's hair back from his face with his fingertips—the tenderness was so deliberate and patronizing that Paul wondered for the first time which of them it was meant to convince.

"Julian?"

"Don't be boring."

Paul felt himself flush. Julian looked down into his face with cool satisfaction; then he smiled, as if it were Paul who really deserved the pity, and leaned down to lift his arm by the wrist.

"Anyway, it's under control," he said carelessly. As he spoke, he turned Paul's hand over and inspected it. "It's not worth talking about, maybe you could trust me for once instead of . . . Oh, Pablo, I sort of butchered you, didn't I?"

Reflected in Julian's face, Paul could see his own helpless fury. He saw Julian's bitter impatience, but also his willingness to forgive Paul the anger he so unconvincingly pretended wasn't there. There was no saying what would happen if Paul let himself snap—*You don't trust me, you don't need to, how am I supposed to trust you?* But Julian allowed him to feel it, and he decided magnanimously that putting Paul in his place wasn't worth his time. They could have a few happy moments together now, so long as both of them agreed not to talk about anything that mattered.

"Hard to trust you if you're going to maim me," was all Paul said, but he could see in Julian's face that he knew it wasn't really a joke.

DURING THE long hours they were apart, Paul tried to think of ideas for the game. They were unserious, or at least most of them were. Whenever they reunited Julian came with one or two new ideas of his own, skewing as they always had toward the theatrical and implausible—squashing the subject between the rolling shelves in the library's compact storage room, shoving him over the railing of the third-floor mezzanine in a fall Paul quickly assured him was survivable. Julian's favorite ideas of Paul's were the ones that were gory and outlandish, and Paul indulged him whenever he could, just to make Julian burst into horrified laughter.

Paul no longer bruised his arm in the file drawer to stay awake during long shifts at his grandfather's garage. Whenever he was bored, he wandered to the office window and peered out at the workspace in search of new techniques. The garage was fertile ground for ideas, filled as it was with toolboxes and tire irons and other agents of blunt force. He was proudest of his un-orthodox adaptation of the orbital sander (*place foot on subject's chest, apply sander edge to the throat, turn on*). But he found the most practical option in the hydraulic lift. Everyone knew they were dangerous, which meant no one would be too surprised if something went awry and a car crashed down on someone working underneath. It was a solid plan, he told Julian, provided the person you wanted to kill was a mechanic.

The game gave them something to talk about when the fragmentary moments they seized might otherwise be spoiled. They had aligned a break between classes two days a week so they could have lunch together by the fountain, but the hour was far shorter than it had sounded on paper, not least because Julian (in keeping with a long-standing vice of his) was chronically and remorselessly late. If they fell silent too long, Paul's nerves would spark with frustration, even as he knew he couldn't let himself lose his temper, because the minutes and seconds were vanishing too quickly to waste on a quarrel. Often he could think of little to say that wasn't unkind—he just watched Julian eat his dismal lunches of day-old doughnuts or cheese sandwiches, and listened to the irritability in Julian's voice that meant he was also trying not to snap. For a while Paul spited him by feeling sorry for him, and he hated them both for the hour (really the forty-seven minutes) they wasted twice weekly on resenting each other. So one day he took Julian an extra sandwich and apple with his own lunch, and to keep him from rejecting the gift, Paul brought an offering he knew he would like better.

"The bubble-in-the-artery trick actually works," he said while Julian—flushed with humiliation—twisted the stem off the apple and refused to meet his eyes. "But it's got to be a really massive push of air. It looks like a heart attack unless they look more closely. It's supposed to be excruciating."

When Julian looked up and smiled, there was a shade of sadness in his face that Paul found almost frightening. But his voice was easy and fond, and when he brushed his fingertips along Paul's forearm, it felt as intimate as a kiss.

"God, you're a nightmare," he said.

Paul tried to bring an idea every day, even when Julian himself seemed for the moment to have exhausted his creativity. The most sensible ideas had to wait for the days Julian was in a vicious mood, because if he could aim his frustration at an imaginary victim, there was less chance he would turn it toward Paul. When he could tell that Julian just needed a laugh, he tried to make his ideas messier and more ridiculous. He often accompanied Julian on late-night visits to the laundromat, where the sickly green light turned the shadows under his eyes into bruise-dark smears. Julian would pace and smoke and assemble a makeshift dinner from the vending machine, and Paul would follow him, voice tamped down to an undertone, explaining his newest plan in vibrant clinical detail. He could never resist puncturing his own ideas, no matter how self-evidently implausible they were—but that made Julian laugh too, and Paul tried not to care that the joke was at his own expense.

When the garage's potential started to wear thin, Paul tried to find new possibilities at the forest research station, where he was taking a second-year wildlife ecology practicum for his major. But there were fewer options there—potential methods still existed, but they replaced straightforward brutality with a sterile, academic fussiness that Paul found aesthetically displeasing. There were any number of solvents, of course, that would cause a swift and nasty death if a subject were forced to ingest them— but this option lacked flair, and the certainty of detection made the simplicity seem facile rather than elegant. Most of Paul's ideas there would never be feasible in practice, nor did they approach the cartoonish whimsy of Julian's favorite offerings. It felt to Paul like a failure of creativity, the same as his inability to follow Julian's line of reasoning when he theorized about the mistake that had doomed Kazlauskas to ruin.

The practicum instructor was a postdoctoral fellow named Carrie Sullivan. She wore nearly the same glasses as Paul, and was an older version of the kind of bird-boned, practical-looking girl his mother was always pointing out to him. Sullivan's dissertation had tracked the local population decline of a once-abundant species of hummingbird, and she delighted in telling puns that made the students groan in protest. On days when Paul couldn't borrow a car from his grandfather's loaner fleet, he could call Sullivan first thing in the morning; she would pick him up on the way out to the preserve, driving an ugly olive-green pickup with a faded McGovern sticker on the bumper.

Paul bore her no ill will, which was the other problem. The game worked far better if he could picture a specific subject, which was easy at the garage. He hated one of the mechanics, Carl, for the way he talked about his wife as if her every word and movement repulsed him—it was as if he'd been born to be crushed under a broken lift, and Paul privately worked through the plan in far more detail than he afforded most of the others. And now and then there were bad customers, blond suburban housewives or their crew-cutted husbands, who took one look at Paul's grandfather and didn't bother to conceal their suspicion.

But his practicum was mostly conducted in small groups that spent companionably quiet hours in the forest collecting samples and taking notes. Paul liked Sullivan, in a distant and businesslike fashion that he even extended to a handful of his classmates. A few of the other students annoyed him with their obsequious vying for Sullivan's attention, but even the worst of them were idealists. Nobody majored in ecology for the money, and all of Paul's classmates were sensitive to the consequences of thoughtless complacency. During lunch they would gather and lament the bad portents they'd found in the field—ponds filled with dead fish, soot-blackened butterflies—and Paul would feel with sudden vehemence that these people were his peers, even if they might never be his friends. It felt perverse to bring them into the game, and so it remained an abstract and idle musing that did little to cheer him during his hours there.

"Maybe it just means you need to pop a few coal mine owners," Julian suggested once. "Go where the money is. It's usually a safe bet whoever you find there is worth killing."

It was one of the evenings when Paul had followed him back from work, but they didn't have much time left before Paul's mother would expect him home. Julian was lying on his bed already, still dressed, head pillowed on the side of Paul's waist. This was the nearest he had come in weeks to acknowledging his parents to Paul at all, even obliquely, and it grazed so close to the memory of summer that Paul had to force himself not to flinch. He didn't dare pursue the subject in detail; he could barely even allow himself to think about it. He tried to believe that all he pitied Julian for was his exhaustion—the shock of adjusting to a world that Paul had always taken for granted.

Half expecting Julian to hit him for it, Paul loosened his tie for him and slowly pulled it free. Julian didn't protest. He just glanced up and smiled, and he looked so weary and unguarded that Paul believed—if only for a moment—that there was something in him that Julian needed.

"I thought of one today," he said, while Julian squirmed drowsily out of his shirt. "I think it's kind of your style."

Julian threw the shirt on the floor and settled against his waist again. "Try me."

"The Chem department has one of those big old-fashioned autoclaves that start automatically when the door shuts," said Paul. "We could stick Brady from Ethics class in there and steam him like a dumpling."

"Ugh, *Pablo!*" said Julian, delighted. "That has to be the worst one you've ever thought of."

4.

HE WAS getting better at giving his family the lies they wanted. That wasn't the same as the lies becoming easier.

It wasn't Julian's kind of lying. Paul couldn't invent a new reality from whole cloth, much less pretend to believe it. But he'd developed a surprising intuition for which fragments of himself his family could tolerate, and he was able, with effort, to slice away every extraneous truth until only the acceptable parts of him were visible.

They all wanted to see different things, though their desires lay within the same tight constraints. His mother wanted the piece of Paul that was fond of Laurie, the one that would pick up a quart of milk on the way home without being asked; the Paul who could muddle dutifully through *please, thank you, nice to meet you,* but not the Paul who found it exhausting. His grandparents wanted his sense of justice, his agreeable ear for talk of labor unions and black civil rights and every other way they had spent their lives trying to heal the world's wounds. He could also keep his grandfather happy with idle chatter about baseball and Watergate and his grandfather's park-bench chess games. His grandmother preferred him when he listened, placid and uncomplaining, to historical facts and funny anecdotes she had told dozens of times before.

But they liked him best, all three of them, when they could see the part of him that was shy. Everything about him that worried them could be explained by shyness, benignly and cleanly. He just couldn't slip up and let them see any shard of truth that might complicate it.

The performance was exhausting. Julian tried to explain to him that what he was doing was not lying but "code-switching"; like most liars, Julian had a very narrow definition of what lying actually entailed. But to Paul the difference was semantic. If code-switching deserved its own name, it wasn't because it was any different from lying; it was because this particular type of lying was so much more agonizing than the others.

There were moments, out of sight of anybody who might object, when the forsaken honesty would swell forth in a rush. When his mother wasn't looking, Paul stopped forcing himself to return the neighbors' false smiles when they engaged him in small talk. They already thought he was unfriendly, had thought so since he was a little boy, when shyness really was his most glaring transgression. He was finally giving them what they had always asked of him, and he delighted in watching them regret it. He also stopped feigning indifference toward Carl at the repair garage, not bothering to hold his face steady during a tasteless joke or a vicious remark about his wife. Carl must have complained, because Paul's grandfather pulled him aside one day to inquire about it. Before he could stop himself, Paul enumerated the reasons for his disgust so vehemently that it startled both of them. (Carl, clearly having been chastised, abruptly stopped mentioning his wife at work at all.)

And one night, when Paul was bicycling home from the library through streets slick with rain, a car nearly struck him as it was running a red light. A year before he would have been paralyzed, alight with anger and fear but incapable of action. Now, though, he didn't give himself a chance to think. Before the car could peel away, Paul whipped a bottle of soda from his knapsack and threw it at the back windshield.

He didn't register what he'd done until the car screeched to a halt, its back window cratered and sweating pebbles of broken bottle glass. Paul fled, blood glittering with adrenaline, until he'd gone two miles off course and was certain the driver had lost his trail. When it was all over he felt perfectly, exhilaratingly calm, and that night he slept so soundly that the incident might as well have been a bad dream. The only thing that nagged at him, distantly, was how little the near miss had managed to upset him.

What hung heavier in his memory was a chance meeting about a week later. It was Rosh Hashanah, which meant the synagogue's basement social hall was crowded with the sheepish strangers from other neighborhoods who only materialized on high holidays. Paul's grandmother was paying rapt attention to him, which meant he'd sanded himself down to a sliver rather than worry her.

She had picked out a girl for Paul to meet, which was becoming a habit of hers. Today's offering was slim and solemn, hair a deeper red than Paul's own, with a father who was supposed to be impressive in some way that Paul hadn't bothered to commit to memory. "Find a way to let her know how smart you are," his grandmother said as usual, as she gave him a slight push to send him on his way. "Good girls know how important that is."

As it happened, he never spoke to the girl at all. He was putting off the conversation as long as he thought he could get away with, dawdling by the carafe to fill a Styrofoam coffee cup drop by drop, when a corduroy elbow bumped against his arm. "Excuse me," he heard, from a voice whose familiarity should have warned him to look away. By the time they recognized each other, they had made eye contact, and it was already too late to escape.

"Paul Fleischer!" Professor Strauss, inexplicably, seemed

delighted to see him. He was unchanged, down to the arthritic twitch of his hands and the bleach spot on the plaid cuff of his shirt. "It's such a small town this time of year—semester off to a good start, I hope?"

Paul didn't relish the idea of making small talk with Strauss, but he felt the red-haired girl's presence behind him and could see his grandmother over Strauss's shoulder, making small frantic gestures for him to extricate himself. He felt a defiant thrill when he realized he could ignore her. And as was so often the case lately, once he began talking, he couldn't stop.

Strauss seemed intent on keeping things light. He avoided the topic of the Ethics seminar, instead asking politely about Paul's new classes. He seized immediately on the subject of Paul's field practicum—he must believe it was a safe avenue of discussion.

"It's good to get out of the classroom and spend some time outdoors, I imagine." Strauss glanced across the room, toward a middle-aged woman who was chatting with the rabbi—graying dark hair, high cheekbones, professorial shabbiness that resembled his own. "My wife and I are both birders, too, I don't know if I've ever mentioned—wait, no, forgive me, you're the lepidopterist—but there's a kinship, isn't there? Early mornings in the wilderness, life lists, that meditative quality of watching and waiting. If I had it to do again," he added confidentially, "I might study ecology myself just for the excuse to get out there more often."

Paul watched Strauss's wife as he spoke, only half listening. They looked like siblings, in the way married couples often did; Paul wondered if men and women did that on purpose, choosing mates who were otherwise much like them in order to mitigate the other gender's unfamiliarity. He pictured the two of them with matching binoculars and rainproof parkas, trudging together through a meadow and hoping to catch sight of one of the hummingbirds whose epitaph Sullivan had written in her dissertation.

Paul looked down into his tepid coffee, finally pouring in the packet of creamer he'd been fidgeting with for ten minutes. White bloomed up from the bottom of the cup like a mushroom cloud. An irrepressible outrage had started to stir at the back of his tongue.

"One of my classmates," he said suddenly, "keeps finding sick frogs."

Strauss looked a little perturbed at Paul's frankness. A crease appeared at his brow, and he took a deep drink from his own cup, buying himself time to think of something to say.

"I shouldn't say 'sick,'" Paul pressed on breathlessly. "'Mutated' is more accurate. Extra legs, or missing ones, or they're growing from the wrong place. One had a fully formed eye in the middle of its abdomen."

"Good god, that's—"

"Amphibians have very porous skin." Paul wished Strauss would walk away from him midsentence; he wasn't certain he could shut up otherwise. "It makes them unusually vulnerable to industrial pollutants, so they're often sentinel species—the working theory is that there's some sort of mutagen in the runoff from the Coke-processing facility upriver. That class makes me so angry"—a sharp, nervous laugh, anger and panic burning inside him—"because—it's just—I'm getting plenty of empirical evidence toward my hypothesis, that the worst damage humans do isn't rooted in malice but in *thoughtlessness*."

"I do remember that notion of yours. Moral laziness as the root of all ills." Strauss appeared grateful that Paul had given him something to argue against, but there was a wary concern in his face all the same. "I also remember trying to push back against some of the assumptions on which you've based it."

The girl, whoever she was, had gone while Paul wasn't looking. By now the crowd was beginning to thin. Paul was dimly aware of Eddie Koenig and his mother at the periphery of his vision, watching through the gaps between bodies and pretending not to listen in.

"For instance, as rigid as your definition of 'moral laziness' is, I did notice a tendency for it to expand conveniently to encompass every moral framework you don't agree with." Strauss stood with a hand on his hip, the way he did when he felt he'd written a particularly salient point on the chalkboard. "To the Milgram example, for instance—I was troubled by your refusal to accept any counterarguments grounded in the subjects' humanity, no matter how well considered the ethical framework underpinning them. You seemed almost to interpret the very fact of a colleague's compassion for the subjects as a confession to sharing that moral laziness, which is a very dangerous assumption not to question."

"If an ethical framework doesn't hold people accountable for their thoughtlessness, it isn't well considered—if the framework is *objectively wrong*, it doesn't matter if it's well argued or internally consistent—"

"'Objectively'?" Strauss looked uncertain whether it was safe for him to smile yet. "And who determines that, Mr. Fleischer? Not you, certainly?"

Paul felt as if all the blood in his body had rushed to his face.

"There's such a thing as right and wrong." Mortified as he was, he couldn't make himself let it go. "Anyone can determine the difference if they're actually willing to think for themselves.

If what they talk themselves into believing is objectively wrong, then they weren't thinking hard enough."

"And that's another place where your theory becomes conveniently all-encompassing," said Strauss. "It's one thing to blame moral laziness for sins of obedience, but I don't think you can stretch that to encompass the deliberate damage committed by true believers."

"How much damage can they actually do without other people to obey them?" Paul countered, but he would never get Strauss's answer.

"Starting the new year off right by arguing with people?"

Paul couldn't tell how much his grandmother had heard, but she wouldn't be so teasing and cheerful if she'd heard anything she didn't expect. As her thin hand settled in the crook of his arm, Paul chipped away at himself until he was small again. The abruptness of the change nearly made him light-headed.

"My grandson," she said to Strauss, "is *deeply* opinionated. I of course have no idea where he gets it."

"I've noticed, believe me, I used to be his philosophy teacher."

Strauss was still stranded in their original conversation; he watched Paul with a slight frown, less intellectual engagement than parental unease. Then he shook himself and smiled, and both he and Paul focused their attention on Paul's grandmother.

"Manners, Paulie," she said to him quietly, her hand tightening just slightly around his elbow. "This is the part where you . . ."

Then he remembered and introduced them to each other, and the conversation was given over to small talk—the real thing, executed properly, by nice people who knew how it was done. Paul barely said a word until Strauss made one last, disastrous attempt to include Paul in the conversation. "Are you still in touch with Mr. Fromme? I remember you two having something of a rapport."

Strauss saw instantly that he had made a mistake, though he also clearly had no idea why. Paul's grandmother tensed beside him, sharp as a splinter of glass. They didn't dare look at each other, though her hand was still cool and firm against his forearm. Paul tried to sand down his last few spurs of honesty; he tried to narrow himself completely to what his grandmother wanted to see, awkward and friendless and naïve to everything outside his own head.

"Not that much, lately," he answered, and Strauss, somehow, knew better than to acknowledge the lie.

5.

THE WALLS of Julian's apartment were painted French yellow, sickly as a fever. In late afternoon the Indian-summer sun swelled through the windows and warmed the brick outside until the air pulsed. It was maddening for their bodies to be so close. The sticky warmth made his skin cling to Julian's wherever it touched.

"I like asphyxiation," Julian said against his shoulder.

They had barely moved in at least an hour, even to disentangle their hands, but Paul was awake to the point of agitation. The rest of the apartment was a clash of clutter, even without his glasses. In turning its narrow confines into a home, Julian had distilled himself to an unbearable intensity.

"It's clean," Julian was saying, "like you said it'd have to be. It'd be sort of pathetic to do someone in with a pillow or a laundry bag or something, but *strangling* them—it's appealingly dramatic." When Julian spoke, the vibrations echoed in Paul's chest.

"It's messier than it sounds." He shut his eyes, but the sunlight pressed scarlet against his lids; there was no escaping it. "It takes upper-body strength, even if you use a garrote. It takes longer than you'd think, longer than in the movies."

After the clinging warmth of Julian's body against his back, the shock of his absence felt like a chill. Paul turned to follow his retreat. Julian was just near enough that his edges were distinct; everything beyond him was a haze.

"Show me."

It was inhuman, the way the light touched him. The shimmer

of sweat on his freckled cheekbones and at the hollow of his throat, the luminous blood beneath the thin skin of his lips. He looked like a peasant boy in a Baroque painting.

"You're sick."

"So are you." He was smiling, just barely. "I know why you fuck me like you wish you could kill me. I know everything that gets you off, you can't help but show me, there's no part of you I can't see—"

He shoved Julian onto his back and straddled his waist. His self-control had snapped so suddenly that he couldn't keep track of his own movements, but Julian didn't even blink. He watched Paul's face, serene and fearless.

"Doesn't that feel better?" said Julian. "Go on. Show me. Don't be a coward."

Paul had no chance to think better of it. He traced his thumb up the line of Julian's throat. He only pressed lightly, just above the curve of his Adam's apple, but between his knees Paul could feel the breath seize in Julian's chest—muscles tensed, scarred skin frighteningly still.

After a few seconds he relaxed his hand, and Julian drew a sharp inhale.

"I'd need both hands, with my whole weight behind them. It takes so much pressure that the bone in the subject's throat will probably snap." He brought his other hand to Julian's neck. Something flashed through Julian's face, too quickly for Paul to tell if it was fear, but even the possibility was dizzying. "Three minutes—that's how long the human body can survive without air. Maybe the subject will die a little sooner from constriction of the carotid arteries, but I can't count on that if I want to be *thorough*."

Julian's face was more opaque now than calm. When Paul tightened his grip again, this time he pressed harder. He could feel the ribbed curve of Julian's windpipe through his skin.

"He has maybe a full minute," he heard himself say, "before his central nervous system starts to shut down. I have to be able to hold the subject in place for sixty seconds while he's fighting for his life—"

A shiver passed through Julian's body, and Paul let go and recoiled. He was terrified that he'd asked too much of Julian's ravaged lungs—there was a discordant note to his breathing, as if it hurt him to inhale. Julian shut his eyes, and when he opened them again, he wouldn't look Paul in the face.

"I'm sorry." A lock of damp hair clung to Julian's forehead; Paul pushed it back so he could kiss the skin underneath. "Julian, I'm sorry, I thought you were all right."

In the moment before he met Paul's eyes again, Julian summoned a teasing, impatient smile. It was almost convincing.

"I'm fine, dummy." He took firm hold of Paul's hands and brought them back to his neck; his expression didn't change, but Paul could feel his tension. "Try again, I'll do better this time."

"I don't want to."

"Of course you do." He was doing such a close impression of being in control that it was all the more frightening that he wasn't. "You liked it, I knew you were going to. Should I fight back like you said? I'll do anything you say, I want whatever you want—"

"I don't." Paul withdrew his hands as soon as Julian let go. "I don't want to hurt you, please don't let me."

Julian's face quickly shifted to conceal something he didn't want Paul to see. He couldn't tell whether it was frustration or relief.

"You're ridiculous sometimes, but that's all right."

Julian plucked a cigarette and ashtray from the dresser and lay back against the pillow; Paul didn't dare touch him at all, much less join him, until Julian pulled him down impatiently by his arm.

Julian hadn't quite relaxed, but he pretended he had. He was retreating into their usual pattern, the one that called on Paul to need reassurance and on Julian to forgive him for it. The performance was comforting, though it had never felt more like a lie.

"I love you." Julian spoke without looking at him. He was watching the ceiling fan slice uselessly through the thick air. "I really do. I wish you could tell."

Paul was startled by the force of his self-disgust. "You shouldn't say that," he said before he could stop himself. Julian didn't answer; he drew a deep, slow breath and shut his eyes, and it was only by the set of his jaw that Paul could tell how furious he was.

They didn't speak for a long time. There was no sound but the occasional sigh of a passing car and the tinny click of Julian's wristwatch beside Paul's ear. He felt sick from the heat, but he couldn't make himself leave.

"You're probably right, about my idea for the game," Julian said. "It's messier than I thought."

6.

IT WOULD be the last time Julian came to pick him up at the research station. Paul never had to ask why. He could tell afterward that it had shaken him, and he wished he couldn't. He didn't like to remember that Julian was capable of fear.

As always, Paul was the last student to leave, too precisely attentive to his notes to rush out the door with the others. "I'm nearly done," he insisted whenever Julian tried to hurry him along. But the pressure to move quickly just made him second-guess himself more, until he was so mired in doubt that his pace slowed to a crawl.

"It's good enough," Julian told him. "You're going to get an A anyway, you might as well leave it."

He had a light scarf tied at his throat, though Paul knew that by now the bruises had faded to almost nothing. Paul idly contemplated strangling him with it.

"It's not about grades. I want my data to be useful."

"I'm sure it'll make all the difference," Julian answered with a pointed yawn. "With all your undergraduate might, you'll single-handedly save the world—"

The door clattered and scraped and Sullivan stumbled inside. She was rattled and grim, her ponytail coming apart in loose dark threads.

"Couldn't wait around for a park ranger," she said when she saw him. "Here, help me."

Paul registered the animal shape in her arms only after the scarlet flash of the wound in its flank—the hanging pelt, matted fur, bright raw flesh. It was a young gray fox, not much larger than Laurie's cat. Sullivan held it firm, one arm braced beneath its body while the other hand held its head still. Paul thought it was dead until he saw the small pained breaths that moved its chest. As if it could feel his observation, it shuddered suddenly in Sullivan's arms, wild-eyed and snapping.

"—Need to sedate him," said Sullivan, while Paul grabbed a pair of gloves and hurried to help her move the fox to the lab bench. "*Mammals*, Christ—sorry—the dosing formula is different for mammals, let me think—hon, we need you over here."

When Sullivan addressed him, Julian shrank back and shut his eyes tight. "No," he said, though he wasn't arguing with her; he didn't appear to have heard her at all. "Please don't, I can't, he's going to die—"

"He's not going to die." Sullivan spoke very patiently, the way she might have coaxed an anxious child. "He's not, but I need you to help us, okay, hon? Just for a few seconds."

After a long moment he obeyed, though he looked as if he might faint. Gingerly, he pinned the fox at its neck and hip. She hurried over to the supply cabinet, wringing her hands in her shirt. When Paul took Julian's place he could feel the harsh patter of the fox's heartbeat in each hand, one at its chest and the other around its throat. It thrashed again, frantic, too strong for how small it was. The curve of its bony spine scraped against Paul's chest; the spasm of movement threw off a thick breath of smells, earth and greasy fur and iron-thick blood. Paul nearly lost hold of it, but he was also stronger than he should have been. He had to be.

Julian hadn't closed his eyes again. His gaze was turned toward the gash in the fox's side, but he was looking through it rather than at it. "Julian," Paul said, but he didn't react.

Sullivan set a vial on the bench and carefully measured the

dose into an oral syringe. Paul had suffered enough ear infections as a child that he remembered those syringes vividly, his mother filling them with a sickly-sweet pink medicine that he always tried to refuse. He knew the fox would clench its teeth against the intrusion because it was what he had always done.

"Good boy." Sullivan nocked the nose of the syringe in a gap between the teeth and pushed the plunger, then held the fox's snout until it choked down every drop. "Good boy, it's all right . . . god, where are all the rangers hiding, they're always underfoot until you *need* one . . ."

It only took a few minutes for the sedative to hit. When the fox relaxed in his arms, Paul moved to arrange it on the table, but the moment he loosened his grasp, he realized it wasn't unconscious. Its toenails clicked on the bench as it tried to stand. When it couldn't stay upright on four legs it sat instead, as agreeably as a dog. The fox looked between Paul and Sullivan with dim interest, as if it had forgotten it had ever been afraid. Then Sullivan pushed gently on its neck until it lay down and rolled onto its side.

It gave Paul an idea for their game, but he let himself forget it for now. He knew it would be a while before Julian would be able to appreciate it.

"Someone got you good, huh?" said Sullivan to the fox. She dabbed its wounded flank with disinfectant. The fox didn't move or make a sound. "Looks like just a flesh wound, though, so hopefully . . ."

Julian had silently drawn up beside him. There was a blot of blood on his scarf, still gleaming red; Julian wouldn't notice it until they were nearly home, and they would have to pull over so he could be sick. But for now he was much calmer. He was moving with such cautious languor that he might have been dreaming. Without asking if he could, Julian pulled off his gloves and petted the fox's ears and forehead. One glassy hazel eye turned upward to follow the motion of his hand.

"Poor thing," he said. "He doesn't understand."

Paul observed Julian's compassion with more unease than fondness. The kindness was sincere, but so was the fascination. Julian could witness suffering and endure it, so long as it was under enough control that he could tease apart how it worked. Once he knew the shape of someone else's pain, he could break off a piece of it—claim it as his own, keep it as a memento under glass—and know they would be grateful to him for taking it away.

7.

THERE WERE signs before it happened, but Julian never allowed him to see them. Paul only recognized them after it was too late.

Of course money was part of the problem. For all that Julian had claimed it was under control, it clearly wasn't. His attempts at budgeting were so haphazard and naïve that Paul couldn't imagine they did him much good—whatever money he saved on food or clothes must have been devoured again by books, and after the start of fall he took to leaving the heat running in his apartment rather than come home to a cold house. He had to be burning through his savings, and the money his brother periodically sent from North Carolina must start to dwindle almost as soon as it arrived.

Paul gave up on trying to broach the subject. When Julian was in a good mood, he assured Paul it wasn't as bad as it looked, with such breezy confidence that he even seemed to believe it. "Rich-people money is complicated," he said. "There are still a few trusts and bonds and things in my name, it would take an act of god for them to take those away. I just can't touch them until I'm twenty-one." Paul never asked what he would do until then, and certainly didn't dare offer advice. Few things made Julian snap faster than having his financial expertise questioned—he'd grown up taking money for granted, and apparently believed that was the same thing as understanding it.

His temper flared at random intervals. An old hobby of making up stories about passersby took on a spiteful tone, without any of the stories' usual humor. There was one woman in

particular—pearls, mauve cardigan matched to her blouse, sandy
hair sprayed helmet-stiff—who passed them on the sidewalk
with a fussy-looking spaniel in tow. "She's going to put him in
the oven the first time he's sick on the rug," Julian said, loudly
enough that she might well have heard him. Paul quickly looked
away into the street rather than meet her eyes.

Julian still came over for dinner whenever he could, but
Paul's family got on his nerves so badly that Paul couldn't figure
out why. Everything on television annoyed him—political talk
shows, bland comedies—but Julian refused to forgo the after-
dinner ritual even when he seemed to abhor it. If one of Paul's
sisters started to tell a lengthy family story, Julian barely concealed his impatience, and would latch on to an insignificant
detail as an excuse to change the subject.

There was one dinner early in October—a Saturday evening,
the first since March that felt as if it might frost overnight. The
kitchen swam with autumn smells, chicken casserole and hot
apple cider and summer dust scorching on the radiator. When
Paul's mother was gathering the dishes she paused at his seat,
smiling a little shyly, and reached down to lift his chin.

"What are you looking at?" Paul protested, and she broke
into a full grin.

"What?" She tapped the end of his nose the way she had when
he was a toddler. "I made a good-looking kid, let me admire."

It would have been merely embarrassing if not for Julian's reaction. He didn't laugh, or even look at Paul at all. He just glared
at his plate, chewing on the inside of his cheek. He barely spoke
for the rest of the night.

There were signs—small, intermittent, easy to ignore. The
pattern never took shape inside his head because Paul didn't
bother to look for it. He'd resigned himself to the way they

skirted around each other's pain and frustrations, not least because Julian had insisted on it.

The call came on a Sunday, when they had hazy afternoon plans to see *American Graffiti*. Paul didn't bother calling ahead before changing out of his fieldwork clothes and catching a southbound bus; both of them were long accustomed to drifting in and out of each other's spaces, as if they were expecting each other. He didn't register Julian's voice beyond his front door until it stopped short at the sound of the knock. It took Paul a fraction of a second longer to realize what it might mean. There was a long pause.

"*Un moment*," Julian said.

The deadbolt slid free. Julian didn't open the door very far. He had the telephone mouthpiece pressed against his palm, the cord knotted through his fingers.

"Didn't we—I mean—" Paul fought the urge to shrink back.

"Go home." Julian spoke in a flat, airless staccato. "It's not a good time."

"Wait, I—"

But Julian shut the door again, and slid the chain lock for good measure. "I'm back," he said. He still sounded as if he was afraid to breathe too deeply. Paul knew he was supposed to leave. He might even have obliged if his heart hadn't been pounding so violently that he could barely move.

Julian spoke to his mother in French. Paul could only understand the long pauses in between, when he could hear Julian pacing; at one point there was the snap and whisper of a match. A few times Julian slipped into English in protest, but his mother didn't let him get more than a couple words in edgewise.

Paul must have stood there for nearly an hour, resting his forehead on the door, listening to something he knew even without comprehending it. He only heard Julian's voice rise once, toward the end of the conversation. Three syllables, none of which he understood, perfectly accented even as his voice wavered.

The silence that followed felt worse than the others. When Julian reverted to English, it was a retreat, as if he could put a barrier between himself and the far end of the line.

"That isn't true," he said, and didn't speak again.

The call ended without so much as a goodbye. Julian threw the receiver into place so hard that the cradle hummed like ringing ears. Paul still couldn't move. He was furious at Julian for telling him to leave, as if he would obey without question. He wanted to take the door off its hinges and force himself inside, to pull apart every hidden working of Julian's life until he knew it well enough to put it back together.

The door swung open abruptly. Paul stumbled backward. Julian had been about to barrel straight through him, but he stopped dead at the threshold when he saw he wasn't alone.

He had his hands in the pockets of his navy-blue raincoat. It was a shade too small for him, the cuffs leaving an inch of bare skin at each wrist, and he looked somehow diminished, narrow-shouldered and thin and younger than he pretended. His face was bloodless except at his mouth and the exhaustion-dark edges of his eyelids.

"I'm out of cigarettes." He lowered his eyes and tugged the door shut; his hands shook as he tried to lock it, but he persisted, patiently, as though he hadn't noticed the problem.

"I'll come with you."

There was no cruelty in Julian's voice. There was no emotion at all. "No. I don't want you right now. Go home."

He gave up on the door and left it unlocked, pocketing his

keys as if he had succeeded. He tried to sidle past Paul into the hallway, but Paul's patience snapped free from its last thread.

"I don't want to." Paul barely noticed how tightly he had seized Julian's arm. "Julian—"

"Do as I fucking tell you."

Paul let go of him. It was all he could do not to recoil altogether. Julian still spoke in a dull monotone, but the words were coming more quickly.

"I will *call* you," he said, "when I'm ready to deal with you. All right? I'll be patient and I'll be nice and I'll tell you how goddamn sorry I am about how much I'm upsetting you. In the meantime I need to go for a walk and put some cancer into my lungs and take a few hours—just a few *fucking* hours—before I have to start managing how *you* feel."

The worst part was that Julian wasn't even trying to hurt him. Paul could tell he hadn't heard the cruelty in the words until they left his mouth. When Julian lashed out at him in the past, each word was precisely calibrated to get Julian what he wanted. But there was no control now, not even a pretense of it. It wasn't that it was the cruelest thing he had ever said; it was that it might have been the first moment of unmediated honesty Julian had ever given him.

Paul had no right to be angry, but he was—the same sour anger he'd always felt as a child when his father chastised him for a transgression of which they both knew Paul was guilty. It was all he could do not to slide backward into childishness and scream "It isn't fair," when what he really meant—what those words always meant—was that he didn't like having to know how fair it really was.

"I was *worried* about you." It was the only thing he could think to say that was actually true, and it still felt like a cheap shot.

For the first time, Julian's eyes fully focused on Paul's face. Even with his shoulders against the wall, he looked hardly capable of staying upright. He was braced as if for a blow, and Paul nearly hated himself enough to oblige him.

"I told you to leave," Julian said quietly. "I can't do it, I can't be *him* right now and I can't stand for you to hate me for it, so please, for god's sake, just go."

He did. It was his own idea, finally, because he could tell for the first time that Julian didn't actually want him to. Leaving mapped perfectly to all Paul's own faults, his all-devouring need and his terror of seeing the truth of it. As he walked away he heard Julian say his name, but he pushed through the front door without turning around.

8.

THERE WAS nothing he could do except prove that Julian's accusation was right. He wasn't capable of anything else. Paul had known that all along—he'd etched it into the white spaces in his journal, between the eager pathetic promises he would never be able to keep. The truth was there in everything about him. Stagnant running times, a body that felt thin as air.

Julian liked to trace his fingertips along the lines of concave skin between Paul's ribs, while Paul held very still and fought the urge to tell him not to look. When he changed out of his clothes that night, he forced himself to examine himself in the mirror. He could feel the ghost of Julian's hands on his rib cage; Paul followed the path of Julian's touch with his fingernails, scraping hard, until blood blossomed just under the surface of his skin.

The next day he searched his flat file and found Julian's favorite of his paintings. Brown wilted flowers and crumbling sunset moth specimens, fruits pitted with mold—a Dutch still life left to rot. It was pretentious and stilted, striving for something it would never reach, and if Julian loved it at all, it was only a fleeting whim he would soon outgrow. Paul cut the canvas free of its stretcher, and with a utility knife and a T square he meticulously sliced it to ribbons.

In the morning Julian had telephoned twice. Paul was out for his run for the first call, and when he returned he found Audrey fielding the second. She was leaning on the wall in the hallway, still in her pajamas, skeptically fidgeting with the phone cord.

When she caught Paul's eye she lowered the receiver from her ear, but she didn't bother covering the mouthpiece.

"It's not even eight," she said. "I thought he went to finishing school or something."

Paul squirmed out of his track jacket and used the inside to dab at the sweat on his neck. His skin felt tacky and gritty, glazed with filth from the polluted air.

"I have my electrodynamics midterm today." Paul tried to make himself sound careless and blunt, the way he imagined Eddie Koenig would be if he turned down an invitation from a friend. But his eye contact with Audrey became a stare, and he could barely feel his face in order to arrange it into the right expression. "I'm headed straight out after I shower. Tell him I can't talk today."

Audrey stared right back at him. This time she did cover the mouthpiece before she spoke.

"Did he do something?" she asked, as if she hoped she could turn the question into a joke depending on his reaction.

Paul folded the jacket over his arm. It was too prim a gesture, not at all belonging to the kind of boy he was pretending to be.

"Nothing's wrong," he said with a shrug. "We don't have to see each other every day."

He headed up the stairs before Audrey could argue. While he passed above her head, Paul thought he could hear Julian's voice in the receiver, but he kept walking rather than risk making out the words.

THE NEXT two nights the telephone rang just before dinner, when Julian knew they would be home. Paul told his mother he would answer, then approached the phone so slowly that Julian might be afraid he was letting it ring.

Both times, he listened just long enough to let Julian hate him. "How long are you going to sulk?" he asked the first time. Paul pushed down the receiver hook without answering, and for a few minutes he listened to the hiss of the dead line while he made one-sided small talk about their statistics exam.

The next evening there was a sharp edge to Julian's voice that Paul had rarely heard before, and he deliberately didn't let himself identify it. "You're being ridiculous," Julian said, very quickly, as if he already knew Paul would hang up on him. "I was upset about *them*, you know it wasn't anything to do with you. Don't be so—"

Emerging from the basement, Audrey nearly caught sight of him tapping the phone hook again, but his hand had fallen back to his side by the time she looked his way.

"He has to work," he told his mother before she could ask, and she clicked her tongue and put two of the raw potatoes back in their basket.

In his head, over and over, Paul spoke to himself in Julian's voice—slightly different accusations each time. While his microbiology classmates chatted through a lull in their midterm, Paul slouched at his bench, chin resting on his forearms, and watched his centrifuge vibrate gently as it spun. He imagined Julian approaching him on his way home, catching him by the arm like a child snatching after a lost toy. That Julian would be impatient and petulant, bored without Paul around to entertain him—not quite tired of being adored, though he would be soon, and they both knew it. "I didn't *mean* it, Pablo," he would say, as if Paul's hurt feelings were the only thing that was wrong. And Paul would follow him home and collapse into his arms, hating himself for how grateful he was for these last undeserved fragments.

But that was only if Julian had anything left to give him. Another variation crept up on Paul that evening—he tried to drown the thoughts out with the music in his headphones, but he felt an echo of Julian sit beside him on the bed, and he couldn't help but listen. This Julian was arrogant and cold, kinder than the first because he was ready to tell the truth. *You're always going to be this way.* (He wouldn't take off his coat. He sat very straight, ignoring Paul's gaze as if he couldn't feel it.) *You're exhausting. It's getting very dull. You don't think this is worth my time anymore either, do you?*

Paul didn't consider skipping their statistics class, because he knew Julian wouldn't, and he wanted Julian to feel himself being ignored. Maybe it would hurt him; Paul didn't mind if it did. But it would hurt Paul more. That was what he really wanted Julian to feel.

Julian was already waiting when he arrived at the lecture hall. He'd settled in their usual spot in the last row, sitting with his ankles crossed on the back of the chair in front of him. When he caught Paul's eye, Julian didn't visibly react. He'd folded every ragged edge back under the surface, as if Paul had only imagined they'd ever been there. Paul paused at the desk, and Julian gave him a prompting smile. When he didn't join him, Julian sighed, and the fondness in his eyes was so patronizing that Paul was sick at the thought that he'd ever tolerated it.

"Don't be dumb, Fleischer."

He was wry and careless. Paul could see his body waiting to shift slightly when he joined him—to lean toward him, break the last of the ice with a joke. But Paul waited in silence, until the slight smile began to falter, then walked away.

HE DIDN'T notice Julian leaving the lecture early. Paul had been sitting toward the front, shielded by a cluster of pony-tailed girls in swim-team jackets. When the lecture ended, the seat in the back row was already empty, but Julian had left behind a book that must have fallen from his bag—it was his careworn chess book, its title nearly ground to powder by the white crease in the spine. Paul scooped the book up and pocketed it, though he wasn't sure whether he wanted to give it back or throw it away.

When he drew close to the bicycle racks, Paul saw Julian waiting for him. There was no escaping him now—he was leaning beside Paul's bicycle, hands in the pockets of his wool coat, beneath a soft vermilion canopy of turning leaves. As Paul approached, Julian drew a deep breath and straightened. There was something unsettling in the way the golden autumn light moved over his cheekbones, a beauty so fleeting and elusive that Paul knew he wouldn't be able to hold it in his memory. *Keep this*, he pleaded with himself, but it was already nearly gone.

"Hey, Pablo."

Paul couldn't make himself answer. He knelt silently to unlock his bicycle. Julian stood over him, excruciatingly close, and rested his fingertips on the handlebar.

"Is it that you want me to say sorry? It's a little kindergarten of you, but I'll do it, if that makes you feel better."

Just being near him slid Paul's eyes back into sharp, unbearable focus. The dying leaves glowing behind him like stained glass—colors searing, brighter than they'd ever been, as if the world was only real again now.

"I don't need you to be sorry."

Paul got to his feet and shoved the bicycle lock into his knapsack. He only realized he was smiling when he saw a flash of fear in Julian's face.

"You were right," Paul went on in a rush. "I'm not worth the effort. I don't give you anything worth having, all I fucking do is *need*, I'm repulsive, it's not like I can blame you—"

"I never said a *word* of that."

"You didn't need to. I know it's what you meant."

Julian's silence was as good as a confession. His face was so blank that Paul could read anything he wanted in his features. He chose disgust.

"I'm never going to deserve you." He couldn't stop talking. Part of him didn't want to. "I know everything that's wrong with me, and I can't fix it, I don't even know how, nothing I try works. No matter what I do, I'm still weak and afraid of everything, I'm not brave like you—"

"You have no idea what I'm afraid of," Julian tried to cut in, but Paul refused to parse anything but the bitterness in his voice.

"Nothing I do is ever going to matter." The longer he spoke, the lighter he felt. "Everything I do is so small and so useless. I'm not like you. I don't even have a shape of my own to hold anything else in place. The world would be exactly the same without me—if I disappeared you'd be the same, as if I'd never been here at all. I'll never matter the way you do, and you know it. You don't *need* me."

Julian had gone unnaturally still. It was intoxicating to believe he was frightened and repelled by this hideous thing Paul had finally revealed himself to be. The thought filled Paul with such sick euphoria that he could hardly feel his body any longer.

"Why do you think I'm here?" Julian's voice was so slow and cruel that his panic was almost undetectable. "I could have decided I could get by without you. It would've been easy. I could have stayed with them and gone to goddamn Georgetown, I could've done everything they wanted, and I would've been fine, mostly—and I didn't. I chose *you*. But that can't possibly mean anything, can it? Because you don't *matter*."

It was a while before Paul could speak. He remembered the paperback in his jacket pocket and removed it carefully, trying in vain to smooth the tattered cover. He could feel the years of Julian's fingerprints beneath his own. It was a long moment before he forced himself to offer it back. When Julian took it, he held it gingerly with the tips of his fingers, then suddenly rolled it tight until the pages touched the spine.

"You're free now. I just helped you escape."

When he tried to wheel the bicycle back from its berth, Julian dropped the book and grabbed the handlebars. He was trying to look bored and exasperated, and when he spoke again he nearly sounded it. He certainly wasn't afraid. Everything about him said so except for the tightness of his grasp.

"I'm sorry, all right?" said Julian. "For god's sake, I should have known you were going to do this, every possible excuse to hate yourself and you take it. If you'd just calm down and listen to me—"

The apology was too spiteful not to be sincere, and Paul was no less pitiful for deciding not to believe it. He wanted nothing less than a plea for mercy, a promise to need him and keep on needing. He wrenched away the handlebars and swung the bicycle around. Julian's hands hung in the air for a moment in the place where they'd been, as if he didn't know what to do with them now. This time there was no pretending not to recognize

Julian's alarm, and Paul took no comfort in how quickly he pulled himself back under control.

"You didn't want to 'manage me,'" said Paul blankly. "So don't."

When he left, Julian didn't try to stop him. He stood under the soft haze of sumac leaves, arms folded around himself, as if he were waiting for Paul to change his mind and turn back.

The world became a blur again; Paul's bicycle wheels barely seemed to touch the ground. The ride home was a blank space in his memory that he would never be able to fill in. He didn't remember pausing at intersections or slowing pace as he descended a hill. Somehow he was home safe, and he must have spoken to his family without worrying them, because then the others were downstairs, busy and unconcerned, and he was alone up in his room. He had no words left in his head, no ideas. He barely thought about Julian at all. All he could think about was throwing himself against a wall, over and over, until he'd smashed himself into shards so fine that the void inside him could finally slip free.

9.

PAUL DIDN'T hear Julian's arrival through his headphones, but he felt it. The record had ended, but Paul was lying very still on his bed, listening to the rustling circle of dust and static. It took him a long time to sit up, and longer still to open his eyes and switch off the record player. He examined his reflection in the mirror on the back of his bedroom door and tried to purge himself of any sign of emotion—when it didn't happen quickly enough, he struck himself across the face, then again, harder. The nervous energy faded into a brisk, stinging calm. He paused at the top of the stairs. He had the idea that he ought to brace himself, but he didn't need to. When he heard the sound of Julian's voice the pain was breathtaking, and Paul accepted it because he knew it was exactly what he deserved.

" . . . my mother, but that's not an excuse. She got under my skin, she always does, I should be used to it by now . . ."

"I'm sure he understands, sweetheart." Paul could almost hear his mother wringing her hands. "Do you still like that blackberry tea?"

"Mrs. Fleischer, that's very kind, but it really isn't necessary—"

As Paul emerged from the stairwell, Laurie darted past on her way to put the kettle on. The cat ambled after her, tail held high. Audrey was lingering in the living-room doorway in her work clothes, wearing one boot and dangling the other from her right hand. She noticed Paul before the others did, and she gave him a shrewd, scrutinizing look.

When Julian looked up to meet Paul's eyes, there was a

split second of quiet. Then Paul's mother turned to follow Julian's gaze, and the moment was over before Paul could understand it.

"I'm so glad I caught you." Julian gave him a cautious, apologetic smile, allowing it to linger long enough for Paul's mother to glance back and see it. "I feel awful, I didn't mean to sound so snappish, my *nerves* are just—god, you don't hate me, do you?"

Paul thought there was something off about Julian's body language, until he realized suddenly that the persona he wore could barely conceal what he was feeling. The fear and sadness and shattering exhaustion were all real and starkly visible. But if Julian couldn't hide his feelings, at least he could weaponize them. Of course he would allow Paul's mother to see past the surface. She was sweet to him and he liked her, and both sides of that fondness could be useful to him now.

Paul couldn't guess what Julian had told his mother, but it didn't really matter. She had so many things she was already pretending not to notice that Julian's flimsy self-defense would barely register. When she looked between them again, echoing Julian's wary smile, Paul knew she had already decided the answer for him.

"I don't think you snapped," Paul heard himself say. "You just seemed tired of everything. I don't blame you."

He wanted the truth to make Julian falter, but if it did, he didn't let it show. Paul felt Audrey glance toward him again, but he refused to acknowledge her.

"Honey, I wish you'd sit down." Paul didn't immediately realize his mother wasn't speaking to him, and it took even longer for Julian to reach the same understanding. "You must be freezing, it's too cold for just a jacket—is the electric blanket still in the hall closet, Audrey?"

Audrey refused to take the hint. "Probably," she said, raising her foot and tugging on her second boot.

His mother flew into a frenzy of affection. She installed Julian on the couch and flitted into the kitchen for a tray of tea and cookies, which Julian insisted (from beneath the inevitable electric blanket) that he didn't need. Paul couldn't hang back without drawing his mother's attention, so he sat beside Julian and fidgeted with his cuffs, gazing blankly at the faded sunflower-print curtains in the front window.

Audrey plucked her coat straight by its lapels. She caught Paul's eye and nodded toward the front door, as if to offer him a chance to escape, but he just stared at her until she gave up and left on her own.

As soon as she'd gone, Julian leaned forward to force Paul to meet his eyes. Up close the ring of lavender around his eyelids looked darker, flushed with blood; the chill had scraped some color back into his cheeks and the rough chapped line of his lower lip. His fragility was frightening, and Paul knew without a doubt that Julian wouldn't let him see it unless he thought it would get him something he wanted.

"We're going for a drive soon," said Julian in an undertone. "You're going to listen to what I tell you this time. The other conversation is closed, and you're going to leave it that way. You're right—I really don't feel like managing you."

Paul gazed back at him, almost through him. He didn't register the words themselves so much as the steady authority in Julian's voice—how unconvincing it was, though it sounded the same as it always had. He had no chance to answer even if he'd had anything to say. Paul's mother returned, and Laurie drifted to the doorway after her to covertly examine them.

The closeness between them was overwhelming, all the more because Paul wasn't sure how long he would still be allowed to feel it. He drifted in and out of the conversation as he lost himself in the restless warmth of Julian's body alongside his.

Piece by reluctant piece, Julian told Paul's mother a story Paul himself hadn't been allowed to hear. There were details Julian hid from her—he skirted around the reason his parents had tried to tighten their grasp, so deftly that Paul's mother didn't seem to notice the elision. But everything else felt true, or nearly. Julian was tired and unmoored and overwhelmed, everything Paul's mother would expect him to be. There was so much arithmetic he had never been taught how to do, so many costs of getting by that he'd never known to anticipate, and he didn't know where to start when it came to learning them. At least he had some padding in savings now, thanks to Henry— "Poor Henry," Julian said, and seemed to mean it, because the phone call from their mother had been to announce that he'd been caught. Julian would be all right, he claimed. That was the part Paul least believed. He wasn't sure how much his mother believed it, either.

At one point Paul's mother cut into the explanation mid-sentence; it was the only time she interrupted him.

"What's your mother's name?" she asked, with a familiar piercing frankness that had lain dormant for so long Paul had nearly forgotten she was capable of it.

Julian paused. He couldn't seem to make sense of the question, and it took a moment for him to decide that it didn't matter.

"Delphine."

"Delphine," she echoed. She contemplated the name without

elaborating, but Paul could see her making an enemy of it, this lone elusive trace of a woman she would never meet.

Paul would have expected his mother to divest Julian of every other detail, but she was careful. She pressed just lightly enough to draw out the generalities, chipping away at her own worry until she was satisfied that Julian wasn't in any immediate danger. Paul remembered this was how she had dealt with his father's quiet dark moods years ago, offering meals and distractions and letting the most painful parts of the truth go unspoken. If Paul hadn't known better, he'd think she couldn't detect the worst of it at all. She let Julian pretend to be unhurt and unafraid. She monitored his progress through the cookies and chided him if he stopped eating, and whenever he evaded a question she let it lie for a while before finding another way to ask it. Paul had forgotten she was capable of moving so deftly when she needed to.

By the time his cup was empty, Julian decided he'd put her at ease. She let him believe it.

"Is it okay if we go for a drive?" The deference in his voice was the first flash of artifice he'd shown all afternoon. "I'll have him home for dinner, I promise."

"You'll *both* be home for dinner," she said, and Julian started when she leaned forward to squeeze his arm. "It's a standing invitation, it always is. Today I insist."

She forced Julian into an overcoat before they left—one that had belonged to Paul's father, gray wool, poison-sweet with naphthalene and pipe tobacco. As they were driving away Julian shrugged it off. He rolled down the window and lit a cigarette. It was his old brand, richer-smelling and more expensive. Paul didn't dare ask where he was getting the money.

"I was worried she'd keep us there too late." Julian leaned

back in his seat and rested his fingertips on the chrome frame of the side mirror. "But this should work out perfectly."

Beneath his languid posture Julian was still so uneasy that Paul could hardly bear to look at him. He yearned for Julian to claim his authority again, even if it was unconvincing. But Julian was still human and volatile and impossible to predict.

"I'm supposed to listen." Paul could just barely hear himself over the whip of the wind past the windows. "So say what you need to say."

"Hm?" Julian took the cigarette between his two forefingers and brought his hand back to the steering wheel. There was a trace of a tremor in his hands—when he looked toward Paul he broke into a strange grin, edgy and feral, as if he were afraid of what might happen if he stopped smiling. "Oh, I don't have a speech or anything," he said breezily. "You never like those. You're such a goddamn scientist, you always need empirical evidence."

"Evidence of what?" Paul asked before he could stop himself, and Julian burst into such sudden wild laughter that Paul shrank back in his seat.

"Anyway, I got you a present." Julian took a long, shaky pull from the cigarette. "It's not terribly portable, at least not yet. But I think you'll like it."

There at last was the authoritative confidence, every note false and flat. For an agonizing moment Paul couldn't imagine why he'd ever been taken in by the performance—it was so obviously a lie, pretentious and childish and transparent.

"Julian, I'm not angry at you." It wasn't quite true, but it should have been. "It isn't about what you do or don't give me, it's about everything I *take*, I don't need you to give me anything else when I know I don't even des—"

"If you say the word 'deserve' one more time I'm driving us off a bridge." He gave another brittle laugh. "God, you're so boring when you get your feelings hurt and decide they have to *stay* hurt . . ."

Paul didn't dare protest. He restlessly tugged his sleeves over his hands. Julian, unconcerned, leaned forward and switched on the radio.

"You're going to love it, Pablo," he said. "Please just trust me. This is something I want to give you."

He turned the radio up too high for Paul to answer without shouting. They wended through the familiar spaghetti junction of residential streets north of the colleges, not speaking. Once they had passed through Bloomfield, Paul had only a dim idea where they were—north, far north, enough to have traded the muddy metallic scent of one river for another. Julian turned down the radio and idled the car in a crumbling asphalt lot next to a playground. He was watching one of the houses across the street. It was shabby and brown and nondescript, with a scuffed armada of old cars parked in the gravel drive.

"It shouldn't be too much longer." Julian lifted his cuff to check his watch. "I don't see his car, but this is about when he gets home."

Paul watched him stub out his cigarette and switch off the engine. Julian rested his fingertips on the lower lip of the steering wheel and took up a silent piano concerto against the wheel's leather seam. Paul couldn't bear his nervousness, so he looked away, toward the house's rusting chain-link fence and sagging front steps.

"Aren't you going to ask?"

"I'm afraid to."

"Don't be," said Julian with a smile. "It's right up your alley."

A pea-green sedan had appeared at the corner. It pulled to a halt in the driveway, headlights flicking dark.

"There he is," said Julian, but Paul hardly heard him. The driver stepped out of the car, burdened with a bookbag and a sack of groceries. It only took Paul a moment to recognize him.

"Oh," he heard himself say. He couldn't tell how much he understood when he started to speak, but by the time the word had finished forming in his mouth, he knew.

Brady was in a sour mood; it was clear even from a distance. He kicked the car door shut and set his bags on the hood, then stalked across the uneven lawn to move the trash bin back from the curb.

"You mentioned him as a joke a while back." Julian's voice was quiet and merciless. "But he'd be perfect. He's already all but confessed that if Milgram asked nicely he wouldn't think twice. Banality of evil wrapped up with a bow. And *petty*," he added with sudden vehemence. "God, that's what always made me loathe him, the way he wound you up on purpose and then acted smug when you got angry . . ."

Paul watched Brady's hands heave the strap of his bookbag back over his head. Six months ago he'd found those hands fascinating—the unrefined broad-fingered masculinity that he knew his own hands would never grow into. But he thought now of an older memory. General chemistry, first semester, Brady serving as the student assistant. The incongruous delicacy of those same hands as he demonstrated, with fine well-practiced movements, how to use a burette.

"We might find a way to electrocute him. Ramp the shocks up bit by bit, just like the experiment," Julian said. Paul could feel Julian watching him, ardently, eagerly, but he was too transfixed to meet his eyes. "I know it's kind of involved, I know you like it more practical—but the *symmetry* of it . . ."

Brady propped the grocery bag on his hip while he pulled the front door closed behind him. Paul stared even after he was out of sight, at the dim flickering porch light and the brass house number ringed by tarnish. When Paul forced himself to look away, he saw a patch of dying sunlight break between the tree branches and fall across Julian's face. As if for the first time, Paul noticed the slim golden ridge of hazel at the inner edge of his irises.

"You haven't said anything. Don't you like it?"

He didn't know how to answer. It would be unforgivable to do something so trivial as to *like* the coolness in his chest. There was something almost sexual about it, the unbearable tension and the fearful desire for the moment it would snap.

"Wait." He only saw the flaw after he spoke; it took a moment longer for the disappointment to catch up with him. "It can't be him."

Julian looked as if all he could see in Paul's face was spite. "What?"

"I'm sorry." Paul knew he was right, and he hated himself for it. "I'm sorry, but it can't be him."

"Why not?" Julian looked toward the closed front door. Beyond the threshold Brady would be putting away bean cans and chiding his roommates for not bringing the trash can back from the curb—forever oblivious to his own maddening, undeserved luck. "You hated him, I remember how much you hated him—"

"That's why." Paul tucked his arms around himself to keep his hands from shaking. "You remember I hate him, and so will everyone else in that class. That's *motive*. Motive gets people caught. It can't be him."

"For Christ's sake!" There was something painfully uncalculated and desperate about Julian's frustration. "Why bother *doing* it if there isn't a motive?"

"There can't be a detectable connection to us, it's too dangerous, it's safest for us if he's a stranger—"

"So we would have to just pick up some random person off the street and hope we lucked into someone who's actually worth killing? Great, you're right, that's a much better plan."

That *had* been calculated, which was a relief. Paul didn't even try to fight the expected response. He looked away and drew back.

"Of course not, for god's sake." He couldn't decide whether he was trying to placate Julian or pick a fight. "All I'm saying is, he has to be a stranger—that doesn't mean there's no way to tell what kind of a person he is, there's got to be a way to do this safely and still have it *mean* something."

"It's *barely* a motive!" said Julian despondently. "You argued with him a few times, months ago, in a class where people are supposed to argue. What kind of cop would ever dig that deeply?"

"My father, for a start," Paul said.

Julian had no answer to that. He closed his mouth and sat up straight; he was very still, staring across the street at the darkening shape of Brady's front door. Then he blinked hard, raked his hand back through his hair, and keyed the ignition.

Paul turned in his seat to watch Brady's house recede behind them. It looked no different from its neighbors. It didn't conceal anything that couldn't be found behind millions of other front doors. If not for class rosters and long memories it could have been Brady, easily and cleanly, but only because Brady could have been anyone. They were everywhere, silent and safe be-hind opaque walls, waiting for an atrocity to which they could consent. Paul had known it his whole life, even before he could put it into words. He'd always been so small and helpless in the face of what the world was; no matter how he raged, nothing he knew how to do could ever leave a mark.

They turned onto an overpass headed south, soaring over a gleaming stripe of unmoving headlights. Pollution-orange sun-light seeped through the windows and set fire to everything between them, clothes and skin and particles of dust.

"It was almost right." His voice sounded strange in his head, grown-up and certain.

Julian gave him a wary sidelong glance. But for the first time since they'd met, Paul was confident Julian wouldn't be disap-pointed in him. He trusted the inevitability of their understand-ing each other.

"It'll be someone like him," he said. "They're everywhere. He couldn't help but reveal himself, so it won't be hard to find another one. It doesn't even occur to them to be ashamed."

Julian's eyes flitted back to the road, but the tension in his body broke, and Paul understood at last that the offering wasn't a challenge or a dare but a declaration of trust. Amid all the weakness Paul couldn't conceal, Julian had somehow seen the potential for something better, something fierce and vital and worth loving. It wasn't just an entry in a private game. It was evidence of what Julian saw in him, of his potential to leave a mark on the world that could never be erased. It was a relief and a horror to be known so perfectly.

10.

THE PROCESS was all Paul's design. He drew up a flowchart on graph paper one morning and brought it with him to review with Julian over lunch.

Julian burst out laughing the first time he saw it—"I'm sorry, Pablo," he said with giddy horror, "I'm sorry, it just looks like a poster at a fucking science fair." But Paul didn't retreat, even though his face was burning. Once he might have been too humiliated and self-conscious to hold his ground, but he reminded himself that Julian thought he was capable of better.

As they talked through the steps, elbow-to-elbow at the tiny Formica dining table, Julian's nervous laughter gradually subsided. They would gather information in stages until the options winnowed down and they had enough data to make their final decision. It was a good process, precise and well considered, everything it needed to be if they were going to make this count.

"You're taking this so seriously." It was the first time Julian had managed to speak without laughing. There was something different in his face now.

"Of course I am," said Paul. "We have to. Otherwise it won't mean anything."

They had to choose carefully—just the right weak point where they could leave their indelible mark. A single person, their pliant and obedient opposite, who carried atrocity inside him like a loaded gun.

THE FIRST step was easy. Paul had known it would be. The candidates were countless, their names suspended in the microfilm of back issues of the local papers. Dozens of names, hundreds, more than they would ever have time to investigate.

Some appeared as bystanders—innocently turning up the hi-fi to drown out months of the neighbors' screaming, then just as innocently proclaiming shock when the man next door finally killed his wife. Paul culled other candidates from letters to the editor, where they signed their full names because they were proud of what they'd written. It was sad for the families, they wrote, but those longhairs at Kent State should have known what they were inviting on themselves. Agent Orange saved some American troops, and so did the atomic bomb; the collateral damage was the other side's problem, not ours.

The My Lai courts martial had summoned the worst of these—the letters were so vile Paul often couldn't finish reading them. The villagers weren't really civilians, and even if they were, slapping any soldier on the wrist was too brutal a punishment. The soldiers had descended into savagery at Calley's orders, and they couldn't disobey their senior officer; Calley was just following Medina's instructions, and so on, up the chain of command, until somehow the massacre wasn't anybody's fault at all. Orders were orders—you couldn't fault a soldier for following orders.

If they could have made their decision with perfect objectivity, any of the candidates would do, but they had to be practical, and that meant a second step of disqualifying any candidates who might make them waver. The subject had to be a man, because otherwise their motive could be mistaken for common brutality; for similar reasons, they promptly abandoned any address that mapped to a black neighborhood. Sometimes the problem was simply that too many years had passed, and the names were no longer listed in the telephone directory at all—Paul always hoped those candidates had died on their own, destroyed by excruciating disease or the weight of their own shame, but there was no time to spare to search the obituaries.

Julian quickly stopped participating in the first two steps. He had no patience for them, and anger didn't invigorate him; all it did was make him squeamish. Often Paul attended to this task alone, while Julian clocked into work and spent a few hours nearby shelving books. Other times Julian kept him company, sitting with his back to the screen and paging through his dog-eared copy of *L'Etranger* with endearing ostentation.

"I trust your judgment," he told Paul, unconcerned. "It's the same as mine, anyway. You're just more *decisive* about it. Play to your strengths—I'll play to mine."

Paul only worried about it at the very beginning, and even then only a little; Julian's enthusiasm returned so decisively after the first two steps that Paul quickly forgot his worry that he was really going it alone. The third step turned out to be Julian's favorite.

They never forced a lock. Most of the candidates kept a spare key near their front doors. Under a welcome mat or a planter, usually; once they even found it in the gap between the exterior wall and the mailbox. If they couldn't find a key, they struck the name from the list and moved on to the next. There was too great a risk that Paul's penknife would leave a sliver of metal inside the lock, or that a tiny scratch left in the brass could be matched to the blade. (Not that either of them knew how to pick a lock, anyway. Neither had been the right kind of boy.)

Julian took to it like a naturalist setting foot for the first time in the Galápagos. Paul never tired of watching him work—the way he carefully stepped over magazine piles or strewn clothes, the fascination with which he examined family albums and desk drawers. Paul never lowered his guard, because a candidate might bring his mother home from church early or return from the bar after just one drink. But Julian's unhurried enthusiasm steadied him, helped him see past his own nerves. Among the banal ephemera of the candidates' lives, Paul began to see fragments of beauty and promise—the first bright strokes of their masterwork.

Paul's watercolor sketchbooks filled with paintings of wood-paneled basement apartments cast in stark shadow by blaring, forgotten televisions; October sunlight pressing through dented blinds; dingy kitchens with wallpaper and curtains stained by decades of nicotine. Paul planned to turn the sketches into oil paintings, a companion piece to the project that only he and Julian would ever understand. Each iteration brought them closer; even the names they struck from the list added a layer to the palimpsest. Nothing went to waste.

The "fact-finding missions," as Julian called them, helped them eliminate any remaining candidates of whom they were uncertain. It was agreed that either of them could strike a name from the list for any reason, without being asked to explain. Certainty was essential. They were carrying something new between them now, the intoxicating relief of believing and being believed, and Paul knew how fragile it was. Any doubts, no matter how arbitrary, would undermine their ability to rely on each other.

Sometimes it was self-evident why a candidate couldn't be used. Alfred A. Lucci had turned his refrigerator into a shrine to a long-dead child, papered over with photographs and yellowing crayon drawings. But other times it was completely inexplicable. Now and then one of them would catch sight of some innocuous object—a toothbrush, a drinking glass—and become so anxious that they had to leave. Paul knew better than to question any rejection, no matter how much it annoyed him that he couldn't find a reason for it. There were still enough candidates who made neither of them balk. He trusted—forced himself to trust—that they'd know the perfect one when they found him.

Paul kept researching all the while, but the list of names gradually distilled. Eventually the remaining candidates became the topic of jokes and gossip, as if they were mutual friends neither of them much liked. "Tony probably never misses an episode," Paul would say if he saw an ad for a mindless sitcom; "Looks like Lou's been here," said Julian, when they found a soggy *Penthouse* magazine crumpled at the base of a chain-link fence. The jokes were never particularly funny, but they still drove each other into hysterics. More than once Paul's mother came to his room to check on them, curiosity disguised as wry concern. "You boys are having way too much fun up here," she always said, and they had to avoid each other's eyes to keep from laughing even more.

The method still wasn't settled, but both their suggestions had become straightforward and blunt. It had to be clean and bloodless and quiet, quick enough to avoid a struggle. There was no overpowering the subject physically—the candidates were all grown men and often tough ones, ex-soldiers and steelworkers and former cops. It had to surprise or incapacitate, or the situation would turn against them before it began. That left only a few options, each with its own complications that had to be foreseen and accounted for. Simplicity was almost prohibitively complex.

"I like the ones that double as disposal methods," Julian said once. Paul had returned to his microfilm research, compulsively as erasing and redrawing an imperfect line in his sketchbook. Until he'd spoken, Paul had assumed Julian was completely disengaged—he was reading idly in the next chair, ankles crossed on the opposite desk, Camus now replaced by Dostoevsky. Paul glanced sideways at him, but Julian's eyes were still on his book.

"Saves us having to lug the bastard around afterward," Julian went on. "No cleanup necessary, just"—he made a soft, descending whistle, bringing his fingertips down to mimic the subject plummeting from a great height—"*splat!* Show's over, good job, gentlemen, and we're home in time for Carson."

They were the only people in the library basement, but Paul still glanced over his shoulder to make sure no one had overheard. A book cart sat near the bank of elevators; he kept expecting one of Julian's fellow pages to appear beside it, sharp-eared and alert, nothing like a real bystander.

"You're not wrong. I just don't know how easy it is to convince a live subject to stand there and wait to be pushed."

"There are many paths to persuasion," said Julian loftily. "Once he's dead, we're down to just lugging."

It was a well-established problem that needed a conclusion, but the detour from the flowchart annoyed him. He'd broken the process into discrete parts for a reason; he didn't like to be distracted, especially at a stage when he was working without Julian's help.

Paul had returned, inevitably, to the courts-martial. He couldn't let the subject go, even as the sources began to run out. With the *Post-Gazette*'s archives spent, he'd moved on to the *Tribune-Review*, and he'd already reached the point of the Calley verdict. There were enough names by now, but he wanted everything he could find—each opinion-page apologetic, each letter to the editor, an exhaustive catalog of moral cowardice. He wanted every available scrap of data, so he would know they had arrived at the best possible decision. It was a matter of scientific rigor, he told himself. Though of course he knew that wasn't all it was.

The microfilm reader lingered on the dregs of a feature about Calley's conviction. Paul couldn't stomach reading the articles from start to finish, so he just skimmed them for names. This one waited in obscurity, toward the bottom of the very last column. Paul had only realized recently that his meticulousness was a strength; without it, he might never have seen the name at all.

Charlie Stepanek has followed the Calley trial closely, discussing it with other veterans at his neighborhood bar in Polish Hill. The soft-spoken 27-year-old takes a nuanced view of the verdict. Stepanek himself was called to testify at the 1969 court-martial of his commanding officer, Cpt. Alden Beach, who was convicted that November of ordering the torture and murder of three Vietnamese noncombatants. The incident at My Lai, Stepanek says, is remarkable only for its scale. He believes similar events are more common than most Americans think.

"They have to court-martial a guy now and then," said Stepanek, who agreed to a brief interview during his lunch break from his job at Wright-Howe Freight & Logistics in South Shore. "But if they want to be fair, they'd have to arrest half the armed forces or stop arresting anybody."

Stepanek demurred when asked how he believed Calley

should be sentenced, citing a lack of familiarity with criminal law. Before ending the interview, however, he suggested that civilian critics might not understand the reality of combat conditions on the ground.

"I don't think anyone likes what [Calley] told his men to do," he said. "I didn't like what my C.O. did. But I also didn't think it was unusual. I still don't. It was war."

Paul slowly lowered his pen and reached for the notebook. At the edge of his vision he saw Julian look sideways at him, but Paul didn't meet his eyes.

"Got a live one?" Julian's voice was light.

"Maybe not for long."

Charles Stepanek (Polish Hill). Paul made a note after the name as he always did, though this time he knew he wouldn't need help remembering. *Nothing unusual. More common than you'd think.*

The first step was complete. Next they would find Stepanek's name in the directory, and then follow the map to his address to assess complicating factors (if there was a wife, a guard dog, a busy home street). Paul couldn't afford to be impatient.

They wouldn't say his name aloud until after the third step—until they'd scoured his house for any evidence of humanity and found nothing worth considering. Only then would they have a mutual friend. Until then, Charlie Stepanek was a ghost.

II.

JULIAN HAD found the bridge by chance. He showed it to Paul on a map from a Chevron station, an unnamed blue line across the Mon. It was only a few miles from the city, but the land around it was wild, swathes of it too ravine-sliced and remote to be worth the expense of developing. There was a long steep road, slick with wet leaves, where Julian handed Paul the keys because he didn't dare drive it himself. Sparse shabby houses sat on the ridge at the far side of a deep fold in the earth, but once they reached the top of the road, the trees shielded them from view.

The freight company that owned the bridge had gone bankrupt three years ago, and a nearby steel mill had followed. It loomed dark on the opposite shore, fenced and shuttered. Between them was the bridge, and the wind, bitter cold, whistling and sighing through its frame.

"You're afraid of heights," said Julian, neither pitying nor cruel. "Aren't you?"

Paul shut the driver's-side door with his shoulder.

"It's perfect," he said. "You don't have to worry about me."

The steel trusses were caked in rust. Their skin and clothes always reeked of it after they visited, a smell that lingered long after they'd gone home. Paul had to throw away one of his sweaters when a powdery red streak on one sleeve refused to come off in the wash.

He got better with practice, but it never became easy. Some days he made it out to the center without reaching for Julian's hand; other days they had to walk together, arm in arm, while

the wind howled against them. The railings were low, only up
to Paul's hip, and when he looked down ("For god's sake, Paul,
don't look down") he could see the rushing gray-green of the
river between the slats. He could never have walked it on his
own. Alone, his head still swam when he stood in high places;
he didn't trust his own balance. But on the bridge his head could
be clear because Julian's was; his steps could be surefooted and
steady because Julian's were. Paul had him to trust now, and
Julian trusted him. He no longer needed to try to trust himself.

On his best days, his bravest days, he didn't hesitate. The
hardest step was always the first one he took after a pause. Self-
doubt grew in moments of stasis; it couldn't take root if he kept
moving.

"I'll be able to do it when it's time," he would say, though Julian never asked. "It's only because I know I don't really need to."

Julian just smiled, not quite reassuringly, and turned toward
the wind. The river breathed beneath them, and they walked.

IT SHOULD have been more conspicuous, the secret they carried between them like two children playing at spies. It glowed
in their skin, filled their horizon with colors no one else could
see. Before now he'd never liked the way they looked together,
because next to Julian he'd felt graceless and undeserving. But
there was no longer such an agonizing asymmetry. When he
saw their reflection in a shop window or a windshield or the
rust-flecked bathroom mirror in Charlie Stepanek's apartment
in Polish Hill, Paul didn't see the weaknesses and imperfections in his own body. Instead he saw how the secret held them
together—made them vibrant and too-alive.

(The first time they visited the bridge, Julian asked Paul to pull over partway down the hill so they could take a picture. Julian had brought his little Japanese camera, still half full of black-and-white film from his freshman photography class. He put it on the roof of the car and set the timer, and they waited hand in hand under a canopy of leaves. Before the shutter clicked, they locked eyes and couldn't keep from smiling. As if they couldn't see anything beyond each other; as if they couldn't believe their luck.)

They were wild and delirious and invincible, and it was strange that no one else could see it. But even Paul's mother had given up on looking at them directly—she was determined to go on liking Julian at all costs, no matter what she had to ignore. They moved like ghosts through the halls of the strange apartment complex and parked unseen for hours across from the shipping depot. They were the authority on whether or not they were visible, and no one dared challenge them.

They made a game of concealing the secret, talking around it with code words and jokes even when they were alone. Speaking too frankly was fatal to productivity—once it began, they would try to one-up each other with violent honesty, until they were both so giddy and overwhelmed that they couldn't get anything done. So Julian's notebook was nicknamed "the football," after the briefcase full of launch codes that was always within snatching distance of the President's hands; the police, rarely mentioned, were "mutually assured destruction."

The most vital unspoken rule was never to use the word *kill*, so of course Julian gleefully broke it. He would finish unrelated sentences with ". . . and then we kill the bastard," which always startled Paul into laughter. But when they discussed it seriously, the word could derail the entire conversation, and Julian knew better than to use it as anything but a joke.

So the final phase of the project was not a killing, certainly not a murder, but an endgame. The code name fit better, anyway, because a murder necessitated a victim. An endgame had only victor and defeated, and even those were beside the point. It was a coup de grâce born of pure reason, that could only live by destroying. The subject, now that he'd been chosen, was no longer "the subject." Instead he was "our friend"—a friend whose voice they had never heard, glimpsed only from a distance through Paul's binoculars. They'd circled one name in the end, and there was no need to say it out loud.

Audrey was the only one who could see any change in them. She took to asking where they were going, though Paul's mother was content to let Julian whisk him away for hours without explanation. ("You always hated it when Dad asked you," Paul pointed out, but she only shrugged and replied that she was curious.) Now and then some fragment of dinner-table conversation would remind them of the project, and they would fall into a nervous laughter that made Audrey raise her eyebrows. She might not be able to name it, but she was the only person who could even tell a secret was there.

She seized the chance to confront him the first time they were home alone together. She hadn't planned it, Paul could tell—when she heard him descending the basement stairs with a basket of laundry, there was a note of alarm in her voice.

"Hello?"

Paul paused midway down the staircase. A pungent sandalwood smell rose from below, from the candles Audrey liked to burn to cover up the smell of grass. He rolled his eyes and continued downward. "It's just me," he said. "Ma's still out."

Silence—Paul thought a rather chastened one. He spotted Audrey past the cloth curtain over the laundry-room doorway.

She was putting on a record and staunchly pretending there was nothing of interest between her thumb and two forefingers.

"You know Ma's going to have an aneurysm if she finds out you're still doing that in the house." Paul flicked on the washing machine and pushed open the curtain. Audrey flashed him a rude gesture, and he put his tongue out with deliberate child-ishness. He felt like he was getting away with something, fall-ing back into the role of the pedantic little brother she expected him to be. Lying came easily now, without even a flicker of dis-comfort. It felt natural, as if he were meant to have been living a bisected life all along.

The autumn chill had swept through the rest of the house before settling in the basement. Audrey wore her sheepskin coat and knee-high boots. The space heater coughed under the weight of the cold.

"Is Julian here?" She threw herself back onto the couch and exhaled a mouthful of smoke. When Paul shook his head, she motioned for him to sit down.

He felt no fear. He was already certain she couldn't see him, so he knew it was safe to dare her. He looked her in the eye and folded his hands, just barely bracing himself.

"I've been meaning to talk to you about him," she said.

She tapped ash from the end of the joint before leaving it to rest in the tray.

"Look," she went on. "I know he's having problems with his family right now, and it's not that I don't sympathize. But my first priority is *you*, and I'm worried about what you're getting into."

An odd urge to smile, so sudden that he barely managed to suppress it.

"When you hang out together," said Audrey, "do you feel like he actually likes you for who you are, or does he make you feel like you have to impress him?"

This time he did smile—and then laughed, incredulous, which she didn't seem to expect. *You don't see me. You can't. You never could.*

"Stop being such a fucking teenager and listen to me for a second, will you?" she said tartly. "I've been seventeen, okay? I know there's a type that acts like perfect little angels around adults, but in private they make you feel like you *owe* them something for being your friend. And you don't owe him anything. I don't care how horrible his parents might be—if he makes you feel bad about yourself, there's no excuse."

She fidgeted with her hair and avoided his eyes, as if she found her own sincerity ridiculous. He pitied her, watching her love and fear for the fragile child she saw in his stead.

"You want to turn it into something simple and boring and pathetic." He could tell she had expected him to be defensive; she couldn't make sense of how calm he was. "It isn't like that. It isn't anything anyone else could understand."

"Well, I'm sure you're right," said Audrey. "I'm sure no one else in *all* of human history could *ever*—" But she stopped herself, sighed, and leaned forward to take a long drag from her joint. "Ugh, whatever. It's your life, you're entitled to make your own mistakes, just . . . *if* I'm actually right, I want you to know you deserve better and you don't have to put up with it."

She couldn't see him any better than anyone else could. Whatever her gut told her, she would morph it in order to preserve the illusion of what she thought he was. They had nothing to fear from her; the secret was safe.

When Julian arrived the next morning, neither his mother nor his sister asked where they were going. As they were leaving, he could feel Audrey's gaze behind them, so he laced his hand through Julian's and refused to look back. The stories his family told about him weren't the affront he'd always thought they were. They were a shield. He had never realized before how much power they gave him.

"WITH YOU," Julian said, "the line between clever and fussy is *vanishingly* fine."

The car was idling so they could warm their hands in front of the heating vent. Paul lowered the binoculars and turned to face him, but Julian wasn't looking at him; he was taking a sip from the thermos, shoulders squared against the chill.

"It isn't fussy," said Paul. "Do you have a better way to get him to move under his own steam instead of bowling straight through us? And if you say 'just make it look like a mugging' one more time—"

"Yes, yes, I know, 'introduces too much volatility to the situation.' *I* think you just don't like it because you think it's vulgar."

"Well, it is." He refused to be abashed. "The point isn't just getting away with it, the point is making an *example* of him."

"Fussy," said Julian, and Paul lifted the binoculars again rather than argue.

He watched Stepanek hop down from the back of a truck and dust off his ungloved hands. Paul never managed to hold their friend's face in his memory. Stepanek's every feature faded as soon as he was out of sight; Paul often had the strange feeling that he was already forgetting the face even before he was done looking at it. There were only a few photographs on the walls of the grim bachelor apartment, all featuring Stepanek in a group—three buzz-cutted children in a Sears family portrait, a uniformed mass of shoulder pads and football helmets, sweat-streaked war criminals grinning arm in arm on the deck of their patrol boat. Paul had seen his face in person more times than he could count, but no matter how closely he examined the photographs he could never decide which figure was him.

But he was a big man, solidly built, a full head taller than they were. That detail never faded, because it posed a serious problem.

Julian elbowed him gently and handed over the thermos like a truce flag. He'd cooked the minestrone himself, part of his ongoing project to save money by learning to cook; predictably, he'd left it on the stove until it disintegrated into oversalted mush. Paul didn't particularly want to accept the offering, but it was endearing, the way Julian tended to his comfort as if it mattered as much as his own. There was such a reflexive, unguarded sweetness to the gesture that Paul decided not to notice the defects in its particulars. He drank enough to satisfy Julian's concern, then handed it back with a nod.

"All right," said Julian bracingly. "Let's have a look and see how much trouble you've gotten us into."

In Paul's pocket the vial had grown warm with the heat of his body. Julian took it from his hand and inspected it, as if he might unearth some understanding from a years-old prep-school chemistry class.

"It won't put him under completely." Paul was proud, and defensive because of it. "Just enough that we can get him to do what we need him to do—walk out onto the bridge, maybe even jump. And he won't feel pain. That's the main reason they use it, when there's no time to prep a full anesthetic. It gets used a lot on battlefields."

"Maybe he's had it before." Julian said it without compassion.

"How did you even get this?" he asked. "Don't they keep this kind of thing locked away?"

"I was getting something else out of storage for my microbiology lab. Yes, my name's on the log sheet," he added before Julian could ask, "but hundreds of others will be too, by the time anyone notices it's gone."

Julian bit his tongue and didn't argue. "Will I trip if I see how it tastes?" he asked instead. Paul shook his head, so he carefully unscrewed the cap and tapped a drop onto his fingertip. When he tasted it, he winced, then shrugged.

"Could be worse," he said. "Kind of bitter and soapy, but I guess if it was diluted enough he might ignore it . . ."

Paul took the vial back and tightened the cap before pocketing it again. "It means we don't have to change the method," he prompted. "We just give him some coffee or soup—something warm—he'll appreciate it, it'll probably be cold outside. Put it in the cup itself, not the thermos, so he can see us drinking from it and won't get suspicious. And if he doesn't take it," he went on, prouder and more defensive by the moment, "it means we can safely abort. Nothing to cover up, no reason for him to be suspicious, no *volatility*. It's—"

"—Clever," Julian conceded. "A little fussy, still. But clever."

In the distance, one of their friend's coworkers was telling a joke. The rest of them laughed, but their friend only smiled. When the others went inside the warehouse, Stepanek dawdled to tie his bootlace before joining them.

Paul looked away because something about the moment irritated him. They were there because of Stepanek's very forgettability, his eagerness to surrender his conscience to the crowd. Paul preferred it when their friend blended in with the others.

It made it easier to remember what he represented—what he was still capable of doing if the right person gave the order.

"He's built like a goddamn quarterback." Julian's gaze followed Stepanek until he disappeared into the warehouse; then he looked at Paul, skeptical and wary. "Are you sure there's enough in one bottle to bring him down?"

It was beginning to annoy him that Julian was still second-guessing him, but he held his tongue. It was a necessary part of the process, even this late in the game. Julian wasn't asking anything Paul hadn't asked himself already; he should feel better, not worse, knowing that he had an answer for every question.

"The dosage formula is very straightforward," he said. "It's the same one Sullivan used for the fox. It'll be more than enough."

12.

THEY CUT their afternoon classes the first Wednesday in November, two weeks to the day before the start of the holiday weekend. Come endgame it would be a little different—no work or classes, an entire day to account for each other's whereabouts and collect receipts for Julian's little green ledger. But it was an acceptable deviation, as long as the rest of the dry run followed the plan to the letter. There were always details that couldn't be anticipated, but they had to hew close enough to the plan to ensure there would be no major surprises.

"What did you tell your mother?" Julian asked when he picked Paul up outside the Biology building.

Paul pushed his knapsack into the back seat and slammed the door. "I had a whole spiel planned about prepping for our stats final, but she didn't even ask. I shouldn't have bothered."

"I can't figure her out," said Julian; Paul only shrugged.

"She likes you," he said, and gave Julian a wry smile. "God only knows why."

At first it felt like a game, gathering the pieces of an alibi they never planned to need. First a pair of ticket stubs at the art-house theater, where they whispered and roughhoused and covertly kissed through a dispassionately European black-and-white film neither had the patience to follow. Then a receipt from the bookstore, where Julian bought Paul a book of Shirley Jackson stories and himself an incomprehensible novel by Andy Warhol. It was the latter purchase that triggered an expansive, almost-unserious argument while they were waiting in line. They were boiling with talk and laughter, play-acting fiercely as versions of themselves that were immune from fear, and an eruption was all but inevitable. Their quarrel drew dirty looks from the other customers, but adrenaline had cured Paul of all his self-consciousness.

"We should've saved that for the endgame," Julian remarked while they were leaving. "People would remember us."

"I'm sure you'll think of something else to be wrong about by then," said Paul, unabashed. "His work is just so *pretentious*, I don't see why you—"

Julian wheeled around on the sidewalk. There was something off about his body language, but it took Paul a few seconds to recognize it.

"It's like the worst kind of jazz," said Julian. Paul burst out laughing—it was a facsimile of Paul's own voice, his vehement gestures, made unfamiliar at first by the cigarette between Julian's fingers. "That's what it is, it's self-referential and all about technique and theory, and for all the bright colors there's nothing *alive* in it—"

Paul almost couldn't recall how much it had hurt, the first time he saw the shape of himself echoed in Julian's body. For all the lingering awkwardness and clipped, too-sharp consonants, Paul barely recognized the person Julian was imitating. He had already become something more.

"Well? All it does is make critics feel clever." Paul gave him an agreeable shove. "Stop party-tricking me, you creep."

"Whatever, you love it."

As he spoke, Julian relaxed back into his own skin. He pushed his cuff up his wrist and looked at his watch. The faint tension that appeared now was entirely his own.

"Getting to be that time," he said, exhaling in a rush. "Shall we?"

A little less talk now; a little less playful. Their energy hadn't ebbed, only remembered its purpose. They parked midway up Polish Hill and walked the rest of the way. The narrow avenues were bounded by a chaos of trees and devouring vines, cast in shadow by a sun that was already setting. It was steep and wild here, unlike Paul's own neighborhood even at its most neglected. Before they chose their friend, Paul had made a few sketches of the vista outside the apartment—the low moss-stained wall, the steep drop into the woods, and the shining freight tracks far below. The drawings were rough-hewn and verdant, rendered with a grace he hadn't known he'd possessed. He'd had to burn them with everything else.

Their friend worked swing on Wednesday nights. By the time they arrived, he'd already gone, but so recently that there were still echoes of him. There was a fresh glister to the motor-oil stain on the asphalt parking lot. They let themselves in with the key he kept under the doormat, looped on its tongue-colored gumband. Inside, a faint ghost of aftershave traced his path around the house, from the bathroom to the bedroom to the door.

As always, Julian paused in the kitchen to pet the little brown terrier, then pulled a piece of jerky out of his pocket and coaxed the dog up on its hind legs. Paul turned to the wall calendar, crooked on its nail and open to November's photograph of a mountain in Alaska. There were X-marks up through the day before. Paul uncapped the red marker, hands a little clumsy in their gloves, and he mimed crossing out the Wednesday their friend would never see through.

That touch had been his idea; it would buy them a false

alibi for Thanksgiving, so that the receipts they collected on Wednesday might never be important. When he'd suggested it, Julian called it "elegant." The word, whenever Paul remembered it, made the inside of his chest glow warm.

"Then we lock up after ourselves and get back to the alibi." Paul put the marker back into its cup. "That's painless enough, as long as nobody sees us."

"Remember." Julian gave the dog's ears a final rumple and stretched his arms. "Bystanders—they're fucking useless. I'm not worried."

One more receipt, this time from the family-favorite Chinese restaurant near his grandfather's garage. It would have looked strange for them to eat in silence, so they talked, but it was a rehash of a conversation they'd already had, about afterlives— whether they would even want one, and how any heaven's stasis would be agony for anyone who had lived a fully realized life. They didn't choose the topic on purpose, and in two weeks they would have to opt for something less fraught. But it was comforting to retreat to a familiar dialogue, debating the merits of eternal recurrence and whether there was any practical difference between a selfhood and a soul. It steadied Paul's nerves before he'd even noticed they needed steadying.

Then, at last, the repair garage. From the line of numbered hooks mounted alongside his desk, Paul selected the key to a customer's nicotine-steeped Chrysler. He tailed Julian back to his apartment, parking at the bottom of the hill and out of sight; he didn't take off his gloves until after he'd followed Julian inside and set down the keys.

Amid all the failsafes and meticulous logistics, they had failed to anticipate the sheer boredom of waiting. Over the long hours, the walls of Julian's apartment contracted, and they paced past each other like two caged lions. The sound of his own voice made Paul snappish and uneasy, so he eventually stopped speaking altogether; Julian couldn't stop, chatting aimlessly and relentlessly about anything but what was really holding their attention. They tried to break up the monotony by playing chess, but the games all inevitably devolved into ugly stalemates. The other obvious solution yielded only slightly better results, and eventually they decided to abandon that effort rather than go about it halfheartedly.

"Did I ever tell you," said Julian after a while, "my sixteenth birthday got ruined by the fucking hurricane last year?"

Paul didn't answer, but Julian didn't seem to notice.

"The storm surge flooded the cellar and everything," he said, and tapped a fresh cigarette against the palm of his hand before lighting it. "We were stuck inside for hours, wondering if the trees were going to fall. You're bored out of your goddamn mind, but you can't *relax* because there's a hurricane outside, and if you let your guard down for a second the winds might get stronger and tear the house in two—or at least that's the kind of monkey-brain magical thinking you catch yourself doing, even when you know better."

"Our basement flooded, too." Paul felt a brief flare of annoyance that Julian still wouldn't stop talking. "It's going to feel worse when it's actually endgame," he added a little unkindly, "so you'd better get used to it."

"I'll just take a fistful of your mother's reds next time," said Julian.

At a quarter to eleven they left. The nights were growing bitter, but the reek of stale tobacco in the Chrysler was so overwhelming that they rode with the windows down. When they reached the warehouse there was a cathartic flurry of tasks devoted to ensuring they'd given themselves enough time to set the stage.

Paul had learned the first trick from his grandfather—it could be used, quite innocently, to pop the hood on a customer's car if another mechanic had wandered off with the keys. All it took was a well-placed bent wire through the front grill. The second trick he hadn't dared ask about, but he couldn't imagine that it didn't work. He knew little about cars, but he knew what the oil pan did and how to fill it. It didn't take any great wisdom to know how much damage would be done by adding a few ounces of sand.

"I'm going to need a second pair of gloves," he said suddenly. He braced his hand on the hood and turned to face Julian, all but invisible past the shivering beam of his flashlight. "Otherwise I'll get engine grease on the steering wheel. I didn't think of that, for god's sake, why didn't I think of that?"

"Let's not spiral into self-loathing, if you please," said Julian with deliberate carelessness. "See? This is what the rehearsal is for."

The pay phone across the street had to be left intact for now, but Paul examined it anyway. There had to be something unbreakable he could use to smash the receiver—and there was, an empty metal shelf whose directory book was long gone. The glass was etched with graffiti; his skin was lit in fluorescent green.

Beyond the booth window he saw Julian leaning against the Chrysler, hugging his arms in the cold. Paul kicked the door shut and hurried across the empty street to join him. Through the dark and distance Julian had appeared almost afraid, but by the time Paul reached him, the look was gone, if it had ever been there at all.

"How much longer?"

"About half an hour. Still bored?"

Julian shrugged.

While they waited, Julian browsed restlessly through the stranger's glove compartment—unfurling fast-food napkins, uncapping lipsticks to scrutinize their color. But he was quiet, even solemn. When he ran out of artifacts to examine, he shut the glove box and wrung his hands; Paul gently pulled one hand free and held it, but Julian didn't relax. Somewhere in the distance, a church bell tolled midnight.

Their friend left work late. He was alone and forgettable, round-shouldered in the cold. Paul only watched him for a moment before looking away. His place in the story was well-established; there was no need to dwell on it.

Stepanek's car rattled to life and disappeared into the dark. Paul pulled the Chrysler up alongside the place where it had been. Julian opened the passenger door and leaned out, one gloved hand braced against the ceiling.

"Hey," said Julian. "Are you okay?"

A symphony of urban silence. The buzz of the streetlights; traffic, thin after midnight, each vehicle a lonely sigh in the distance.

"No matter what mood he's in, I'm patient with him. He's having a rough night." Julian spoke with his best stranger manners, as if he were still addressing their friend. "He gets in the car."

"If he doesn't?" Paul didn't doubt him, but he had to ask. The practice would be worthless if they didn't account for everything.

"Then we tell him 'good night' and go home," said Julian. "But he's going to get in. That's why we like our friend so much—he doesn't ask a lot of questions."

Paul drummed his fingertips on the steering wheel. Then he nodded.

"He gets in the car." There was a trace of a stammer, but he no longer feared Julian would laugh at him for it. "He has a nice hot drink, and we drive."

They were no longer restless. He'd never seen Julian so still. There was a presence beside them, a body-thick heaviness to the quiet; they wore the skins they used when they knew someone was watching them. When they veered from the route to Polish Hill, the last fragments of conversation faded into silence. There was nothing to say, anyway. They were well past that.

It was a forty-minute drive, out to the suburban snarl of railyards and ramshackle houses. The chill sliced past the open windows. When they turned up the hill and into the woods, the world's last sounds were smothered by the trees. Outside the car, the air was sweet. Moss and smoke; the warm smell of rust. There would be hardly any moon in two weeks, but for now it was high and shining. Its reflection shuddered in the river below. The bridge was bright angles and shadow. He wasn't afraid of it; he never had been.

"One," said Julian. They approached the railing side by side. The presence walked with them, obedient and yielding.

"Two." Paul watched his face through the ghost that stood between them. There was already the shadow of a transformation inside them. How could Paul brace himself for the real thing when the transcendence was already too terrible to bear? It would be like looking at God.

"Three."

13.

HERE WAS the truth: it was the happiest they had ever been. He would never say that to himself afterward, but he always knew. Even when the time came that he despised himself for knowing it. Even when he reached desperately backward in his memory to find a joy he could still yearn for, an innocent and untarnished *before* that had never existed.

No longer was there any danger in being gentle with each other. It was a relief to be able to trust, and the relief made everything else simple. Love was so easy they could take it for granted, so transcendental that they would never dare. They talked on the phone late into the night and hid notes in each other's pockets like lovesick children; whenever they reached an empty stretch of sidewalk they drew together to hold hands, reflexively synchronized. Of course they would promise each other everything. Of course eternity would yield to them once they'd earned it.

At a certain point they stopped talking about the plan. The logistics were set, and there was little else to say; it dropped beneath the surface. But it touched everything that belonged to them—everything they read, everything they believed, every idea they brought to each other to be dissected and loved. It was the key to their freedom from the world of obedience, the catalyst that would help everything else fall into place. Every hope for the future hinged on what it would help them become, and Paul never questioned it, not once. They were happy, and the plan was inextricable from their happiness, and he would never be able to forget that both things were true.

Each day was shorter and darker, but they hardly felt the cold. They barely slept, and when they did, they didn't dream. Instead they told each other the things they dreamed when they were awake. How they would never be apart, how they would take care of one another. How they would seal themselves off from everything outside and distill themselves to such purity that no one else could ever touch them. How this, in the end, was the only thing they wanted.

Any other happiness dimmed beside it. It was unblemished by fear or reason, a joy in impossible things—the belief, hopeless and unwavering, that the center could hold.

14.

"... TOMORROW, THANKSGIVING Day, when families across this nation will be ..."

He was a small child, walking the beach at Cape May with his father at his side. Past a veil of fog stood a rusted railway bridge, collapsing into the sea. Lying in the sand was a seagull, long dead, its eyes and breast and belly hollowed out by flies. A voice came from the place inside its chest where its tiny lungs and heart had once been. Beneath the roar of the sea the voice was faint, and the words didn't make sense no matter how closely he tried to listen.

His father didn't want him to linger—"Don't look," he said, and covered Paul's eyes. But then Paul heard the gull's voice more clearly, and his father was no longer there.

"... marked, in retrospect, not only the death of a charismatic and promising young President, but the death of our innocence as a ..."

His eyes opened, and the breaking waves receded. The split-flap numbers clicked softly into place, two minutes past his alarm. The radiator creaked and snapped, but the room was still frigid. He reached for the sweater hanging from his bedpost—an old brown pullover of his father's, still sweet with pipe tobacco and aftershave.

Familiar smells, familiar sounds, a life still marred by all its old fractures and disappointments. This was the day he would reforge it into something smooth and whole.

"So as we gather around the family table to give thanks, let us remember our fallen—"

He switched off the radio and got up to stand beside the

radiator. As he tried to wring warmth into his hands, he could picture their friend doing the same, hunched over the baseboard heater in his dark apartment across town. He would be wearing a terrycloth robe, the wine-colored one that hung from the back of the bedroom door. The terrier would dance at his heels until he opened a can of horsemeat for it in the kitchen.

Nineteen hours—Paul couldn't stop himself from doing the calculations in his head. Heartbeats, one hundred thousand; eighteen thousand breaths, seventeen thousand blinks of the eye. The numbers were finite, but so were the ones that measured any life. The only difference was being able to reckon them with any precision.

It was still dark when he returned from his run. While the household stirred to life outside his bedroom door, Paul hung his bath towel over the keyhole and pulled his sport bag down from the closet shelf. He forced himself not to rush, to lay everything out across his bed carefully to ensure that he didn't forget anything. He kneaded his lower lip between his thumb and forefingers and went over the list in his head. Matches, two changes of clothes, toothbrush, aspirin. Tennis shoes, penknife. Baseball bat, wrapped end to end in grip tape to hide the bright green paint. An extra pair of socks.

He waited till the last moment to retrieve the vial. He crept across the cold floor on gooseflesh and bare knees to unlock the paint box under his bed. Paul resisted the impulse to hide it in his bag right away, like a guilty child burying a broken piece of china. He set the vial out on his bedspread along with the everything else, between his spare glasses and his thrift-store driving gloves. One final inventory, then he packed it all away.

He left the bag at the foot of the stairs, beside the shoe pile and the constellation of oval-framed childhood photographs.

He followed the voices to the kitchen, where Laurie and his mother had already finished breakfast. They were assembling Laurie's sack lunch, their mother trimming the crusts from her peanut butter sandwich. Laurie smiled at him, her flower-printed knapsack hanging from one shoulder.

It could have been any other morning. Laurie chatted aimlessly until her friend Miriam summoned her outside with a shave-and-a-haircut knock. His mother always found fault with his scrambled-egg technique, so Paul waited to make his breakfast until she'd migrated to the sunroom to watch the morning news. Eventually Audrey drifted up from the basement, yawning and ruffling the loose tangle of her hair. In tinny strains from the open sunroom door, the television took up the lament for the long-dead President. Audrey set down her mug and settled in with her breakfast, a pickle spear and a liverwurst sandwich cut into triangles.

Paul knew he had to put something in his stomach. Hunger would only make him shakier and more nervous. But it was as if he were swallowing clumps of wet cement. He minced his eggs down to gravel with the side of his fork, and the bulk of them went cold and uneaten. He waited until the others were distracted by conversation before getting up to scrape his plate over the bin.

"The official story is full of holes." Audrey was in a cheerful, combative mood; she had earlier tried to engage Paul in the same conversation, and was still annoyed at his lack of interest. "I'll buy that Oswald was the triggerman, but the whole Castro connection, you'll never convince me—"

"Don't be morbid, Audrey," said their mother. She was still curled up in the wicker chair in the sunroom, half-obscured face turned toward the television. "I don't like it, people turning that tragedy into a parlor game . . . Paul, do you remember your card?"

Being directly addressed sent a shock through his hands. "My what?"

"That sweet little card you made for the Kennedy children." Her voice was almost wistful. "You were so worried about them. I wonder if they still have it."

"Oh." Paul couldn't summon the memory; he didn't have the nerves to spare. "I doubt they ever saw it," he said. "It probably went straight in the trash."

He hadn't planned to leave as early as he did, but he couldn't bear to stay in the house any longer. The air was too thick with a past he would soon be rid of. The boy who lived here didn't deserve a goodbye.

He intended to take the bus, but Julian was waiting for him at the corner, windburned in the cold, leaning on the hood of his red Chevrolet. His hands were in his coat pockets, his scarf knotted close at his throat. Between gray earth and low sky, he was the only thing that shone.

Paul came near enough to kiss him, but he didn't quite dare. They watched each other's eyes for a long moment; then Julian grinned and sidled free to open the driver's-side door.

"It took me ages to get dressed this morning." Julian gave a brittle, nervy laugh and scraped his fingers back through his hair. "I nearly had a nervous breakdown over *socks*, of all things. I couldn't stop laughing, having to decide what goddamn socks to wear the day I go out and—"

"Endgame," said Paul. "The day of the endgame."

Julian drew a sharp breath, as if to suppress another laugh. Then his unsteadiness vanished as quickly as it had appeared, and Paul soon forgot it had been there at all.

HE KNOWS what he has to do, even if he can't remember why.

It's dangerous; it will kill him if he lets it. It itches and burns like hay, so deeply that he feels it in his teeth and throat more than in his skin. It loops around his arms and over his fingers, and he is so afraid of it that he almost forgets his mission. But he doesn't forget. He refuses to forget.

He can pull it, little by little, through the unseen clumsy knot that holds it in place. He knows he must. He tells his hands to keep pulling, even when he can't feel them and can't be certain they're still attached to his wrists. He cannot forget how to move. It will kill him if he lets it.

His every breath flows to his hands because they are all that's left of him now. This is the most important thing he's ever done.

They haven't noticed. Whoever they are, they haven't noticed. When they glance at him they jitter and laugh, and they make remarks to each other that jumble together into nonsense before they reach his ears. Side by side they are twin angels on a headstone, cold and terrible and immutable. They were boys once, he remembers, but they aren't anymore.

Are you sure he's still with us?

Should be. His eyes are still moving.

Beneath them the world rocks back and forth, and he is on his riverboat in Vietnam, and the sun glares and the air clings and sweat slicks down his back. The boys are boys again and there are even odds they'll both be dead within the week. The green smell of the swamp rises like steam, and there is a cloud of blood in the murky water, it's his mistake, it's his fault—

—No. He's sorry, he's so sorry, but he can't stay. What he has to do is too important.

Then something gives, buckles like a knee. The loop of rope is large and loose.

Something is stirring far away. He remembers his legs. But no, he can't move them, not yet. He can't let them see, the two stone angels. When he moves one wrist an inch farther from the other it is a secret they don't see. He must keep the secret. He has to wait.

The world is still.

The car doors open and the rain chatters like teeth. He holds the secret tight and grasps the rope so they won't see it fall loose. They hold him at each elbow and ask him to walk—not tell, ask, Would you walk with us? Thank you, Charlie. Just a little walk.

Charles Raymond Stepanek Jr., Petty Officer Third Class, two-six-eight, four-one—

They walk him out into the rain, and the trees shine from the headlights and slice like knives into the pitch-black sky. He forgets how to speak again before he even registers he remembered.

Their grasp is breakable and spider-thin. They aren't angels; they're children. His body only walks because it expects to walk. He will make his body expect something else. The secret can save him. It's the only thing that might.

He lets the rope fall. Lets his wrists come free. The secret is out.

He twists away. He staggers forward.

He runs.

Part IV

I.

WHEN HE was six or seven, Paul saw a sparrow kill itself against the kitchen window. It didn't die right away. He remembered dropping his mitt and looking down at it in the grass. Spine twisted, tiny frantic heart pumping blood loose into its cerebellum, the short-circuit spasm of its wings. It wasn't a bird anymore. Dying turned it into something else, fluids and electricity—membrane and follicles and little hollow bones. He knew even as a child that it would be kinder to kill it, but he didn't know how, so he just watched until it was over. The stillness afterward was a mercy. He remembered that. He wouldn't have been able to put an end to it now without the memory.

The crush of panic had been too thick for him to hear the rain, but he could hear it now. He shivered at the remnants that found their way down to him through the trees. He got to his feet and wrung his gloved hands on his shirt. There was no question that his clothes would have to go, but they were so drenched there was no hope that they would burn.

"Hey."

Julian hadn't moved. He was still standing with his back to a tree trunk, eyes shut. The bat lay between them in the mud. Paul kicked it into the shadows as he approached. It was a distraction Julian didn't need.

"Julian." Paul pressed his fingertips to his forearm, just hard enough to guide his hand down from his mouth. "It's all right now. You can look."

It took a long time for Julian's eyes to open. He breathed as if he were playing dead, small sixteenth-note breaths.

He looked past Paul, then at him. He closed his eyes again, hard, but only for a moment.

"All you did was knock him out," he said. "Right?"

The barest pause before he could summon his voice. "I didn't check."

"It has to be both of us," Julian said again. His eyes didn't focus properly on Paul's face. He looked very young. "Paul, please, it has to be both of us, *tell me he's still alive—*"

Paul took hold of both his hands, certain the calm would pass between them, somehow.

"I didn't check," he said. "We can't ever know for sure. So it's still both of us. Okay?"

Julian drew a sharp inhale, held it, exhaled slowly. It wasn't enough to steady him, but they couldn't wait around for better. All Paul could do was promise wordlessly that the stillness inside him would find its way to Julian eventually.

"It's not that far to go." Paul looked over his shoulder. Every ugly detail blurred; all that remained was equations, distances over rough terrain, weights and measures. "Fifteen, twenty yards," he said. "It'll be easier once we get to the bridge. Then it's just far enough to get out from over the shallows. Do you think you can do that?"

Julian didn't answer. For a long silent moment he stared at the inescapable shape of it just downhill, stark and cold in the headlights. Then he laughed.

"Lazy bastard," he said, "isn't holding up his end of the bargain at *all*."

Paul could never remember afterward how they managed it. There were only fragments, as if he'd woken briefly while sleepwalking. The downpour reaching them at full strength when they emerged from the trees, sloughing down in frigid sheets that flattened their hair against their scalps. The chill in his chest, so thick he might have drowned in it. Julian having to pause once they reached the bridge, choking suddenly on the cold air—but that didn't stop either of them from dissolving into horrified laughter when Julian lost hold of the left ankle and the leg landed on the rail with a sickeningly decisive *thump*.

Other sounds lingered, but he could never recall the collision of flesh against water. He remembered only the quiet afterward, the concentric circles of impact radiating over the surface of the river. Even without his glasses, he could see the pockmarks of the rain.

The bat would have floated if they'd thrown it in the river, so Paul scraped a trough into the mud and buried it under damp soil and leaves. The bat had been a failsafe they were never supposed to need, and because of it they had to deploy contingency plans—but they were still *plans*, orderly as clockwork, nothing improvised. There was something peaceful about falling back on them. It meant even the deviations were under control.

Julian retrieved Paul's canteen from the glove compartment and poured it over Paul's hands so he could scrub away the worst of the contamination. ("Your face," said Julian suddenly, as if he were noticing for the first time. There was a delirious threat of a laugh in his voice, so Paul knew better than to ask for details.) They took turns holding the subject's umbrella while they changed into dry clothes; the old clothes and gloves went into a Kaufmann's shopping bag, topped off with rocks and destined to sink in one of the other two rivers.

For a long moment Julian sat behind the wheel, holding it as if he feared it might slither alive. Then he slid over to the passenger's seat and looked out at Paul with unfocused, glassy eyes.

"You drive," he said. "I can't, I can barely feel my hands."

Paul crumpled the subject's umbrella into the shopping bag and moved inside to switch on the heat. Every sound was needle-sharp. The growl of the engine coming to life. Windshield wipers whining, bright rattling rain.

When he finally put his glasses on, the world gleamed with detail, and he lost all sense of depth—it was like looking at a painted illusion and then leaning in too close to see anything but brushstrokes. He could feel every fold of fabric against his skin, every goose bump and fine hair on his forearms. But the details didn't fight with each other anymore. They didn't cling to his limbs and pull him downward. They washed through him like a symphony.

After the edge of the woods was the steady thrum of street-lights and darkness. Beside him Julian stared forward into the street, holding very still. He had his thumb and two fore-fingers pressed to his lower lip, fingernails skating over the thin chapped skin.

"How are you doing?"

Julian looked at him as if he'd forgotten he was there. Behind his hand, his face shifted slowly into a grin.

"I'm fine." His voice was a rising singsong, teasing and impatient. "How about you? Feeling okay? Need me to hold your glasses so you can throw up?"

Paul wasn't sure if Julian wanted him to smile. He couldn't quite parse the remark, as if it had been intended for someone else. "Do I *look* like . . . ?" he said, distantly curious, but Julian burst out laughing before he'd even finished speaking.

"Jesus, look at you." Julian's eyes were wide, alight with something too shimmering and elusive for Paul to name. "Nothing can touch you, you're high as a fucking kite. Hold out your hand."

Paul raised his hand from the gearshift and held it outstretched, flat and steady.

Julian let his hand fall from his face and lifted it to hold next to Paul's. It was shaking so hard that he couldn't keep it in place for very long.

"You scare the hell out of me," said Julian. He darted over to kiss the side of Paul's neck; his smile didn't fade. "You really do."

They were back in the city, now. The car crept along a side street thick with houses, then ducked beneath the dim arch of an underpass. Julian rested his head on Paul's shoulder. His pulse was so strong and quick that Paul could feel it through his shirt.

A sharp detour north. They idled on the Sixteenth Street Bridge to drop the shopping bag into the river. Paul wanted to do it himself, so he could revel in looking down from the height and feeling no fear. But Julian followed him, clambering over the railing onto the pedestrian path.

A single car passed behind them, not stopping, headed in the opposite direction. Julian took Paul's hand and stared down into the black of the water. The city light cast his face in sickly yellow.

"We should go." The other car didn't worry Paul, but it reminded him that he was capable of worry. "So we can . . ."

Julian's fingers threaded through Paul's and squeezed tight. It was something he liked to do in bed, when Paul pinned him down and let him feel the teeth behind every kiss. Out of context it was painfully intimate, far more so than any less chaste gesture would have been.

"I know," said Julian. "We just need a moment to breathe."

It was the first time he could believe Julian when he spoke this way, as if they were one mind, one heart, one pair of lungs.

The car returned to the repair garage. The lot was eerie and gleaming beneath its floodlights on the deserted street. Julian wiped down the steering wheel and any other surface they or the subject might have touched, while Paul went inside to write the car's new mileage in his grandfather's records. It was past two by now, and Paul's muscles were beginning to ache, as badly as they ever had after a punishing run. But he felt cool and soft, like an empty garden beneath fresh snow. He imagined a deep and dreamless sleep, and how he would wake to find the world new.

He nearly let sleep overtake him as Julian drove them back to his apartment. He was just on the edge of dreaming; the street signs appeared nonsensical until he focused long enough to sort out the letters. He watched Julian absently light a cigarette and blow the first breath of smoke slowly through the part of his lips. It hung like a cobweb in the dark.

When they returned at last to the apartment, they showered together in the too-bright light, and the last evidence of the earth left their skin. Julian cleaned the remnants of mud from Paul's face as reflexively as he had from his own fingernail beds. They moved together automatically and without hesitation. They watched each other's eyes, rested their foreheads together as if from opposite sides of a mirror. Their bodies belonged to each other because they were the same body. They had been just one person, long ago, but had been cut from one another before they were born.

Paul nearly succumbed to fatigue the moment he collapsed

into bed, but Julian's voice pulled him back from the ledge. "Stay with me. Paul, wake up, I need you."

He was too exhausted to do more than acquiesce, but that was all Julian asked of him. He wrapped his arms around Julian's neck and tried to pull him beneath the surface, into the dreamlike peace.

"I love you." Julian's mouth was snow-soft against the side of his neck; he spoke nearly too quietly to be heard. "I mean it. Like crazy."

Paul believed him. He couldn't remember ever doubting.

2.

HE LOOKED the same as he always had. He'd expected to see a change, even if it were so subtle that only he could see it. A mature sternness about the eyes, something strong and resolute in the line of his jaw. It nauseated him when he caught sight of the mirror and saw the same face. The dark hangdog eyes, solemn and grim; the boyishness at his outlines, the soft movements of his hands and the uncertainty of how to hold them. He still looked like his father's son. Worse, he looked like his mother's.

The house whirred with voices. Even from the upstairs hallway he could smell the holiday—sweet potato, maple, toasted walnut, the crayon-pink scent of Laurie's strawberry perfume. Familiar and festive smells, artifacts from his old life. The world went on as it always had, mistaking him for the weak and obedient boy he'd left to die in the woods beside the bridge. He would have felt better if he could see even a glimmer of the truth in his own face. He never wanted to forget that they were wrong.

Mushrooms were hissing in the frying pan. Laurie and Paul's mother assembled a sweet potato casserole at the table, and Audrey gestured with the spatula as she talked, recounting a political article she'd read in one of her magazines. Their mother's apron wasn't long enough for her, so Audrey wore their father's old woodworking apron over her jeans.

Only Julian took notice of his return, half turning from his plate of uneaten toaster waffle. He'd been so restless since they arrived at Paul's house that it was clear he'd barely slept. His eyes were too bright and shadowed deeply underneath. There was a chemical edge to his movements, as if caffeine and adren-aline were the only things keeping him upright.

As Paul sat beside him, Julian met his eyes with madden-ing caution. "Are you all right?" he asked under his breath. It wasn't the first time he'd asked, and it was wearing on Paul's nerves. He made a face in response, and Julian rolled his eyes and turned back to his plate.

The question, like the shape of his body, belonged to the ver-sion of himself Paul had abandoned. The state he was in de-fied easy judgment. It wasn't *all right*—it was something better, more alive. If his serenity was fading a little at the edges, he would just work harder to maintain it. The flutter of unease in his chest was just muscle memory; as he settled into his better self, it would be replaced by something new.

He felt like a convalescent awake after weeks of delirium. His whole body ached. He was ravenous, so exhausted he could barely speak.

"Do you have plans for the rest of the day, sweetheart?"

Paul had eaten a full breakfast without complaint, so his mother's concern had shifted to Julian. When panic passed through Julian's face, she looked at him with anxious pity.

"I thought . . ." Julian fired Paul a sidelong glance and wrung his hands. It was such a rare gesture of uncertainty that it broke through Paul's calm and landed hard on his nerves. "I mean, Paul sort of—"

"He's coming with us." Everyone looked at him now. Before last night it might have made him falter. "You said he's always welcome."

"He is." His mother reached across the table to squeeze Ju-lian's forearm. The gesture made him jump. "You are, always, of course you are—Paulie, do you want to step into the living room for a moment?"

"Not particularly."

There was a burn of red in his cheeks and at the edges of his ears—another reflexive remnant he would have to unlearn. That Julian needed to be accounted for all day was nonnegotiable. Perhaps Paul shouldn't have trusted the solution to be this simple without confirming his assumptions, but it was too late now to abandon it.

His mother gently let go of Julian's arm and pressed her hands together. "It's just that it's at your auntie's house." She gave him a heavy, plaintive look. "And she—well—no one's going to be *expecting* him."

"I can probably still get a flight to New York." Julian pretended he didn't mind one way or the other, but the alarm hadn't quite left his voice. "My friend Joy—ugh, never mind, they go to the Keys—"

"It's one more chair," said Paul curtly. "There's always enough to feed an army, so what's the big deal?"

His mother's fondness for Julian was a weapon she'd willingly given him, so she had no right to be angry with him for using it. She pursed her lips, and Paul watched her resolve crumble. Behind her Audrey was watching them, prodding inattentively at the mushrooms.

"Well," his mother said wearily. "I guess I'll have to let Hazel know."

Another piece of the calm chipped away. Paul tried to seal it back into place, but it was gone, and without it he couldn't figure out how to settle back into his new skin. Details began to sting again, so slowly and insidiously that he didn't notice in time to stop the slide. Food smells clung in his throat. When the hall telephone rang, inevitably, the trill of the bell was a shade too loud to ignore.

None of it should matter, and it didn't, exactly, but that didn't stop him from noticing it. He saw the way his grandparents' faces fell when they caught sight of Julian in Hazel's doorway. He felt the way the air swelled with quiet when he entered a room, and the way it contracted again after he left. Some of the family pretended not to mind Julian's presence—his uncle Harvey, in particular, was as scrupulously friendly as if Paul had helped him win a bet. But the others addressed Julian with polite dismissiveness, the way they might have spoken to a door-to-door salesman. Paul knew, without wanting to know, that they were assembling a story to tell each other behind his back; it didn't matter, but it struck him at full strength. How-ever fiercely he tried to ignore it, he couldn't stop himself from seeing.

But more than anything else, he noticed Julian. The way he jumped when people spoke to him. The way he laughed at jokes a little too quickly, the slight overearnest edge to his smile. How he would dart out onto the deck to smoke, backed into the corner of the railing as if someone might creep up behind him and push him over. How he rubbed at his exhaustion-heavy eyes and chewed his cuticles; the way he always kept one eye on the door.

"If I don't get to ask, you don't either," said Julian, when Paul inevitably let his concern overpower him. He was trying for a playful tone, but the results didn't convince either of them. "I'm just tired, Pablo. You can't know what it was like, watching you sleep like the dead—I had to keep checking to see if you were still breathing."

Paul might have thought Julian was angry if he hadn't hung so close. He refused to be left alone. As Paul made his obligatory loop through each cluster of relatives, Julian hung half a step behind and rolled his disposable cup between his hands. If Paul so much as retreated to the washroom, Julian leaned against the wall outside and waited for him. But Julian barely spoke, even to him. He answered Paul's questions in monosyllables, not meeting his eyes.

His cousin Debbie, ever the showman, waited until the toasts at dinner to announce she was expecting her first baby. It was Audrey who took the brunt of it, the *Oh isn't that nice for them* and *Aren't you looking forward to having your own someday.* She didn't even pretend to absorb it gracefully, which gave Paul a reluctant measure of comfort. ("Listen, I could go out and get pregnant right now," she told their grandmother with her eyebrows raised, "but I wouldn't enjoy that any more than you would.") In years past, Paul might have been pulled into it. They would have teased him about nonexistent girlfriends and assured him that some ill-defined *it* would happen for him, someday, when he was a doctor. But today they addressed him with a silence too pointed to ignore. Another layer of calm stripped away. What remained was so translucent now that Paul had to remind himself it was still there.

Past the gaps in the curtains, the rain turned into snow. They were hard little flakes, cold enough they might stick. Beside him, Julian was rolling a green bean back and forth across his plate, which he'd filled very lightly, then barely touched. The exhaustion had left him brittle and diminished; he smiled when he met Paul's eyes, but he didn't grow any less pale.

Being out among others already was a mistake; compared to subjecting themselves to this acid bath, the need for an alibi felt frivolous. He brushed his hand against Julian's under the table. Julian tensed and remained that way for a while, before he finally took Paul's hand and seemed (almost, not quite) to relax.

Paul wanted the snow to thicken, to continue without pause until he and Julian were stranded together somewhere far from here. He pushed the temperature lower and summoned a blizzard. Snow would cover the roads and the driveways and the parking lots. It would cling to Julian's apartment windows and keep them warm inside. They would have a few days of stillness, and the calm would return, even as the slush along the banks of the Monongahela slowly congealed into a translucent sheet of ice. Then there was the soft thump, the dark thick shape, of something buoyed against the ice by the currents underneath.

Suddenly nobody was speaking. There was a near-inaudible ring in the air, the echo of his fork slipping from his hand and clattering onto his plate. Every face turned toward him. The meal in his stomach was a dense wet weight.

"All right, Paulie?" his grandfather asked. Paul hated the way his voice sounded, as if he'd been waiting for this moment all along.

"I'm fine." Paul didn't dare look at Julian. He rose as slowly as he could and forced himself to smile. "Just a little tired."

He hid in his aunt's bedroom and curled up in the corner of the window seat. He tried to push the image away, but it wouldn't leave. It became another new part of him, undetectable in the shadow of his reflection in the glass.

He started at the sound of the door, but he didn't turn around. He didn't want Julian to look at him until he remembered how to be serene and untouchable. He didn't want him to see how little he had really changed.

The door shut slowly. Julian touched his shoulder, then pushed his fingers through Paul's hair. Paul expected his fingers to draw tight and pull. He wanted Julian to strike him across the face; he imagined the icy tone his voice would take when he told Paul to pull himself together, and how reflexive and natural it would be to obey.

But Julian leaned against the window seat and gently lifted Paul's chin. There was only the dim glow of the streetlights outside, but Paul could see that he was close to smiling.

"There's the Pablo I know." He brushed Paul's hair back from his face. "I was worried I'd lost you."

He wasn't sure what made him collapse—whether it was the accusation of weakness or the realization that he was too exhausted and overwhelmed to prove it wrong. The world was too loud again, and he felt pathetic and small, and the shame was more than his body could hold.

"You're okay." Julian held him close and pressed a soft kiss to his hair. It was the first time all day he'd been calm. "You can trust me now. You're safe, I'll take care of you. I don't need you to be brave."

3.

JULIAN STILL wasn't sleeping—that much was clear. He was glassy-eyed and inattentive, his movements as jittery as a bird's, and he smoked so relentlessly that his new carton of cigarettes was already crushed and slack. Paul was deliberately incurious about what was wrong, but a memory lingered in his head even when he refused to see why it was important. How Julian had looked at the wounded fox, as if it forced him to remember something he wanted to forget. Julian's squeamishness was a quality that Paul had always considered rather childish; today it infuriated him, even if he couldn't currently see any evidence of it.

They'd met at the delicatessen for a lunch neither wanted to eat. Yesterday's snow hadn't lasted long, and the rain sloughed far too loudly against the window and through the gutters. The amber glass shades on the overhead lights, the faded cartoon of a whale printed on the side of the salt carton—this place was too familiar, too comfortable, a relic of his life before. Being here made him feel young and useless.

"It's strange not having to go Christmas shopping," Julian mused. "Except for Joy, I guess. Do people give presents for Hanukkah?"

"Just little ones. It isn't worth wasting your money."

"You're as much of a mother hen as your Ma," said Julian. It stung like a slap, but it wasn't cruel enough that Paul could treat it like one.

He watched Julian sugar the last of the coffee into a slurry. For only the second time since they met, Julian was in the process of losing at chess. Paul could hardly count it as a win, because Julian barely paid attention to the game—he was hemorrhaging material and blundering into simple traps, though for the moment he still clung jealously to the black queen. Everything about Julian was fractured by exhaustion, and knowing how unkind he was being only added to Paul's annoyance. He yearned for an excuse to pick a fight, but Julian was in one of his strange gentle moods and refused to give it to him.

"So how much is your grandfather paying you, anyway?" Julian asked, as if it were a subject they'd already been in the middle of discussing. He was doing a careful impression of being bored by the question, but the cracks in the veneer were visible even if Paul couldn't quite see what was behind them. It instantly put him on the defensive.

"About fifteen dollars a week," he said flatly. "I don't see why that matters."

"Just curious." If Julian heard the edge in his voice, he was pretending not to notice. He made a move so nakedly wrong-headed that Paul suspected he was losing on purpose.

"I've just been thinking," he added carelessly, "it might be easier to keep the money thing under control if I didn't live alone."

It took a moment for his meaning to click into place, and when it did, Paul wished it hadn't. His reflexive, cowardly reaction was to imagine how this idea would be received, how ruthlessly his family would decide to be hurt by it, how his grandfather might even hire someone else in Paul's place rather than bankroll the arrangement.

When he forced himself to bury this fear, the suspicion that replaced it wasn't much better. The offering felt the same as the set of oil paints had, overly generous and tailored to overwhelm him, as if it were supposed to remind Paul of how weak he was for wanting it.

Julian crushed his cigarette in the ashtray; before he retreated, his fingertips came to rest, just briefly, on Paul's wrist. Paul smiled to hide his dismay. He reminded himself that they trusted each other now, even as he looked at Julian's shadowed eyes and poorly combed hair and wondered with senseless spite whether that was a mistake.

"It would have to be after my birthday," he said, and looked down at their hands so he wouldn't have to see the relief in Julian's face. "Just so there's no . . . I don't know, so no one can do anything to stop me."

Julian didn't argue the point, though for the first time all day he seemed to want to. He pulled the impatience beneath the surface so quickly that Paul barely had time to recognize it.

"Poor Pablo," he said kindly. "Ruminating, as always."

They didn't finish their game. On their way out Julian pocketed the black queen, as if it belonged to him as much as his wallet and keys. He rolled it between his fingers as Paul drove, too overtired and fretful to get behind the wheel himself. The rain had grown heavier, thick with fragments of snow; Paul switched on the radio to drown out the drum of it on the roof.

"Pull over here," said Julian suddenly.

They were cutting through a lightly traveled stretch of the park, empty under the heavy skies. Paul expected Julian to kiss him, and he tried to believe this would steady him. But Julian only lifted his chin and studied him.

"I've always loved this place right here," said Julian, and he touched Paul's face just beneath the outer corner of his eye. "Something about the slope from your eyelids to your cheekbone, the way the skin here catches the light. It makes your eyes look so dark and serious."

Feeling this visible put Paul in such agony that he knew he couldn't speak without snapping. Instead he shut his eyes and forced himself not to flinch.

"It always makes me a little sad when you laugh," Julian went on. "The way it sort of takes you by surprise. I love it, it has that sweet sincerity that's the best part of you, but it still kills me how you never seem to expect it. All I want to do is make you happy, and you're the unhappiest person I've ever met."

"Stop." He was relieved when he heard the anger in his own voice because it was less humiliating than pain. "Please stop—"

"Everything hurts you." It wasn't an accusation, but it should have been. "You just keep hating yourself, no matter how much I try to show you that you shouldn't. I just want you to trust me, I want you to believe me when I tell you—"

"*Shut up*, Julian."

Julian recoiled as if Paul had hit him. Paul grasped the steering wheel and pushed his shoulders hard against the back of his seat. He could feel his heartbeat in the space behind his eyes.

"I don't need you to talk like that," he said wretchedly. "I'm not some pathetic—I don't need you to *coddle* me, okay? Just stop, I don't want it, I want you to believe I have self-respect and instead it's like you think I need some kind of a reward for good behavior so I don't go to pieces."

If they were going to fall backward into the roles they'd played before, the least Julian could do was snap at him. He'd always been so quick to put Paul in his place, to remind him with devastating mercy how little his emotions actually mattered. But the long sleepless hours had sanded the sharpness from Julian's teeth. *You scare the hell out of me.* The look Julian gave him made Paul wonder for the first time if it might be true.

"I love you," said Julian—uneasy, distant, as if he were reminding himself. "By now you ought to be able to let me fucking tell you."

HE DIDN'T expect it, except in the sense that bracing himself for the possibility felt all but identical to expectation. The fact that it wasn't inevitable only made the dread worse—it could have followed him every day of his life, the chill of fear when he opened the morning paper and the slow climb back into functional uncertainty.

When it happened, it didn't surprise him. The only feeling he could name was a perverse, shattering relief, even as he had to brace his hand on the key table to keep himself from collapsing. His insides had felt loose and unmoored, as if the interstices weren't strong enough to hold his organs in place. But now his body had something to anchor it—evidence, however hideous, that Paul still existed outside his own head.

The headline came on Saturday, while the family was preparing to leave for services. Front page, just above the fold, holding its own amid the turmoil in Greece and the screaming panic over the price of oil. He'd gone all day yesterday without knowing it was already true. Early morning, before he'd even left for his run; some unfortunate stranger he hoped never to meet, out for a walk along the riverfront with her dog.

"Identity has not been disclosed," the article said. Not "unidentified." They already knew who he was.

"Any good indictments today?"

Audrey zipped her jacket as she approached. When Paul

didn't answer, she took the paper from his hands and inspected every headline except the one that mattered.

"This new paperboy, I swear to god," she said to no one in particular. "This whole edge is papier-mâché, he always leaves it sticking out into the rain."

Paul retreated to the living room just long enough to hide his shoes under the couch. He sidled past Audrey and hovered in the kitchen doorway; his mother had set her purse in one of the chairs and was rifling through it for a throat lozenge.

"I'm thinking of sitting it out today." His calm sounded so tinny and false that he didn't dare believe it was convincing. "I've got an article I need to finish reading for journal club."

"Don't you want to hear how Bobby Koenig is doing at William and Mary?" called Audrey from the hallway. Beside her, Laurie quickly turned away to hide her smirk.

His mother straightened; the lozenge clicked against her teeth and gave a glimmering smell of false cherry. She lifted his face, frowning, and leaned up to feel his forehead.

"You look a little pale," she said, in her familiar tone of faint accusation. "Are you sure you're not coming down with that bug?"

"I'm fine," said Paul, but it was convenient for her not to believe him.

He forced himself to wait, long after the trio of black umbrellas had bobbed out of sight at the far end of the street. His hands wore a greasy sheen of newspaper ink; even after he washed them, he thought he could see traces of it etched into his fingerprints. He left a note telling them he was going to the library, and he took his bicycle out into the cold.

He'd forgotten his gloves, but when he noticed, he didn't turn back. A bitter wind picked up, and when he coasted downhill the cold air snapped through his clothes. The rain pilled on his glasses and snaked through his hair until the thrum of his heartbeat made his whole body tremble. He endured it to punish himself, and to prove to himself that he could; those were the only two reasons he ever chose to do anything worthwhile.

It was weeks too soon. He repeated the protest in his head, though he knew it was every bit as useless and self-damning as "It isn't fair." Every moment of doubt he'd felt in the aftermath, every bodily betrayal and senseless lash of temper, every weakness—it all made sense now that he knew he must already have felt the mistake. Some unconscious part of him must have pushed around with its tongue and found it there, like the knot of a new tooth beneath the gums.

He should have seen it; it should have been part of the plan. But he found it buried in the third or fourth contingency, amid the frenzy of the fallback position they were never supposed to need. He'd read in a book that drowned bodies, real ones, would almost always sink. Four liters of water in their chests weighed more than enough to pull them down, and only decay eventually brought them back to the surface. The subject was supposed to follow them out onto the bridge in a haze of his own obedience. Filling his pockets with stones would have been an added complication, a chance for things to go awry, so Paul hadn't even suggested it. It was inelegant and unnecessary— provided the subject entered the river with his lungs still desperate to breathe.

There was no bike rack at Julian's apartment building. Paul walked his bicycle up the steep dead-end road and chained it to the front railing. The tobacco-brown bricks were slick and dark, broken gutter coughing filthy water into the street. Inside the vestibule the light was flickering; the chessboard grid of the linoleum was smeared with mud, as if someone had dragged something inside.

He let himself into Julian's apartment as quietly as he could, in case he was finally sleeping. It was so stiflingly warm that the water on his glasses turned to steam. Paul lingered in the kitchen to peel off a layer of clothes. A bowl sat in the sink, full of tepid milk and bloated kernels of uneaten cereal.

Julian was indeed fast asleep. One slack arm hung over the edge of the mattress; Paul recognized the olive-green sleeve as one of his own cardigans, left behind back in October and then forgotten after every visit since.

Paul intended to curl up in one of the papasan chairs and wait, but when he draped his wet clothes over the radiator, Julian jolted awake.

"It's just me," he said. "Go back to sleep."

For another moment Julian stared at him in alarm, as if he hadn't quite finished dreaming. Then he sighed, rubbed his eyes, and lifted the edge of the blanket.

He already knew. Neither of them acknowledged it; there was no need, and it wouldn't change anything.

Paul should have been eager to prove that he was still strong and unafraid and no longer needed Julian to take care of him; it should have been so self-evidently true that he didn't have to prove it. But he slid under the blankets and rested his head on Julian's arm. He couldn't remember ever being the person he'd decided to become.

Against the scrim of Julian's skin, the cardigan was bright with witch hazel and camphor and kitchen steam, smells Paul barely recognized as belonging to his own body. It was uncanny in the same way as the smell of the Fleischers' empty house after a week in Cape May—the sudden sharp awareness of something long familiar. Julian pulled him close and settled against the mattress again. Neither of them relaxed.

"Do we know what we missed?"

To explain the mistake would mean admitting that it hadn't really been both of them, for all that Paul had promised they would never know. To Paul it was an academic difference, but he knew, even without understanding why, that Julian would take it badly. Uncertainty had made Paul needlessly spiteful for days; he owed Julian kindness more than he owed him the truth.

"Water is denser when it's cold," he answered. "It's my fault. I didn't think of it."

"Don't worry. It doesn't matter." Julian yawned and closed his eyes. "I don't think it'll make much difference, anyway."

"Not much," said Paul, and for a long while both of them pretended to sleep.

4.

HE PUSHED his run earlier every day, first to five and then to four. Every morning before the others woke, he would creep into the nightlight-dark bathroom and fill the tub with cold water. He'd read somewhere that the Spartans had done it to acclimate their soldiers to pain, and that the same principle once applied to mental patients. He held himself underwater until his muscles were taut and screaming. When he held his breath and lay back he could hear only the exhale of the water.

He never became solid. There were soft places on his body that would never fill in with muscle. ("You're such a stringbean, look at you," Julian would say, closing one hand easily around his wrist.) Every smell and sound landed in him at full force, until his skin felt as if the slightest pressure could dissolve him. A single teasing barb from Audrey was all it took one Sunday to reduce him to furious tears—she retreated in bewilderment while his grandparents stared, so alarmed that at first they forgot to pity him. But of course he was *sensitive*. He'd always been sensitive. Paul had never given them cause to expect better.

Each morning he slid down into the crushing cold, and when he emerged he told himself it was one more thing he had endured. Each morning would glaze another layer onto his skin; one day, if he persevered, it would be thick enough to withstand anything.

IT HAPPENED constantly now, and the humiliation fed it like oxygen. Once the tears started coming, it was nearly impossible to stop—and there was never a good reason, nothing he could articulate without feeling even more pathetic. When he took inventory of the day, with its accumulation of small agonies that he should have been able to tolerate, the whole thing felt senseless. A truck horn blaring close enough to make his ears ring, the film of dirt the rain left on his skin, one too many of Julian's condescending endearments. It shouldn't have sanded him so raw, but here he was, and of course Julian refused to pretend not to notice.

"You weren't lying about wanting to, were you?"

Paul kept his eyes shut and tried to pretend Julian wasn't there. But Julian, as always, reacted to the first sign of weakness by pulling it free and inspecting it. There was never any escaping him.

"No, I did, it's just overwhelming sometimes—I'm being stupid, I'm sorry, please just ignore me."

He felt Julian lean up to kiss his forehead. It was all he could do not to shove him away.

"I'm never going to *ignore* you. You wouldn't be here if I didn't like looking after you. It's just that you've been—"

"Don't." Paul curled forward and folded his arms tight. "Please, I don't want to talk about it."

Paul heard the beginnings of a sigh, but Julian quickly smothered it. He broke away and got up from his knees; Paul opened his eyes, watching him untuck his tie from the front of his shirt and shrug back into his cardigan.

"I'm sorry," he said again. Julian rolled his eyes and retreated into the kitchen.

Paul dragged the back of his wrist over his eyes and pushed up from his chair to refasten his belt. He heard the refrigerator opening, then the hiss and snap of a bottle cap.

He couldn't say afterward what made him do it. Julian concealed his exasperation, and he was very kind, in the way that told Paul how much resentment hid just out of sight. Paul reluctantly worked through the ginger ale Julian had given him, while they sat side by side at the head of the bed and Julian read aloud from a translation of Akhmatova.

"You should tell me about the others," Paul said.

Julian trailed off midsentence. His face was steady, but Paul could tell he'd heard a note in his voice that he didn't like.

"The other what?" he asked indifferently. He turned his eyes back to the page, expecting to find his place again once he'd dismissed the question. Paul could feel himself smiling, but he didn't know why.

"Before me," he said. "The other boys like me. What happened to them?"

Julian went very still. He made no attempt to hide his panic.

"There's never been anyone like you." His voice was faint and almost pleading, but Paul didn't stop.

"You know what I mean," he said patiently. "It's all right, Julian, I don't mind. I'm not jealous. I'd just like to know about them."

Julian adopted an affect of haughty disdain, far too abruptly to be convincing. He sighed and paged through his book. "This is the most boring game of yours," he said, "and you come up with *endless* variations on it, it's really quite—"

"I want to hear how you talk about them," Paul said over him. "How you describe them. It's all right if you want to make fun of them. It won't upset me if you hurt them, it's better if you did, I know there's no way they could have deserved you."

Julian gave a miserable laugh.

"I'm so goddamn sick of hearing about what you think people *deserve*. Christ, is that why you're asking? Is it because you want to feel superior, or do you just want something new to accuse me of when I'm not paying enough attention to you?"

Paul hated himself more with every word, but he had never felt less like crying. He would rather be cruel than weak, even if Julian found weakness easier to manage.

"It's as if you respect me less, now." There was a bitter false brightness in his voice that frightened him. "You treat me like I'm delicate. You used to hold me to a higher standard—you used to respect me enough to show me you thought I was capable of being better than this—but now it's as if you'd rather I failed. *Tell me*," he said, "tell me what happens when people fail you. I'll be strong enough to handle it, but I need you to *expect* me to be."

Slowly and with meticulous calm, Julian let his arm fall from Paul's shoulders and put a few inches of distance between them.

"My roommate at prep school," he said. His voice was flat and airless. "He used to climb on top of me when he thought I was asleep. He didn't even take off his clothes, it didn't *count*, I only let him do it because he was a little good-looking and I felt sorry that he didn't have any other friends. Is that the sort of thing you wanted me to tell you? Do you really think I rate you about the same?"

"I don't have any other friends, either. Maybe you feel sorry for me, too." When he finally wanted to stop talking, he couldn't remember how. "I know what you're doing, you tell little pieces of the truth and hope I'll mistake them for the whole thing. Your mother told me there was more than one, and that you got rid of them all."

"She's a fucking liar," said Julian.

So are you, he could have replied, but at last his voice had failed him.

He wanted to apologize, but he knew Julian would reach into the wound and tear it deeper rather than console him. Julian gave him a long, pitiless look, then pulled his knees to his chest and turned away.

"Go home, Pablo," he said blankly. "You were right. I think I liked you better before."

5.

HE COULD tell how dire the fight had been because after smaller ones they didn't give each other the chance to recover. Even if they couldn't yet stand the sight of each other, they always drew together again, compulsively. When Paul went to his old high school for his morning run, he expected Julian to appear by the track—windburned and smiling, his double-breasted wool coat buttoned to the chin. He would have brought one of his silent peace offerings, a thermos of hot chocolate or a new book. They would park in a deserted place, and while they were in the passenger seat Julian would keep his hand braced against the ceiling, and afterward they would pretend to forgive each other until it stopped being a lie.

But when Paul finished his last lap, the parking lot was still empty. He walked home in the cold; whenever he reached a familiar corner, his chest swelled with hope and panic, but it was early and the streets were quiet, and he shouldn't have expected anything else.

At nine o'clock Paul called him, so promptly that he could still hear the church bell tolling at the far end of the line. He wanted Julian to laugh at his desperation, but Julian cut off his apologies before they'd left his mouth.

"Tomorrow. There's no point, you have class today anyway." Julian's voice was edgy and impatient; he still wasn't sleeping well. "Sorry, Pablo," he added, and this time there was a half-hearted veneer of fondness. "Maybe we can go for a drive this weekend, just a day trip somewhere—this city is making me crazy, I'm so goddamn bored . . ."

Paul sat for a long while at the base of the stairs, phone cord pulled taut around the banister, listening to the low whisper of static after the click. Audrey paused in the foyer to look at him. He forced a smile and waved her off, and she sighed.

Later it was supposed to snow. The sky was flat gray and the wind bitter with coal smoke. Paul borrowed a loaner car from the garage to drive out to the research station, what would be his last field practicum of the semester; before he left, he had to flick the windshield wipers to scrape away a thin black film of ash.

He hadn't slept well either, though he couldn't say why. The hours were the same as they usually were, but they had passed too quickly. On the drive out of town the scenery flitted through him, as if he'd never seen the beauty in it and never would. He tried to listen to the news, but the radio was broken. The forest was muffled by winter, clouds grazing the canopy.

The research station lay beyond a sharp bend in the road, concealed by a thick stand of trees. Paul was among the last to arrive, but he noticed the car right away. A black Ford, the same model his father had driven.

He knew what it was, what it meant, before he could brace himself to know. He flipped down the visor mirror and studied his face, certain he would have to correct something. His skin felt mask-tight, but he looked no different than he always did.

The station's generator got temperamental in the cold, and the lights were guttering. His classmates turned at the sound at the door, but Sullivan only looked at him for a moment. Her brow was creased, shoulders squared; she'd forgotten to take off her parka.

Even without the badge clipped to his lapel, Paul would have recognized the stranger as a police officer. There was always a commonality to the way they carried themselves, a peculiar combination of alertness and businesslike disinterest. He was a black man in his early forties, neatly bearded, with round wire-framed glasses. Like all police officers he wore a fortress around himself, as much to keep himself contained as to hold any dangers at bay. Paul could nearly put a name to his face by imagining a black band around his badge. The detective glanced at Paul, and his gaze lingered just a moment longer than it should have. He might have been doing similar calculations in his head, trying to remember the face of a red-haired boy he'd seen at a funeral two years before.

Paul joined his classmates at the worktable. One boy leaned toward him and answered the question before Paul could pretend he needed to ask.

"It's some kind of a drug theft thing," he said at Paul's ear. "Apparently no one told him we're all boring eggheads out here."

"Pity if the final gets canceled," a girl whispered, and everyone but Paul shared a bleak laugh.

He looked away and busied himself unzipping his backpack. Sullivan and the detective spoke so softly that they were drowned out by every rustle of his classmates' clothes.

". . . Public Health and the medical school have their own supply, and it's all accounted for," the officer said. "It's only the biology department that uses that one."

Then Sullivan, a few moments later, after a symphony of shuffling papers. She fidgeted with the end of her ponytail as she spoke. ". . . Doesn't necessarily mean it was one of ours. I'm sure some enterprising physiology student could read up on it even if . . ."

"I understand, ma'am—Professor, excuse me." The officer's

smile was diplomatically impatient. "But since this is the only facility in your department that . . ."

Paul's classmates were nervous and giggly, and he had to give up on listening. He opened his field notebook to a back page and ground his pencil to a stub as he blacked the graph paper square by square.

Sullivan's conversation with the detective hit a lull, and she relaxed just enough to remember to take off her parka. The detective smiled again, but he shrugged off his own coat and folded it over his arm. He wore a canvas-strapped wristwatch, and the effect of his crisp suit was undercut slightly by his comfortable walking boots. He struck Paul as a dangerously practical man.

"I was wondering," he said, a little less quietly, "if I might be able to chat with your students."

Sullivan blanched. Then she wrung her hands, slowly, as if she couldn't quite feel them.

"It's a standard formality—we're checking in with *everyone* who's done work out here," he said, as if this ought to reassure her. "I mean, it can wait, but it's more efficient when we don't have to do it piecemeal, so I'd sure appreciate it."

Sullivan acquiesced with her face and shoulders before the resignation reached her voice. She clasped her hands tight, then let them fall.

"These are smart kids," she said, "and all of them are here because they want to make the world a better place. I don't think you're going to find what you're looking for."

The final was not canceled; Sullivan gave them the packets to take home, though a few of Paul's classmates got started on theirs for want of anything better to do. In alphabetical order they were called back to the storage annex, where the detective had set up a pair of straight-backed chairs. The first few students were in and out quickly—he only wanted names and addresses, they promised the others, and threw themselves back into their chairs as if they no longer had to worry. But Eisenberg, one of the upperclassmen, was kept in the annex for a good half hour. He emerged looking more irritated than shaken, but the others greeted him as if he'd returned from a battlefield.

"What was that all about?" one of the girls demanded, but Paul didn't get a chance to hear the answer.

"All right, Mr. Fleischer," said Sullivan. His blood chilled; she had always called them by their first names. "You can go on in."

When he entered the supply room, the detective rose to shake his hand, a little ungainly in the confined space. Paul had to remind himself where his own hands were; he was overwhelmed by the flickering light and the nearness of the walls.

"I'm Detective Benton," the officer said. His handshake was firm and cool. Paul stared at the rims of his glasses to simulate eye contact and tried in vain to return his smile. "You look a little familiar, have I seen you somewhere?"

His mouth might as well have been full of sawdust. "Um— Paul," he answered. "Fleischer. You probably knew my dad, sir."

Behind the shine of his glasses, a familiar expression flitted through Benton's face—remembering a story, then remembering how it ended. It wasn't quite sympathy. Paul might have liked it even less if it were.

"Of course. You look a lot like him. He was a good man," he added, as if to put Paul at ease. "Good cop, too, but the other thing's a lot less common. How's your mother doing?"

"She's all right, sir. Thanks for asking."

Benton didn't sit until Paul did. He unbuttoned his blazer and leaned back in his seat; behind him the open shelves glittered with specimen jars.

"Fleischer," he said. He lifted the cover of his notepad and glanced down, just long enough to put a knot in Paul's stomach. Then he nodded, just barely, and flipped to a fresh page.

"So what other classes are you taking?" Benton asked. "Anything in the biology labs?"

His name, of course, was on the log sheet of the supply room in the life sciences building. It was alongside dozens of decoys, but not nearly enough—not the right ones.

"Microbiology." His mouth stumbled over the *M*, one of his childhood enemies; he hoped the weakness would make him seem harmless. "I mean, I was, I just had the final on Tuesday."

"You like it?" asked Benton conversationally, and he gave a brief courteous laugh when Paul shook his head. He looked at his notepad again, and Paul held his spine straight to keep himself from squirming. "October thirtieth, about noon," Benton said, "you stopped into the supply room for 'agar'—not sure if I'm saying that right, I majored in poli sci—"

"The stress is on the first syllable, sir," said Paul, and immediately realized he should have kept silent. He could no longer pretend to be a cipher; yielding even a fragment of his personality gave Benton a reason to remember him.

"I had a feeling." Paul wished Benton would stop smiling. "Do you remember if you saw anything funny that day? Anyone acting as if they weren't supposed to be there?"

He had given Paul a chance to lie, so welcoming that he knew it was a trap. Julian might have taken the risk and spun a clever story, an *I'm sure it was nothing* and a description of a stranger too hazy to be of any use. But Paul knew from their chess games that Julian was prone to flashy gambits that he didn't quite have the skill to manage. It was better to be cautious; he couldn't afford to give Benton another inch.

"I don't think so," he said. He spoke in a flat monotone; he hoped it would pass for boyish indifference. "Just people I see around all the time."

"Are you sure?" Benton prompted, and Paul was certain now that he was baiting a hook. "Your classmate, Mr. Eisenberg, wasn't he there around the same time?"

Paul attempted an apologetic smile. He couldn't tell if it was a mistake.

"I see *him* there all the time, too, sir," he said. "It wouldn't have registered."

He wasn't kept much longer, which did nothing to reassure him. There were no veiled accusations or questions about his whereabouts. Instead Benton offered a few banal, inexplicable questions about school, as if he were a second cousin visiting from out of town who didn't know Paul well enough to ask anything more insightful. He wanted to be reminded how many sisters Paul had, and whether Paul was the one with the butterfly hobby; then he was curious how Paul collected his specimens, and was surprised, as people often were, that he didn't use a killing jar.

Just as Paul feared that the conversation had taken a dangerous turn, Benton rose and extended his hand again. He held a business card between his two forefingers, and Paul only belatedly registered that he was supposed to take it.

"Well, I'm glad you and your family are holding up well," said Benton kindly. "Pass on my regards to your mother. That number's my direct line, just in case you happen to remember anything."

It occurred to Paul, almost too late, that an innocent person would wonder what was going on. Not every civilian would dare to ask, but he was supposed to be inured to the mystique of the police. They were the men who invited his family to backyard cookouts and went to Pirates games with Paul and his father—sometimes brusque or vulgar, but never intimidating, not to him. He had been too circumspect and deferential, nothing like a police officer's son. He couldn't imagine it escaping Benton's attention.

"Those must have been some drugs they stole," he said.

This time Benton didn't smile.

"I'm afraid it's much worse than that," he said. "Sorry I can't get into detail. But I really hope, if you remember something, that you'll give me a call."

When he emerged, Eisenberg had already gone, and the other forebears were preparing to follow him. Sullivan greeted him by gingerly patting his shoulder. They exchanged a look, incredulous and uncomfortable, as if they were trapped at the same awkward party, and Paul had to stifle the giddy urge to laugh.

"You can head home if you want," said Sullivan. "The exam is due on Monday at five—hopefully plenty of time for everyone to get their heads screwed back on."

She was trying to remember her adult authority, the way Paul always had to when he was touring a group of young children through the botanical garden. He felt monstrous watching Sullivan try to shield him from whatever she knew—as if she absolutely trusted that he had some kind of innocence to preserve.

"I'm going to get some air first, I think," he said.

Paul walked unseeingly into the cold, until he was deep

enough into the trees that he could no longer see the station behind him. One glove had fallen from his pocket, but rather than turn back to find it, he threw its mate into the dead leaves. He found Benton's business card in the same pocket, already beginning to flake from friction. It announced Benton's first name as Anthony; the police department coat of arms was printed in black and yellow inks that didn't quite align.

He crumpled the card and cast it aside. Then he hit himself as hard as he could. He tried again, methodically, until the numbness finally left his face. He had to deliberately drum himself into a panic. The scale of the disaster was so immense that he could barely accept it as real.

JULIAN'S APARTMENT hadn't been empty for long. The radiator was turned down, but it still clicked with heat. There were two crumpled hot chocolate packets on the counter, and the kettle was warm.

The chill hadn't left Paul's bones, but when he refilled the kettle and set it to boil, the smell of the steam was so sickening that he quickly shut it off again. Instead he filled his mug with half a can of Dr Pepper and three fingers of bourbon from the freezer. That wouldn't do much to settle his stomach either, but he swallowed a revolting mouthful. It cheered him up to think how much he would regret it later. When he switched on the stereo and sat down to wait, Paul finally noticed what was amiss. There were two chocolate-stained cups on the coffee table, one kissed at the rim by sherbet-orange lipstick. The color appeared again in the ashtray, around the end of a spent cigarette—a strange one, all white, lollipop-stick thin.

Julian's day planner lay open on his dresser, a grocery receipt clipped to the page (ginger ale, mandarin oranges, pancake mix). Beneath it, in Julian's familiar flowing cursive, two notes: *JG plane 11:15a* and *PBT 6:00p.*

Julian had arranged the intrusion in advance, and hadn't bothered to tell him. Even though the visitor was someone Paul knew, even though her presence breached between present and past in a way too jarring not to acknowledge. They were no longer supposed to have secrets, and the very insignificance of this one frightened him. He imagined worse things that Julian might be keeping from him.

Paul switched off everything but the stove light and dropped back into his chair. By the end of the Françoise Hardy record he'd drained his drink, every sickly-sweet, musty drop of it. He made another and forced himself through as much of it as he could, until the world churned around him and he knew he would throw up if he tried to finish.

He didn't remember falling asleep—there were no dreams, even bad ones. But the clack of the deadbolt startled him upright. The soreness in his face had worsened, and his teeth ached as if he'd been clenching them.

The door swung open, and they spilled in with the light. The girl was watching Julian over her shoulder, laughing. It was Julian who saw him first. The tension took hold of his body, visible even in the dark.

Joy Greenwood turned to follow Julian's gaze. She made a small *Oh!* of surprise and picked her way toward Paul through the clutter. When the lights flicked on, Paul saw that she was flushed and beaming, unsteady in her knee-high white boots.

"*There* you are, lovely." She leaned up and flung an arm briefly but firmly around his neck. She smelled like peach perfume and sloe gin. Her white suede trench coat was lined with real fur. "I didn't think I'd get a chance to see you, Julian said you wouldn't be able to come with us."

"I didn't think he could," answered Julian before Paul could speak. "Or that he'd want to, particularly."

It was taking Julian longer than usual to fit his pieces together. He was slow following Joy inside, and his smile had an impatient edge that he would normally have tucked away unseen. He was trying to pretend that he hadn't been drinking. For a hideous instant Paul could see himself through Julian's eyes—hands shivering, weak and fearful in the wake of his own failure. Of course Julian could tell something was wrong.

"It was only the *Nutcracker.*" Joy was suddenly intensely concerned that his feelings might have been hurt. "I promise you didn't miss anything, it was all drearily provincial."

"I—it's fine. I don't really like things where people dance around in costumes."

"Oh god, Julian, he's such a *boy*, how can you stand it?" Joy flung herself into a chair and lit one of her cigarettes; her hands were a flurry of flame and gleaming jewelry, graceful despite the drink. She looked up at Paul with a fond smile, and he felt a pang of guilt amid the frustration.

Julian was in the kitchen, filling three glasses with ice. When Paul drew near him, he took a long, slow breath. By the time he met Paul's gaze, his eyes were defensively opaque.

"I don't want to hear it." He turned on the faucet so that Joy wouldn't hear them.

"You need to get rid of her."

Julian wore a grim, tight smile that reminded Paul of Mrs. Fromme. "I'm not going to be cruel to her." He handed Paul a glass of ice water and turned back to the sink. "She's my friend. I'm entitled to those."

Paul was still a little drunk himself, but he didn't bother to try and temper it. "You didn't even tell me she was coming." It wasn't the point, but it was easier to make himself angry than to admit what the point actually was.

"I thought I might avoid one of those charming meltdowns you have when I pay the slightest attention to anything besides you." Julian filled another glass without looking at him. "If you're trying to convince me I made the right decision, you're doing a stellar job."

"Juli, do you have enough cigarettes?" There was a faint conciliatory note to Joy's voice, as if she'd picked up on the tension. "I can pop out to the gas station for you."

"Stay put, you lush, you'd never find it. I don't want to have to fish you out of the river."

The drink in Paul's stomach turned syrup-thick. He set his glass aside and took hold of Julian's arm.

"Something is wrong." Even at an undertone, he could barely keep his voice from breaking. *"Please*, Julian." Julian was stone-faced, eyes wide, so tense he might snap. Paul had thought it was anger. As Julian smiled again, unblinking, he suddenly recognized it as fear.

"I know," said Julian. "Wait."

Joy was sitting at the outermost edge of the curved cushion, elbows on her knees, chewing at a loose flake of orange nail polish between puffs from her cigarette. She gave Julian a worried, puppyish look; Julian shook his head and touched her shoulder, and she relaxed back into her seat. It wasn't unlike the moments that sometimes passed between Paul and Laurie, the wordless and ineffable exchanges of meaning that accompanied long years of familiarity. His understanding of Julian felt abruptly small.

The two of them sat together in the other chair and spent

a while putting Joy at ease—or rather, Julian did, while Paul just tried to make his monosyllabic replies sound as friendly as he could. After a few gentle attempts to include him in the conversation, Joy decided to leave him be. She and Julian chatted about the artistic defects of the ballet production and her family's plans for Christmas. Julian had his arm around Paul's shoulders and reached up now and then to touch his hair, but neither of them looked at each other; Paul knew if he saw the fear in Julian's face again, he might not be able to keep his own from boiling over.

Finally they found an excuse to step out—hot chocolate, breakfast cereal, something forgettable that could have waited till morning. Before they left, Joy caught Paul by the wrist. Julian, rather than wait beside him, returned to the kitchen and gathered up his wallet and keys.

"Listen," said Joy in a plaintive undertone. "I know he's hopeless at showing it, and god knows he can be a pest, but—he really is wild about you. I don't doubt it for a minute."

It was such a small fragment of evidence that Paul couldn't quite piece together what Julian might have told her. Even if he could, he wouldn't know what to feel. Dread swelled into his every corner; there was no space left for him to feel anything else.

Julian led him to the very bottom of the stairwell, to a basement landing outside the padlocked grate door of a boiler room. Paul watched him light a cigarette. In the stark light he looked thin—there were shadows beneath his cheekbones that Paul didn't remember being there before. Paul lingered on the second stair. He could only bear the sound of his own voice by ignoring it in favor of the smaller other sounds around it, the creak of the boiler and the thrum of the lights.

Julian worked slowly through the cigarette as he listened, not speaking. He shook free a flake of ash. Paul couldn't see his eyes in the dim light—just the sickly shade underneath them, the spidery interlace of his eyelashes. When Paul fell silent, Julian exhaled slowly and crushed his cigarette against the heel of his boot. He folded his arms and paused before speaking. *Look at me*, Paul pleaded silently, but he didn't.

"Well. I guess this is what the alibi is for."

"Should we go over it?" *Look at me. Fucking look at me.* "I'm just worried that—"

"There's no need for them to talk to *me* at all," said Julian. "Remember? Charlie marked off Wednesday on his calendar like a good little soldier. You have an airtight alibi that doesn't rely on me in the least. You're safe."

Paul's hands fell to his sides. There was no mistaking now that Julian was thinner than he'd been before. Paul didn't know why he hadn't noticed sooner. The cruelest thing was that there was nothing unkind at all about his smile—it was the same one he wore when he was being reassuring and gentle, *managing* him, and wanted Paul to know it.

"What a face." Julian was relaxed and cajoling, as if he could trick Paul into believing nothing was wrong by pretending it was true. "Chin up, Pablo. It's nowhere near as bad as you had me thinking it would be."

All Paul's energy went toward keeping his feet rooted to the ground, and there was nothing left to keep his voice from shaking.

"The day before, though—we're supposed to have each other covered for the day before, you said, you *promised*—"

"For Christ's sake. Don't be an idiot." Julian was annoyed now, and incredulous. "I'll talk to them if *necessary*," he said tersely, "though I'd appreciate the courtesy of a warning if you think it's coming. All I was trying to do was remind you of your first line of defense, which is frankly much more credible than whatever I'd be able to give you. Would you like to calm down now?"

Paul drew a sharp breath and held it until he could remember how to exhale. Julian dropped the stub of his cigarette and joined him on the stairs. He put his hand on Paul's shoulder, as if to reassure him, but as he drew closer he tightened his grasp.

"You already know," he said at Paul's ear, "what I'm willing to do for you. Maybe you can start counting that in my favor going forward. Okay, Pablo?"

He didn't wait for an answer. He just smiled again—a bracing, expectant smile—and brushed past him on his way back up the stairs. Paul didn't try to follow him. He sank down to sit at the bottom of the basement steps, listening to Julian's footfalls overhead as he headed out into the snow.

6.

JULIAN HADN'T said where they were going, and Paul hadn't asked. They'd planned it in advance, supposedly, though Paul had no memory of it; the two days that had passed since then might as well have been years. "We're going for a drive, remember?" Julian had prompted, while Paul stood in the doorway in his nightclothes and realized he was too exhausted to contradict it. Even if it was a lie, it meant Julian was in control; if Julian was in control, that meant at least one of them was.

In his weakness, Paul had yearned for the old order of things. He'd missed the way Julian would decide what would happen and what was true, and proceed as if Paul already agreed with him. Of course you'll wear the blue sweater, of course you'll let me pay for lunch, of course you want to kiss me. Of course we're going for a drive, and of course you'll go back inside and change so we can get out of town before rush hour. "Don't keep me waiting," Julian had said, and he didn't.

They were traveling west, beneath the cloud-rippled sky and flat silver sun. Julian followed the highway across the state line, and for hours they sped past decaying places where even Paul struggled to see the beauty—white dormant soybean fields, ragged trees glittering with snow, the low rooflines and yellowing roadside signs of Pentecostal churches. Paul couldn't make sense of what they were doing here. He could feel Julian steeling himself against it, the way he always did when they drove through places where neither of them were welcome.

But there were no bitter comments or scathing jokes. Julian was quiet, steering one-handed with the sunlight at his back.

His right arm was draped over the back of Paul's seat, but they didn't quite touch.

"You look better," said Paul. "How are you sleeping?"

Julian looked at him sideways—puzzled, or pretending to be. Paul understood belatedly that it had been a deliberately needling question, just shy of picking a fight. Julian smiled as if they were teasing each other, and Paul knew he was trying to neutralize the threat.

"Joy left me a few 714s," he answered, so dryly that Paul couldn't tell if he was kidding. "I woke up at four in the afternoon yesterday, it was marvelous."

"It's better though, isn't it?" Paul felt a sudden and violent compulsion to keep talking, though the sound of his own voice was infuriating. "Isn't it sort of a relief now that something's finally gone wrong? I think it is at least, I always knew that if something went wrong it was going to be my fault, and now I finally—"

"Pablo."

Julian seemed to know he'd spoken too harshly, and with visible effort he recalibrated; then he traced his fingertips down the side of Paul's face. It was the first time either of them had touched the other all morning.

"That subject is getting so tedious." Julian held Paul's face for a moment even after he'd turned his gaze back toward the road. "It's going to be fine—if you can't trust yourself, then at least trust me. That's all I want to hear about it today. Agreed?"

It wasn't that Paul believed him; he felt so far from the world of tangible things that he didn't believe in anything. But in the imperious remove of Julian's voice he remembered how he'd felt in the early days, when he still thought Julian was unbreakable. He remembered his faith in the steadiness of Julian's hands and in the way winter light lensed through the thin skin of his wrists, and it was enough—or nearly enough—for Paul to feel self-contained.

"I want you to do something for me," said Julian. He glanced at Paul again but didn't let his gaze linger. "I want you to let me be nice to you today. I don't care if you don't think you deserve it."

He knew what he deserved, and it wasn't kindness—it was the dread that Julian's affection would vanish with the last of his patience. But Paul didn't protest, because part of letting Julian be kind to him was pretending to believe it would last forever. He answered instead by taking off his glasses and resting his head on Julian's shoulder. The world beyond the windshield faded away to formless undulations of gray. When Julian turned to kiss his forehead, Paul caught a sharp unfamiliar smell at his throat—perhaps a new shaving cream he barely needed, or a different brand of soap. The change unnerved him far out of proportion to its actual importance. Even Julian's smallest details threatened to slip through his grasp.

"We'll be all right," Julian said, and Paul wondered which of them he thought needed the reassurance. "I'll show you. We're nearly there."

Around noon they reached a town where the water tower was painted with a name Paul nearly recognized. The town looked like a painting from one of his mother's jigsaw puzzles—well-loved clapboard houses with bright paint and white trim, tall healthy trees along the edges of the streets. Even in the snow, with tire-troughs in the slush and flags taken inside for the winter, it was picturesque in a way he wouldn't have thought Julian liked.

"I know," said Julian, as if Paul's apprehension was too obvious to ignore. "When we came here to visit the campus, I almost balked, but there's a bigger town up the road, and it would only be for a few years."

The college was one of the tony handful where neighbors on wealthier streets liked to send their children—the kind of place where long-haired students staged sit-ins and rallies, but not the kind where they might be shot for it. When he and Julian stepped out into the empty parking lot, Paul involuntarily imagined Julian's parents accompanying them. Mr. Fromme would collect arbitrary details to find distasteful, some of which he would jeer at in the moment and others he would hold in reserve to hurt Julian with later. The picture of Julian's mother was more impressionistic—she would be quieter and far crueler, able to convey the depth of her skepticism by the delicate way she removed her gloves by their fingertips.

"You've got to imagine it in the fall," said Julian.

The campus was empty for winter break. It was as archetypal in its way as the town that surrounded it, like something out of a brochure for the faraway expensive colleges Paul had never considered attending. Frozen walkways wandered beneath a vaulted ceiling of bare branches, and the façades—stone and red brick, Harvard in miniature—were half hidden by veins of ivy. They didn't see another soul. Every window was black.

Julian led him by the hand and explained the plan. It crackled with downsides and imperfections, which Julian might have included on purpose so it would seem more likely to come true. They would have to share a dorm room for at least the first year, and Julian knew they would both go crazy from being unable to escape each other. The student body was nebulously Episcopalian and lily-white—"About ten Jews total," Julian joked, "and it sounds like you know all of them." The town would be unbearably boring, and of course no sane man aspired to live in any of "these awful flat states that start with a vowel."

But Paul really had to imagine it in the fall. (He pretended he could.) He would have no trouble getting in; there was a biology program, and even a decent art division, just in case he decided to double-major. He would be able to enjoy the preserve nearby, with a thick forest full of butterflies; the town up the road had a Chinese restaurant and an art-house theater, and even what Julian's parents had humorously failed to recognize as a head shop. Not perfect—it wasn't Vermont-or-Maine, not yet. But it was a start.

Julian had it all planned, their future of petty frustrations and collegiate joys. Paul suspected he'd even built a road map of their inevitable quarrels, tiny curlicue detours from which they would easily return.

It was cold, but not bitterly so, and they didn't return to the car right away. When Julian tired of walking, they sat on a bench alongside the duck pond. Yellow-stalked cattails leaned and folded at the shoreline, and the ice was still carved with skate marks from the students who had since gone home for the holidays. Julian turned up his coat collar. Paul zipped his parka up to the chin.

"Do you actually like it, or are you just humoring me?" Julian's tone was light and teasing, but when he went on, Paul could sense the unease underneath. "I've been to a million other colleges if you don't like this one. This one's just, you know, it's closer to Pittsburgh than the others. And since you have a family that's actually *worth* visiting, I thought . . ."

A shiver moved through Paul like a chill in the wind. When he tried to imagine the two of them here, he could only see them at a distance. He watched them wander the long path around the campus green, walking in step as they always had, alone together under a shining September sky. Not as they were now, nor even as they had been at the beginning. They were the people they should have been for each other's sake, so far out of reach now that Paul barely recognized them. The better Paul grieved as much as he did, skin so thin around his father's absence that the pain left him breathless—but in the parts of him that Julian held in place, he believed somehow that his shape would hold. The other Julian might be opaque to the world outside, but with Paul he held nothing back, because somehow that Paul forgave him for being capable of fear. Paul couldn't stand to imagine them for long. These were the only versions of themselves that had ever stood a chance of surviving.

"I like it—I do." Paul spoke as soon as he could summon the words because he couldn't bear to hear the uncertainty in Julian's voice. It didn't matter if it was a lie.

Julian exhaled hard. Then he smiled, with such wary and blazing relief that it hurt to keep meeting his eyes.

"I wanted to show you it was real," he said, and Paul almost shied away when Julian touched his face. "It's always been real for me, every second—anything else I've ever loved is so wrapped up in you now, you're all that's left. Promise you believe me, I'm so goddamn exhausted trying to convince you, I don't know what else I can do to make you see it."

He had promised to let Julian speak without arguing; the promise was the only thing that kept him steady. There was no revering him anymore. Only love remained, and it was a fragile thing that Paul had been desperate not to see. He couldn't stand to look at the truth, even now. All they were—all they had ever been—was a pair of sunflowers who each believed the other was the sun.

Of course he said yes. Of course he made every promise Julian asked of him, because they'd hurt each other enough, and it was the only mercy he could offer. It didn't matter. He knew what waited for them back in the city, and he knew nothing they said to each other today would hold.

The sun sank behind them as they left. Julian drove with the window rolled down. Now and then he would shake his cigarette ashes out into the wind, that careless movement he must have borrowed from his mother. His fingertips were red from the cold, and he was euphoric and radiant with hope, and Paul imagined the inevitable moment the dream would fall down around them.

They drove past an abandoned barn that a tornado had ripped in two. Julian watched it as they passed, turning in his seat to get a better look, as if he couldn't parse it. Then he lowered his sunglasses and turned back to the road.

"You shouldn't look so sad," he said. It was less of an accusation than he pretended. "Are you sure this is really what you want?"

Paul shut his eyes and tried to find a plausible lie. "It is," he said. "I just didn't know we would have to go so far away."

Julian chewed on the inside of his lip, just long enough for Paul to see the grim shape of what they carried between them.

"I think 'far away' is what we're going to need for a while."

7.

THEY CAME back for him the day after Christmas.

The garage was open, but business was slow. The pair of them appeared at the far end of the building, framed from behind by bright light and snow. Paul looked reflexively toward them, putting on his glasses as he raised his head, because their arrival was the first unexpected movement in hours. He nearly looked away again, but he recognized Benton, first by his profile and then by his boots.

Paul wasn't surprised to see them. He couldn't tell if he was afraid, because the first and most overwhelming thing he felt was the absence where his boredom had been moments before.

His grandfather approached them, wiping grease from his hands. Then he stopped short.

Carl wheeled himself out from under the car he was working on, out of sight of the others, pretending not to listen in. Paul's grandfather loomed over the two detectives with his hands on his hips, but Benton's partner said something that made him glance involuntarily toward the office. Benton followed his gaze and turned to march through the garage. When Paul's grandfather tried to follow, the partner stepped into his way to intercept him.

The pencil had fallen from Paul's hand. When he looked down at the ledger, the numbers churned like the surface of a river during a storm.

Detective Benton's face appeared on the other side of the reinforced glass. When he caught Paul's eye, he waved, as if they were friends, and let himself in through the office door.

"Hi, Paul." He spoke with the sort of sterile amiability that Paul used himself, not infrequently, in conversations with his classmates. "Got a minute?"

Paul told his face to smile. The muscles moved, but he couldn't feel them.

Benton didn't say how he'd known Paul was here. He had a vision of Benton stopping by the house to ask his mother— and then a far worse one of an unmarked car following him, unseen, for days or even weeks. He watched without blinking as Benton glanced around the office with placid disinterest. He didn't sit down; he leaned on the file cabinet with his hands in his pockets.

"You handle this all by yourself?" Benton asked. He was pretending to be impressed.

Paul's tongue felt too dry and thick to move, even after he spoke. "Just helping my grandfather keep things under control. The last manager left a real mess."

"Doesn't look like a mess anymore," said Benton, and he flashed Paul one of his inscrutable smiles. "So listen, Paul, this shouldn't take long . . ."

His grandfather had freed himself from Benton's partner. He appeared in the doorway, his face grim, though he gave Paul a reassuring nod and rounded the desk to stand behind him.

"I'd like to know what this is about," said his grandfather quietly. His hands came to rest on Paul's shoulders. Paul didn't dare look at him; he didn't want to see how much the question might have been directed at him.

"We're tying up some loose ends in an investigation. There was a drug theft at your grandson's college." Benton dispensed the half-truth with an easy confidence that rivaled Julian's. "Paul isn't a *suspect*, we've only talked to him as a witness—we're just trying to narrow our focus and make sure we build a good case. I'm surprised he didn't mention it," he added, as if his surprise were both genuine and trivial.

Paul felt his grandfather's gaze; he had to steel himself to turn and meet his eyes. "I didn't want Ma to freak out," he said quickly. "It didn't seem like a big deal, and she's been doing so well lately that I—"

"You're not in trouble, Paulie." His grandfather squeezed his shoulders. Paul bit his tongue and looked away.

Benton's partner was in no rush to catch up with them. Paul could see him through the open door, strolling around with his hands in the pockets of his peacoat. He was younger than Benton, with a lean face and untrimmed black hair. He leaned down to chat with Carl as he worked (or feigned working) beneath the squeaky-braked Chevelle. Paul stared until he couldn't bear it any longer, trying to imagine the kind of answers Carl might give. (*All right, I guess. Funny kid, though—quiet. He's the boss's grandson, so . . . Yeah, now that you mention it, I guess he might know how to sabotage an engine.*)

"I was hoping you could firm up a few things for us," said Benton. Paul snapped his gaze forward and tried, once more, to smile. "Just for the record, where were you around Thanksgiving?"

"What is this?"

Paul's grandfather still had a U-shaped scar on his scalp where a police baton had struck him decades ago, when he was a young man trying to save the world. He sounded increasingly as if he was remembering how it felt.

"Paul's never been in trouble in his life," he went on, "and you—"

"Well that's not *strictly* true," said Benton, in a conspiratorial tone that didn't match the polite distance of his smile. "There's the matter of his, ah . . . abrupt exit from high school."

"Self-defense," said his grandfather coldly. "Do you look up school records on all your *witnesses*, Detective? Did you happen to notice he was a goddamn model student while you were digging around in there?"

"It would be very helpful," said Benton as if he hadn't heard, "to hear your whereabouts on your Thanksgiving break. I'm sure we can wrap this up painlessly."

"He was with his family all day," his grandfather said. "As you might expect. There are over a dozen witnesses who would be happy to confirm it, if you insist on wasting their time."

"No need, Mr. Krakovsky. I'll take you at your word."

Benton opened his leather-bound notebook and clicked open a pen. He turned his gaze to Paul—keen but impassive, offering no hint of what he thought an innocent person would do.

"The holiday break starts on Wednesday, doesn't it?" he said. "Maybe you could tell me about that day."

For a single, interminable second, Paul lost the ability to speak.

Of course they'd discussed the possibility that the police might pull apart the false time line they had tried to create. They'd kept the receipts from the day, just in case, paperclipped into Julian's little green balance book. But they hadn't rehearsed a script, because Paul would never be able to speak it convincingly, and it would look suspicious if they remembered too many details of an unremarkable Wednesday from weeks before. In the absence of a concrete road map, Paul was briefly but sickeningly certain that they had made a terrible mistake—that he was even less capable of improvising than reciting a lie from memory.

"Let me think," he heard himself say. He could have wept from relief at finding his voice at all. "It was a while ago."

His grandfather gave his shoulders another gentle shake before letting go. Of course his grandfather was another un- wanted variable. Suspicious of Julian, deliberately kept in the dark about how often they still saw each other—Paul didn't trust him to keep his face steady if he heard the truth. But there was no avoiding it. His grandfather had appointed himself as Paul's protector; he would hardly be swayed by any efforts to get rid of him.

"I think . . ." He paused, pretending to search for the memory of a dull day in November. ". . . yeah, I was with a friend." He felt his grandfather tense, but he forced himself to keep speaking. "I stayed over the night before Thanksgiving. I can't really re- member what we did, I think we went to the movies, that kind of art-housey place down the street from the Hillman Library."

"Does this friend have a name?" Benton adopted a gentler tone after a few words, clearly for his grandfather's benefit. "We'll just have to chat with him to confirm. We should be able to clear all this up."

"Um—Julian." Paul wrung his hands and tried to think of an inconspicuous way to warn him. "Julian Fromme. I can call him if you like."

"Nah, I've got to drop by the station in a bit, you could just give me his contact information." Benton flipped to a back page of his notebook and held it out to Paul, bracing the book against his palm rather than letting Paul take it. "We'll try to get it squared away this afternoon—speed things along," he added with a glance at Paul's grandfather, "so we can get out of your hair."

Paul carefully wrote Julian's phone number and address, in

a tight too-neat hand that barely looked like his own. One or the other of the detectives might stay behind and follow him; he couldn't dare run to a pay phone and call Julian before they arrived. With wild and senseless spite, he decided not to care if Julian was angry. If Paul had to improvise, so should he.

The other detective was waiting in the doorway. Paul realized with a start that he didn't know how long he'd been there.

"There were 'a few' in for minor repairs over the holiday weekend," he said to Benton. "The kid's in charge of the records, apparently."

"This is Detective Marinetti," Benton said, as if he were reminding his partner of his manners. Marinetti looked at Paul with a nod and a smile, but he didn't say another word.

"So the cars that come in for repairs," Benton added, turning back to Paul. "Where do you record their plate numbers and mileage and everything? We just need to know about the cars that were here over the holiday. Do you know where we could find that information?"

Under any other circumstances, Paul might have laughed. It seemed like a deliberately ludicrous question, calling attention to the careful order Paul had imposed on the office over the last several months. The offending record binder was in plain sight on the shelf behind him, labeled *REPAIRS 1973 OCT–DEC* in crisp block lettering. But his grandfather's patience finally snapped.

"You said this was about a theft." His voice was so cold with fury that Paul wouldn't have recognized him. "What would my business records have to do with it? My *private* business records," he said, "which I think, if you check the Bill of Rights, you'll find you still need a warrant for."

"We didn't mean any offense," Marinetti started to say, but

Paul's grandfather drew himself up to his full, massive height. Marinetti didn't recoil, but he seemed to think about it.

"They're just doing their jobs, Zayde," Paul tried to interject, but no one appeared to hear him.

"My son-in-law," said his grandfather, "gave twenty years of his life to you *police*. He could have done anything, and that's what he chose, god knows why. You drain every ounce of life from him, and then you have the *gall* to come in here half-cocked, treating his son like a goddamn criminal."

Paul couldn't bear to look at his grandfather, so he fixed his gaze on Benton, on the arc of tube lighting reflected on the surface of his glasses. He tried to look the way an innocent person might—a little defensive, mostly confused. But his face resolved into the stony blankness that it always did when he was desperate to conceal the truth. To an unfamiliar eye, it would look like defiance.

"We've cooperated more than enough," his grandfather said. "Come back with a warrant."

Benton didn't even blink. Paul's father wouldn't have, either.

"Well," said Benton evenly. "Hopefully it won't come to that. Like I said—just tying up loose ends."

"Our lieutenant," Marinetti added, "doesn't tolerate a single undotted *i*."

"I can think of a number of things my son-in-law wouldn't have tolerated." Paul could all but hear the look on his grandfather's face. "Is that all, gentlemen?"

Benton's smile sent a shiver through him. "For now," he said. "Thank you. We'll find our own way out."

Paul's grandfather watched them leave from the doorway. He had his arms braced at either side of the doorframe, as if they might turn around and try to push back inside. Paul sat very still until they were gone, and then he lost the strength to hold his weight upright. His grandfather turned toward him, but Paul slid down in his chair and clasped his hands over his mouth. He could feel the slick mass of organs inside him; one might slither out if he parted his lips.

"All this for *drugs*," said his grandfather with venom. "For god's sake . . . Paul, come on, now. Sit up, let's have a look at you."

He tried to pull his spine straight. His grandfather lifted his chin to inspect his face, and his gaze was so absolutely void of suspicion that Paul had to shut his eyes.

"Pull yourself together," his grandfather said kindly. "Don't take it so hard, you aren't in any trouble . . . Take a deep breath, think how ridiculous this is, *all* of us know better."

Paul didn't have any more lies in reserve, even silent ones. He could only open his eyes when he pretended he was dreaming. He accepted his own despair and his grandfather's bracing impatience with the same resignation he would accept the chaos of a nightmare.

"Please don't say anything to my mother," he said quietly. He scarcely heard his grandfather's reassurances over the rush of blood in his throat.

HE SHOULD have trusted his grandfather to give his mother a prettier version of the truth. By the time the explanation reached her, it was trifling, even funny. Could they imagine their Paul getting mixed up in drugs? They couldn't, either of them; he was a good boy, a nice young man, if anything *too* averse to rule breaking. It would blow over, and in a year or two it would make a good story. Of course neither of them were worried. He shouldn't be either, but he was sensitive, easily shaken. It was a character flaw they had always made a point of forgiving, and this time was no different.

The telephone didn't ring all evening, and Paul didn't dare phone first. The police might be there when he called; even if they weren't, Julian's nerves would be at least as shaken as his. Paul had to get himself back under control, or at least shield himself behind anger. Until then—until he knew he could withstand whatever Julian said to him—he didn't trust himself to endure what was coming.

His family demanded that he recover quickly, with all the warmth and kindness that made them difficult to disobey. The next day was Laurie's birthday, and by early afternoon the house was cluttered with girls, each hallway a gauntlet of perfume and fringed-jacket elbows. Paul wended between empty corners and picked at the wax-paper mouth on his cup of fruit punch, and whenever his mother or grandparents glanced toward him he smiled, because he was supposed to smile.

Julian, as always, arrived late. Paul watched from a distance as his mother sidled through the crowd to greet him. He'd brought a gift wrapped in green foil, along with a pink pastry box from a French bakery downtown. He laughed at something Paul's mother said before she'd finished speaking, and she beamed and squeezed his arm. He was ferociously cheerful and fraying at every edge.

When Paul approached, Julian smiled, unblinking, and caught him by the shoulder. "There you are, Pablo," he said. "I have the funniest story to tell you."

Paul's mother bustled away to put Julian's boxes in the dining room. The thrum of piping laughter and pop music was ruptured by a sudden, exuberant scream; Paul started, but Julian didn't flinch.

"Upstairs," said Julian. "Now."

There were two whispering girls sitting on Laurie's bed, heads bowed together, cross-legged in their matching white boots. When they caught sight of Paul and Julian one of them sprang to her feet to close the door, watching them gleefully through the narrowing gap until it clicked shut. Julian waited for her to disappear, then pushed Paul into the bathroom and locked the door.

Julian was round-shouldered and tense. There was barely any space between them, but Julian seemed determined not to touch him; he pushed his back against the wall opposite Paul instead.

"You didn't warn me." His fury was all the more lethal for how quietly he spoke. "I told you to *fucking warn me.*"

"I didn't get a chance." Paul's voice was so wheedling and childish that he wished Julian would hit him. "You stuck to the script, didn't you?"

Julian threw him a disgusted look and broke his gaze to lean over the sink. He fumbled for a cigarette and lit it, inelegantly, with one shaking hand.

"Julian."

Julian exhaled a mouthful of smoke through his teeth. Then he straightened, and he met Paul's gaze with eyes so cold and distrusting that the two of them might as well have been strangers.

"Of *course* I stuck to the *fucking* script."

"So what went wrong?" His voice pitched with panic, and he tried to flatten it again. "Wasn't it—"

"I wanted a chance to brace myself." Paul almost didn't notice Julian wasn't answering the question. "That's all I wanted.

We've built everything else about this around what you need, around your fucking *variables*. You owed it to me to give me this *one* thing."

There was a chime of little-girl laughter down the hall, muffled by the doors between them. Paul tried to decide whether he should cling to his defensive anger or swallow it. Julian looked away and flicked ash into the sink.

"How bad was it?" asked Paul quietly. He pushed his hands into his pockets and leaned harder against the wall.

"It's not about it being *bad*." Julian pronounced the word in a ruthless caricature of Paul's accent. "For Christ's sake! It's as if you're worried I'm going to tattle on you for shoplifting, it's like it still hasn't occurred to you that *I'm* part of this just as much as you are, and maybe I have a little more on my mind right now than reassuring you every goddamn second of your life—"

"Oh, poor you, it isn't like I'm the one they're actually asking about, I can't possibly—"

There was a knock at the door, too soft and uncertain to belong to any member of Paul's family. "There's another one in the basement," he called, more sharply than he intended, and the intruder scampered away.

Julian's cigarette had gone out. He crushed it on the counter rather than relight it. "It's both of us." There was a crack of desperation in his voice. "It's always been both of us, it's mutually assured destruction, that was the entire point. And it didn't do me a damn bit of good, did it?"

Paul wanted to hurt Julian enough to make him angry again. It was only after he spoke that he knew he'd accidentally landed on the truth.

"It's only mutually assured destruction if you think I'd drag you down with me." His voice was slow and precise. "But I wouldn't. You know that. I don't even think you did it on purpose, but you've made sure of it. You survive this no matter what."

Julian looked at Paul with something that could have been pity as easily as horror. At first it appeared he couldn't speak, and then as if he'd decided not to try. Paul folded his arms and stared at the wall. As Julian brushed past him, he touched Paul's hip with his fingertips, but Paul couldn't bring himself to meet his eyes.

Julian left the door open to the hallway. Paul heard him pause at the head of the stairs and murmur something to himself over and over, trying a different tone each time, as if he were praying. Then he took a deep breath and descended, and when he spoke aloud, Paul realized he'd been rehearsing.

"Where's the birthday girl hiding?" It was an imperfect performance, but the others weren't primed to expect perfection, and they likely wouldn't notice. "I need to give her her present . . ."

His family would notice his absence if he avoided them much longer. With meticulous care, Paul reassembled himself. He knew the reflection in the mirror was his, but it was only a philosophical understanding. When he made his face blank and straightened his back, he felt a distant surprise that the boy in the mirror was doing the same thing.

He didn't see Julian downstairs, and didn't hurry to find him. He drifted through the chattering chaos as if he were no longer attached to his body. When an aunt turned to address him or one of the young guests bumped into him, he reflexively smiled. He didn't remember a word of his conversations; neither would anyone else. At long last, he didn't exist, even to himself.

But his mother—she existed. She was in a good mood, flushed

and cheerful, holding court in a flowery chiffon cocktail dress she hadn't worn in years. She would catch Laurie long enough to scoop her into a kiss on the cheek, then let her go, laughing, and tell a teasing story that Laurie was meant to overhear. Paul recognized his mother now—not the phantom she had been for two years, but *her*. He had nearly forgotten her, and her return now felt so sudden and so fragile that he feared the slightest pressure might send her away again.

He imagined—forced himself to imagine—what might happen if she learned everything he was and everything he'd done. He imagined how the grief and terror would make her tentative colors fade again for good.

"Honey, I swear," he heard her say. "The more you smoke, the less you seem to eat."

His mother was talking to Julian, trying to ply him with a wedge of cake, split down the center by a bloody stripe of jam. As she was talking, Julian met Paul's eyes, and the despair in his face was so naked that it felt impossible that she wouldn't see it.

"Ugh, sorry." His voice caught up to the persona faster than his face, but just barely. "I had a late breakfast."

His mother followed Julian's gaze and beckoned for Paul to join them. He and Julian stood two feet apart, the air between them snapping with static. If his mother could sense it, it didn't show in her face.

"You're getting so thin," she accused, and when Julian wryly thanked her, she winced. She spoke more quietly then, as if to keep passersby from listening in; Paul wasn't certain even he was intended to hear. "Did something happen with your parents? You've been so out of sorts lately."

For the first time, it seemed possible that Julian couldn't maintain a lie. "He's fine," Paul cut in, too tersely.

Even in the worst moments of that long shattering day in Maryland, Paul had never seen Julian look so on edge. He was the one who was never supposed to be a liability. If everything were to go wrong—and Paul had imagined it against his will beforehand, again and again, even in at the heights of their euphoria—if it were all to go wrong, Paul was supposed to be the one to fall apart. Julian was supposed to be rational and cool and ruthless, willing to put a knife between Paul's ribs until the pain shocked sense back into him. He should never have let Paul doubt that he was in control.

Paul's mother couldn't make sense of it, and Julian tried not to give her a chance to. He pulled a laborious smile and finally accepted the plate; she watched him as he gingerly took a bite, then swallowed it as if it chafed in his throat.

"You're so sweet to worry," he told her. "It's nothing dire. I'll survive."

They hung together as long as they had to, until his mother—less reassured than she pretended—wandered out of sight to attend to another guest. Julian let his face fall. He turned his paper plate upside down in the trash bin and pushed it down with his fingertips, until it sank between the napkins and gift ribbons. Then he fled into the crowd.

"Julian," Paul tried to protest, but he was already out of sight.

Detail returned in a rush—crumpled eclairs and birthday candles and sugar-bright cake frosting, a glancing tang of heavily sprayed unwashed hair. Chatter and high laughter, the bass currents of his grandfather's voice in the distance, the cat—never shy—chirping and complaining as it circled the visitors' legs. The empty hanukkiah still sat in the window, forgotten in the chaos of party preparations; when Paul cut through the living room, he paused to return it to its box, so reflexively that he barely noticed he was doing it.

He wasn't looking for Julian; all he wanted was cold air and quiet. But he found the front door yawning and the welcome mat dusted with snow. Julian's satchel lay on its side, books and cigarettes scattered as if he'd shaken them free. He was sitting on the bottom stair, windbitten, shaking, drawing rapid gulping breaths. Snowflakes clung to his shoulders and his hair.

When Julian saw him, he didn't even try to pull himself together. Paul reached for his arm, but he jerked away and Paul let his hands fall to his sides. Something like shame moved through Julian's face, and he looked away into the street.

"I fucked up," he said.

Paul reached down to pull Julian around by his shoulders. "What do you mean? How did you fuck up? *Julian.*"

Another inhale, sharp and deep.

"My lung is collapsing." He spoke in a stuttering staccato, and Paul was afraid he might cry. "They told me I was high-risk, the fucking accident—I remember what it's like, it's like I'm caught on the barb of a harpoon, I can *feel* it—I can't breathe, I'm going to fucking die—"

It would be better if Julian was right, and the problem was simple enough to solve with a few days in the hospital. The truth was worse; that was how Paul knew to believe it.

He became his father because he needed to be. He sat on the steps beside Julian and held his shoulders.

"Breathe out, then hold your breath," he said. "Then breathe in slowly."

Julian made a noise too pained and furious to be a laugh. "*Fuck you.* I need to go to the hospital, please, don't you dare—"

"Do it."

Julian shut his eyes and covered his face, but he did as he was told. There was no spasm of pain, either on the exhale or the inhale, though if Paul had mentioned this he knew Julian would have summoned one. He took the air in as smoothly as he ever had—there was the rasp of cold and pollution, the familiar imbalance in right and left, but he was healthy and strong and his body held itself together. He was the same fierce creature he'd always been; the difference was that he couldn't remember it.

"You're all right," Paul said, but his voice was incapable of reassurance. He sounded as if he was trying to win a fight. "I get them sometimes, you're just breathing too fast, it'll go away."

Julian looked at Paul and smiled.

"Of course," he said. "You know how it sounds. How people breathe when they're really dying."

Something shuffled behind them, and they whipped around in unison. Audrey stood in the doorway, hand braced against the frame. The light was better behind her than in front of her, but Paul could see the shadow of a frown.

"What's going on out here?" Her gaze flitted between them, but when it reached Julian it lingered.

"Just getting some fresh air." Paul didn't stammer. "We're fine," he said. "You can shut the door."

A pause. Another long look at Julian. Julian set his jaw and said nothing.

"Well, come in before you freeze to the doorstep," said Audrey. "I don't want to have to chip you off with the shovel."

"We're *fine*, Audrey. Please give us a minute."

The hinges wheezed as the door closed. Julian looked into the street and choked down a mouthful of cold air. Paul touched his back.

"Tell me what went wrong." Resignation was nearly as good as calm. "Julian. Look at me. Tell me what happened. We can't fix it if you don't tell me."

Julian sat up straight. For a long moment he shut his eyes, hands curled like the claws of a fallen bird. Then he turned to Paul. "'What went wrong.'" His smile was ruthless. "I don't even know where to start."

He shrugged off Paul's arm and flung himself up the steps, just long enough to gather his belongings. When he emerged, he kicked the door shut behind him and pushed a handful of the spilled cigarettes back into his satchel. Paul tried to follow him, but the look Julian gave him stopped him in his tracks. Julian's wool coat was folded over his arm. His hands shook, but his spine was very straight. He was terrified and luminous with fury.

"I should never have let you convince me that this was what you needed from me." He was cold and sharp. "Maybe that's what went wrong."

Paul didn't speak; he couldn't. Julian opened up the car and threw his bookbag inside.

"I want to be alone. Not that you ever care what I want." Julian lit a crooked broken-necked cigarette and flicked the match into the gutter. "I'll call you when I can stand the sight of you. Don't hold your breath."

He didn't try to stop Julian from leaving. He just watched. For a long while after the car pulled away, Paul looked blankly at the place where it had been, a patch of damp asphalt ringed by snow.

8.

HE WAS letting his family believe he was sick, and it wasn't quite a lie. He'd skipped his run, and he threw up the few bites of breakfast he'd managed before his stomach turned. It wasn't much evidence in his favor, but it was enough to give his mother something benign to fret about. Even Audrey didn't dare ask him what was really wrong; now and then she came close, pausing at the sunroom door and looking at him with her lips barely parted, but at the last moment she always thought better of it.

Laurie put a cushion over his legs and curled up on the couch with him to watch game shows. The blunted weight of her head on his shin was more comforting than he expected it to be, as much an echo of his childhood as the tulip-printed cushions on his mother's wicker chair. His mother was steaming a pot of rice in the kitchen, and he knew she would be by soon to serve it to him plain, in his old soup bowl with its motif of peaceable rabbits. The excuse bought him a day at most; eventually he would have to come up with something better.

If he shut his eyes, Paul could imagine sliding backward, becoming the simple and incomplete creature he had been before he ever heard Julian's name. But the illusion always fell apart and his shame and dread returned in waves, and he pressed his forearms against his churning stomach to punish himself for wanting to cry. When the phone rang, Paul knew it wasn't him; he wasn't confident it ever would be. He didn't remember at first that he had other things to fear.

His mother had been preparing a familiar tray of sick-day

food. He heard her peel back the foil top of the cup of apple-sauce before hurrying to answer before the third ring.

"Hello?" Then, inevitably: "Papa, what's wrong?"

Laurie was asleep. Paul carefully slid his legs out from under the cushion and sat upright.

It wasn't a long conversation. His mother's interjections were incredulous and inscrutable. "Of course," she said quickly, "we'll be right there." She hung up without saying goodbye.

There was a thick, unbearable silence as she paused in the hall, gathering herself. Then she hurried through the kitchen to fetch him.

"Paul," she said, and only when she saw him in his T-shirt and green high-school tracksuit did she remember he was supposed to be sick. She winced, but hastily put on a brave face. "Honey, I'm sorry, but we need to go talk to your grandfather. It can't wait."

Audrey had rushed upstairs to intercept them. She was al-ready carrying her shoes. "Ma, what's going on? Is everyone okay?"

"It's—there's been a misunderstanding." Paul's mother pushed him gently but sharply toward the door. "Go upstairs and look through your father's Rolodex, call the garage when you find numbers for his friends in the DA's office—*home*, we need home and office, they might be off work for the holidays—"

Whatever Audrey had been expecting, that wasn't it. Paul looked down to pull on his shoes before she could meet his eyes.

"What . . . the *fuck* kind of a misunderstanding?"

Their mother didn't even remark on her language. "It's noth-ing, it's ridiculous, we're going to sort it out—the Rolodex, honey—"

It was windy, dry snow catching on the gusts, but his mother forgot to tell him to put on a coat. He zipped up his sweatshirt and chased her to the car. She was floating on fear, moving as smoothly and swiftly as if she were dreaming, and he nearly slipped on the sidewalk trying to keep pace with her. She wasn't looking at him; they had driven several blocks before he realized it was on purpose.

"Ma?"

Several wispy locks of hair had fallen free of their knot. Paul watched the muscles work in her face and throat—watched her swallow hard and bite the inside of her cheek. When she finally looked at him, Paul wished she wouldn't. She'd had the same look after his father died, a hopeless and primal despair at not being able to lie to him.

"Is it that drug thing again?" He tried to make his tone guileless and exasperated, but from the inside it sounded like a sing-song imitation of a child. "I don't understand why they . . ."

She looked toward the road. Her fingertips just barely touched the steering wheel.

"Someone died, honey," she said. "They're trying everything they can think of."

The litany of *even if* was so familiar by now that he could have laughed at his own desperation. *Even if they hunt down every car it could have been, they won't find any proof of which one it was. And even if they do—even if* . . . He was running out of ways to finish the sentence. When he found his tongue, he didn't have to fabricate the panic in his voice.

"But that's *insane*. All that happened was I signed into the storage room at school the same day someone stole something from it, I don't understand why I—"

"No," said his mother with sudden vehemence, and he'd never in his life hated himself as much as he did then. "No, honey, don't ever defend yourself to me, I know my baby wouldn't get mixed up in something like this."

At the garage the police were gone, but their chaos remained. Paul lagged behind his mother and watched through the office window. His grandfather stood amid the mess with his hands on his hips, until his mother drew near and seized his arm with both hands.

Paul's careful ordering of the office was completely destroyed. Binders lay open in piles, their pages crushed by careless hands. His grandmother stalked restless circles around the office booth with her bony arms folded tight, tugging at her Magen David pendant. When she reached the office door, she stopped and stared inside.

"I'm going to find out what clown of a judge they got to sign the warrant," she said, "and I'll canvas *every goddamn door* in this city to get him voted out."

When she caught sight of Paul, her face didn't soften, but she set her jaw as if she were holding back furious tears. As he passed her, she reached up and combed her hand briefly through his hair; inside the office, his grandfather nodded and patted him on the shoulder. No one spoke to him; Paul couldn't tell if they were trying to shield him or if it was an attempt to give him space.

"It was a veteran," his grandfather told his mother. "Some poor kid who was in Vietnam. They're grasping, it's all politics, the papers are getting worked up and it's an election in November. I can't think of anything more cynical."

Paul hardly heard them. It felt imperative, somehow, to put the office to rights. He smoothed a crumpled ledger page and closed the book to press it flat, but his grandmother spoke so sharply from the doorway that he jumped.

"Leave it," she said. "We need to take pictures."

Paul lowered himself silently into his desk chair. He saw suddenly that the repair manuals were all missing, and he couldn't make sense of it until he remembered the engine of Charlie Stepanek's car. The police might be combing through the manuals at that very moment, paging through the sections on oil pan maintenance to dust fruitlessly for Paul's fingerprints.

". . . overdose," his mother was saying in an undertone. "You'd think they'd go after the drug dealers, not . . ."

"It wasn't that kind of thing, Ruthie . . . No, later, I don't want to worry him."

The uppermost desk drawer was just slightly open, and Paul pushed it shut before he remembered what was inside. He kept a photograph there, one he had taken on the trip home from Maryland. Julian alone, solemn and round-shouldered in the summer rain, leaning against a roadside fence with the gray-blue mirror of Chesapeake Bay behind him.

Paul opened the drawer again, but he already knew it would be gone.

9.

HE MUST have made an excuse, but he didn't remember it and doubted the others would either. By then they'd returned to his mother's house, and all three adults were preoccupied by the tedious business of calling on his father's prosecutor friends for favors and explanations. They pretended in a clumsy, fiercely loving way that Paul himself was beside the point.

Before he left, he slipped upstairs to comb the contents of the paint box under his bed. He would have to leave a few secrets inside, to give the police the satisfaction of discovery without finding anything they could actually use. He sat cross-legged on the floor and forced himself to choose a few memories he could live without. He couldn't bring himself to read through the notes Julian had given him all autumn, because even from the corner of his eye they were so raw and revealing that he couldn't understand why he'd never seen them for what they were. He crumpled them in the bottom of the box and left them there, underneath some failed sketches and a fold of glossy Baroque painting reproductions he'd torn from a library book when he was fourteen.

But the journal was too dangerous to leave behind, even though he hadn't written about the plan. And there were letters and photographs too precious to allow the police to take, things he would be desperate to find again if he ever had the chance.

He gumbanded them inside a shopping bag and took them outside. The street was quiet, every car empty and long familiar, but he still paced the sidewalk and looked through every windshield, making sure he was alone. He still wasn't certain no one would see him, but he was anxious about running out of time and had to decide not to care. He hid the bundle under the Koenigs' front steps, in the gap behind a warped board that had pulled away from the bottom stair.

He barely remembered how he reached Julian's apartment. Afterward he had a faint impression of the sky clearing, sunlight diffusing white through the bus's dirty windows—and that there had been a car, an ugly blue Ford, that he'd thought was following him until it creaked into a side street and vanished. He remembered waiting at a crosswalk for the light to change, calmly imagining buying a book of matches and setting himself on fire. But every other detail slipped away.

Paul's key still worked, which surprised him, but the chain lock trapped him in the hallway. It was nearly a minute before Julian came to the door. Paul could only see a slice of him—dressed haphazardly, pigeon-toed in his thick winter socks. When he saw Paul, he didn't conceal his dread. But he wasn't surprised. Somehow that was worse.

"Please let me in. It's an emergency."

The door shut in his face, and there was a long pause before Julian freed it from the lock. Paul waited for the door to open, but it didn't. When he let himself in, Julian was waiting in the kitchen. He didn't look at Paul; the only indication that Julian had registered his presence was the second glass he took from the dish drainer.

Julian filled each glass with a splash of bourbon from the freezer. His hands were moving strangely, as if they wanted to shake but couldn't remember how.

Paul couldn't wait any longer to be invited to speak. The

words tumbled out in a rush, before he could arrange his thoughts and remind his mouth not to stammer.

"They searched the repair garage—they must've guessed what we did with the cars. They got a warrant, which means the alibi didn't work, which means there's something you didn't tell me, maybe you lied when you said you kept to the script, you always say you never lie to me but I can't believe it for a second—"

"I've always told you the truth." Julian handed Paul one of the glasses and contemplated his own before swallowing the bourbon like medicine. "Every word I've ever said to you was true, not that you've ever believed that, either."

Exasperation plumed through him like radiation. "That isn't the same thing as never *lying*. You lie to me all the time, you keep things from me so you can control what I know and get me to act the way you want. Hiding the truth is still lying, and you'd know that if it weren't so fucking convenient not to."

Julian filled his glass again; he didn't bother to pretend it was anything but an excuse to avoid Paul's eyes.

"Are we not allowed to have secrets?" he asked evenly. "How did your father die, Paul, as long as we're telling the whole truth?"

"Oh, he killed himself," said Paul with furious false cheer. "You know damn well, but thanks for making me tell you. Do you want to know what caliber of bullet he used? Should I tell you what a .38 does to the back of your head?"

He didn't give Julian a chance to answer; he didn't want an apology he couldn't accept.

"Your turn. Tell me what went wrong. Tell me how bad this is."

Julian leaned back, one hand braced on the counter and the

other holding the glass at his side. It was a deliberately open
stance, incongruously at ease.

"I *did* keep to the script," he said. His tone was meticulously
careless. "As much as I could, anyway. I've been doing this all
my life, you know, talking strangers into liking me. Under ideal
circumstances, it would have worked."

Paul felt sick enough already without the drink. He set it
aside untouched. "Why weren't they ideal circumstances?"

Julian looked away, toward the window. He finished off his
drink. "The problem," he said, "was that I couldn't stop thinking about the dog."

"What *dog*," Paul started to say, but by the time he finished
speaking, he knew.

He'd never paid it much attention, but Julian had. He remembered Julian sitting in Stepanek's kitchen and pulling treats
from his coat pocket, while the little brown terrier stood on its
hind legs and grinned at him.

"You didn't." All the air had left his lungs. "Please tell me you
didn't."

Julian gave an odd, clipped laugh.

"Well, he wasn't supposed to pop up again so quickly, was
he?" His smile was agonizing. "It was supposed to be weeks.
Maybe the neighbors would hear her barking, but we know all
about good Samaritans, don't we? She might have starved to
death before anyone came. But of course when I went to check
on her on Friday, well . . ."

Paul's body forgot how to support his weight. He sank slowly
into one of the dining chairs.

"I'm not an idiot, mind you," Julian was saying. "I saw the
cop cars parked halfway around the block, and I kept walking.
Didn't even flinch. But they did see me, and one of them was

one of *them*—the white one, the one who looks kind of like Serpico. I have no goddamn idea how he remembered me, much less recognized me, but when they came by to ask about your alibi, he clocked me right away and wanted to know why someone who lives in Hazelwood would be out for a walk in Polish Hill. I thought I covered for myself all right by pretending I'd been up there trying to buy grass, but . . ."

"You can't. You can't have been that stupid, it's just a dog, it's just a *fucking* dog—"

"She couldn't help who her owner was. She didn't deserve to be collateral damage. I couldn't stomach it, not on top of everything else." Julian spoke as dispassionately as if they were just analyzing a chess game—the defensive panic underneath was almost imperceptible. "You didn't even notice the problem, and I knew you wouldn't care if you did."

"So you just—unilaterally, without even thinking it through for five seconds, because of course you're so goddamn brilliant you don't *have* to think—"

Julian laughed again, just shy of hysterical. "Sure," he said. "It can't be that I just took a calculated risk."

Paul's stammer had grown so thick that he could barely push the words through his tongue. "You know what I think really happened, Julian? I think you *want* us to get caught." It sounded truer the longer he spoke. "You always need people to know how clever you are," he said in a rush. "I've seen you, the way you'd always show off in class, all your games and your party tricks—you *live* for attention. You couldn't *stand* to just get away with it, you needed someone to know you were clever enough to pull it off—"

"I knew you'd find a way to spin this into me victimizing you," said Julian coldly, "but you're really outdoing yourself."

"*Tell* me it isn't true. Look me in the eye and fucking tell me."

The remaining pieces of Julian's calm looked like they would hold fast to the bitter end.

"No, Pablo. Because I don't have anything to prove," Julian said. "That's you. It always has been. *Après toi.*"

It was excruciating how Julian poisoned his contempt with affection. The way Julian pronounced his nickname felt like a sharp kiss before pushing him away.

"Don't." Paul grasped desperately for anger. "Please don't, it's your problem we need to solve, don't try to make this about me—"

There was a snap of movement in Julian's body, a crash of shattering glass, but through the dizzying churn of his vision Paul couldn't quite put them in order. He had recoiled, somehow—hands up to shield his head, the panic of a baseball hurtling toward him high and inside (what a funny thing to remember now). Then Julian was speaking, as if he could barely breathe around the words.

"It's *always* been about you," he said. "It's *always* been about you. Your revenge, your Nuremberg gallows by proxy, your grand philosophical point we were supposed to make so you could keep yourself from feeling the real reason. It was your fucking delusion that if you just made yourself strong and cold and heartless and everything you aren't—if you could just make yourself 'better,' if you could destroy every part of you that's worth loving, then you wouldn't ever have to be afraid again. That was what you needed me to do, and I would have done anything, god help me, I would have done *anything* for you. I thought you'd finally trust me if you knew I'd kill for you, and it still isn't enough, I don't know why I thought it ever could be enough, nothing ever will be. And I'm never going to get it out of my head, I can't, I can't forget the *sounds* he made and how you just—like it was nothing—"

"It wasn't *nothing*, it just had to be done—Julian, please stop—"

"—and I had to see you like that," said Julian, "this poor beautiful boy who can be so sweet and gentle when he can bring himself to trust me, who wants to save the world because he feels all the ways it hurts, he feels *everything*—and you felt it, you felt everything he felt and you *loved* it."

Don't say that, Paul tried to say, don't say that, neither of us wants it to be true. But all that would come out was the word *Don't*, too soft and wavering to be intelligible.

As he watched Paul's eyes, Julian's face flooded with pity. It did nothing to soften the revulsion.

"You loved it." He said each word with ruthless precision. "It's the happiest I've ever seen you."

What Paul wanted, impossibly, was to comfort him—and he despised himself because he couldn't tell whether he wanted to ease Julian's pain or just spare himself from knowing he'd caused it.

"Please—Julian, please look at me. It had to be done."

Julian drew a sharp breath and slid to the floor. When Paul approached, Julian met his eyes with such raw hatred and fierce, senseless love that Paul wished the shame could kill him.

"It had to," Paul said hopelessly. "He was an *example*, it had to be done, he said he didn't even think it was strange to be ordered to kill little fucking kids, he would've done anything they told him to do—and there have to be consequences sometimes, there *have* to be, or they'll never learn."

It should have given Julian some comfort, because it was the only thing that gave Paul any. But nothing changed. He looked at Paul as if he'd never seen him clearly before.

"You're so certain," he said distantly. "Incomplete evidence, inferences clearly rooted in bias—not your best work. And here I was, doing everything I could to help you *stay* certain, because I thought I'd finally found a way to love you and have you even notice I was doing it."

Julian suddenly grinned, as if to keep himself from crying.

"How sick is that?" he said. "I'm just as much of a monster as you are."

It would have been easy to walk out—to wander for an hour or two, get some fresh air and clear his head, and then come back expecting Julian to stitch both of them back together. But he didn't deserve to reap the benefits of cowardice. He was supposed to be brave now, or free, or a real man, or whatever the fantasy had been. The least he could do was look directly at what he'd done.

Paul sat alongside Julian on the kitchen floor. There was a long moment that they didn't touch, or even look at each other. Paul could feel them staring at the same patch of wall, the scar of the glass in the yellow paint. When Paul breached the distance he expected Julian to recoil, but he didn't. Paul had barely touched his arm when Julian collapsed against him. He lay with his head on Paul's lap, hardly making a sound but for the scattered rhythm of his breathing.

Paul's heart was somewhere far outside him. He remembered the things Julian had once done to bear him through his own grief, and he mimicked them one by one, a mechanical performance of kindness for this boy he barely knew. He held Julian close and stroked his hair, and he didn't dare speak. *It's all right*, Julian had always told him. *You're all right. I like looking after you.* But there was nothing Paul could say now that stood any chance of coming true.

THE SUN set. Long shadows and stripes of ember-orange sunlight swung across the floor and then faded; at some point the phone rang, probably Paul's family looking for him, but neither of them got up to answer it.

He could feel Julian forcing himself back under control, summoning the will to move. Paul watched him sit up and push himself to his feet, but it felt impossible that his own body might follow.

Julian didn't look at him. He tapped out a cigarette, lit it, and sat propped on his elbows at the kitchen table. His shirt hung close against the depressions beneath his shoulder blades and the sharp profile of his seventh vertebra. Paul had a keen, agonizing memory of the taste and texture of Julian's skin— the path from rib cage to scapula, up the rhythmic line of his spine. The soft firm incline between shoulder and neck, where the lightest touch from Paul's lips could bring his every defense crashing down.

Paul settled on the kitchen floor beside him and let his arm drape along the length of Julian's thigh. Julian looked down at him, face barely visible in the dim light. He set down his cigarette and threaded his fingers through Paul's hair.

"Okay," said Julian. "Let's talk."

The pragmatic coldness still hadn't left him, even if Paul could see now how much effort it took. Paul might be paralyzed by fear and grief and indecision, but Julian put the most ruthless part of himself to work. Somehow, despite everything, Julian had found something like a plan. "Let's talk" meant that Julian would talk, so Paul shut his eyes and listened.

"Near as I can tell, we don't have much to worry about from them. You and the stolen sedative, even their seeing me on the sidewalk—it's nothing but a couple of nasty coincidences, as far as they can prove. They aren't going to find anything in the car—no, they really aren't, we talked it to death, I know we did that part properly. They don't have *anything* they can put in an acetate envelope and show to a jury as Exhibit A, and they never will."

Paul opened his eyes. Julian gazed toward the window; he picked up his cigarette again and relit it left-handed.

"So their case is D.O.A.," said Julian. "They're going to need a confession, which means they have to get us to turn on each other. A day, maybe two, so they have the chance to search all the cars—but eventually they're going to get fed up and bring us in. So you're going to have to trust me a little while longer, Pablo, or all of this is going to fall apart."

Paul stopped waiting for him to make eye contact. He rested his head on Julian's waist; there was something maddening about the way their bodies felt against each other, like two jig-saw pieces that almost fit.

"So what do we do?"

"The boring thing," said Julian. There was a bleak smile in his voice. "What Henry would advise us to do, god help us, with all the force of his 1-L wisdom." The muscles in his torso shifted as he moved to tap his cigarette in the ashtray. "We invoke our fucking Miranda rights and let the lawyers sort it out. It still isn't a guarantee, but it's the best avenue we have. And then it's over, one way or the other."

It was humiliating and sensible and absolutely unfussy. He knew it was the best option, and he hated it.

Julian let his hand slip free. His fingertips grazed the back of Paul's neck, and then he withdrew his touch.

"I need to know what's going to happen after it's over."

It was the cruelest thing Paul could have said, and he didn't trust himself enough to decide whether it was on purpose. He endured the silence as long as he could, then looked up at Julian's face.

"What do *you* want to happen, Pablo?" said Julian. All the vibrant energy had left him.

Paul couldn't answer the question. There were too many answers. *I want to go far away, start over, pretend we can wake up from this. To stop hurting you, and to hurt you so badly the scars will never fade. Never to see you again. Never to see anything but you.*

"I believe you now," he said. "I believe you, I trust you, I don't need you to prove anything to me anymore. I just wanted this to last forever, I was missing part of myself my whole life until I met you—I just wanted you to feel the same way, I wanted to feel like something you couldn't replace—I couldn't go back, I'd die without you, I just wanted to be *worthy* of you—"

Julian turned in his seat and pulled Paul up by his collar to kiss him.

They barely reached the bed. Neither of them expected it would ever happen again—there was no playfulness left, no attempt at grace. They were as clumsy as the first time and as ravenously tender. Too-eager teeth brushed skin, bruises echoed after fingerprints. But there was no cruelty left. It had always been easier to hurt Julian than to endure his sincerity—the gentleness in his voice, the way he would collapse into a kiss. Paul made himself endure it now. He let Julian push him back against the mattress, welcomed his weight on top of him, even

as he forced himself to feel how little Julian was really in control, and how clear it was that he never had been.

They drew it out as long as they could. Even when it was
over, they pretended it wasn't. They held each other close, ungainly and barely moving, air shivering in their lungs like water. Then Julian pulled back and rolled to the side to lie next to
him. Paul's hips ached, and there was the gnawing pressure of a
sob inside his chest, but when he tried to release it he couldn't.

"I hate you so much." He could barely hear his own voice,
but he knew Julian could. It wasn't true except in its intensity,
but that was enough. Julian was tense as if he were holding back
a shudder. He nodded, just slightly, but he didn't speak.

10.

A DAY, maybe two. Waiting, blindfolded, for the firing squad to load their rifles. Word drifted back from the friendly prosecutors, in their living rooms full of sweatered screaming children or their in-laws' condominiums in Florida—precise and confident reassurances they were in no position to give. His grandparents threw themselves into their righteous fury; it left them no space for fear.

Paul's mother told him over and over that she wasn't worried, either. One night she burned a snarl of spaghetti to the bottom of the pot, and the next morning withdrew at the last minute from her New Year's Eve plans, but she wasn't worried. She didn't tell Audrey and Laurie why the garage records had been raided—"investigative overreach," she quoted one of the lawyers, and by some absentminded oversight she failed to mention Paul's part in the drama at all. But she wasn't worried, not at all. It was a rough patch, but a mercifully surreal one. They would all look back on it with bewilderment, and one day they would laugh.

There was no sparing them, even by letting his bicycle drift into traffic. The police would never relent—they would still want Julian, and all the remnants of evidence they thought Paul could still give them. They would come tearing into a house in mourning, and once and for all they would destroy his family's memory of the obedient son they'd never had.

In the final days of his life, Paul's father had been as kind as he ever was. He told each of the children in turn how proud he was, and leaned down at breakfast every morning to kiss the crowns of their heads. The night before it happened, he pushed the kitchen table to the side of the room so he could tease Paul's mother into dancing with him. He was happier than he'd been in weeks, and it was such a pleasure to endure his affection and deliberately inept jokes that no one questioned where the change had come from. They should have seen it for what it was, but they hadn't. They still didn't, now that Paul found himself compelled to do the same.

Relentlessly, he made himself useful. He washed all the windows and laundered the curtains and cleaned the neglected flue so they could have a fire in the hearth on New Year's Eve; when his mother abandoned her plans, he hurried out before the butcher closed to pick up a parcel of lamb. If he kept busy, Audrey couldn't ask why he looked so miserable, and he wouldn't have to feel his mother watching from the corner of her eye and wondering the same thing. He was helpful and kind, in the bashful, self-effacing way they expected of him. It wouldn't read as an apology until it was too late.

Paul turned in early on New Year's Eve, but he didn't sleep. He knew what morning would bring, even if he had no rational way of knowing. For hours he watched the ceiling and listened. Audrey had long since left for her party, but he could hear the television humming below as Laurie and his mother watched the special on ABC. Now and then there was a stray firework, until at midnight they erupted like a Russian symphony—then scattershot quiet, and the others coming upstairs for bed, and the rustle of the house settling.

After days out of contact, he didn't know what Julian was doing. It was like waking up to his own pinched, unfeeling arm draped over his body.

When he got up for a glass of water, he found his mother awake. It was nearly two. She was sitting up with one of her historical novels, yellow light angling past her half-open door. He tried to creep by unseen, but she looked up at him and smiled.

"Hey, little bug," she said. "Can't sleep?"

He shrugged. His mother set her book aside and hooked her reading glasses in the collar of her nightgown. He didn't argue when she beckoned him inside. He told himself it was an undertow of compliance that pulled him in, because even that was less damning than admitting he wasn't quite through being a child.

He couldn't remember the last time he'd touched his parents' bed—it was years ago, long before his father died. He couldn't meet his mother's eyes, but she didn't appear to expect it of him. When he sat at the edge of the bed, she put a soft, bracing hand on his shoulder. The air in her room held a faint musk of woodsmoke from the fireplace below. Paul knew his black-and-white baby portrait hung by the door, but without his glasses he couldn't see it.

"You've been so down the last few days." Her worry always carried an edge of gentle accusation. "You're not letting that silliness at the garage get to you, right?"

He couldn't answer. He didn't know anymore what might happen if he tried. He imagined the irresistible compulsion to tell her everything, how he would twist her love for him past its breaking point.

She rubbed his shoulder. He could hear her preparing for the next question, summoning her nerve.

"Did something happen with Julian?"

He'd had time to brace for it; it shouldn't have landed as hard as it did. "Nothing." He barely opened his mouth as he spoke. "It was my fault. Just a stupid fight."

"Oh honey, I'm sorry," she said, and left it at that. It occurred to him that she might once have been relieved, eager to push Julian out of their lives and declare the problem solved. But the only thing he could detect in her voice was a wary, deliberate sympathy—not quite what it aspired to be, but still far from anything he would have expected.

They sat in silence for a long while. His mother let go of his arm and opened her book, but the pages never turned, so he knew she wasn't reading. Paul stared at his hands and drummed his fingernails against his water glass.

When he got up to leave, she caught his hand just long enough to squeeze it. "You can always talk to me," she said gently. "About anything, okay? We all love you no matter what."

He only met her eyes for a moment, because that was all he could bear. It would have been easier to hurt her before, when he still saw her as a wound that never seemed likely to close. But he saw a human being now—kindly crow's-feet eyes, buckling paper skin on the backs of her hands, flesh and bone. He hated her, hopelessly, for refusing to deserve this.

He remembered hurrying back to his room, but he didn't remember going to sleep. Without any time passing it was morning, almost too late. His sheets clung, damp with sweat as if he'd slept off a fever. From the kitchen below he heard the toaster pop, then the hiss of something in the frying pan. His heartbeat was frantic. He had very little time.

The only thing left under his control was the project's aesthetic dignity, and Paul attended to it with all the care of washing a corpse. He put himself meticulously to rights, because he owed it to the day to be presentable. He ran the shower autoclave-hot, scrubbed his nailbeds red, even combed a bit of pomade into his wet hair to make the curls look less unkempt. He dressed with great care, as if he'd been told he had to make a good first impression. He remembered the police station being cold, so under his corduroy suit he wore a blue roll-neck sweater that Julian had always liked. He didn't have any polish for his good shoes, and wasn't sure they were even the kind that ought to be polished, but he still tried to buff down the white creases of stress in the veneer. At all costs, he had to remain calm and self-contained. He mustn't do anything to embarrass himself.

The knock sent a shock of quiet through the house. Paul took one last look to make sure his bookshelves were neat and ordered. Then he plucked his bedspread straight at the corners, folded his hands, and sat down to wait.

The front door opened and did not close. The men's voices were calm, businesslike; when his mother made a quiet sound of protest the men politely softened their tone, but they did not reassure her. A dutiful pause. Then the clatter of many footsteps up the staircase.

There was no knock before Paul's bedroom door swung open. Several men stood outside, but only Benton entered. He paused in the doorway with his hands on his hips, and for the first time Paul caught sight of the holster at his side. When Paul met his eyes Benton smiled, a grim and knowing funeral smile. His overcoat was dusted with snow.

"I'd tell you why we're here," Benton said, "but I think you already know."

Paul looked back at him, blank-faced, and did not speak.

"We'd like to make this as easy for everyone as possible," said Benton, slowly and calmly as if he were reasoning with a child.

"Your father deserves for all of us to handle this respectfully, I think you'll agree with me on that. We can do this quietly. No handcuffs, for your mother's sake—and it gives the neighbors a little less to talk about. You have a choice to make, Paul. You're a smart young man. I think you'll make the right one."

Paul couldn't remember holding his breath, but it shook when he exhaled. He looked around his room and imagined distantly how it would look to these strangers—the Leonard Baskin reproduction above his bed, the favorite specimens in their shadowboxes, the dark curtains printed with galaxies and stars. He wondered what state they would leave it in. He wondered if he would ever be back to see it.

"Could you please ask them to be careful with the specimen drawers?" The urgency of the question caught him so off guard that he couldn't stop himself from asking. "They're delicate, they shouldn't be pawed through, and the drawers need to be opened gently."

For the first time—and it would be the last—Paul saw a flash of unmediated emotion in Benton's face. He collected himself quickly, and the look was gone before Paul could name it.

"I'm sure we can accommodate that," he said. "How about you?"

Paul smiled, very weakly, then decided he shouldn't have done it. "Just a moment, please," he heard himself say. "I need to get my coat." They were all watching him—not as if they expected him to try something, but as if they'd never seen anything like him before.

The army parka wouldn't give the right impression, so he settled for a handsome raincoat that was only really warm enough in the fall. It had been a gift from Julian, one of the ones he'd clumsily disguised as hand-me-downs. It didn't smell like him any longer. Paul wouldn't have taken much comfort if it had.

Benton wrapped a firm hand around Paul's arm. He smelled of electric-green cologne and fresh wool.

"Good choice," he said. "Let's go."

One of the officers took Paul's other arm, and the others parted to allow them to pass. There were more of them than he'd expected, waiting to set to work ripping the house apart. Paul didn't bother to count them, or to try and place their faces. All he saw was the way they turned to watch him pass, the way their faces shifted. This wasn't the sort of trouble officers expected of their sons. Their boys were supposed to crash their cars, get caught with drugs, treat girls unspeakably—simple crimes of excess, nothing they couldn't ignore. Paul watched them search for their own sons in his face and find nothing.

He felt Benton glance over, so he fixed his gaze straight head. He lifted his chin and straightened his back and wore his face like a mask. Better to be arrogant than afraid.

His mother was in the living room, still in her dressing gown; Laurie huddled close to her, clinging to the cat. Paul had never thought they looked alike before, not with Laurie's face so like their father's, but they were mother and daughter when their expressions were the same.

"There's been a mistake," he said. "I have to sort this out." His mother made a soft strangled sound into her hands, but his voice remained steady and distant; he couldn't allow himself to feel anything. "I'm sorry about this." Benton led him away before either his mother or Laurie could answer, but Paul hadn't expected them to speak. It would take all their energy to convince themselves of the lie.

Then there was Audrey, waiting by the front door. There was no fear in her face. If there had been, some other feeling had chased it away. When she met Paul's eyes, it was as if she were seeing him for the first time. He couldn't remember why he'd ever wanted to be seen.

"Paul," she said quietly. "What the hell did you do?"

II.

NEARLY TWO years ago Paul had sat for the last time in the principal's office, mother at one side and grandparents on the other. His future was pulled from his grasp and reshaped without his permission, but he'd barely heard the conversation over the clamor of the too-tight necktie at his throat. It was a similar room to this one, cold and cheaply furnished, with peeling paint and high ceilings. City funding and century-old buildings always reacted to each other the same way. They were places you only came in order to feel helpless.

At the places where the wrought-iron grate touched the window frame, the sill was streaked with rust. There was a dent in the surface of the two-way glass; every movement in the room eddied and swirled as it passed.

"So how does it work?"

Paul doubted either of the uniformed officers were supposed to speak to him, but one of them couldn't restrain himself. His companion said nothing, but he chewed his gum a little harder, lips parted, and watched. When Paul didn't answer, the officer snapped his fingers beside his ear. Paul looked up before he could stop himself. Blond, thickset, hair clipped tight against his scalp—but young, no more than a few years older than Paul. His name was Trumbauer, per the lettering on his shirt. He belonged at the bottom of a river.

"I'm talking to you," he said, and smirked. "How's it work? The Bonnie and Clyde thing—ha, more like Bonnie and Bonnie . . ."

Paul shut his eyes and summoned the image of a gash erupting across the man's face. Bone splintering inward, blood shuddering through. When he opened his eyes again, he was nearly able to graft the fantasy over the shape of Trumbauer's smile.

"Christ, look at him, he's *shaking*."

Trumbauer looked to his partner. The other uniform folded his arms and clacked his gum, and his mouth drew slowly into a grin. Paul pressed his hands flat against the table and shut his eyes again.

"*Someone's* got to be the girl," said Trumbauer leeringly. "Is it you? I bet it's you, it's always these uptight buttoned-up little faggots you find bent over in the bushes—"

The impact sent searing currents through his fists and up his arms. He should have smashed Trumbauer's face against the table instead of his own hands, but he was too much of a coward. His pain was a relief—too easy, but it would have to do. He thrummed with untapped adrenaline, and nothing outside his body could reach him.

"Whoa, easy, *easy*." Trumbauer tried to grab his shoulders as if to wrest him back under control, but Paul recoiled.

Something was happening at the door behind him. Paul didn't bother to look. He sat up straight and lifted his hands to examine them. He held one hand in the other and clasped them tight.

When he finally looked up both of the uniformed officers were gone. Where Trumbauer's partner had stood, there was now only an empty stretch of white plaster and the caged face of a wall clock. The presence behind him was slow to approach, but Paul didn't turn around. Detective Benton sidled past the table and sat in the second tarnished folding chair. He had un-usually lithe hands for an adult man, long-fingered and thin, nails trimmed in straight lines. He'd come in alone. Paul didn't need to wonder where Marinetti was.

"Anything broken?"

When Paul shook his head, Benton smiled, a calculated operation that moved his mouth like clockwork but didn't reach his eyes.

"Sorry about that." Benton pushed up his cuff to glance at his watch, then folded his hands on the tabletop. "I can't pretend we recruit these guys from charm school." Paul gingerly pressed his palms to the table and said nothing. Benton kept talking, as if they were chatting over the punch bowl at a dull party. "Truth is, every department needs them—ex-Army and football burnouts who won't ever pass the detective exam, but who are good for a couple decades of corralling speed freaks and knocking down doors. You know the type. Kind of guy who isn't going to ask a lot of questions."

Paul knew what came next, and he held his face still. It wouldn't quite pass for blankness.

"Sort of like our friend Charlie Stepanek."

Benton had already decided not to believe him. Paul didn't even try to make it convincing. "I don't know any Charlie Stepanek."

Benton looked mildly surprised, as if Paul had forgotten the name of a mutual acquaintance. "Sure you do," he said. "Light brown hair, cute little dog named Lucy. A year and a half in Vietnam, doing god-knows-what. Big guy, bigger than I think you estimated, since you didn't get the dosage quite right. *That* Charlie."

Paul looked at the stretch of table between their hands and mapped every dimple and scratch in the paint. He pictured rust fanning outward from each defect, spreading like an algae bloom.

"Look up," said Benton quietly. "We already know what happened, Paul. That's not why you're here. We don't need a confession, not with everything we have. I'm trying to help you."

Benton's every word and gesture was so measured and deliberate that there was nothing to distinguish the truth from the lies. Paul wasn't afraid he would fall into the trap of believing him. Benton was a different kind of liar than Julian was, and didn't even seem to care whether he was believed. The real weapon was uncertainty; the lies themselves were just a byproduct.

"You played baseball in school, didn't you?" Benton was saying. "Lefty pitcher with a mean swing—jurors love it when we tell them the killer was left-handed, it makes them feel like they're on TV. Any idea where your old bat might be?"

He promised himself there was no chance they'd found it, but he knew he couldn't trust himself to tell the truth.

"I don't play anymore. I gave it to Goodwill."

"When?"

Paul didn't look up. "Who on earth," he said tonelessly, "would remember something like that?"

Benton gave him a long, unblinking look. "Ice cold," he said, with the barest pause between each word. "That's what the prosecutor is going to tell the jury. You're not doing yourself any favors—it's better, a lot better, more sympathetic, if you let us see you're as scared as I know you are.

"The bat," Benton added, as if it were an afterthought. "It was green, wasn't it? School colors."

It took all Paul's strength to keep his face from moving.

"There was a bit of paint transfer," said Benton. "He wasn't in the water long enough for it to wash away. Very distinctive shade of kelly green."

That was a lie. Paul took hold of the certainty with both hands. The paint could never have made contact at all—Paul had foreseen the problem and had taped over it meticulously, without so much as an open seam. It was a lie. Everything Benton told him was a lie.

"I gave it away," Paul said again. "Months ago, I don't remember when. I don't know what else to tell you."

Paul fixed his eyes on Benton's face and listened to the small sounds that cut through the silence. The click of the second hand on the wall clock, the tinny trill of Benton's wristwatch breaking each second into tenths. Benton's breathing, and his own. The barely perceptible pressure of someone's presence behind the glass.

"You've got to help me out here, Paul," Benton said. "Because the story they're telling out there is the kind that could keep you from ever seeing the light of day again. They're saying the two of you just wanted to see if you were smart enough to get away with it. And—they think I'm crazy," he added, glancing toward the two-way glass, "but I don't think that makes sense. Maybe for some entitled rich kid, but not for you. I knew your father, and I know the kind of son he would raise, and I don't think for a *second* that they're right about why you did this."

When Paul's eyes fell, Benton leaned forward to catch them again; it was something Julian had done countless times.

"Maybe you can explain to me," said Benton, "what exactly the arrangement was between the two of you."

His whole body flared hot. "Thank you for tidying that up," he said acidly. "I almost couldn't tell it was the same question that meathead asked before you came in."

Benton pulled a fleeting smile—more of a wince. Paul felt a savage impulse to lay out every detail, to drag Benton's distaste out into the open so neither of them could pretend it wasn't there.

"Hardly," said Benton delicately. "No, this is about what you *expected* of each other—specifically what he expected of you. Because your feelings on the matter are obviously sincere, and I'm sure he found that very useful." Paul fixed his eyes unseeingly on the wall. *"He's* of a type, too, I hate to tell you." Benton spoke with patient, calculated compassion. "My mother used to give piano lessons out in Bradford Woods, she could tell you some stories. These people are like children. The whole world revolves around them, so they think they can take whatever they want from it. And they know if they get in any real trouble Mom and Dad will come bail them out. So he knows how wrapped up you are in him, and how much you want him to feel the same way . . . and then one day he gets bored, because *no one* tolerates boredom worse than the idle rich, and he decides he wants to try something new . . ."

"You don't know anything about him." Stop talking, he pleaded, please stop talking, but the words guttered out like a free bleed. "His parents don't care about him, he's nothing like them—they made him choose and he chose me, it isn't like you're saying it is, it isn't *vulgar,* we understand each other better than anyone else ever has and you're making it sound like we're just using each other—"

"Well, you were a hell of an efficient way to piss off his parents." Benton didn't even blink. "Like I said—I think you're sincere, which is part of your problem. But I also think you've probably noticed the same thing I have, even if you don't want to. Sooner or later," he said, enunciating every word, "his parents are going to show up with some hundred-dollar-an-hour lawyer they pried out of the wheel well of an ambulance. And you've given them *everything* they'll need to pin this entire thing on you."

Paul bit his tongue.

"I've been doing this a long time," said Benton slowly. "People like him don't go to jail. People like you do. You're supposed to be in this together, right? He's probably told you as much. So why does all the concrete evidence only point to you?"

Paul felt a tear slide down his cheek, but brushing it away would mean trusting himself to move. Benton leaned forward and set his hand on his forearm, the way his father might have done.

"I know you didn't want to do this." Benton's sympathy almost sounded sincere. "I *know* you didn't. Sure, you've got a bit of a temper, but that's just self-defense—against guys like Charlie Stepanek, which maybe you thought would make this easier. But you're not cold-blooded. You're a smart kid from a good family, and you'd never do something like this on your own. This was always about him, and what he made you feel like you had to do."

Paul shut his eyes tight. He would doom them both if he allowed himself to move. He could feel Benton pitying him, reading shame and despair into his face, casting him as a love-sick child who barely questioned his orders before acquiescing. *How dare you,* he said silently. *How dare you tell me I couldn't have chosen this.*

"You deserve to have a life after this, Paul," said Benton. "He's taken so much from you already. Don't let him take that, too."

He'd never once said Julian's name. When Paul noticed the omission, it echoed through him like a chord, and at last there was no doubt left inside him. Benton was telling himself stories about two strangers Paul had never met. Julian would protect him. Paul owed it to him not to fall apart.

He lifted his chin, folded his aching hands, and looked straight into Benton's eyes.

"I'm invoking my right to counsel. That's the last thing I'm going to say."

Benton was grim. He exhaled; it was nearly a laugh.

"Have it your way," he said.

12.

JULIAN WAS on his third cigarette. He smoked one-handed, elbow propped against the table. He'd laced their fingers together so tightly that Paul could feel the way their heartbeats moved almost in rhythm. Now and then Julian pressed his side against Paul's arm, and Paul shut his eyes and tried to synchronize their breathing. Then Julian would squirm and sigh and rake his thumbnail over his eyebrow, and Paul fell out of sync with him again.

They'd had the same thought, Paul could tell, because even by his standards Julian had dressed for the day with exceptional care. But he carried a keen lingering smell of spearmint. In the hallway Paul heard two uniforms laughing about Julian being sick at the sight of an autopsy photograph; Marinetti, at least, had taken pity on him and found him a toothbrush. Almost none of the stress was still visible in Julian's face, but the effort was. Whenever he forgot to look away, Paul's eyes landed on the mirror—its ruthless portrait of two suicides tethered together at the throat.

". . . No eyewitnesses, no getaway car, no *motive* for god's sake. Am I missing something, or are you trying to get an indictment for murder because your detective saw a teenager going for a walk?"

At Paul's other side, his mother brought one hand to her face, wedding rings glinting, and shut her eyes. Paul touched her arm, and she reflexively clasped his hand in hers, but she didn't look at him.

There was no sign of the Frommes, nor the sleek expensive

lawyer Benton had promised. There was only this crooked-tied old friend of Paul's father whose white eyebrows feathered outward like venomous caterpillars, and whose good, sensible questions had demanded good, sensible lies. Paul was trying his best to ignore him now. He had command of the situation, or so he'd promised Paul's mother once she was allowed back in the room. Paul could only hold himself together if he pretended not to notice the one-act play unfolding at the far end of the table.

Piece by tedious piece, the lawyer and his unsmiling counterpart sparred over every detail. Benton stood in the corner with his arms folded, frown deepening the longer he listened. His partner, feigning indifference, leaned against the door and examined his nailbeds. Marinetti wore his sidearm in a shoulder holster like Steve McQueen; something in the affectation reminded Paul of Julian, and it occurred to him how neatly each detective had paired off with the suspect he could more easily pretend to understand.

". . . One of only a few people with access to the drug and knowledge of how it is used."

"Whoever-it-is made a hash of it, Sal, are you *sure* you're looking for someone with 'knowledge'?"

So softly that Paul almost didn't hear him, Julian started humming. He'd been doing it off and on all day, never quite long enough for Paul to place the tune. This time he glanced sideways at Paul, nearly smiling, so Paul closed his eyes and hummed along a quarter-note behind. He abruptly recognized it as "Me and Julio Down by the Schoolyard," and he had to lurch forward and cover his face to keep from collapsing into hysterics. Benton gave them a long, sharp look that Paul forced himself not to see.

It was sick what a comfort it was to be together again—for all the long desperate days that had separated them, and how little hope they had for the future to be any better. It was a comfort that Julian would still want to tease him; it was a comfort that he had taken Paul's hand first, and that even hours later neither of them was willing to let go.

His father's lawyer friend was winding down his argument. Paul saw him check his watch and sigh. The prosecutor's shoulders sagged, and with stone-faced urgency he paged through his folders. *Their case is D.O.A.*—Paul hadn't believed it, and he still wasn't sure he could, but in the lawyer's weary Yinzer drawl the nasty coincidences stopped sounding like much at all.

Paul couldn't ignore Benton any longer. He was still looking at Paul; once he spoke, Julian abruptly lowered his eyes.

"There's still the baseball bat." An ugly silence echoed. Even without looking, Paul could feel his mother tense; Julian grasped Paul's hand tighter.

The lawyer didn't blink. "The one you never found?" he said, as if the problem were long solved and its continued discussion was beginning to bore him.

"The one that's *very* conveniently gone missing." Benton's frustration pushed up against the confines of his self-control, but it didn't break through. "Left-to-right swing, just like your client's, but by some strange coincidence—"

"He gave it away nearly a year ago," said the lawyer, checking his watch again, "which people sometimes do with things they don't need anymore. Not to mention that if I read the coroner's report right, it was only a cylindrical object the *size* of a baseball bat—I'm sorry to get gruesome, Mrs. Fleischer," he added, because she'd made a quiet strangled noise, "but it could just as easily have been a pipe."

"Hell if it was," Marinetti muttered, but Benton gave him a warning look and he fell silent again.

"I'm going to be late for dinner," the lawyer went on, as if he hadn't heard. "Christ, Sal, are we really doing this? It gets dismissed the second a judge claps eyes on it, you don't want to waste the court's time any more than I do."

Paul didn't register the shallowness of his own breathing until the prosecutor and detectives disappeared behind the mirror, and he drew a sudden deep inhale. His mother slowly let her hand slide free of his arm. He expected to see relief in her face, but her eyes were glassy. She swept one fingertip under her lower lid, but there were no tears there to catch.

"I'm so sorry about this." Julian's voice was raw-throated and little-used all day. Paul turned quickly, but Julian was leaning forward, looking down the table toward Paul's mother. "It's all my fault," he said, so miserable and eager for absolution that he hardly seemed to be wearing a mask at all. "Trying to buy grass of all things, it was so *stupid*, if I hadn't gone up there none of this would have happened."

At first Paul's mother didn't parse what he was saying. When she finally focused on Julian's face, she was bewildered, then pitying, but there was something elusive and frightening in her eyes. "I don't understand why your parents aren't here." Her voice was so vague and faraway that any warmth faded away across the distance. "Someone needs to be looking after you."

"They're probably in France for Christmas," he said. Julian was asking her for something Paul wasn't sure she could still give. "I don't want their help, anyway. They've been very clear that I'm not their problem anymore."

Paul couldn't bear to look at his mother any longer; it took enough of his nerve just to look at Julian. "He has me to look after him," he said.

When the door into the hall swung open, Benton was alone. He'd pulled all the anger back inside, but Paul could feel it, and he knew what it meant. He told himself to be relieved, but he couldn't even imitate it anymore.

"Well?" asked the lawyer, but he'd already clicked his brief-case shut.

Benton looked from Paul to Julian and back again. Then he lifted one hand to shield his eyes from the setting winter sun.

"We'll be in touch," he said, and he stepped away to let them pass.

HE HAD braced for every possibility but this one. There was supposed to be a world outside for them to unite against, and they were supposed to forgive each other once they knew no one else would. He was ready for anything but the fog that hung between them now as they sat in the back of the family car, waiting for Paul's mother to come drive them home.

She was talking to the lawyer, and had been for a while. In the rearview mirror Paul could see her, standing on the police station steps in her purple winter coat. The lawyer was one stair above her, headless in the reflection. Paul couldn't understand the hopelessness in her face, the way she hugged herself as she spoke. "He's a good boy," she had told the lawyer, and then the police, over and over, in a voice so small they could pretend to ignore her. "You're out of your minds. Both of them are good boys." It hadn't occurred to Paul before now that she might not believe it.

"I can't stay in this city." Julian sat in a slouch, one leg crossed over the other, a coil-tight caricature of repose. Cigarette number four wasn't allowed to burn inside the car, so he turned it between his fingers and tapped it against the armrest. Paul could picture every point in the constellations of his freckles. Paul saw a faint impression of his teeth at the side of his neck, a mark that Julian's skin had already almost forgotten. "I don't care where we go." Julian stared straight ahead, unblinking, but he nearly managed to sound indifferent. "Anywhere. I just want to get in the car and drive until I forget what the air here tastes like. I wake up in the middle of the night and feel like I can't breathe, I just want . . ."

It was agonizing how little the word *we* surprised him. Refusing Julian would have been a kindness, and Paul knew himself too well to try. All he could do was need. Even if they never forgave each other; even if it ruined them both.

"It should be a real city," Paul said quietly, and he hated Julian for refusing to flinch when he touched him. "I know you'd like that better than Vermont-or-Maine. I don't care either way, you're all I need, I'll go anywhere you want."

It was a handsome silk lining for the inside of the shadowbox they would trap each other in, and both of them knew it. But Paul could tell from his smile that Julian almost didn't mind.

"Maybe Montreal," he said. "You'd like it there. I could teach you French."

Paul sensed his mother approaching before he let himself see her, a dim violet shape moving past the glass. She slid into the driver's seat, as slowly and gingerly as if her back ached. "You'll have to help me navigate, sweetheart," she said to Julian, but she didn't look either of them in the eye.

They ghosted through the quiet streets, hardly speaking. Paul rested his head on Julian's shoulder and watched the snowflakes melt on the windshield. The city was a jagged, verdant dream already slipping from his memory. He wished he could believe anything better would replace it.

When his mother pulled to a halt in front of Julian's building she leaned forward, clutching the steering wheel, and looked at it with bleak dismay. She didn't turn off the engine or even pull the parking brake; she was as eager to leave as Julian was. Paul followed Julian out of the car, but his mother jerked her door open and grabbed him by the sleeve.

"No," she said. Her voice was shaking, and she looked as if she might cry, but Paul had never seen such flinty resolve in her eyes. "No, Paul. You're coming home."

Julian stood on the steep sidewalk, one hand still outstretched toward Paul's wrist. He looked between them with badly concealed panic. Paul took his mother's hand, imagining he could pacify her if he clasped it tenderly enough.

"I'll be back in a few days to get my things." He just had to make himself into a convincing enough authority on the truth. "We have to leave, it doesn't matter what really happened, they'll never leave us alone if—"

"No," she repeated. "This isn't a negotiation. You're seventeen. You're still a child. You don't get a vote."

Paul was too incredulous to be angry. She'd never issued him a direct order in his life—hundreds to Audrey in the depths of her adolescence, but never him. He tried to think her ridiculous, this tiny round-faced woman trembling in her purple coat. But he couldn't dismiss her. He couldn't even make himself break her grasp.

"For god's sake," he said in exasperation. "You know you can't actually stop me, right? What are you going to do, call the police?"

Her jaw was a tight line. "If I have to," she said quietly. "If you make me."

"Mrs. Fleischer." Julian had fallen back, hands hanging at his sides. But he approached her again, as if it took all his courage to do it. He touched the open driver's-side door; it was a long, sickening moment before Paul's mother forced herself to look at him.

"Please," he said, and for the first time Paul saw her flinch. "I don't want you to think . . ."

"I don't." She gave him a rueful, bracing smile. "Oh, Julian," she said. "I hope you can find someone to take care of you. I mean that. You need it so much."

One obstacle shattered, then the next. She looked back up at Paul and tugged gently on his sleeve. "Front seat," she said. "I want to be able to look at you."

Paul tried to promise Julian without words that he would wait it out—until his birthday, past it, however long it took. But Julian was looking straight through him.

Paul's mother backed the Buick down the hill, out into the holiday-emptied street and the shivering light of the streetlamps. It would have been better for her to hate him, but when he searched her face he couldn't find hatred, or even anger. Instead she grieved, with her entire body. It was nothing like the way she grieved for his father. It was worse.

"It wasn't a year," she said. They were nearly home; he'd stopped waiting for her to speak. "I remember. Your bat was still under your bed a few weeks ago."

Of course there were reasonable explanations. She expected them, and he gave them, and they went through a ritual of pretending. It didn't change anything. Nothing ever would.

13.

JANUARY 6, 1974

I've only just had the chance to slip across the street. I was afraid they would have fixed the board or god forbid found the archive behind it but it's all still here, and I ought to hide it somewhere but I can't stand to let it out of my sight. Even if I can't bear to look through it, even if I never can, I need to know that it's still there and within my grasp and real, it was real, it was always real.

The rest of the house is nearly back to normal but I'm leaving my room the way it is. I have to pick across the floor to get to my bed over a bunch of clothes they threw out of the closet and a dresser drawer no one bothered to pick up. I like to sit there and look at the destruction until I feel like I'm boiling from the inside out.

(The specimens are all intact and the drawers are neatly closed. Very considerate. It isn't quite the absolute dismemberment I deserve.)

It was so arbitrary the things they took. My copy of Eichmann in Jerusalem *is in an evidence locker somewhere and probably will be forever because apparently it proves something to someone. A few drawings too but not even the ones you'd think—some sketches of J., a few forest landscapes, like they deliberately chose things they knew I would miss. But of course "[t]he items you have requested are determined to have continuing evidentiary value"—it was a form letter with my name typewritten in after the fact. Something about it made me think of Jean*

Valjean and his convict papers. How impersonal it is when there's hardly anything more personal than what they've taken from me.

But I have my archive now. They didn't leave me any other photographs. Every other trace of him is gone.

JANUARY 21, 1974

No school this semester. I didn't fight it.

They haven't decided what to do with me yet. They have to keep me from him obviously. Their other objectives remain unclear, probably even to them. What possible action can they take without admitting that they think it's true? House arrest is the only solution they can stand because there are benign reasons for it that they can feed to my grandparents and pretend to believe themselves. I've been so delicate lately. I'm not coping well with the stress. I've suffered under the malign influence of a friend I should never have trusted. (By necessity nobody tries to articulate what he might have influenced me to do.)

It's better if I stay home and rest. On her way home every Thursday Audrey stops at the library and picks up some books for me—braving the public would obviously be too much for me right now. If I'd like to go for a run one morning someone would be happy to accompany me to the track but it's such nasty weather lately so swimming would be better. I'm safest and happiest when I'm surrounded by walls and by people who love me unconditionally and who aren't afraid of me, they promise.

One fine day I will feel better but not yet. It may be years before that miracle arrives.

FEBRUARY 3, 1974

She's been taking her pills lately to get to sleep. She slept through the entire call.

It was so brief, just seconds, and it only made the emptiness grow wider. We didn't talk about anything real, just I love you I miss you I can't keep doing this. What is "this"? Neither of us wanted to say. So we pretended "this" is just being apart because that is a binary condition with a theoretically easy resolution.

But I've done some archival reading today. I know what this is, what it's been from the start and how hard I worked to keep it that way. I know that nothing about this is easy and nothing about this can be resolved.

We can't keep doing this. It will kill us if we keep doing this.

FEBRUARY 17, 1974

Dear fucking diary, today I put my forearm on a hot burner on the stove and leaned on it with all my weight until they pulled me back.

I don't think I decided to do it. If I had I would have done it properly without anyone in the room so they would've had to take off the arm. How it really happened: room full of people (mother, sisters, grandparents). The burner wasn't hot enough for third-degree burns. The E.R. doctor said if I'm lucky and I care for it right it might not even scar.

They are moving more quickly now. Laurie is staying with grandparents "until things" (until I) "calm down." And there is an appointment on Friday that I'm not supposed to know about but it isn't at a hospital yet—some doctors apparently still make house calls. The doctor hasn't been told the whole story and I'm not to take the liberty. We are still playing the make-believe game about how delicate I am.

No one will speak to me directly. My mother has been crying since she got off the phone, back to her old standbys. Audrey is the only one who can stomach helping me change the dressings, but even she's run out of things to say to me.

Fuck them. They wanted crazy. They're getting it.

STILL FEBRUARY I THINK.
There is sufficient data. No more putting it off. Time to talk conclusions.

   -

FACT: The current state of things is intolerable.

FACT: The state of things is changing. Some things have yet to give and others are in the process of giving. He will run out of money eventually and have to go somewhere I'll never be able to reach him. My family is already inching toward it and soon they will finally pull the trigger and do whatever the good doctor recommends. The police

(Let's not dwell on the police. Any action on their part is unacceptable.)

The status quo is intolerable for us, and as time marches forward the odds increase that a new status quo will emerge. It will be worse. In all likelihood irreversibly.

But inevitably

FACT: Being apart is an abhorrent void. It would consume us alive.

CONCLUSION:
Self-evident. Isn't it?
This is the only choice we have. When he needs to he will understand.

He couldn't swim until his arm healed, so they had to let him run. Audrey always accompanied him, reading a music magazine on the bleachers while he circled the track. But she didn't follow him when she thought he was just headed to the men's room. For a few moments every morning he was able to reach the bank of pay phones, and he could pause just long enough to open the directory in the second booth.

No matter how early it was, the day's note was always waiting, tucked between the pages advertising the local travel agencies. Paul wrote his answer on the other side and hurried back to the track.

Tell me where and when. Soon. I can't do this anymore.

Sunday, 6 a.m., old Esso station west of Laurie's school. Backroads + rural border crossing, harder for anyone to follow.

Julian always took the notes away by the next morning, as if he knew Paul might not be able to resist keeping them. Instead, late at night while the others were sleeping, he would take one of Julian's old letters from the archive and try to memorize the shapes of the words.

Cashed out savings—OK for gasoline, then hostel but not sure for how long.

I'm not worried. We'll be all right.

If you haven't forgiven me I hope you can pretend for a while. I'll do anything to make it up to you.

Stop—it's going to be better now. There's nothing to forgive.

No note on Wednesday. Thursday, another torn scrap of fine paper grayed by the newsprint—a sliver of the stationery with the nautilus shells.

Tell me you still love me.

He heard it in Julian's voice—that note of false carelessness Paul had only recently recognized for what it really was. It wasn't about control and never had been. It was as simple as Julian waking from a nightmare and reaching for his hand in the dark.

Paul turned the paper over and picked up the pen tethered to the pay phone. *Always*, he wrote, and then couldn't stop writing.

By the time he ran out of space his handwriting had devolved into a scrawl. The word echoed like a scream from edge to ragged edge.

14.

IT WAS still early when he decided he couldn't wait at the house any longer. He couldn't remember sleeping. In anticipation of his escape he'd made a production of getting up in the middle of the night and taking the cold medicine out of the bathroom cabinet. He left it out on the counter, a ring of red still puddled in the measuring cap—hopefully a convincing excuse for why he wasn't getting up for his run. Before he left he rolled up a spare sheet and arranged it like a body under his bedclothes, because they wouldn't do it in the movies so often if it didn't work now and then. It should have felt silly and childish, as if he were sneaking out to break curfew, but whenever he tried to laugh he couldn't.

He imagined the fury and the panic and the vain search for a note, the desperate arguments over whether or not to call the police. *He might be anywhere by now,* they would say, but he knew his mother would know—his father had primed the canvas. He wondered how long they would wait for him before they gave up hope and covered the mirrors.

He stood outside the house for a long time, knapsack over his shoulder, watching for the blaze of a light or a fluttering curtain. But there was only the buzzing porch lamp and the green glow of Laurie's nightlight behind her blinds. No one felt him there. No one came to stop him. He didn't linger.

For nearly an hour he waited alone at the meeting place, under the canopy and out of sight of passing cars. Now and then a flash of red passed beneath the streetlights and hope cut through him like lightning before fading away.

It was four minutes to six when one of the glimmers of red slowed at the crossing. Julian was only ever early when he was afraid. The Chevrolet swung into the lot and idled on the cracked asphalt. Past the glare of the headlights Julian was a gray shadow behind the windshield, barely visible, not yet tangible. Paul straightened, shouldered his knapsack, and walked toward the lights.

At first all they could do was stare at each other. It was the longest they'd been apart since summer, and there was no accepting the reality of him. Even when Paul kissed him, it felt like a dying dream.

"What happened to your arm, Pablo?"

Julian was sick again, his usual winter bronchitis; when he rested his forehead against Paul's there was a menthol glint to his breath. He took Paul's hand and pushed up his sleeve, following the gauze along the length of his forearm. For a moment Paul bit his tongue and endured it, then let go of Julian's hand and covered the bandage again.

"I burned it." He tried to smile, but Julian's face still fell. "It's all right. I'm not going to do it again."

"You'd better not." Julian affected an imperious carelessness Paul couldn't believe he'd ever found convincing. "It has to be better from now on," he said. "We have to start from scratch. You're not going to try to make me hate you as much as you do, not anymore. You're going to let me take care of you, even if you can't stand to do it yourself. Promise me."

He couldn't lie, not directly, because Julian could always tell. But Paul could see his desperation for comfort, and he knew the answer was true. "It will be better, Julian," he said.

Paul drove. They followed the rural route, north through sleeping farmland and the gentle waves of foothills. Even as the early light crested the horizon, the mist was slow to lift. They didn't speak much, but it was a grateful and reverent quiet. For the first time in months there was something like peace between them. It was a blessing to find that peace again, in the moments before they preserved it forever under glass.

Julian lit his last cigarette and crumpled the empty pack into the glove box. When he rested his head on the window frame the gesture laid bare the left side of his throat, the shifting muscle when he swallowed and the soft beat of his pulse.

"Can I try that?"

Julian looked at him with a weary, skeptical smile. "I'm giving it up," he said. "My lungs are enough of a mess already."

"I know," said Paul. "I just want to see what it's like."

Julian paused, then braced his forearm across Paul's shoulder and held the cigarette to his lips. Paul knew he would be sick if he took the smoke all the way in, so he held it in his mouth, the way Julian had when they first met. It was bitter as burnt coffee, unpleasantly cloying, but he released the breath with a slow grace he'd never been capable of before.

"I know," Julian said. He kissed Paul's temple, very lightly, then leaned back and rolled the cigarette along the edge of the window to scatter the ashes. "People talk themselves into the strangest things when they want to look impressive."

His heart had been racing since they left the city behind, but he pretended it was because of the smoke. When they passed the first road sign for the forest preserve, he let one hand slip from the steering wheel, and he held it to his throat until his pulse steadied. He was afraid, but it wasn't from cowardice. They were nearing the only perfect and absolute thing they were capable of finding.

When they reached the little town just outside the park

entrance, Paul drove through without stopping. Breath by breath, he made himself light.

"Is it all right if we stop in here for a little while? Just to stretch our legs."

There was no suspicion in Julian's eyes. In the end, there wasn't any difference between trusting someone and under-estimating them. "Tricking me into going *hiking* at a time like this," Julian said, already acquiescing. "My lungs are full of wool, but I'm all right if we don't walk too far."

"Not far," Paul answered. It shouldn't have been so difficult to return Julian's smile.

It was usually summer when he came here. He'd come with his father, then alone, and it was familiar as a recurring dream. The footpath was carpeted now with dead leaves and frost, but he remembered the woods chattering with birdsong, path fringed with bright ferns, wildflowers alongside the creek like smears of blue pastel.

They kept close, speaking very little, hands clasped tight. In the bleak quiet Paul could hear Julian's every breath. He was dressed more casually than usual, as if to blend into a crowd. Corduroy trousers, tennis shoes, soft brown sweater under his wool winter coat. Not quite warm enough, not suited to the trail. But he didn't look unhappy. Paul hoped he really wasn't.

(He tried, without knowing why, to remember what Charlie Stepanek had been wearing. But the memory had left him, if he'd ever had it at all. It hadn't seemed important.)

Paul didn't let himself think too far ahead. He knew better. Julian understood him, and he would read the truth on his face before Paul was ready for him to know it.

The ravine was marked on trail maps, but from the path it was barely visible. Past the brush of a soft incline it plunged deep into the earth. As a child Paul had strayed from the path to get a look at it, trying to prove to himself that he shouldn't be afraid, and he'd nearly reached the edge before he could see it at all. A sheer, unforgiving drop, down to crumbling boulders and a dying creek. Afterward he memorized the bend in the trail alongside it, and whenever he drew near it, he felt the pull of the void. At one time the fear had been enough to make him reluctant to return. But he was braver now, not least because of Julian.

Even for winter the woods were still. Paul let go of Julian's hand and walked a few paces ahead. He took off his gloves, and he brushed his fingertips one by one over the fragile gray things that would survive around them. The rough belly of an oak, the bristling hair of a low pine, the silvery foam and fragile fingers of lichens. In the chill and the living quiet, he wasn't afraid anymore. After a lifetime of yearning and trying not to yearn, he imagined the relief of surrendering.

Julian wasn't far behind him—cold-chafed, still so thin, but as magnetic and as heartbreaking as he'd been the first time their eyes met. Paul could feel himself smiling. Never in his life had he felt so safe.

"Come and see," he said, and he reached for Julian's hand.

Julian didn't move.

He knew.

They could see each other clearly, and the knowledge was absolute and irreversible. He knew, and he didn't understand, and it was agony to see what it did to him. Paul wanted to cut the comprehension from his own body and graft it into his, because without it he was suffering.

"Julian." Paul took a cautious step toward him, as if he were approaching a wounded animal. "Julian, wait, let me—"

But he ran.

Paul couldn't avoid seeing the parallels. City dwellers in the wrong sort of shoes, unused to ragged terrain and the maze of trees. The pursuit didn't last long this time, either. Stepanek's drug-numbed feet had skidded on a blanket of wet pine needles; for Julian, it was a root across the path. Even a momentary fall was enough, because Paul was always faster. He'd been doing this all his life. Only now did he see the cruelty of the imbalance. Julian turned and sat up on the path, but he couldn't get to his feet before Paul reached him. When Paul moved forward, he scrambled back.

"Pablo." His voice didn't sound anything like his own, or else it was the first time it ever had. "I'm sorry about the dog, I'm sorry, it was all my fault—Pablo, *please*, you have to let me make it up to you, I'll do whatever you want—"

Paul didn't want to touch him, not until he could make him see. "I'm not—Julian, I'm not doing this to hurt you, it's not a punishment—"

Julian had backed right up to a tree, but he couldn't take his eyes off Paul long enough to find a new path. "We'll start over." He was despondent and furious and still grasping, hopelessly, for any reason to forgive. "We were going to start over, we were going to be all right, I was finally going to make you happy—I love you, I love you so much, I'll do anything for you, please believe me, please give me a chance—"

"I believe you." Paul reached down as if to help him to his feet, but Julian recoiled. "This is *because* I believe you—it's both of us together, it was always going to be both of us—it's too late to start over, we can't survive together, and it was me, I know it was, I'm so sorry—this is the only way we can fix it, it's the only way we won't ever have to be apart—"

"We wouldn't be apart or together or anything else, it isn't being *anything.*" Julian tried to get up again, but the twisted ankle wasn't ready to support his weight. "You know that, you can't help but know that, you know damn well your father and his family aren't *together* now, they're just fucking dead—"

He wasn't losing his temper, or at least that was what he told himself. He pretended there was no rage and shame pulsing through his nerves. The problem was that Julian didn't understand—the problem was that Paul was terrified and stammering and couldn't keep pace with an argument. He wasn't brilliant enough to explain in a way that Julian could accept. He wasn't lashing out; he was cutting their losses. He promised himself it was a mercy.

At first Paul took hold of him hesitantly for fear of hurting him, and it was a mistake. Julian nearly managed to break free. His elbow cracked a cobweb across the left lens of Paul's glasses, and there was pain, there must have been pain, but there was no time to feel it. He caught Julian by the neck and pulled him back down, and when he tried to twist away again Paul pinned him to the ground with one knee at his chest. Under the weight of his body he could hear the force of the air knocked from Julian's lungs.

Before he placed his other hand at Julian's throat, Paul threw his glasses aside. It would be dishonest to keep hiding himself behind them.

"I just wanted you to trust me." There was no hope or defiance left in Julian's face. Seeing him like this was unbearable. "Pablo, please, I don't want to die."

Three minutes without air. Another minute after that, maybe two, to double back and find the edge of the ravine.

"I know," he said. He shut his eyes tight and told himself to be brave.

For the first time he remembered Stepanek, every detail that he'd arrogantly given himself permission to forget. Blood gushing dark from the back of his head, jaw clenched, body in spasm. How for the first time Paul had felt indifferent to what either of them deserved. He realized that he'd murmured something soothing to Stepanek before he finished it—*It's all right it's almost done it'll be over soon.* A gentle lie for the unhearing ears of this thing that was already no longer a man.

He imagined Julian's body the same way, given over to fractured synapses before the final stillness. It was an abomination, and it always had been. For Stepanek it had been no justice. For Julian it would be no mercy.

When he opened his eyes, Julian's were waiting to meet them. His fear was so absolute that Paul knew it would be there forever. There was something absent in his eyes; Paul couldn't remember what they had looked like before. He'd never told Julian how beautiful they were, because he had thought it self-evident. He'd believed that of far too many things.

Paul leaned down and pressed his lips to Julian's forehead. Julian made a strange sound, almost like a sob. For a long moment Paul held him there, still wanting only to breathe him in. Then he let go and allowed Julian to push him away.

Paul heard the uneven footfalls, back toward the countless roads to a world outside the two of them. But couldn't force himself to watch. He tried to believe that the smell of him lingered. But there wasn't much to it—just soap and cigarettes and bone-deep, aching familiarity.

He didn't know afterward how long he lay there in the mud and dead leaves, alongside an absence he should never survive. He wanted anything but to have to withstand it. But he had yielded to every other monstrosity that would accompany him for the rest of his life, and he yielded to this. He promised himself that death would be better. But he survived, and he would go on surviving. It was as reflexive as breathing.

He walked along the shoulder of the highway. He couldn't remember following the trail back, or finding his knapsack by the side of the road where Julian's car had been. He returned to the town outside the park and its dingy Greyhound station, and he took the 12:37 back to Pittsburgh. It was only when he saw his reflection in the window that he noticed the pebble of shattered lens embedded in his check, glistening red like a pomegranate seed. He picked it out, then spat on his hand to wipe the blood from his face. None of the other passengers paid any attention. Bystanders never changed.

When he set his knapsack down by the door, he thought for a moment that the house was empty. But then Laurie was running down the stairs and his grandparents and his mother were hurrying out from the kitchen, and everyone was talking over each other so relentlessly that he couldn't have understood them if he tried. Audrey was in the kitchen, holding her chin with her fingertips. The contents of his desk drawer were spread over the kitchen table. There was his journal, lying open next to the butter dish; there, the blurry smear of Julian's handwriting on nautilus-shell stationery.

"What in god's name," he heard her say. He left them all behind and shut himself into the sunroom. They didn't try to stop him. Their shadows clustered in the kitchen, barely moving, and the house became very quiet again.

Now and then he saw Laurie's face on the other side of the French doors. Neither met each other's eyes, and she watched him as if he were a rattlesnake trapped under a bowl. Beyond her Paul couldn't see much without his glasses, and he didn't try. There was movement in the kitchen, until there wasn't. Where voices should have been, there was only the inaudible whisper of conspiracy.

He settled onto the couch and wrapped his arms around his chest. A few yards to his right lay the stretch of bare earth where the garden shed had been; the place of his father's death sat with him like an old friend. Gradually his body remembered the gnaw of the burn in his forearm and the throbbing cut under his eye. He didn't mind. He absorbed the pain into himself along with the rest of it.

The sky was growing dark. He didn't know what he was waiting for, but he waited. He knew it wouldn't be long.

THE WORLD outside the sunroom had arrived at a decision. Soft voices in the living room, one-sided telephone conversations. They knew what they were going to do, and in the silence he could hear them summoning their nerve. The door clicked open. There was Audrey, all sharp edges, hands on her hips and hair pulled back. Their grandfather hung back in the shadows behind her. In the dim light his eyes were uncomprehending, and Paul made himself meet them.

"Your friend's phone has been busy for hours." Audrey's voice trembled but didn't break. "We're going to go check on him. All three of us."

Perhaps he should have argued—accused her of overreacting, asked what she feared he'd done. He didn't. By now there wasn't much point trying.

He hadn't even taken off his boots. He shrugged back into his muddy coat and realized he hadn't stopped shivering. Audrey stepped backward when he stood, bracing herself as if she might have to stop him from running; he looked away, for her sake rather than his own, lowering his gaze to fasten the buttons.

His mother and grandmother were waiting by the front door, arm in arm. His mother held his knapsack, still packed; she had probably checked to make sure he'd remembered a toothbrush. She looked unbearably small, but she didn't need her mother's arm to hold her steady. Paul had never seen her spine so straight.

"Where am I going?"

His mother didn't answer the question. She looked straight at him, bright-eyed and brave. Something warm and over-whelming broke free inside his chest, far too late to matter.

"It's for your own good, Paul," she said quietly.

After his grandfather took the bag from her hand, Paul leaned down to kiss the top of his mother's head. The gesture seemed to take her by surprise, and she made no move to em-brace him in turn.

Audrey's hand settled on one arm, his grandfather's on the other. Paul squared his shoulders and stood up straight.

"I'm sorry, Ma." He played the words back in his head, listen-ing to the way his voice didn't reach any farther into his chest than the very tops of his lungs. He knew his voice would sound this way from now on—the inside and the outside of him would never be allowed to touch.

"Let's go, Paul," said Audrey.

His grandfather drove. The snow was young, and the world was quiet. Audrey navigated, narrating every turn of a drive Paul could have taken with his eyes shut. He watched the pass-ing streetlights, their bright halos of falling snow. He watched for the hilltop glimpses of distant bridges.

Julian's car wasn't there. Paul could all but feel Audrey's dread. "It's a Chevy," she said to their grandfather. "Little red two-door. Are you sure we didn't pass it?"

Audrey led the way, across the dirty chessboard tiles and up the winding stairs. There in the second-floor hallway the door hung open, lamplight spilling across the carpet. She froze, and their grandfather gently squeezed her shoulder. "We'll give you the all-clear once we know what's inside," he said, and she swal-lowed hard before nodding.

The apartment was empty; of course it was. The telephone receiver swayed in the circulating air, skimming the floor like a hanged man's shoes. The floors were strewn with books and the open mouths of fallen drawers. Audrey sidled past and shuffled through the wreckage, but Paul's grandfather didn't let go of him.

There was an envelope waiting on the dining table, propped up against a drinking glass to ensure it would be seen. Audrey noticed it as soon as Paul did, and picked it up before he could reach it. Even without his glasses, he could see his name written on the outside. Not *Pablo*, not anymore; his full name and address, printed clearly, as if the post office would have to find him.

Audrey held the empty envelope between her fingers and examined what was inside. One was a photograph, the other a page torn from a book. Paul recognized the photo. It was the one they'd taken on the drive down from the bridge, underneath the low canopy of leaves.

"What does this mean, Paul?" Audrey asked him.

She handed both papers to him, but she meant the book page. To her the chess notation would be an incomprehensible cipher of numbers and letters. Paul would have struggled to read it himself, but he'd all but memorized the game—all the times he'd watched Julian replicate the endgame on his portable board, trying to pinpoint the moment the outcome was inescapable.

Paul looked at the boys in the photograph as if he'd never seen them before. Eyes locked, hands entwined just beneath the frame. They were windburned and beaming and younger than he could ever remember being.

The other two were talking quietly, as if to keep Paul from hearing. But he wasn't listening. The letters on the book's page seemed to run together.

U.S. Open 1970—Kazlauskas v. Kaplan—Championship Final.

The opening move was circled in red.

I CONCEIVED of these characters in 2011 and began seriously writing *These Violent Delights* in 2013, but I have been trying to tell this story in various forms and iterations since I was a teenager myself. Along with many other members of the post-Columbine generation, I spent my childhood being told by the culture at large that adolescent anger was a latent threat of violence—that the alienation and sense of grievance living inside me could erupt at any moment into monstrosity. I was terrified of my own anger and of where it might lead me, perhaps without my even realizing it.

This likely explains why, after learning about the Leopold and Loeb case in my early teens, I was briefly but intensely enthralled with it—not aspirationally, but because I recognized enough basic similarities that I could see them as what I feared becoming. I was queer, Jewish, isolated, and both too smart for my own good and nowhere near the visionary genius I thought I was—and for a time this let me imagine that my own misanthropy could spiral out of control in the same way. The finer details of the Leopold and Loeb case turned out not to interest me (by now I've forgotten most of them), but I retained my fascination with the places in the case where I had seen some reflection of myself. This resulted in a book that ended up being more thematically concerned with those surface-level commonalities than with the actual case. With the skeleton of the plot squared away I was free to write about queer alienation, the provisional whiteness of Jews in America, the lonely arrogance of clever young adults.

The most prevailing concern of *These Violent Delights*, of course, is the kind of toxic and identity-consuming romantic friendship that many queer people experience in their teens. While obsessive love is clearly not bound by gender or orientation, there is, I think, a dialectic of both wanting and wanting to be that is specific to same-gender relationships of this kind. My own experiences of these relationships felt like another latent threat I carried inside me, one that fed off my alienation from the outside world by affirming it. Here, too, one can find the beginnings of this theme with the Leopold and Loeb case, but the greater spark of my inspiration—and in many ways the impetus to write the book—stemmed from the 1954 Parker-Hulme murder case in New Zealand. I learned of it in 2010 from the film *Heavenly Creatures*, whose emotional texture and tone have been a much more direct influence on this book than the murder as historical fact. This is another case I have never researched in deep detail, and which I have used solely as a jumping-off point for basic plot beats and themes.

While both these crimes have clear reflections in the plot of *These Violent Delights*, the characters, events, and dialogue are wholly invented, and are not intended as either factual record or as speculation on "what really happened." This book is fiction, and all fiction is more autobiography than anything else. What the story records, ultimately, is the deep fear I once carried about my loneliness and what it could do.

ACKNOWLEDGMENTS

THIS BOOK exists because of the people who believed in it. My incomparable agent, Caroline Eisenmann, understands this book to an almost uncanny degree—she has been a force of nature, as fierce an advocate as I could hope for, and I have never doubted for a moment that *These Violent Delights* belonged in her hands. The book truly found its shape under the guidance of Erin Wicks, whose sharp editorial eye is matched only by her unwavering compassion. I'm forever indebted to Erin for pushing the book, and me, as far as we could go; thanks to her, *These Violent Delights* is as close now to its ideal self as it ever could be.

I am also deeply grateful to the rest of the team at Harper Books. Many thanks to Nikki Baldauf in managing editorial and Caroline Johnson and Leah Carlson-Stanisic in the art department for all their work in bringing this book into the world; to Katherine Beitner and Kristin Cipolla, Tom Hopke, and Leah Wasielewski for helping it find its readers; and to Jonathan Burnham and Doug Jones for giving it a home.

Ollie Levy read and critiqued several iterations of this book, and listened patiently to countless hours of the frustration, self-doubt, and general fretting that writers euphemistically refer to as "bouncing a few ideas off you." Ollie has a particular talent for asking piercing, insightful questions with such diplomacy that I was always delighted to help the book answer them. I must also offer a special commendation to Wyn Tarbell, who has probably spent more time reading this book than anyone else—including the very first shaky fragments, which I'm certain would never have evolved into a book without Wyn's early kindness and support. Many other lovely friends have read along and helped this story reach the page. My deepest thanks to Marissa Beverly, Lindy Bolzern, Chrissy Ebbert, Arden Harbert, Kae Hunter, Gabriel Lippincott, Trina Luciano, Briana Pipczynski, Alex Max Schaffner, Jessie Taylor, and A.M. Tuomala—their encouragement has meant the world to me.

Writing my art history master's thesis was as rigorous an education in writing as any MFA, and to a great degree this is thanks to my committee head, Kelly Dennis. In terms both funny and exacting, she gave insights into pacing and thematic focus that have been invaluable in writing and revising this book—not to mention helping me develop a deep appreciation and thick skin for constructive criticism. (After sitting at her desk first thing in the morning, watching her red-pen through my thesis pages line by line, editing has been a piece of cake.) Every "great, galloping Germanic sentence" is better for her mentorship.

Many other teachers have helped shape me as a writer, as a thinker, as a person. My deepest gratitude goes to Ken Allan, Margaret Breen, Anne D'Alleva, Anke Finger, Naomi Hume, Melanie Feinberg, and Andrea Roth. And I dedicate this book in part to the memory of David Heller, a brilliant professor and deeply kind man who deserved a much longer life than he was given.

Finally, and with boundless love, I thank my mother, Leslie Nemerever, for supporting me unconditionally through this process and for all my life. I've told her before and will tell her again that she gave me a wonderful childhood, suffused with art, imagination, and delightful strangeness. She has always encouraged me to follow my passions wherever they might take me, and I've learned so much from her own drive to discover and create. I truly could never ask for a better mother.

To these people, and to the rest of my friends and family: I am so glad and so humbled to have you in my life. Thank you for everything.

—MN
January 2020

I RECOGNIZE that this book was written on the ancestral lands of the Duwamish, Mohegan, Tonkawa, Chimakum, and Klallam people.

ABOUT THE AUTHOR

MICAH NEMEREVER studied art history and queer theory at the University of Connecticut, where he wrote his MA thesis on gender anxiety in the art of the Weimar Republic. He is a prolific home chef and an avid amateur historian of queer cinema. He lives in Seattle, Washington.